PRAISE FOR *THE COURT OF SHADOWS*

"Dixen excels at concocting unexpected detours and jaw-dropping cliffhangers. Anne Rice fans will be especially enthralled."
—*Publishers Weekly* (starred review)

"Fantasy fans who like their speculative fiction filled with vampyre aristocrats and plenty of twists along the way will enjoy taking a bite out of this series starter."
—*Library Journal*

"*The Court of Shadows* has intriguing world-building and a protagonist with true, merciless grit. You're rooted in the familiar, yet there are enough twists to break your expectations. Jeanne is vicious in her determination, and the king is utterly fascinating. I NEED TO SEE HIM WITHOUT THAT MASK!"
—Charlie N. Holmberg, *Wall Street Journal* bestselling author of *The Paper Magician*

"I loved it! The tension, the intrigue, the undercurrents of revolution, and above all else, a warrior girl who still wants to love and be loved. This will be an immediate classic. Bravo!"
—Amy Harmon, *Wall Street Journal*, *USA Today*, and *New York Times* bestselling author

"Seductive, thrilling, and deliciously dark, *The Court of Shadows* brings the glamour and danger of eighteenth-century Versailles to life. This is historical fantasy at its finest!"
—Kass Morgan, bestselling author of *The 100*

T0282278

THE
COURT
OF
MIRACLES

VAMPYRIA
BOOK II

THE COURT OF MIRACLES

VAMPYRIA
BOOK II

VICTOR DIXEN

Translated by Françoise Bui

AMAZON **CROSSING**

Text copyright © 2021 by Éditions Robert Laffont, S. A. S., Paris
Translation copyright © 2024 by Françoise Bui
All rights reserved.

Previously published as *Vampyria: La Cour des Miracles* by Éditions Robert Laffont in France in 2021. Translated from French by Françoise Bui. First published in English by Amazon Crossing in 2024.

Published by Amazon Crossing, Seattle

www.apub.com

Amazon, the Amazon logo, and Amazon Crossing are trademarks of Amazon.com, Inc., or its affiliates.

ISBN-13: 9781662505737 (hardcover)
ISBN-13: 9781662505720 (paperback)
ISBN-13: 9781662505713 (digital)

Cover design by Kimberly Glyder
Cover illustration by Colin Verdi
Interior maps illustrated by Misty Beee
Interior character list illustrated by © Loles Romero

Printed in the United States of America
First edition

For E.

Remotest wood, silent, dark, and deadly fearsome,
Is yet a refuge from Paris, now so tiresome.
Wœ to him at many a street's bending waylaid,
Amid the constant din that leaves the soul
dismayed!
Across my threshold I step and wearily tread.
The western sun an ember barely glowing red.
Slumber beckons, gladly do I my candle snuff,
But still the city screams inside my head:
"Enough!"
—Nicolas Boileau, "The Embarrassments of
Paris"
(in the year 1666 of the Christian era)

*

By light of the moon,
Firmly shut your door.
When descends the gloom,
Vampyres will soar.
Poor homeless Pierrot,
His blood they will steal.
Leaving just marrow,
A grim ghoulish meal!
—Popular song heard at dusk in Paris
(three and a half centuries later, in the year
299 of the Shadows)

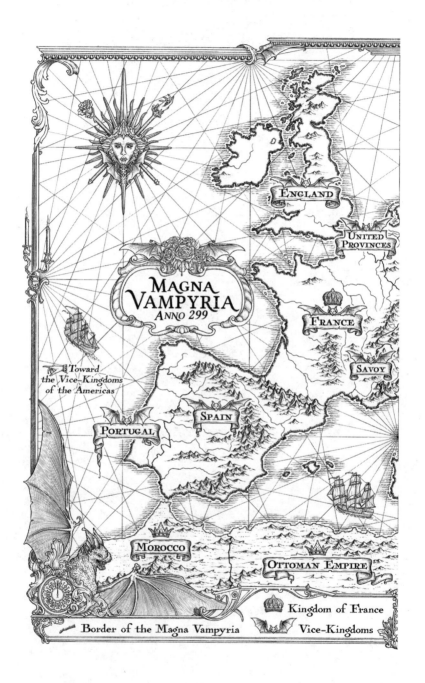

MAGNA VAMPYRIA
ANNO 299

ENGLAND

UNITED PROVINCES

FRANCE

SAVOY

Toward the Vice-Kingdoms of the Americas

SPAIN

PORTUGAL

MOROCCO

OTTOMAN EMPIRE

Kingdom of France

Border of the Magna Vampyria   Vice-Kingdoms

DENMARK

SWEDEN

RUSSIA

PRUSSIA

POLAND

GERMANY

CIMMERIA

SWITZERLAND

AUSTRIA

MOLDAVIA

VENICE

TRANSYLVANIA

PIEDMONT

WALLACHIA

TUSCANY

NAPLES

OTTOMAN EMPIRE

MOREA

Allied States

Terra Abominanda (last known border)

BEEE FECIT

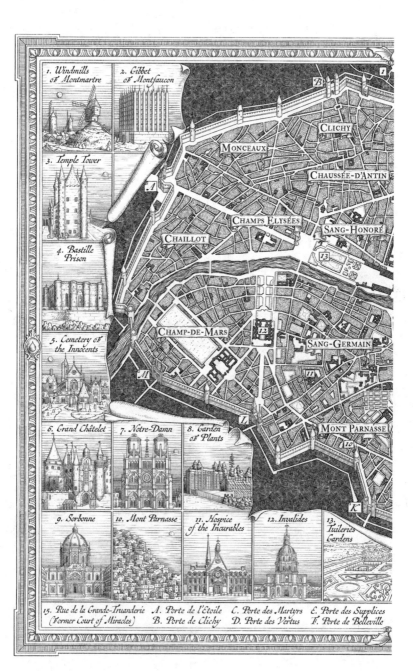

1. Windmills of Montmartre
2. Gibbet of Montfaucon
3. Temple Tower
4. Bastille Prison
5. Cemetery of the Innocents
6. Grand Châtelet
7. Notre-Damn
8. Garden of Plants
9. Sorbonne
10. Mont Parnasse
11. Hospice of the Incurables
12. Invalides
13. Tuileries Gardens

CLICHY
MONCEAUX
CHAUSSÉE-D'ANTIN
CHAMPS ELYSÉES
CHAILLOT
SANG-HONORÉ
CHAMP-DE-MARS
SANG-GERMAIN
MONT PARNASSE

15. Rue de la Grande-Truanderie   A. Porte de l'Étoile   C. Porte des Martyrs   E. Porte des Supplices
    (Former Court of Miracles)   B. Porte de Clichy   D. Porte des Vertus   F. Porte de Belleville

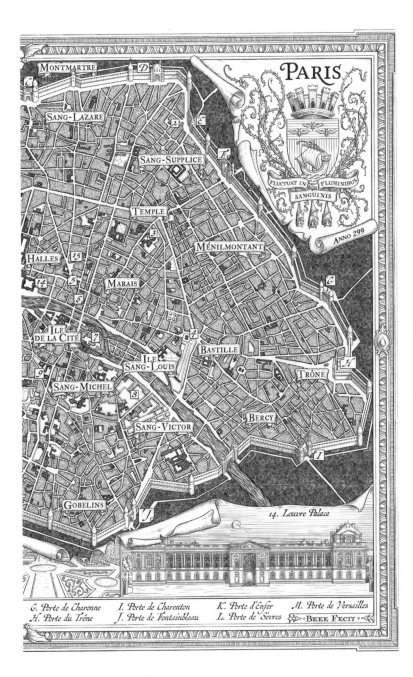

PARIS

FLUCTUAT IN FLUMINIBUS
SANGUINIS

ANNO 299

MONTMARTRE
SANG-LAZARE
SANG-SUPPLICE
TEMPLE
MÉNILMONTANT
HALLES
MARAIS
ILE DE LA CITÉ
ILE SANG-LOUIS
BASTILLE
TRÔNE
SANG-MICHEL
BERCY
SANG-VICTOR
GOBELINS

14. Louvre Palace

G. Porte de Charonne   I. Porte de Charenton   K. Porte d'Enfer   M. Porte de Versailles
H. Porte du Trône   J. Porte de Fontainbleau L. Porte de Sèvres   BEEE FECIT

MORTAL CODE
CODEX MORTALIS

Edict of
LOUIS THE IMMUTABLE,
KING OF SHADOWS
LUDOVICUS IMMUTABILIS,
REX TENEBRÆ
issued as law for governing the mortal commoners
of the fourth estate of the realm,
throughout the kingdom of France and its
vice-kingdoms of the Magna Vampyria.

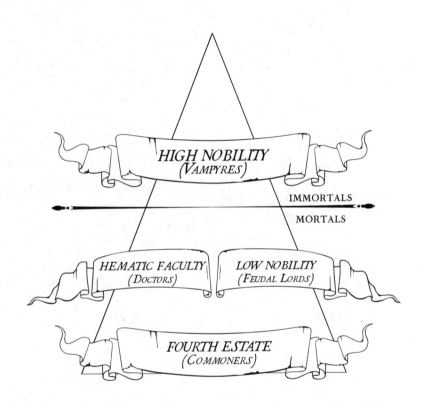

PREAMBLE

By the grace of the Shadows, the realm of the Magna Vampyria is divided into four estates. The immortal estate: vampyres of the high aristocracy. Three mortal estates: feudal lords of the lower nobility, doctors of the Hematic Faculty, and commoners of the fourth estate. The articles below concern this last tier of mortals.

Art. 1: OBEDIENCE, *OBOEDIENTIA*

From cradle to grave, commoners remain under the protection of the vampyres, in return for which they owe total submission and the following obligations:

Art. 2: SEQUESTER, *SEQUESTRUM*

During daytime hours, for as long as the sun shines, commoners are forbidden from going farther than one league from their bell tower.

Art. 3: CURFEW, *IGNITEGIUM*

During nighttime hours, as soon as the warning bell tolls, commoners are forbidden from leaving their dwellings.

Art. 4: TITHE, *DECIMA*

Every month, commoners are required to donate one-tenth of their blood.

Art. 5: SANCTION, *SUPPLICIUM*

All who violate the above articles will be executed.

SQUIRES TO THE KING
OF SHADOWS

Diane de Gastefriche
Alias Jeanne Froidelac
Born in the Auvergne, France

Suraj de Jaipur
Born in India

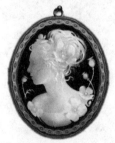

Proserpina Castlecliff
Born in England

Rafael de Montesueño
Born in Spain

Hélénaïs de Plumigny
Born in Beauce, France

Zacharie de Grand-Domaine
Born in Louisiana, the Americas

SOME REBELS BELONGING TO THE FRONDE OF THE PEOPLE

Jeanne Froidelac
Alias Diane de Gastefriche
Born in the Auvergne, France

Raymond de Montfaucon
Grand equerry of France and coordinator of the
Fronde of the people

Orfeo
Mute abomination without a past

Naoko Takagari
Daughter of the daytime ambassador of Japan

The Fronde Rebels
Secret network in Europe and the Americas

THEY AWAIT YOU IN THE PARIS OF THE SHADOWS

Alexandre de Mortange
Viscount of Clermont

Edmée de Vauvalon
Marquise of Vauvalon

Raoul de Montfaucon
Royal executioner

Ézéchiel de Mélac
Minister of the armies and governor of Paris

Sister Vermillonne
Hospice of the Incurables

Sterling Raindust
Attaché to the embassy of England

I

INTRUSION

Nothing is more vulnerable than a body at rest.

In sleep, we all become defenseless newborns again.

Same as this girl who's stretched out in the middle of a huge bed, one much too big for her.

Everything is still, except for the stain that fans out like the corolla of a flower on the sleeping girl's nightgown. A blossoming blood rose. Its petals unfurl slowly on the silk that's punctured where her heart is.

The more the flower reddens, the more the girl's face goes pale.

Her lips turn visibly whiter.

The color of her forehead blends in with the gray of her hair spread out on the pillow.

Deep in her surprised, frozen eyes, I see myself reflected as in a mirror . . .

. . . and I understand that this young corpse, it's me!

I wake with a jolt, my hand pressed on my chest right at the spot where I was stabbed.

A nightmare!

Under my clenched fingers, my heart thumps wildly. I'm alive.

The storm pounds just as savagely behind the heavy curtains of my bedroom.

I wriggle out of my sweat-drenched sheets and drag myself across the dim room. As a squire to the King of Shadows, I've been given one of the most spacious apartments at the Palace of Versailles. I grope for the chair of my dressing table and let myself fall into it. Then I turn the knob of the oil lamp to awaken the sleeping flame. A bronze clock appears in the halo of light, revealing that it's five o'clock in the morning. On the threshold of winter, in late November, there are more than three hours left before sunrise. I can't afford to waste another minute of sleep, a precious commodity in my new life as a squire. At precisely eight o'clock, I'll have to be in front of the king's mortuary chamber, along with the other five squires, for the ceremony of the Grand Retiring.

Hastily, I unscrew a jar containing pills made of white willow and pop two into my mouth to fight against the pain that's battering my brain. For as long as I can remember, my excess of black bile has left me prone to chronic migraines . . .

As I wait for the pills to take effect and return me to Morpheus, I study my creased face in the mirror. The palace craftsmen carved my initials—*D* and *G*, for Diane de Gastefriche—in the gold frame. It's the name under which I've been known here for the last month, the name of the girl who foiled an attack against the king. Little does the Immutable suspect that my real name is Jeanne Froidelac; that I'm not the daughter of a baron from the countryside but a mere commoner whose family was massacred by royal dragoons; that I've come to Versailles not to serve him but to undermine his empire from within.

In the dead of night, the immensity of my task crushes me. I know that my bogus identity hangs by a thread. If it were to be revealed one day, I dread to imagine the tortures I'd be subjected to. Since my arrival at the court, I live in a state of anxiety that disturbs my sleep and brings on gruesome dreams . . . like the one that just jolted me awake. I think about this as I scrutinize my reflection even more, searching for details that could betray me. Under the mass of gray hair that I've gathered into a braid, is my bearing haughty enough? My large, watery eyes disdainful enough? My soft lips sufficiently pinched?

I force myself to imagine a proud baronette in the mirror, but I end up seeing only a lost peasant girl, an orphan who's totally alone in the world . . .

. . . *alone, really?*

Didn't I detect a movement behind my head, right in the corner of the mirror?

I furrow my brows to better probe the reflection of the room. Far from the weak halo of the oil lamp, the back of the chamber is nearly obscured in darkness.

Still, I think I see one of the large velvet curtains stir gently.

It can't be a draft. I'm sure I closed the window before going to bed last night.

Then a certainty bursts into my brain, dissipating my migraine like a cold bolt of lightning: *someone's crept into my bedroom!*

I freeze on the chair, my stomach in knots.

My nightmare was a warning.

"Who's there?" I bleat in a high-pitched voice that sounds like a lamb about to be bled.

No response.

But the way the velvet curtain suddenly stops moving confirms my suspicion. Someone's there, hiding.

Beneath my nightgown, a shiver of panic runs through me. The fine silk fabric won't offer me any protection against a sharp blade or pointy canines. It'll redden, just like in my dream. As for my squire's sword, it's stored in its sheath at the back of a closet, at the other end of this oversize room.

"I'm warning you, if I scream, the Swiss Guards will come running!"

A crack of thunder punctures my words as if the sky itself is laughing at my empty threats. Not only is the storm raging outside, but a vestibule separates my bedroom from the hallway of the palace. Behind the fury of the elements, I can barely make out the music of the night's festivities as it reaches the upper floors. At this very moment, under my feet, aristocratic vampyres are emptying the last of their warm blood-filled glasses before returning to their cold coffins, and mortal courtiers are getting drunk on wine before sleeping off the effects in their soft, cozy beds.

Even if I scream at the top of my lungs, no one will hear me.

With a trembling hand, I search my vanity tabletop for a weapon. My fingers meet only combs and brushes. My arm knocks over the jar of white willow pills, and it shatters on the floor.

It's like a trigger. The curtain suddenly parts, revealing a dark figure.

I jump to my feet and rush to the bedroom door.

But I'm not fast enough. The intruder reaches it first.

He positions himself in front of the door, blocking my way.

I assess him in one quick glance. He's wearing a rain-drenched shirt and patched pants, his face half-hidden behind a large black scarf with holes cut out for the eyes. With an iron grip, he grabs my arm and pulls me violently toward him. With his other hand, he raises a dagger, the sharp edge catching the flare of the lamp.

His lips twist under the hem of his homemade mask.

"Die, you filthy death-licker!"

In the fraction of a second that my assailant takes to insult me, I shift my body weight onto my right leg.

I narrowly dodge the dagger.

Momentarily thrown off balance, the assassin lets go of me.

I curl into a ball and roll until I reach the middle of the room.

A thunderbolt even more deafening than any that came before makes the floor vibrate under my sore palms.

I get up, panting, fully aware that I've only given myself a short reprieve from death. My attacker is still in front of the door, preventing me from escaping.

Already, he's coming toward me—and now I notice a limp in his step.

Limp or no limp, I know he won't commit the same mistake twice. He's not going to be careless and allow me to flee.

"I . . . I'm not who you think I am," I stammer.

My thoughts are going crazy.

Find out who he is.

Guess why he wants me dead.

And above all, buy some time.

The intruder's mouth twists again under his mask.

"You're *exactly* who I think you are," he shouts as he continues forward. "A courtier hungry for fame. A death-licker who dreams of being transmuted into a vampyre. That's why you saved the tyrant!"

I register the steellike hate in his voice; it's as sharp as the blade of his dagger. But I also detect a tremor, like it's a piece of glass that's about to shatter.

My thoughts whirl at full speed. I'm obviously face to face with a rebel who blames me for aborting the attack on the king . . . But what type of rebel am I dealing with?

Does he belong to the Fronde of the princes, those who want to take the Immutable's place on the throne, like Tristan de La Roncière, the champion of conspirators, whom I killed last month?

Or does he belong to the Fronde of the people as I do, harboring the wild dream of liberating the world from the yoke of the vampyres?

His plain attire is a thousand leagues removed from the silk garb of a gentleman. His hunched shoulders have nothing in common with the snooty airs of the courtiers of Versailles. When his hand gripped my bare arm, it felt calloused, like a laborer's. As for the term *death-licker*, it's the one lowly people whisper to designate the mortal aristocrats ready to commit all kinds of atrocities in order to please the vampyres.

"Wait!" I cry, risking everything. "I didn't thwart the La Roncière plot against the king to save the tyrant, as you believe. I did it to save France from an even crueler tyranny!"

The intruder stops a few inches from me.

"What are you talking about, little aristo?" he growls.

"I don't dream of being transmuted," I say, short of breath, my words tumbling forth. "But Tristan de La Roncière wanted to be transmuted to *wear* the crown. Worse: he wanted to abolish the *numerus clausus* that limits the number of vampyres roaming the kingdom. If he'd succeeded with his plan, every mortal aristocrat would have become a bloodsucker, thereby assuring the destruction of all commoners."

The dagger in the assassin's hand begins to shake.

I sense that he has doubts. He's like a sleepwalker balancing on the tightrope of reason. At any moment, he could topple back into a murderous rage.

"You have to believe me," I say, forcing my voice to calm down in spite of my screaming vulnerability.

Since I, like all the squires, drank the Sip of the King, I'm supposed to be even more fearsome . . . but in terms of supernatural powers, the royal blood mostly reinforced my chronic migraines.

"I'm telling the truth," I add, trying hard to keep my voice steady so that I don't inflame this tormented soul.

He sniffles loudly, choking back a sob.

"The truth?" he repeats. "Maybe . . . maybe not." His trembling lips harden again. "The only thing I know for sure is that you killed Toinette, you monster!"

Toinette? The memory of the young servant at the school of the Grande Écurie swirls in my head: her honest, red-freckled face; her shy smile when her eyes met mine in the dining hall; the crook of her elbows scarred by the blood tithe, a monthly ordeal imposed by the Hematic Faculty on all commoners of the kingdom. I remember piercing poor Toinette's veins myself when I was a student there. Madame Thérèse, the governess, had ordered me to bleed the servant in the middle of a banquet in order to fill the glass of the Marquise de Vauvalon, one of the cruelest vampyres at the court.

"Toinette is . . . is dead?" I stammer. "But when I left the Grande Écurie a month ago, she was alive."

"The wounds you inflicted on her got infected. The needle you mangled her with must have been dirty, or worse!"

In horror, I think back to sadistic Madame Thérèse. She held a grudge against Toinette for stealing a pound of flour. Could the governess have given me a poisoned needle to puncture the guilty girl with?

"I—I didn't know . . . ," I sputter, mortified. "I swear it."

But he isn't listening anymore.

"Now it's your turn!" he shouts.

His dagger hurtles toward me so fast—and with such fury—that I don't quite manage to dodge it.

A sharp pain burns my right cheekbone where the sharp steel grazed it.

The maniac limps toward me again so he can deliver a second blow.

Toinette's words come rushing back to me, words she used to try and justify her paltry theft before the merciless governess: *"My parents are ill, and my carpenter brother can't work right now. He broke his leg last month when he fell from the scaffolding that was put up for work on the expansion of the palace."*

The evidence hits me square in the face.

"You're the carpenter, Toinette's brother. I know what it's like to lose a beloved sister."

The blade freezes in the air.

"I lost my dear brother Bastien," I go on, my throat tight. "It's like having a piece of yourself ripped out. Like being amputated of half your soul. Bastien was all that for me . . . until the king's dragoons killed him, just like they murdered my entire family back in my village in the Auvergne."

Toinette's brother—for it's him, I'm sure of it—is so close to me that I can see his eyes tremble through the rough cutouts of his scarf. From confusion. From anger. But most all, from misery.

"The king's dragoons killed your family?" he says, distraught. "You, a squire from a noble family?"

"I told you, I'm not who you think I am," I say again, hoarsely. "My noble birth is just a pretense. An illusion. In reality, I'm the daughter of an apothecary, and even worse—the daughter of rebels."

By confessing that I'm a commoner, I know I'm jeopardizing my life, and yet the words flow out easily. It's my last chance to reach this unhappy soul. I also see myself in him, see the way I behaved in the days after my loved ones were killed. This boy doesn't belong to any secret society. He isn't the emissary of any Fronde, the people's or the princes'. He's just a cannonball of fiery desperation unleashed onto the closest target in this chaotic world.

"I . . . I don't know if I can believe you," he stammers.

His troubled eyes rest on my bare arms, where only a month ago the punctures from the blood tithe were visible, as they are with all commoners. But the infamous scars in the crooks of my elbows faded. The small amount of royal blood that runs in my veins confers on me a speedy ability to regenerate, if not any extra strength in fighting.

"The Immutable's blood closed my wounds," I say, anticipating Toinette's brother's question. "I was forced to drink a sip of his blood to assume the role of squire, but deep in my heart I'll always be a daughter of the people."

Suddenly, I remember the only family object that I've kept. With haste I slip my hand into the pocket of my nightgown and take out my mother's pocket watch. On the backside of the bronze case lid are some engraved words.

"Liberty . . . or . . . or . . . death . . . ," the carpenter says, deciphering the words with difficulty. My guess is that he can barely read.

"It's the motto of the people's Fronde—proof that I'm on your side."

Finally, he lowers his dagger.

His eyes fall on his wet clodhoppers. They're soaking the freshly waxed floor, and it's as if he's suddenly wondering what he's doing here.

"You could give purpose to your grief," I tell him gently. "You could honor your sister's memory the way I honor Bastien's and all my loved ones. You could sabotage the Magna Vampyria at its very foundation."

He looks up at me with big open eyes, his body shaking in disbelief, as if I've just said something blasphemous.

"My name is Jeanne Froidelac," I tell him as I extend my hand.

"Paulin Trébuchet," he responds in one breath.

I force myself to smile at him despite the deep emotion that grips me. "The people's Fronde could use someone like you, Paulin," I tell him. "Join us in the fight for the sake of the fourth estate."

His eyes widen even more.

I have the impression of seeing my own surprise reflected in them, the surprise I felt when I, too, found out about the existence of a revolutionary organization that spans several continents.

"What are you saying?" he asks, sighing. "Don't you know there's no salvation for the fourth estate, no light at the end of the tunnel? There are only the Shadows, all the darker and colder. The vampyres will never step down. Their power only strengthens with time. The earth gets a little bit cooler every year. And the nocturnal abominations multiply like crazy." He gives a disenchanted look at my luxurious silk nightgown. "Maybe you forgot that since you came to live at the palace, but it's always us, the little people, who pay with our lives. Always us who die of hunger because of bad harvests. Always us who quench the thirst of vampyres with our blood. Always us who fall prey to the creatures of the night."

Paulin's lugubrious words trouble me. I know he's right. These last few years the mysterious hold of the Shadows has only solidified its grip over the world. The vampyres' thirst for blood grows a little more each month, and the nighttime breeds even more bogeymen.

"In the suburbs of Versailles, the ghouls have never been so voracious," Paulin says bitterly. "Rumor has it that it's even worse in Paris. The people will end up being bled dry by the vampyres, then devoured by those cannibalistic monsters."

Even if I never encountered a ghoul in my faraway village of Butte-aux-Rats, I know that these scavengers swarm the cemeteries of big cities . . . and that they sometimes even attack miserable wretches who have the bad luck of being out after the start of the curfew.

I shake my head, trying to push away the horrible visions that assail me.

The room is bathed in quivering shadows and echoes of thunder, like nightmares that try to materialize.

"I used to be as miserable as you are, Paulin, but the Fronde saved me," I assure him, mustering all my conviction. "You have to be hopeful again. In secret, a vast network is preparing a revolution against the Magna Vampyria. Not only here in France but also in the Americas. To liberate the entire world from the bloodsuckers. To put an end to the era of the Shadows."

The lightning lets a sliver of white light enter under the bedroom curtains like the cautious hope of a new dawn.

This glimmer of light is reflected in Paulin's eyes, the eyes of a lost soul who wants to believe.

"If this organization really exists, what use could it have for a cripple like me?" he ends up saying.

He looks down at his lame leg.

"You managed to come all the way here, despite your infirmity," I point out. "Our cause could benefit from someone able to penetrate unnoticed into the best-guarded area of the Magna Vampyria."

Under the hem of the scarf that covers his eyes, a pale smile spreads across Paulin's lips.

"I started work again, two days ago, with only one thought in mind: avenging Toinette, even if it means my own death," he confesses. "I took advantage of the storm to slip away from the guards who watch over the dormitory where the workers sleep during the curfew. As a carpenter with a lot of years spent working at the palace, I know which roofs to climb. And I know the servants' corridors, like the one I took to get here."

With his chin, he indicates the curtain from where he appeared. Behind the crimson velvet is the outline of a concealed door I'd never noticed before.

"Hurry and go back the way you came before the guards discover your absence in the morning," I instruct him. "And come back to see me here in a week, at the same time. Meanwhile, I'll have consulted with the coordinator of the people's Fronde. I can't reveal his name—at least, not yet—but I promise that he'll know just how to put you to work."

Paulin inhales deeply. He appears a little taller, a little straighter than before. Such is the power of hope, however tenuous it may be. It heals men and women who seemed broken and helps them stand upright. A desperate person entered my room, but he's leaving as a fighter.

He unties the scarf that hid his face. "You laid yourself open, Jeanne," he says, clearly moved. "The least I can do is show you my ugly mug."

By the glow of the oil lamp, I see a young face with its own smattering of freckles. My heart bleeds: he's the spitting image of Toinette. But his wan smile reminds me of my own dear Bastien's, forever etched in my memory. It's the smile of a boy who finally dares to dream of a different world.

"Nothing will replace your sister, Paulin," I tell him, on the verge of tears. "And nothing will replace my brother. But if you're willing, from now on, let us be each other's brother- and sister-in-arms." I reach out to him and add, "Liberty or death."

He pulls me close in the kind of brotherly hug that I've greatly missed.

While the storm outside rumbles, he repeats with fervor, "Liberty or dea—"

The last word gets stuck in his throat, no doubt from all the emotion.

And the warm shower that rains down on my face must be his tears. I raise a hand to dry them off.

As my fingers brush against his cheek, I feel a warm, viscous liquid. His face is a mask of gloom against the feeble light of the oil lamp.

"Paul . . . Paulin?" I stammer.

By way of response, he lets out a horrible gurgling sound. My hand glides from his cheek to his mouth. A steel tongue has sprung out from between his lips—the tip of the sword that has just pierced his nape and plunged into his palate.

"Traitor!" roars a voice from behind the carpenter.

Horrified, I untangle myself from Paulin's grasp. His muscular arms seem to want to hold on to me so that I embrace death in turn. The steel tongue suddenly retracts from his mouth as the killer abruptly pulls it back.

In the blink of an eye, I catch sight of the newcomer's attire: wine-red livery and a festooned three-cornered hat. He's a Swiss Guard. With dread, I also notice that the bedroom door is open. He must have entered as I was hugging Paulin.

"I thought I heard a noise coming from this bedroom," the Swiss Guard says with a snarl. He wipes the bloody blade of his sword against his boot. "I came into the vestibule and put my ear against the panel to see if you were sleeping. A good move on my part. I overheard your entire conversation, Mademoiselle Diane . . . or, I should say, Jeanne."

He raises his weapon and advances toward me.

"The king's favorite squire is an agent of the Fronde," he growls. "When the Immutable finds out, he'll give you the punishment you deserve . . . and I'll be rewarded as I should!"

While he holds me by the tip of his sword, he tears a length of curtain rope that was hanging on a hook. I have no hope of escaping. This time I'm not dealing with a craftsman with no weapon experience; I'm facing an elite soldier. The Swiss Guards are the best fencers in the kingdom.

He advances toward me carefully, sidestepping Paulin's body without letting me out of his sight. My intervention to save the sovereign has given me a fierce reputation at the court.

"You don't look like much, gray and petite that you are," my opponent says mockingly, yet sounding nervous. "Hard to believe I'm facing a ferocious fighter."

"I don't pretend to be anything other than a huntress who's been plucked from her forests," I blurt out, my throat dry.

"Well, tonight you're going to let me tie you up like a jackrabbit, or I'll skewer you the same way I speared that scoundrel!"

He steps behind me and slips the blade of his sword under my chin. Using his other hand with fiendish dexterity, he binds the cord around my wrists.

"I really doubt that you'd skewer me," I say, breathless.

"Really? If you only knew how many lowlifes I've speared during my years of service."

"You need to deliver me alive if you want the king to hear my confession. But if you bring him only my dead body, you'll get no promotion and no honor. On the contrary, you risk being sent to the gallows for having killed his *favorite squire*, as you said yourself."

"Shut up, traitor!" the Swiss Guard orders.

But I sense that my words have gotten under his skin. His blade moves slightly away from my chin.

Now's my chance.

Whirling around so I'm behind him, I pass my tied arms around his head and fall onto his back. Then, with all my might, I pull on his neck, tightening the three turns of cord against his protruding Adam's apple.

"I . . . what . . . ," he chokes, his breathing cut off.

His sword is doing crazy loops in the air as he tries to stab me. But what had been my weakness has become my strength. My petite body, which the guard mocked only moments ago, is now out of reach.

My feet leave the ground. I grab onto the improvised garrote with all my weight, like a bell ringer holds on to his cord. Instead of ringing, the human bell from which I'm suspended gives a gurgling hiccup sound. The howling storm spirits it off the same way it muffles the noise of our two bodies crashing to the floor.

The Swiss Guard finally releases his sword so that he can bring both his hands to his neck to try and loosen my stranglehold. If he had used his strong muscles to shake me off him from the start, no doubt he would have succeeded. But he lost precious seconds as he clung to his weapon, and now his strength is starting to ebb. He's agitating his fingers, trying in vain to slip them between the taut cord and his purplish neck. My own fingers are clenched so hard on the garrote that they're turning white.

Tighter.

Make him stop talking altogether.

To avenge Paulin, Bastien, and all the victims of the Magna Vampyria.

I suddenly feel a sharp pain on my head. One of the Swiss Guard's hands has slid along the triple-bound silk cord twisted at the back of his neck to grab my hair. He's pulling with all his might—the last ounce of strength from a man who can taste death.

I bite hard on the insides of my cheeks so that I don't scream and rouse the attention of the rest of the palace. As my teeth sink into my skin, the garrote sinks into the Swiss Guard.

His veins swell up like bulging tree roots.

Suddenly, the hand that was pulling my hair goes limp.

The neck beneath my clenched fists stops pulsing.

His big head bobs and falls sluggishly to the side.

Slowly, I get up, short of breath, my fingers numb, sick that I've had to kill to save myself and protect the secret of the Fronde.

The Swiss Guard's inert body bathes in the widening pool of blood that gushes from Paulin's pierced nape. Both of them look as if they've drifted off to sleep, the lowlife and the one who boasted that he skewered them. Frozen in the same eternal sleep as the girl in my nightmare.

Outside, the storm makes one of the shutters bang, sounding like a skeleton's disjointed clacking teeth. It's as if the Shadows themselves were frantically snickering.

2

GRAND RETIRING

"Just as a candle flame attracts moths, you certainly have a knack for attracting rebels, Mademoiselle de Gastefriche," the King of Shadows declares.

The monarch just entered the hallway that leads to the mortuary chamber. He's followed by a crowd of courtiers and the chilled air that signals the presence of vampyres. As with every dawn and every dusk, I'm supposed to wait for him with the other squires. Even this morning, when I've just had a close brush with death. Nothing disrupts the rituals of Versailles, which for three centuries have been as regular as clockwork. It's the throbbing symphony of hell on earth.

"It was surely a coincidence, sire," I say, lowering my head in front of the imposing sovereign, who's clothed in the most precious fabrics. "The rebel entered my room by chance. He could just as well have gone into any other."

To speak of Paulin in the past tense, after just only meeting him, breaks my heart. But I can't let any trace of sadness overwhelm me in front of the king, the courtiers pressed around him, and the five other squires in their dark leather breastplates.

"We don't believe it was a coincidence," the sovereign states as he stops a few inches away from me, towering over me in all his haughtiness.

The deep voice that escapes from his metal lips chills my blood even more than the deathly cold emanating from his person.

Under his large peacock-feathered hat and between the thick curls of his long brown hair glistens a gold face in the image of the sun god Apollo. A face with no emotion or expression, frozen for eternity. A mask that conceals the real face of history's first vampyre, a face that was disfigured during the procedure that granted him eternal life.

"That miserable wretch went after you because he knew how dear you are to us," the sovereign says. "Tell us how you crushed that pest of an insect."

I can feel the eyes of the barons and marquises fall upon me, scrutinizing the gash left by Paulin's dagger on my cheekbone. The eyelids of the mortal courtiers blink with curiosity, while the pupils of the immortals are fixed and retracted at the sight of blood. I also sense that my fellow squires—with whom I'm supposed to form the strongest team in the kingdom—are listening and observing me intently.

"I screamed as soon as the intruder entered my room," I lie as calmly as possible. "A courageous Swiss Guard came running to help, but the rogue slit his throat with a dagger."

He had his throat slit, yes. But I don't say that I'm the one who sliced it to cover up the real reason for his death: strangulation. My instincts told me that that method of death would square better with my story.

"I had just enough time to grab the unfortunate guard's sword and turn the blade against the aggressor."

One of the aristocratic vampyres accompanying the sovereign steps forward. His tall, lean body is loaded down with the weight of many medals, and his gaunt face emerges from beneath the curls of his wig like the sharp edge of a blade: Ézéchiel de Mélac, minister of the armies.

"*Turn the blade against the aggressor*, that's an understatement, Your Majesty," he says. "According to my soldiers' report, your squire plunged the sword into that parasite's neck right up to the hilt. She pinned him like the vulgar moth that you alluded to earlier."

The courtiers roar with laughter at the Marquis de Mélac's words. The king raises a hand, his long white fingers studded with gems, his sleeve festooned with lace from Calais. Immediately, the laughter stops. "They tell us the intruder was a carpenter who worked on our construction sites," he says. "Is that true?"

A small man clothed in black bends so low before the monarch that his gray wig dusts the floor. He's Bontemps XXI, the mortal attendant at the palace, so named because he's the twentieth descendant of the first Bontemps, the manservant who served Louis XIV before his transmutation.

"Yes, sire," he says. "After badly injuring his leg, Paulin Trébuchet was recently reinstated on the expansion team of the palace. That's how the scoundrel repaid our magnanimity: he attacked your people in their sleep."

"No! It was *us* he attacked!" the king corrects in a thunderous voice that rattles the Bohemia-crystal chandeliers. "Anyone who attacks our squires attacks our very being, for our sacred blood runs in their veins."

The members of the assembly freeze in place in the heavily gilded hallway. They seem as rooted to their spots as the antique marbles lining the walls. Squires are a breed apart, halfway between the mortal nobility and the high aristocracy of vampyres. We have only one sip of supernatural blood running in our veins, not enough to become immortal, but as the Immutable just reminded everyone, it's sacred blood. *His* blood.

"The body of that vile rebel will be impaled on the Hunting Wall where the ravens can peck at it," the sovereign decrees. "And every laborer from his dormitory will be whipped until blood is drawn. Until they name his accomplices."

"Uh . . . Your Majesty, it would seem the rebel was acting alone, without accomplices . . . ," Bontemps says softly.

One look from the monarch and he stops talking. The valet draws his wrinkly neck into his shoulders like a turtle into its shell.

"Tell me, Montfaucon, is there a link between this Paulin and the conspirators rotting in our prisons?" the king demands as he turns toward Raymond de Montfaucon.

The latter is a giant of a man, constrained by a long riding coat with a large collar, where the curls of his wig fan out as limply as the branches of a willow tree. Just like me, Montfaucon is a double agent at the court. For years now, he has used his position as director of the Grande Écurie to secretly coordinate the people's Fronde. He recruited me while I was a pupil at his school, and since I've become a squire, I've patiently awaited his orders to serve the cause. My engagement was born out of my family's massacre, but guilt is what motivates Montfaucon. He comes from a long line of executioners who have served the Immutable—a bloody heritage that haunts him to this day.

"There's no link between Paulin Trébuchet and the conspirators, Your Majesty," he says assuredly, his voice raspy. "During our interrogations concerning La Roncière's attempted coup, no one mentioned this miscreant. He was most likely a dreamer with no connection to last month's plot. At most, news of the failed conspiracy might have pushed him to take action."

"That may be, but are we certain all the conspirators were apprehended?" the king inquires.

Mélac puffs his chest out like a rooster.

"Absolutely, sire!" he says. "Thirty-two of those wretches perished on the spot when you appeared in all your magnificence."

Magnificence . . . what a euphemism to speak of the king's face, which was momentarily revealed during the attempted assassination. I was behind him and saw nothing when he briefly removed his mask. No one who did see his face lived to tell about it.

"Sixty-seven other conspirators were rounded up in the halls of Versailles," Mélac continues. "Forty-three more were captured by my troops in the Ardennes, on the La Roncière estate, including the instigator of this evil plot, Blanche de La Roncière, mother of the ignoble Tristan."

The monarch smacks the floor with the tip of his walking stick, like a vengeful Jupiter strikes his enemies with lightning.

"Let us continue to squeeze the prisoners as we do the fruits of our greenhouse, until we extract the marrow from their breaking bones, along with the most complete confessions from their treacherous mouths."

At that instant, the clocks in the hallway chime eight times.

A prelate clad in a long scarlet coat steps out of the sovereign's shadow. It's Exili, the grand archiater of France, head of the Hematic Faculty and the king's personal doctor. His bald, skeletal head, with a bluish tint that stands out against the white fabric of his ruff, has horrified me since the first time I laid eyes on it.

"Eight o'clock just chimed, Your Majesty," he whispers in a hissing, reptilian timbre that makes every hair on my body stand on end. "It's nearly dawn, and day is about to break . . ."

"So be it. Let us disrobe!" the king orders. "We are quite sleepy."

He removes his large hat and hands it to the wardrobe master, who takes it with as much care as if it were adorned with the feathers of an angel rather than a peacock.

An army of valets rush to remove the royal shoulder sling, the jabot studded with precious stones, the walking stick with a mother-of-pearl knob, and the gold thread-embroidered vest. The rigid ritual follows its daily course under the watchful eye of the grand chamberlain, a chubby vampyre with a pompous air who's bedecked in ribbons. For ages, he's been in charge of tending to the king's chamber.

The squire to my right gives me a discreet elbow jab. It's Rafael de Montesueño, a young knight from Castile with brown hair and dark-green eyes. He's the only squire who's been friendly to me since I started my duties at the court. I alienated the only other two girls: Hélénaïs de Plumigny was my chief rival during all the tests leading to the Sip of the King, and I had to betray Proserpina Castlecliff's trust in order to get here. As for the other two boys, Suraj de Jaipur and Zacharie de Grand-Domaine, I hardly know them.

"Everything all right, Diane?" Rafael whispers.

He touches my hand with the fingers of his black-polished nails, the fashion at the court of Spain.

My heart aches. Even if I don't have any scruples about my false identity when it comes to my enemies, I still have trouble hearing a name that isn't my own spoken by those who only wish me well.

"Everything's fine. I just have a small scratch, is all . . . ," I say, brushing my cheek.

"How did that dirty scoundrel dare hurt such a perfect face?" someone behind me whispers, right against the back of my neck.

It's an all-too-familiar voice, full of passion . . .

I turn halfway around and am met with the harmonious features of the viscount Alexandre de Mortange. His face is framed by his sumptuous red hair. This vampyre is hot on my heels as soon as I leave my apartments. My only break comes at sunrise, when he's forced to return to his coffin like the other immortals. The sweet-talker with the face of an archangel is in love with me—or rather, he's infatuated with the girl he believes me to be. He's ignorant of my true identity. He doesn't know that when he annihilated an obscure den of rebels back in the far reaches of the Auvergne, he took part in killing my family. But *I* know it, and I won't ever forget. Mortange tops the list of bloodsuckers that I've sworn to myself I would eliminate as soon as possible.

"If the one who dared lay a hand on you were in my grip, I'd kill him a second time," he says with an amorous ardor that disgusts me.

"Commoners die only once, Alex," I reply, forcing myself to smile graciously. "Only aristocrats can sometimes be reborn in the Shadows."

"Just as well! And you, my dear Diane, you're well on your way to obtaining eternal life. First you thwarted a conspiracy, then you became an amazing squire prodigy, and now you're a killer of rebels. You're racking up heroic deeds, which is positively fabulous. Didn't I tell you that you'd create sparks at Versailles?" He gives me a dreadful complicit smile, then points discreetly with his chin toward the Immutable, still surrounded by his flock of bustling valets. "I bet the king will authorize your transmutation very soon, for services rendered to the Crown."

If Alexandre's ardor repulses me, the future he describes totally horrifies me. The Immutable usually grants the transmutation of a few squires after a certain length of service. For the death-lickers of Versailles, ascending to immortal status is the supreme honor, the holy grail; for me, it's a damnation I have to avoid at all costs.

At that instant, the grand chamberlain's voice rings out, silencing the courtiers' private chatter.

"The king is disrobed!"

The supreme vampyre is now free of his knee-length coat and wide culottes with side ribbons. He's wearing only his shirt, breeches, and silk stockings, all of them black. Instead of bringing him closer to his subjects, this state of pared-down dress simply distances him further. Without the multitude of layers to absorb his coldness, his body disperses a glacial—*arctic*—aura. His unbuttoned collar offers a glimpse of a large white neck shot through with nearly blue-black veins, as if it's rotting. It's no longer blood that runs through the Immutable's veins, it's the Styx itself, the river of the underworld, saturated with Shadows . . .

Under Exili's direction, a small army of doctors in dark shirts and tall conical hats switch places with the valets. They take the sovereign's nonexistent pulse, pat his pale skin, and place fancy bronze instruments on his body to listen inside. I don't know what's being assessed, but for three hundred years the king's health has been a public spectacle. Just like every aspect of his living death. At the conclusion of this baroque ritual, Exili gives his master a crystal vial filled with a ruby-red liquid.

"Your medicine for the dawn, sire. Bohemian blood spiced with the fragrances of the pharaohs. To better invigorate your royal entrails before you sleep."

The sovereign empties the vial between his metal lips in one swallow.

"It's the king's bedtime!" the grand chamberlain cries out.

Straightaway, court ushers extend thick velvet ropes to push back the crowd. While many at the court are allowed to attend the start of the

Grand Retiring ceremony in the hallway, only the highest-level nobility—
including the squires—are accorded the right to glimpse more.

With pomp, a Swiss Guard opens the double-leaf door of the ante-
chamber. Beyond it, an immaculate vestibule stretches out, leading to
the monumental mortuary door made entirely of ebony.

But today, for the first time, its impenetrable blackness is marred
by a white blotch.

A large envelope is nailed to a portion of the dark carved moldings.

By way of address, the missive displays tall handwritten letters:

To the attention of the King of Shadows

From the Lady of Miracles

Most striking of all is the white wax seal that closes the envelope.
It looks like an imitation of the royal seal, except that it represents a
crescent moon rather than the sun—a fearless profile with hollow eyes
and no pupils, a parted mouth that reveals sharpened canines.

Muffled whispers are heard among the ranks of the courtiers.

"Damn!" Mélac swears.

"What an affront!" Exili exclaims.

Bontemps hurries to retrieve the envelope, while the grand chamberlain apologizes profusely.

"Sire, I—I don't understand. No one has access to this antecham-
ber . . . ," he stammers, the ribbons of his attire quivering as he panics.
"Every missive systematically goes through the king's cabinet of royal
mail . . . I'll have this one thrown into the fire."

"Out of my sight, *ex*-Chamberlain," says the Immutable, his voice
as acid as a spurt of vitriol.

He turns his gold mask toward Bontemps.

"Whoever it is, the person who dared plaster that missive on the
door of our room wanted to make a splash and embarrass us in front
of the court. It failed. We will not be intimidated. Read it, Bontemps."

"Ugh . . . now, Your Majesty?" the valet sputters.

"Make us repeat ourselves even once and you will instantly be ceding your place to the twenty-second Bontemps," the sovereign growls.

The domestic unseals the envelope with trembling hands and takes out a letter. He starts reading it aloud before the transfixed courtiers.

> King Louis,
> It is in this chamber that you had a near brush with ultimate death. A plot was narrowly foiled, but how many others are being hatched in the shadows, either here at Versailles or even more so in Paris? Just as the sun cannot shine on every corner, your vigilance cannot be everywhere at once. You need other vampyric celestial bodies by your side to illuminate the world.
>
> We, the Lady of Miracles, have decided to come out of the darkness and make ourselves known to you. We want to offer you such an alliance. From our court in the depths of Paris, we reign over an army of ghouls and abominations whose strength your police were able to measure these last months. In fact, we are already the true sovereign of the capital. So remove your useless army and let us have the city. Other vice-kings and vice-queens are already seated and serving in your name on the thrones of England, Spain, and all the nations of the Magna Vampyria.
>
> Make us vice-queen of Paris and we will be good neighbors—just as the moon shines brightly when there is no sun.
>
> Refuse us, and we will be forced to confront you. But just remember that it is the moon that eclipses the sun, and not the other way around, when these two celestial bodies meet up in the firmament.

As he reads the letter, poor Bontemps turns totally pale. The threats contained in the concluding words make him shiver so hard that his teeth start chattering.

"It . . . it's signed . . . *Hecate, Lady of Miracles*," he concludes, breathless.

The king, who remained impassive as the letter was read, grabs it from Bontemps's hands and brandishes it under Mélac's nose.

"Who?" he roars, his face reddening. "Who is this so-called Lady of Miracles who wants to seize Paris under the pretext of making it a vice-kingdom? Mélac, you are responsible for the administration of the capital—so answer me!"

The minister of the armies is usually sure of himself, but his voice quivers.

"According to L'Esquille, the police lieutenant general, it's just a tale out of Paris . . . a vulgar rumor without basis. It's so absurd, I didn't think it worth mentioning to you. The people say that a new Court of Miracles was formed in the depths of the capital, a court that commands the nighttime abominations. Of course, it's impossible. For one thing, everyone knows that the ghouls cannot be tamed. Secondly, the ancient Court of Miracles was dissolved nearly three hundred years ago."

"A legend does not nail missives to doors!" the Immutable roars. "A rumor does not desecrate the royal chamber door!"

I have the impression that the gold mask shakes a tiny bit. Could it be that the supreme master of the Magna Vampyria is . . . scared? As the letter said, he escaped a close call with death in this very chamber only a month ago. And now an invisible rival has come to challenge him again, offering a deal that sounds a lot like blackmail. A deal that wants to snatch the capital from his empire.

"But sire, this letter is a fantasy without rhyme or reason," Mélac says defensively. "A schemer obviously wants to benefit from the fresh outbreak of ghoul attacks in Paris. She's pretending that she's the one who controls them. Rubbish. The ghouls are nothing more than stomachs on uncontrollable legs, with no objective other than their next gruesome meal."

The grand archiater clears his throat, letting out what sounds like an echo from a deep well.

"This letter is less of a fantasy than you proclaim, Marquis de Mélac," he says softly. "The image of the moon is not an innocent choice. A celestial orb capable of eclipsing the sun isn't just a provocation—it's also the alchemical symbol of the ghouls."

I shiver in spite of my thick leather breastplate. If anyone knows the dark mysteries of alchemy, it's the grand archiater. After all, three hundred years ago, he presided over the terrible ritual that transmuted Louis XIV into a vampyre.

"Alchemical symbol?" Mélac chokes out. "What does that signify?"

"The ways of the Shadows are impenetrable," Exili answers mysteriously. "Whoever wrote that letter pretends to be immortal. She must be an unrecorded vampyre, illegally transmuted and outside the *numerus clausus* of the Faculty. She may even be an especially powerful alchemist. It's true that the Faculty has never been able to discover the origin of the ghouls, and even less to tame them. What if this lady succeeded in doing just that? The name she uses, Hecate . . . belongs to the ancient goddess of the occult moon from the depths. Each month she vanishes from the sky and burrows into the earth. She's the mother of monsters, nightmares, and sorcery."

"With all due respect, Exili, this alchemical mumbo jumbo is ridiculous—" Mélac starts to say.

The prelate's hoarse voice cuts him off. "There's nothing ridiculous about alchemy," he says. "It would explain the recent and coordinated outbreak of ghoul attacks in Paris, attacks you yourself spoke of earlier. Attacks that your troops have not presently been able to subdue. Are you going to wait and let the ghouls seize the entire city before you take action?"

The minister of the armies is momentarily silenced, gut punched and publicly humiliated by Exili's accusation.

He pivots on his red heels—the heel color reserved for aristocratic vampyres—and turns his obsequious face toward the king.

"Sire, I will send all my soldiers in pursuit of this usurper," he hurries to promise.

"The same soldiers who guard this palace where anyone can enter, as if it's a windmill?" the king lashes out.

Suddenly, he leans toward me, the protruding edges of his metal mask catching the candlelight.

"You, Gastefriche. We are so ill served these days that we place greater confidence in a young lady of seventeen years than we do in an entire army. You alone took down La Roncière's secret scheme. Today we ask you to thwart another revolt. We charge you with finding the Lady of Miracles, if she exists."

Found wanting in front of the most elite courtiers of the palace, Mélac glares at me with eagle eyes. His thin lips purse involuntarily, revealing the tips of his pointy canines in all their stiff anger.

A seasoned courtier, he manages nonetheless to restrain this hint of savagery, which is frowned upon at the court. Instead, he gives a bitter, disdainful smile.

"With all due respect, sire, Diane de Gastefriche is only a frail and slight young girl," he sniffles.

"*Frail*, a girl who fought and slew the traitor Tristan de La Roncière?" the king snaps back. "*Slight*, a young lady whose veins proudly pulse with a sip of divine blood, bestowing upon her superhuman powers?"

Shamed, the general lowers his head.

"I . . . uh . . . *frail* and *slight* were undoubtedly not the correct words, sire," he stammers.

"No, they were not, for you're a dunce. Do you happen to know Aesop's fable 'The Lion and the Mouse,' retold by our own good man, La Fontaine?"

"A—a fable?" the minister sputters. "Forgive me, Your Majesty. I admit I'm more versed in army treatises than in literature."

"Well, that's unfortunate. If you read more literature, you'd choose the *correct words* to address your king. And if you had come across La Fontaine, you would know that *there's none so small but you his aid may need*. In the fable, the lion has a mouse companion who gnaws at the nets that hold the lion captive. Here, we have our little gray mouse to slip and scurry through the nooks and crannies of Paris."

Little gray mouse—that's what the Immutable persists in calling me, with a mixture of affection and condescension.

I have to find a way to get out of this mission that has just befallen me. My place is here, at Versailles, where I can spy on the palace, not in Paris, settling the quarrels of power-hungry bloodsuckers.

I execute an awkward curtsy.

"Sire, your confidence fills me with honor, but I am a mere provincial who has never stepped foot in Paris . . ."

"Suraj de Jaipur will accompany you. Our faithful squire went to the capital last spring on our orders to combat the ghouls. At the time, we were unaware that a renegade was organizing their attacks. Suraj knows all the backstreets like the palm of his hand, including the alleyways where the Marquis de Mélac's soldiers are afraid to venture."

As Suraj bows his turban-covered head, I scramble to find another reason not to go.

An idea quickly comes to me.

"There's something else, Your Majesty," I say. "I have to confess that, even with the sip of your priceless royal blood, for now, I haven't noticed any superhuman power in me."

Apart from the horrid nightmares and raging migraines, I add inwardly.

The grand archiater leans toward me and pats my cheek with his long bony fingers, as if I were a piece of fruit he was inspecting for ripeness.

"Hmmm . . . the Sip of the King reveals its powers differently in each subject," he affirms, assessing me with sunken eyes from above his ruff. "With some squires the effect takes longer to manifest itself."

Hélénaïs, who until now was champing at the bit, seizes the moment to make her presence known. She executes a perfect curtsy—far more graceful than mine—then raises her beautiful face, framed by chestnut curls styled à la hurly-burly, toward the king.

"Sire, I would gladly take Diane's place and go to Paris," she says. "The Sip of the King has already given me all its powers. I feel stronger, hardier . . . and, more importantly, much faster."

The king looks at her through the slits of his impenetrable mask.

"You are competing with the Baronette de Gastefriche, Mademoiselle de Plumigny," he says. "It is a mistake. You should know that our squires must suppress all personal sentiments in order to devote themselves to our service."

As always, the Immutable's words are carefully selected. When we competed in the ruthless qualifying tests for the Sip of the King, Hélénaïs accused me of being merely the daughter of a knight banneret, not a baron. After I became a squire, the sovereign confirmed my title of baronette. He just reminded my rival that within the hierarchy of aristocrats, I rank above her. Her claim to nobility is more recent.

"Show us that you can act in concert," the king decrees with finality. "You will, all three of you, go to Paris, each bearing a royal pass. We charge you with finding the Court of Miracles and bringing us its lady, alive—back to Versailles, so that we can hear from her lips how she came to tame the ghouls." The monarch straightens to his full height, looming over the gathered courtiers by a full head. "Our armies will be that much stronger once they are reinforced by a corps of nocturnal abominations available at will. Then we will fully be King of Shadows, commander not only of the vampyres but also of the ghouls. Commander of all the night's creatures, and we will show France, Europe, and the world that no moon will ever eclipse our immortal brilliance!"

He crushes the letter in his ring-laden fist. When he opens it, there's nothing left but finely ground paper.

The voice that escapes from his immobile lips is even more merciless than his fist.

"Our beams of vengeance will shine brightly as soon as tonight. On second thought, the prisoners who plotted with La Roncière have taken sufficient advantage of our prisons' hospitality. They will be executed after dusk, at our grand gibbet. That will serve as a warning to all those who dare defy us. The people of Paris will be given a reprieve from the curfew and be summoned to witness the hanging. May it be an example to them all! Montfaucon, arrange the details with your brother, our royal executioner."

I think I see a nervous facial tic agitate the grand equerry at the mention of the sinister Parisian gallows built by his ancestors. As for his brother, it's the first time I'm hearing about him.

Already, the sovereign turns on his heel.

The two ebony door panels part before him like magic, revealing a room that's entirely black from floor to ceiling. This is where he was transmuted three centuries ago. As with every time that the mortuary chamber opens, I grow dizzy and my ears start to ring. This place is mysteriously exempt from the passage of time, as the frozen hands on the clocks bear witness. It's a black hole that distorts perspectives and swallows up sounds.

An enormous sarcophagus rests in the center of this evil room, oozing with the Shadows. The heavy lid glides on its support without the slightest creak, driven only by the all-powerful will of the Immutable. His back turned to the court, he steps slowly over the thick rim and stretches out on the bed of stone.

The marble lid closes over the royal sepulchre.

The ebony doors shut themselves, hermetically sealing.

3
REUNION

"Hurry," Montfaucon grumbles. "The Hunting Wall will be shutting soon."

He crosses the palace's Court of Honor in long strides, the tails of his long leather coat flapping behind him in the chilled air, his limp curls fluttering over his shoulders.

Suraj, Hélénaïs, and I follow closely behind. It's been decided that we'll spend the day at the Grande Écurie in order to prepare for our mission.

At present, we're dashing toward the gigantic wall surrounding the palace and its gardens. We have to get past it before this lone entry point is sealed off for the next twelve hours. The Hunting Wall, as it's called, is an imposing defensive structure that's supposed to protect the palace and gardens against any forced entry during the day.

"Do you have any springs in your legs?" Montfaucon hurls at us as he darts into the tunnel that cuts across the ramparts.

On the double, we cover the few yards of the torchlit passageway.

As we reach the Parade Grounds on the other side, a seismic tremor makes the cobblestones shake beneath our feet. It's the underground gearwheels turning, activated by the same hydraulic network that supplies water to the fountains at Versailles. Behind us, the enormous limestone-panel blocks close, sliding on their rails. As with each time that the Hunting Wall is set in motion, I have the sickening feeling that the gigantic statues of prowling vampyres that adorn the walls are coming to life. The red glimmer of early dawn illuminates their cruel details—sharp jaws, pointy fingernails, ecstatic eyes. But in the middle of the stone giants, the most horrible sight is to be found at the top of the building: the outline of a human-size body impaled on a hook.

It's the remains of Tristan de La Roncière. For a month now, his body has been exposed to the elements and half-devoured by ravens. It's all that's left of the boy who broke my heart before I chopped off his head. The boy who dreamed of taking the King of Shadows' place and wanted to marry me now serves as feed for the scavenging birds. I look away, troubled. I must not allow myself to think of what could have been.

"Let's go!" Montfaucon shouts, snapping me from my macabre thoughts.

Turning his back to the Hunting Wall and the thousands of immortal courtiers resting in their palace coffins, he leads us to the other side of the Parade Grounds and to the gate of the Grande Écurie.

It feels strange to enter the school courtyard for the first time since I left in October. It was only four short weeks ago, and yet I have the impression that years have gone by. Through the tall second-floor windows all lit with chandeliers, I can make out the boarders, who are having breakfast: the boys in the right wing, the girls in the left wing.

"Jaipur and Plumigny—go have something to eat with your old classmates," Montfaucon orders them. "I'm taking Gastefriche to a quiet bedroom on the top floor so she can recuperate; her night was cut short, and she needs to gather all her strength to face Paris tonight. We'll meet at noon, all four of us, in the room with the mare tapestries, and plan our strategy."

We take our leave of the two other squires and climb the school's grand staircase. But instead of taking me to the attic rooms as he said he would, the grand equerry heads toward a hallway that leads to his office. He shuts and double-locks the door behind us.

I want to ask him questions. So many questions since our last meeting. But he places his large multi-steel-ringed index finger on my lips. "Shhh. Not here."

He goes around his desk and heads toward the books that line the back of the room. On the shelves, old equestrian treatises alternate with formaldehyde-filled jars in which monstrous hands are marinating— hands of ghouls, sectioned off by the grand equerry himself. Montfaucon inherited the bloodthirsty nature of his long line of executioner ancestors and devotes his nights to hunting in the cemeteries of Versailles. Ghouls are his preferred game—and even if I've never crossed paths with those fearsome creatures, the appendages in the jars conjure up creatures that spring from the worst nightmares.

Montfaucon stops in front of a heavy container that holds a hand four times larger than mine. I notice that it has only four fingers, with long yellowish claws at the tips. Next to it is a collection of cracked leather-bound books. Montfaucon pulls on the thickest volume, titled *Nocturnal Abominations and the Art of Hunting Them*. But instead of leaving the shelf . . . the book turns with a click: it's a spring-loaded lever.

The library wall creaks open halfway, revealing a flight of uneven steps that plunge toward the bowels of the Grande Écurie. Montfaucon lights a lantern, then closes the hidden door behind us.

"Just like my room at the palace . . . ," I whisper as we head down the stairs. It seems like all Versailles is rigged with secret passageways.

"True. And the walls have ears. But in the belly of the school, we'll be able to talk without fear."

After a long descent, we finally reach Montfaucon's secret den: the torture chamber where he usually cuts up his ghastly hunting trophies.

He plops down in a chair, next to a wall where saws and pliers are hanging. Then he invites me to sit across from him.

"The last time we were here, I had to stretch you on the torture rack to make you talk," he reminds me as he points to a wooden bed with sinister pulleys above it. "Today, however, we're here as friends, so tell me everything."

Montfaucon smooths his goatee with his gnarled fingertips.

"You are decidedly full of surprises, Jeanne Froidelac," he says in the middle of my story.

The grand equerry may be sorely lacking in warmth, a brute haunted by bloodthirsty impulses, yet his words warm my heart. Hearing him say my real name, with a certain admiration, no less, reminds me of who I am and the goal I set for myself. To serve the Fronde in the name of Bastien, Maman, and all my loved ones. My raison d'être.

"You have an amazing survival instinct," he adds. His eyes glow like coal between the limp curls of his wig. "And what's more, an impressive capacity to kill."

"I only defended myself against that Swiss Guard," I tell him. "It was either him or me. I don't derive any joy from killing anyone, believe me—even if he was the vampyres' cruel servant and had dozens of victims to his name."

"And yet you're such a gifted killer," Montfaucon insists.

I twist in my chair, suddenly ill at ease. The smell of saltpeter that impregnates the damp walls feels suffocating. But what's oppressing me even more than the confined atmosphere is the knowledge that this man is right. Death is dangerously present around me . . .

"Let's not reverse roles," I lash out. "*You're* the descendant of the Montfaucon executioners, not me."

"I already told you that I turned away from my forebears' profession to devote my efforts to help the people's Fronde."

"Yet the king entrusted you to torture the conspirators of the La Roncière plot."

"Just so you know, I didn't touch a hair on their heads. Mélac and his henchmen took them to some prison in Versailles where no one could hear their cries for mercy and made them talk."

For a moment, I think about what he just said, deep in this silent lair where Montfaucon claims to no longer practice his sinister talents, except on ghouls and other nocturnal abominations. How many inhuman cries have reverberated here, far from the surface?

"Maybe you renounced torturing your fellow brethren," I grant him. "On the other hand, you never mentioned having a brother who still seems to run your ancestors' gallows."

The grand equerry grows somber.

"Raoul . . . ," he whispers. "My elder horrifies me. He's everything I've sworn to myself I would never become." He shakes himself like an exhausted horse that wants to chase away a pesky fly. "Let's not talk about him. Ever since he became the Immutable's royal executioner, he's toppled headlong into the Shadows, totally out of reach . . . far from any redemption. Let's focus instead on the person the Immutable ordered you to find. Let's talk about the one who reigns over the new Court of Miracles."

My eyes widen.

"Did you say a *new* Court of Miracles? That means there was already one in the past, just like the Marquis de Mélac said?"

Montfaucon nods in confirmation.

"A long time ago, the Court of Miracles was the secret gathering spot where the most feared outlaws of Paris would meet. Poison trade, contract killings, witchcraft, and human sacrifices: the most odious business dealings took place there. In the first century after his transmutation, the King of Shadows built a wall around the capital. He waged total warfare against the cheats, swindlers, and murderers to eradicate them, so none would fail to submit to the unbending law of the Magna Vampyria. The old Court of Miracles was discovered, and all its members were wiped out."

"The way you describe that seedy place, I don't see what was so miraculous about it."

"Well, it's because after a day of panhandling in the streets of Paris, the fake cripples would walk again and the fake blind beggars would see . . . like a miracle!" A cold smile appears on the grand equerry's chiseled face. "As a phony baronette, you would have been right at home in the middle of all those tricksters."

Coming from the person who's supposed to be my mentor, this new sting pierces me. I know he's boorish and brusque, but I have a hard time getting used to such barbs.

"You know I'm pretending only so that I can serve the people's Fronde," I shoot back, exasperated. "To serve you. I've been twiddling my thumbs at Versailles for a month, just waiting for your instructions. And what happens? The Immutable gives me my marching orders first, so that I can track down this Lady of Miracles and bring her to him."

Far from taking offense that the sovereign blindsided him, Montfaucon continues to smile coldly, all the while kneading his unkempt goatee.

"And that's exactly what you'll do," he affirms. "You'll track her down with your keen hunting instincts. But not to deliver her to the king, no; to drive a stake right through her heart and silence her forever!"

I open my mouth to respond, but at that instant, I hear the creaking of rusty hinges behind me.

Quickly, I turn around in my chair. The heavy studded door to the torture chamber just opened, and the scent of decaying leaves wafts in. Two leather shoes appear on the threshold.

"Orfeo," Montfaucon says. "Come in. I don't believe that you and Jeanne parted on the best of terms the last time you met."

The most bizarre creature I've ever encountered enters the room— the most heart-wrenching too. Under his patchwork leather tunic and hood, his powerful body is made up of human fragments all sewed together. Dark sutures encircle his wrists and the base of his neck. His head, which is grafted to his body, displays a translucent green complexion that's more strange than repulsive. It looks like celadon skin, set with two eyes of jade. A teardrop tattoo appears under the corner of his right eyelid—the sign of Neapolitan outlaws. This brooding and strangely touching face once belonged to a young, anonymous delinquent before unscrupulous alchemists stole it from a mass grave. They created, then abandoned this abomination that Montfaucon took in and baptized Orfeo.

"Pardon me," I say, overcome by guilt.

The grand equerry is right. The last time I saw Orfeo, I treated him like a savage beast. I abused his trust and locked him in this room. But he's not a brute with no brain. A genuine sensitive nature resides behind those watery eyes presently staring at me.

"I . . . I was afraid," I say, struggling to find my words.

Orfeo utters a guttural sound, very low and very deep—but mostly just sad. The alchemists who gave him life didn't see fit to graft him a tongue. Nonetheless, he doesn't need to say a word for me to detect the heartrending tone of his groan.

"I wasn't scared of *you*," I hurry to say, suddenly aware that my words must have wounded him. "It was the situation that made me panic, the countdown to the Sip of the King."

Montfaucon sweeps away my excuses with the back of his hand. "Stop lying, it's cowardly," he berates me. "And it's dangerous for Orfeo. Of course he scares you. He's an inhuman monster. He must never forget that. And he must stay hidden underground."

"I assure you that—"

"Be quiet. Don't go putting crazy ideas in his fogged-up brain. If he were to show himself in public, he would terrorize people, and the Hematic Faculty would cart him off to the butcher the way it does all abominations."

Orfeo lowers his head to avoid eye contact with the person who's both his savior and jailer. But what does Orfeo mean to Montfaucon? Is he a sort of adopted son? Or simply a hunting dog who accompanies Montfaucon on his nocturnal hunts through the cemeteries? In a certain way, they're alike—one is steeped in the shame of his family origins, the other in the shame of what he is.

"Go make some tea to warm us up, and cut some bread for us to eat too," Montfaucon orders the creature.

Orfeo slips off without a noise.

"Where were we?" says the master of the premises. "Ah yes, the Lady of Miracles. I don't know who this renegade vampyre who calls herself Hecate is. This anonymity is a characteristic of illegally transmuted immortals—we know nothing about them. The Hematic Faculty pursues them relentlessly in order to eliminate them since all nonauthorized transmutations are considered crimes of treason. As long as they're willing to live like pariahs, some of the more cunning and vicious among the unrecorded manage to slip through the cracks. They hole up in squalid hideouts and feed on vagabonds."

The grand equerry turns the rings on his fingers, a nervous habit that seems to help him focus.

"To the best of my knowledge, the Lady of Miracles is the first unrecorded to step out of the dark and openly defy the Immutable," he continues. "She must feel particularly sure of herself to be asking that he cede Paris to her."

"To be precise, she's asking to be named vice-queen," I point out. "Why is that so shocking, after all? Other vice-sovereigns rule in the name of the Immutable on foreign thrones."

"As you said, on foreign thrones. Whereas here, it's the capital of the French kingdom and of all the Magna Vampyria that the Lady of Miracles wants to remove from the King of Shadows' direct control. He can't afford such a power play so near to Versailles; it would be a terrible show of weakness to the rest of the world. Especially as other vice-kingdoms, like England, are expressing signs of rebellion lately."

I know that diplomatic relations have been tense between the kingdom of France and the vice-kingdom of England, the latter supposedly a vassal state. On the other side of the Channel, there are rumors that

Vice-Queen Anne is making battle plans. It seems the cohesion of the Magna Vampyria has never been so precarious.

"For the Immutable, granting Paris the status of vice-kingdom would be the first step toward a total secession of the city," Montfaucon asserts. "It would also mean that he couldn't claim the blood tithes from Paris. He'll never agree to such a request, especially as there was an implicit threat."

The grand equerry smooths his rough goatee with his fingertips.

"Who is this Lady of Miracles?" he wonders aloud. "What's the real extent of her alchemical powers? Is she, as she claims, truly able to command the ghouls? Does she have a secret way of subduing those uncontrollable monsters? If that's the case, Louis must never learn the secret—*never*, do you understand?" He looks at me pointedly, as if he wants to imprint his words deep into my soul. "Louis may go by the name *King of Shadows*, but he himself is a product of the Shadows more than he is their sovereign. The true nature of this mystical energy still escapes him, despite the Faculty's painstaking work to solve the mystery. And the nocturnal abominations, those other offspring of the Shadows, elude him as well. But if he managed to seize control over them, then his power would truly become absolute. No Fronde, no matter how organized or resolute, could ever overthrow the Magna Vampyria."

He grabs my wrist, stressing each of his next words in a stirring voice.

"You *must* find the Lady of Miracles before the royal armies do, Jeanne. You *must* destroy her before she reveals to the Immutable by what diabolic means she controls the ghouls. The future of the Fronde is at stake. You'll have to be cunning in order to go behind the backs of your teammates, Jaipur and Plumigny. Those two will pursue a very different objective." He lets go of my arm and adds, "I'm confident that you'll be able to straddle both sides of the fence. After all, you're an expert at that game."

The compliment leaves me with a bitter aftertaste. It reminds me how I've had to lie and deceive to get where I am today. But if it's the price I have to pay to further the cause that my parents believed in so strongly—that I believe in!—then so be it.

"I'll do my best," I promise him.

"No, Jeanne. Your best isn't enough. I know the task is challenging, but you'll succeed. You have to."

Montfaucon's surly voice trembles in a way I haven't heard before, and his eyes glisten with emotion unexpected for a man so hardened.

"Initially, the Immutable was sending you to Paris alone," he reminds me. "But don't forget, the tyrant is endowed with malicious wisdom that he's honed over the centuries. He never makes a decision lightly. He truly believes you'll be able to bring him the lady. And I believe you'll be able to destroy her." A slight smile appears on his lips, all the more precious because it's so rare. "I . . . I don't quite know how to define it, but ever since you came into my sphere, I sense the Fronde is experiencing renewed hope. You're a ray of sunshine in the Shadows. Although I never met your parents, just knowing you, my guess is that they were good-hearted people. And although I'm childless, if destiny had given me a daughter, I would have wanted her to be just like you."

His confession takes me by surprise and touches me deeply.

My throat tight, I can only utter a strangled "Thank you."

Montfaucon removes one of his many rings—the one from his right little finger.

It's a steel band decorated with a large round black gemstone.

"This is my most precious possession," he says. "In the hollow of this onyx stone are a few drops of *essence de jour*, which was clandestinely distilled by an alchemical lab of the Fronde in Andalusia."

"*Essence de jour . . . ,*" I repeat, softly.

Once again, I'm overwhelmed with emotion. In the secret laboratory of their apothecary, my parents also conducted alchemical experiments on behalf of the Fronde. I never knew anything about the exact nature of their work, but I like to believe that they created substances with equally poetic names.

"*Essence de jour* is an alchemical quintessence, time consuming to distill, with a small concentration of sunlight. Even in a sun-filled country like Spain, it takes a full year to synthesize one drop. You can imagine that it's highly prohibited by the Hematic Faculty. Just possessing some is synonymous with a death sentence. You'll have to conceal the secret nature of this ring during your mission—until the moment comes for you to use it."

I examine the ring that's in Montfaucon's palm. Strange to think that a gemstone as dark as night holds a few drops of daylight . . .

"Once you've reached the heart of the Court of Miracles, you'll simply have to turn the onyx stone on its bezel. Three times to the left, then three times to the right: the mechanism will open onto the secret compartment where the essence is stored. The essence will instantly evaporate, releasing a brief burst of blinding light."

"Enough . . . enough to kill a vampyre like the Lady of Miracles?" I whisper.

"No. Only enough to disorient her for a few seconds, and also to disperse the ghouls who hate the light more than anything. That will clear the way for you to deliver the fatal blow to their mistress. To that end, I'll give you a stake made of the finest wood. And you'll send that unrecorded back into the void from which she should never have emerged."

The grand equerry drops the precious ring into my hand. It was made for his pinky finger, but I have to slip it all the way to the end of my middle finger to make it stay securely. And so it takes its place next to the signet ring, stamped with the Gastefriche coat of arms, that I took from the real baronette before coming to Versailles under her assumed identity.

"Remember, Jeanne, only use this trump card at the last possible moment. You get only one shot," Montfaucon counsels me. "And close your eyes when you unscrew the onyx so you're not blinded too."

Just then, the door to the underground room creaks again behind my back. Orfeo enters, bringing our discussion to an end.

"Put the provisions on the rack," the grand equerry orders as he quickly dries his moist eyes.

"Tell that thing to let me go!" says a clear voice.

Montfaucon and I shoot up from our chairs. Instead of tea and bread, Orfeo has brought a young girl with porcelain skin, her black hair knotted in a thick bun.

"Naoko!" I yell. "What are you doing here?"

The daughter of the daytime ambassador of Japan, Naoko Takagari, was my only friend while I was a student at the Grande Écurie. She was also the only boarder who knew the secret of my double identity.

"I saw you arrive at dawn from the dining hall window," she says, casting a frightened look at Orfeo from under the edge of her bangs. "I was racing down the big staircase of the school to come talk to you when I crossed paths with Hélénaïs. She told me you'd been the victim of an attempted murder and that you were at death's door."

"In her dreams!" I shout, welling up with a rush of rage.

"I arrived in the hallway just as you were rushing into the grand equerry's office," Naoko goes on. "I spied on you through the keyhole and saw him lead you down this hidden staircase." She raises a finger to the gold pins that adorn her bun. "I . . . I picked the lock to follow you."

Montfaucon steps forward menacingly, the top of his wig brushing against the cobweb-covered vaulted ceiling.

"And what did you think I was going to do, Takagari?" he asks, reddening. "Chop your friend to bits?"

By way of response, Naoko eyes the cheerless room where instruments of torture are neatly aligned.

"As a consequence of your indiscretion, you will never leave this place," he thunders. "This room will be your tomb. Orfeo, lie her out on the rack!"

Montfaucon turns toward the workbench and grabs an axe.

"No!" I yell as I grip his coat sleeve.

"One well-placed blow is all that's needed to detach her slender neck. It'll be painless. I assure you she won't suffer."

"You swore you'd renounced torture!"

"It's not torture. It's an execution."

He places his enormous left hand over my shoulder to keep me at a distance, all the while brandishing the axe in his right hand.

"That little snoop overheard our conversation," he says. "I'm not about to let her report back. The secret of the Fronde prevails over any other consideration."

"I swear that you can trust Naoko!" I shout, hoarsely. "If you really think of me as a daughter, listen to what I'm telling you."

"Your youthful sentimentality leads you astray. When you're older, Jeanne, you'll understand that the killing of Takagari was the only good decision. Now, Orfeo: on the rack!"

I shout and I rush at him, but nothing gives—and by the glimmer of the lantern, the grand equerry's face is twisted in a cruel grimace, wholly transfigured. It's as if the cursed blood of the executioners of Montfaucon has gone to his brain, sweeping aside all scruples, all ability to listen.

With a gentleness that's a far cry from his master's brutal manners, Orfeo pushes Naoko forward and delicately places her cheek against the rack. Yet behind his measured actions, I sense there's an overpowering strength against which my poor friend cannot fight.

"Naoko knows about my double identity, and she never betrayed me!" I shout. "It's proof that she's worthy of our confidence."

"Actually, it's proof that you're truly imprudent. Allowing a student to come and go with that knowledge could sink you, and me as well," Montfaucon says as he raises the axe a little higher.

Overcome with panic, I go for broke.

"At least undo her bun so that the blade doesn't slip on her hair."

Montfaucon's feverish eyes gleam with a brighter . . . crazier spark.

"Ah, that's good, you're learning fast!" he rejoices. "Did you hear, Orfeo? Undo her bun."

Naoko cries out in distress—as if any violation of her hairstyle constitutes a fate worse than death.

"No! Not my hair!"

But she's no match against Orfeo. He grabs the tip of the long red wooden lacquered hair stick that closes Naoko's bun and pulls it out in one stroke.

Naoko's long black hair falls in silky cascades down both sides of the rack.

Montfaucon's axe stays suspended in the air.

"What—what evil spell . . . ," he sputters, rolling his round eyes like saucers.

The bloodthirsty flicker that lit up his eyes is replaced by astonishment, the same reaction I experienced not that long ago, when I saw the back of Naoko's neck for the first time. For there, behind her bun, my friend conceals a horrifying secret: a second mouth that stretches monstrously from one end of her ears to the other. A carnivorous evilmouth, greedy for fresh flesh, its oversize lips seemingly smiling at the grand equerry.

"Voilà, now you know Naoko's secret!" I rush to say. "She's burdened with an abomination that would send her to her death if it were known. Didn't you just tell me that the Hematic Faculty expedited abominations to the butcher?" I swallow, trembling, pushing down the guilt of having betrayed my friend's secret, if only to save her. "Her life is now in your hands. If she dares repeat even a word of the conversation she overheard between us, you only have to speak a word of your own to end her life. You're even."

4

CURSE

"I didn't have a choice," I say to Naoko. "It was the only way to stop Montfaucon's axe."

After a lot of pleading, I finally convinced the school director to spare my friend's life. He agreed, on one condition: Naoko has to live as a recluse in the depths of the Grande Écurie. At least until the master of the premises trusts her enough to let her resurface. For now, he's gone to the aviary to send a homing pigeon to his brother, Raoul, concerning preparations for the evening's hanging. He left us alone in a room that adjoins the torture chamber; it's a small cell with a rusted metal bed. From now on it will be Naoko's dwelling.

I can't make out her expression under her black bangs, which she hurried to finger-brush into place when she redid her bun earlier. She's avoiding my eyes.

"It might have been better if that axe had done its job . . . ," she says softly, finally talking again. "The blade would have shut the evilmouth once and for all, and put an end to my cursed life."

"Don't talk like that!" I tell her. "You've managed to live with that . . . that anomaly for sixteen years."

Naoko looks at me with her large black eyes.

"And for how many more years? On the night of the Sip of the King, when I came to the palace for the first time with the other boarders to attend the ceremony, I sensed the evilmouth growing more restless than ever behind my bun. It was as if the aura of all the vampyric courtiers had woken it up, stirring its insatiable appetite, sweeping aside all the meditation exercises I've forced myself to do each night since childhood to put it to sleep."

She puts her trembling hands on her knees, which are squeezed together under a beige silk skirt painted with exotic flowers.

The prospect of joining the court has always terrified Naoko. What she just told me confirms her fears. The concentrated presence of the Shadows seems to have a diabolical stimulating effect on her strange growth.

"Listen to me," I say as I place my hands on hers. "Ultimately, today's misadventure might end up being a lucky break. If you'd stayed up above, you would have had to join the court at the end of the schoolyear next summer, along with the other seniors. But now you'll be spared from that. Montfaucon will find a way to explain your disappearance to your father, the ambassador. Accident, runaway, maybe he'll even pretend that the ghouls whisked you off, I don't know. What I do know is that you're being offered a new life."

There's something absurd in talking about a *new life* within the confines of this narrow cell, where the air is thin and where Naoko is now essentially buried.

Nevertheless, a small smile appears on her softly painted carmine lips.

"You think so?" she whispers.

"I'm sure of it."

This girl is the most solitary creature I know. For such a long time, she concealed the secret that consumes her. Her mother died in childbirth, her father became like a stranger, and since I left, she has had no friend at the Grande Écurie. She'll cope with being cut off from the outside world because she was already living on a different plane.

"I promise to come see you every day," I say with fervor.

"Don't make me any promises," she replies. "You're about to leave for Paris. And in the past, you already made promises that you broke. Right up to not revealing the existence of the evilmouth."

"I did that to save your life, Naoko," I repeat, overcome with shame for all the times I lied to her, same as I did to many others I considered my friends.

But there was nothing reproachful in her tone.

"I'm not asking you to visit me every day. Only that you remember me once your mission is over"—her pale eyelids flutter an instant, like a moth's wings—"and that you remember Toinette, who you told me vanished."

Naoko's selflessness touches me deeply. Her life just got turned upside down forever, and yet she's thinking of a poor deceased servant that everyone at the Grande Écurie has probably already long forgotten.

"Toinette always took care to set aside a plate of vegetables for me. At every meal," she recalls. "She didn't know that my vegetarian diet was part of my battle plan to weaken the evilmouth, but she was nothing but thoughtful toward me. She didn't deserve to die so young."

"Toinette will be avenged," I vow.

Naoko sighs. "*Vengeance*, that seems to be the only word you utter, my dear Jeanne. You're stubborn like a mule. But is that what's most important? Is that what Toinette would want?"

Her question leaves me speechless.

She makes me remember the person I was after my family was killed.

At the time, I threw myself headlong into wanting blind vengeance because I didn't see another way of giving purpose to life without my loved ones. But since then, I've matured. And my understanding of the world has broadened. It's no longer a matter of snatching a personal revenge at any price. Even if honoring the dead remains important, I've opened my eyes to what's most precious, and most fragile, too—the fate of those who are still alive . . . and who are suffering. What drives me now is wanting to carry my parents' torch and fight for the millions of anonymous people that the Magna Vampyria crushes each day under its heel. Just like Maman and Papa did, in secret, all the way from Butte-aux-Rats.

Beyond the destruction of those responsible for my tragedy, I want with all my heart to build a better world. After an endless winter, spring must bloom. Once the Shadows are dissipated, the light will return to the world. That's my ideal now. And Naoko reminded me of it, just as I was about to let old demons get the better of me.

"You're right, Naoko, it's not what Toinette would want," I say. "Her parents are still alive. I imagine they'll soon be crying their eyes out right now in some dilapidated cottage in the outskirts of Versailles. Not only for their daughter but also for their son who's no more. The best way to honor Toinette is to protect them. To make sure they're not wanting for anything. I'll ask Montfaucon to discreetly send them a portion of my squire's wages each month."

As I say this, I'm filled with the opposite of the seething vengeance that has so often poisoned my thoughts. I feel a calm, soothing resolution. This sense of serving others, rather than the law of retribution, is strangely liberating.

"Now, that was well spoken," Naoko congratulates me. "Who knew that feisty Jeanne Froidelac could one day hold such a sensible discourse?"

"Anything's possible, Naoko, and stubborn mules can be made to see reason."

I slap my backside with my hand and let out a *hee-haw*.

Naoko smiles gently at my silly antics. She has a knack for bringing out the best side in me. Then she glances at the small clock hanging above the bed, the only device that will allow her to follow the passage of time in her confinement. The two hands are nearly vertically aligned.

"It'll be noon soon," she says. "It's time for you to join the director and the other two squires as planned." She gives me an encouraging look. "Go on. And be careful of Hélénaïs. She was already a viper at school, so the Immutable's blood probably makes her even more venomous."

I squeeze Naoko's hands one last time before I knock three times on the thick door of the cell. The panel opens on the mute guard that Montfaucon assigned: Orfeo, holding a lantern in his fist. He closes the door on Naoko, then escorts me in silence toward the spiral staircase that rises to the surface.

Once we've reached the top of the steps and before I enter the Grande Écurie, I turn toward Orfeo and finally have the nerve to look squarely into his strange watery jade-colored eyes.

"Even if the grand equerry said you were an inhuman monster, I'm sure that deep inside he doesn't think that. And neither do I."

Orfeo's long black eyelashes begin to flutter.

The tattooed teardrop under the corner of his right eye creases slightly.

Already he's turning away his bare head to hide it in the dimness of the staircase.

With a caress to his cheek, I stop his shame-filled reflex. His skin is as cold as death against my palm. But I don't withdraw my hand—and after a few seconds, I sense veins pulsing with life under the flesh of my fingers. Contrary to vampyres, who have a big void in their chests, a heart beats in Orfeo's large torso.

"Several weeks ago, you gave my loved ones a decent burial," I say softly. "I'll be forever grateful."

In fact, Orfeo detached the remains of my family from the Hunting Wall, where the king had their heads impaled. He buried them in a secret spot that only he knows, sheltered from the voracious appetite of the ghouls. Montfaucon likes to say that his protégé can hear the bones of the dead sing and that, in turn, he plays them lullabies on his harmonica to soothe them.

"You took care of those who were dearest to me," I whisper, getting choked up. "You gave them eternal rest. It's my turn to give you something now."

I remove my hand from his cheek and slide it into my pocket, from which I take my mother's watch, then hold it out to him.

"This is for you. It may look like just a broken watch, but, to me, it's the most priceless treasure, for it belonged to my mother. This treasure belongs to you now."

I place the small round pendant in the center of his large palm and gently close his fingers over it.

"Goodbye, Orfeo."

I run off, relieved of my most precious possession, yet enriched by the most beautiful gift in the world: the pale smile that, for the first time, appeared on Orfeo's bloodless lips.

"Well, Gastefriche, you're late," Raymond de Montfaucon says the instant I enter the office filled with equestrian tapestries. "Didn't General Barvók's lessons in the art of courtly manners teach you that punctuality heads up the list of good manners?"

He's seated at a small table with Suraj and Hélénaïs. Servants have placed a lunch of cold meats and raw vegetables on top of it. The grand equerry is once again treating me like a former student and not a rebel, in order to deceive my companions. But whether he wears the uniform of the school director or of the rebellion, he's just as gruff.

"Please accept my apologies, monsieur," I say. I hug the walls covered with thick tapestries depicting mares, the Immutable's terrifying vampyric horses, until I reach my place. "My nap lasted a little longer than planned."

"Let's hope you'll sleep less soundly when you get to Paris. In the slums, those who slumber too deeply end up robbed of their money . . . or their life."

In the light of the bright flames burning in the fireplace, Hélénaïs's amber eyes narrow in disgust. I recognize that expression: daughter of the wealthy Lord of Plumigny, principal purveyor of the kingdom's poultry, Hélénaïs has a dreadful horror of commoners.

"Are you saying we'll have to visit the slums of the city?" she asks, outraged. "Is that really necessary?"

"And where do you suppose you'll find the Court of Miracles, Plumigny? In a cozy boudoir at the Palais-Royal? Between two ballrooms at the Opéra? You'll need to venture into the underbelly of the City of Shadows."

"City of Shadows?" the heiress repeats in a high-pitched voice as she plunges her lovely nose into her salad plate so she doesn't meet the grand equerry's glowering eyes.

Montfaucon nods, grumbling into his goatee.

"That's the nickname for Paris. In the king's lifetime, when he was still only Louis XIV, he started developing the public lighting for the capital. Paris was known then as the City of Light throughout Europe. But since his transmutation, the Immutable had lanterns and torches removed from most of the streets. After all, what's the point in lighting the roadways when the human livestock is confined to stables after curfew?"

Montfaucon superbly plays the part of merciless nobleman, a role he honed as he evolved among the sharks at the court.

"If the king entrusted you with this mission, it's because he assumes you'll know how to infiltrate the most obscure recesses of the city," he goes on. "The very places where the soldiers of the Royal Watch themselves don't dare go. You should know that the rule of law and order in the capital is assumed by the police lieutenants. In the past, they reported directly to the Immutable. But for dozens of years now, the monarch has grown uninterested in the day-to-day affairs of the kingdom in favor of more esoteric pursuits."

I myself had noticed that the Immutable spent the better part of his nights in the company of Exili and his archiaters, all of them contemplating the stars from his observatory. Concerns more pressing than terrestrial events attract him to the heavens . . . like the crazy project to reconquer daytime thanks to the alchemical science that many in the corridors of Versailles speak of in hushed tones.

"As minister of the armies, Ézéchiel de Mélac fought to regain oversight of Paris and thus consolidate his influence at the court. The scandal of the letter plastered to the mortuary chamber constitutes a serious blemish to his reputation. And the king's public rejection this morning looks a lot like a fall from grace. So don't expect any real help from the police once you get to Paris. Mélac will have only one goal: put roadblocks in your way so that you don't find the Lady of Miracles before he does."

Using the tips of her cutlery, Hélénaïs fiddles with her leaves of lettuce as if she's trying to dissect them.

"Excuse me, monsieur, but how are we supposed to find the Lady of Miracles without anyone's help, in a city we don't know?"

"Not unknown to all," the grand equerry says. "As the king reminded us, Jaipur, herewith present, knows the capital well. Especially its cemeteries, as he and I both share a common passion for hunting ghouls."

Suraj bows his head. Under his ocher-colored turban, his face remains impassive. He's the most aloof of the squires and the most experienced too. Of the six who served the king before my arrival at the court, he's the only one who survived the La Roncière plot. Hélénaïs and I are new, but Suraj already has one year of royal service under his belt.

"With all due respect, monsieur, it isn't passion that drives me to hunt the ghouls of Paris," he corrects in his deep, foreign-accented voice. "It's a sense of duty. Last spring, His Majesty sent me to the cemeteries of Paris to fight those creatures who attack commoners. Until now, I was unaware that a criminal controlled them in order to coordinate their attacks." He tightens his fists over his cutlery and harshly adds, "The flesh and blood of the people belong to the crown. The ones who steal these—be they mortals, vampyres, or abominations—must be mercilessly punished."

Montfaucon cuts himself an enormous slice of wild boar pâté as he clears his throat with scorn.

"Don't act so righteous, Jaipur," he says, sniffling. "The *sense of duty* you cloak yourself in is a passion like any other, the most pernicious of all. It's an all-consuming intoxication that disguises itself under the guise of cold necessity."

Montfaucon opens his large jaw and stuffs it with the chunk of pâté. He proceeds to chew loudly. Then, in one gulp, he empties the glass of dark-as-molasses wine into his gullet.

"The conspirators of the La Roncière plot were likewise motivated by a *sense of duty*," he continues after wiping his mouth on the back of his shovellike hand. "Duty for a perverted idea of honor, duty for an outsize sense of self-importance. Poor fools. They were victims of their own blindness, dragging their families and allies down with them."

He pulls the plate of cured meats toward him from the center of the table and plants his fork in it, spearing three thick pieces of ham and four pickles.

"Enough talk, let's eat," he orders us. "We'll set out for the Gibbet of Montfaucon in one hour, along with the convoy of prisoners."

A funeral procession.

That's what the long convoy stretching out before me reminds me of. On the main winding road from Versailles to Paris, dozens of carts are being pulled by heavy draft horses. Their hooves strike the icy road in a solemn manner. Tick . . . tock . . . tick . . . tock . . . like the mechanism of an impassive clock, where every beat marks another step toward the fatal outcome.

Dozens of prisoners are crammed together in carts that are exposed to the glacial November wind. Only a few days ago, these same men and women, who dreamed of taking the king's place, were clothed in the finest fabrics, the most shimmering silks. Today, their hands bound, they're wearing only bland shirts whose tails lift up with the wind. Some of them huddle against one another as they weep, looking for a little warmth. Others contemplate the bare trees that go by them, their eyes fixed and dazed, as if they've already turned into frozen corpses.

Soldiers dispatched by Mélac are closely escorting the convoy. As for the minister of the armies, he's traveling aboard the lead carriage in an armored coffin. He won't be stepping out of it until nightfall.

The other two squires and I, clad in our black leather breastplates lined with fur, bring up the rear on our horses.

I can feel the powerful muscles of Typhon, the stallion I rode to train for the equestrian portion of the Sip of the King, beneath my legs. I was happy to be reunited with him in the stables earlier. Right now, the heat from his body warms my heart.

Suddenly, at the bend of a craggy hill, the city comes into view, and my heart freezes.

Paris!

Capital of the kingdom of France and all the Magna Vampyria!

A huge wall soars around it for leagues on end—not white and sculpted like the Hunting Wall but gray and bare. The pale sun, already waning, stretches out the shadows of the sharp crenellations, above which rise plumes of black smoke. Here and there, large gates where tolls are levied open in the facade, leading to roads that branch out to all the corners of the kingdom.

"The outer rampart!" Montfaucon announces gloomily from high atop his smoky-brown steed. "That fortified wall is the longest in all the Magna Vampyria."

My stomach knots up at the idea of the countless masses who live packed together in the enclosure, as the law requires.

We reach a dark river straddled by a large wooden bridge.

"The Seine," Montfaucon grumbles.

"The water is so murky," I say. "As if the Shadows themselves flowed in its bed."

"It's not the Shadows," the grand equerry replies. "Upstream from Paris, the Seine is crystal clear, but as it flows through the capital, it gets filled with the detritus of human life. What you see flowing here, under the Sèvres bridge, is the residue of industry, the human waste of the multitudes, the ashes from the wood and charcoal that must be burned each day to heat a million commoners who'll never leave the walls of the enclosure."

A million subjects. Since I come from a small village populated by hardly a hundred souls, that crazy number makes my head spin.

The convoy begins to make its way across the Sèvres bridge, causing it to crack under the weight of the steel-covered wheels. Over the guardrail, I can see ice slowly drifting into the inky river. The terrible winter is almost here.

"In fact, the other river that flows out of Paris toward Versailles and the rich residences of the vampyres on the Île-de-France is not black but red," Montfaucon says darkly. "Hence the motto of the city: *Fluctuat in sanguinis fluminibus*."

No need to know Latin to guess what the motto imposed by the Magna Vampyria means: the capital of this empire floats on a river of blood . . .

As we move on, we hug the rampart wall from the north, up to the hill where a slew of windmills soars. Their sails turn slowly in the chilly wind, calling to mind the arms of scrawny giants trying to tear at the clouds.

"Night and day, the village of Montmartre grinds a great deal of wheat to nourish the people of Paris," our guide says. "But the windmills have been turning more slowly these last few years, due to bad harvests caused by frost."

"It's like the grain that gets thrown to the poultry in the battery cages at Plumigny," Hélénaïs says from atop her chestnut horse. "When there isn't enough wheat, the chickens have to make do with barley mixed with pebbles. Maybe we could feed the Parisians bread with gravel?"

What an odious comparison between the intensive breeding that made her family's fortune and the commoners kept caged up to generate megagallons of fresh blood. I clench my teeth, holding back the scathing remarks that are on the tip of my tongue. I suffer through the squire's babbling in silence until we reach the northeast edge of the capital. The plain of Saint-Denis stretches out on the horizon, surrounded by ramparts that are equally gloomy—the northern banlieues of Paris. A large toll gate stands in front of us: our destination.

"We've arrived at the Porte du Supplice," Montfaucon announces. "Wait for me while I go negotiate our entry. Even with a letter bearing the royal seal, the administrative formalities can take some time and be as torturous as the word *supplice* implies."

His horse breaks into a gallop toward the portico, which is shut by a heavy iron portcullis and watched over by guards armed with halberds.

Unable to bear another second of Hélénaïs's conversation, I press my thighs against Typhon's flanks so that I can get away until the portcullis opens. As I make my way past the twelve carts that are stopped one behind the other, single file, I feel the weight of the prisoners looking at me. I don't dare glance at their reddened eyes, some of which are punctured, a consequence of the rounds of torture in the jails of Versailles.

Whispers hoarsened by cold, resentment, and fear surge in my wake.

"It's her . . ."

"It's the squire who saved the king . . ."

"It's the traitor who killed Tristan de La Roncière . . ."

Suddenly, spit lands right in my eye.

Blinded, I pull hard on the reins.

Typhon rears up.

I fall with a thud on the cold-hardened ground.

"You think you're different than us, but you're wrong!" roars a voice burning with hate. "You saved the tyrant because you hope to be transmuted, admit it. May you burn in hell, you slut!"

The hushed whispers turn to furious shouts. A rain of spit lands on me from the carts, smudging my cheeks, gumming up my hair with thick phlegm.

"Bitch!"

"Whore!"

"Hussy!"

"Death-licker!"

None of the soldiers come to my aid. They're all sold out to Mélac. The grand equerry warned us that they wouldn't lift a finger to help.

"Enough!" a voice suddenly proclaims amid the onslaught. It's a female voice, endowed with such authority that the shouts come to a complete stop.

Wiping my forehead with the back of my sleeve, I raise my eyes.

A tall lady appears before me at the front of one of the carts, her long blonde hair floating in the wind. Her hands are bound behind her back, like those of the other prisoners, but this in no way diminishes her haughtiness. On the contrary, she looks like the figurehead on the prow of a victorious vessel, like the mermaids without arms that adorn the finest warships.

"Leave her be," she orders her unfortunate companions. "Stop behaving like wretches. Don't forget who you are—the crème de la crème of the nobility hailing from the provinces. Despite the affronts we were subjected to, the Immutable will never be able to take that away from us."

I get up in the middle of the renewed silence, not knowing what to say to the woman whose fate I sealed when I saved the king.

"Thank you, Madame . . ."

"Blanche de La Roncière," she says, identifying herself.

My stomach somersaults.

Her ash-blonde hair . . .

Her deep-blue eyes . . .

And especially her haughty bearing, marked by determination and melancholy.

This woman is the spitting image of Tristan, my most burning love, my most tragic mistake, so it seems right that this is his mother.

Words rush from my lips. "I . . . I'm sorry . . ."

"What for?" she answers, lifting her chin. "Winners don't need to apologize. Has the wolf ever said it was sorry for devouring the lamb, the eagle for swooping down on the rabbit?"

In a sudden painful memory, I have the impression I'm hearing Tristan speaking through his mother. This declaration of faith that makes strength a unique virtue. This volition of power that crushes everything in its way. This is why I stopped Tristan before he could ascend to the throne, where he would have ruled with even less mercy than the Immutable.

"The law of the jungle is still the best." Blanche de La Roncière hammers away, the harshness of her words in sharp contrast to her harmonious face, whose beauty time hasn't altered. "You were stronger than my son, Diane de Gastefriche. You were stronger than all of us gathered here. Defeat is the destiny of the weak, and I'm not asking for your pity."

A smile spreads across her cold blue lips. This woman is the brains that masterminded the La Roncière plot. She represents everything I abhor—the arrogance of the powerful for whom the people are merely livestock—but her lack of emotion jars me. And her personality reminds me of my own mother: two strong women waging battle from diametrically opposed sides.

"No, I'm not asking for any pity," she says again in the middle of the silent yet attentive prisoners. "I'm merely asking you to lend me an ear. For I have a few words to whisper into it, in Tristan's name. A few words that will change everything."

My blood freezes.

What secret is Blanche de La Roncière talking about? Could she possibly know my real identity? Yes, Tristan discovered that I was a commoner, but he swore he wouldn't speak of it to anyone before marrying and transmuting me. What if he lied? What if he opened up about it to his mother in a letter? And what if she now plans on blackmailing me to save her life?

I absolutely need to know what's what and protect my cover at all costs.

I dust off my outfit, straighten out my slimy hair, and walk slowly up to the cart without taking my eyes off the prisoner. All around me, the silence of the condemned suddenly feels meditative. Yes, there's something religious about it, as if I were walking down the aisle of a church toward the woman who could have been my mother-in-law.

Madame de La Roncière leans over the edge of the cart, still retaining her grace in all her shackled distress.

"I'm listening," I tell her.

"I know who you are," she whispers, her frozen lips brushing against my cheekbone.

My heart pounding in my chest, my breathing hindered, I stand on tiptoes to collect her words in my ear so that no one else can hear them.

"You're an even more ambitious aristocrat than I was, willing to do anything to be transmuted."

I allow myself to breathe. My cover is safe.

"But I'll do anything to stop you from attaining eternal life," the prisoner continues. "May my last words be stamped on your brain: I curse you, and Tristan will come back to avenge me."

Before I have time to react, Blanche de La Roncière's malediction turns into a savage bite. Her teeth close in on my scalp, tearing from me a piercing cry, along with a thick knot of hair.

5

EXECUTION

In the red light of the setting sun, the Gibbet of Montfaucon looks as if it has shot up straight from hell.

It's an enormous square structure composed of forty stone columns with large crossbeams between them. All this on twenty successive levels. Hundreds of alcoves rise from the different sides, all of them empty for now, like gaping mouths awaiting meager crumbs. Located at the top of a hill, the gallows overlook the entire city, offering a three-hundred-and-sixty-degree view to the people of Paris.

The public is congregated at the bottom of the structure, surrounded by armed soldiers. There are more people than I've ever seen in my life, a human tidal wave that makes Versailles look like a small provincial town. The esplanade and adjacent streets are so dense with people that it's impossible to see the cobblestones. From where I and the other squires stand on the wooden dais of the grandstand at the foot of the gallows, I can't distinguish the thousands of faces turned toward us. They're just pale, anonymous dots.

"You must be relieved to be perched high, out of reach of their spittle," Hélénaïs whispers next to me.

My attempt to slip away from her earlier turned into a disaster, and my scalp is still stinging.

"The aristocratic rebels who took part in the La Roncière plot sure have it in for you," she adds in a murmur. "But I doubt the lower classes have much love for you, either, not since you saved the Immutable. It can't be easy to be loathed by everybody."

"Listen, Hélénaïs, the king told us to bury the hatchet and work together," I say, sincerely wishing for us to peacefully coexist.

The beautiful heiress shoots me a deadly look from between her silky curls of hair.

"Oh, I could put on an act and pretend that I've patched things up with you," she says. "But deep down I'll *never* forgive you for reading my correspondence."

During the height of our rivalry for the Sip of the King, I did actually pick her closet lock and rifle through her personal belongings for anything that might prove compromising. That's how I found the letters from her father, full of harsh admonitions to promote the Plumigny name at the court. I also learned that she had an older sister, a certain Iphigénie, who had failed in carrying out the very same mission. It seems that Hélénaïs hasn't gotten over my indiscretion.

"Here's the young lady who's giving me so much work," scolds a voice behind me, so deep that the floorboards under my boots shake.

Quickly, I turn around and see two figures in the light from the torches affixed to the columns of the grandstand. The first belongs to the grand equerry, the second to an even larger man. A titan whose face is hidden behind a black leather hood.

"Squires, may I present Raoul de Montfaucon, my older brother, His Majesty's royal executioner," the grand equerry says, clearly ill at ease.

I've always known the director of the Grande Écurie to be sure of himself, intimidating and full of arrogance. But today, in the presence of his executioner brother, he suddenly seems diminished.

"A hundred and ten to execute in a single stroke," Raoul de Montfaucon says with relish. "It's going to be a big evening, and all thanks to this snippet of a girl."

THE COURT OF MIRACLES

The titan leans over me, covering me with his dark shadow.

"Raoul, don't forget you're speaking to one of the king's squires," Montfaucon reminds him.

"I'm not forgetting, little bro. On the contrary, I've come to pay my respects."

He extends his enormous leather-gloved hand toward me.

I place my trembling fingers in it, though he could crush them just by closing his palm.

But he's content to lower his masked face to kiss my hand.

As he straightens, I stare into the slits of his hood, where I can see two protruding, bloodshot eyes . . . the eyes of a madman.

"Bring me the Lady of Miracles," he whispers. "Tonight it's a mass slaughter, a rough-and-tumble job without refinement. But on her, I'll use my most subtle tortures, the most painful and drawn out, until she confesses all her secrets to the King of Shadows."

As if to emphasize his sinister words, a deluge of bells rings down over the cramped rooftops of Paris. It's dusk, the hour when the warning bells toll from all the church towers of the capital to announce the setting sun. Anxious whispers rise from the crowd below. Under normal circumstances, commoners would be rushing to get home before the curfew. But tonight is an evening unlike any other.

While Raoul de Montfaucon slips off to tend to his tasks in the wings of the gallows, a man in a brown coat approaches us. He's sporting a thin brown mustache and undereye circles that he's tried to hide beneath a layer of concealer.

"Thomas de L'Esquille, police lieutenant general," he says, introducing himself. "Welcome to Paris. I have four rooms ready at the Grand Châtelet where you can spend the night after the hanging."

I detect a tremor in his voice when he says *spend the night*, as if he needs to catch up on sleep too.

"Three rooms will do," says the grand equerry. "I won't be staying. I'm returning to Versailles right after the executions to tend to my school."

63

L'Esquille nods, agitating the curls of his long wig, which match the color of his coat.

"As you wish. The hanging is about to start." He checks his pocket watch. "Yes, it's time for the Marquis de Mélac to awaken."

He steps toward the dais and coughs to clear his hoarse voice.

"Ahem . . . people of Paris!" he bellows, his voice echoing from church tower to church tower. "By special edict of the king, you've been summoned to stay out and witness the execution of the miserable conspirators who dared defy the crown. Let this be an example to all dissidents, starting with the usurper who calls herself the Lady of Miracles. Be warned. All subjects, far and near, who participate in her vile sedition will be mercilessly pursued and executed. Such is the law of the Magna Vampyria. Such is the will of the sole ruler of Paris: Louis the Immutable." L'Esquille turns ceremoniously toward the steel coffin that was transported from Versailles and now rests in the center of the grandstand. It's surrounded by soldiers standing at attention. "I have the honor of inviting the Marquis Ézéchiel de Mélac, His Majesty's minister of the armies!"

The heavy lid opens in a single motion.

A lean body bolts upright like a mechanical devil springing from its box: it's Mélac, clothed in an ancient armor that gleams under the torches. The pectoral and abdominal muscles sculpted into the steel stand in contrast with the marquis's gaunt face. A lace jabot shoots out from under his pointy chin, falling onto the breastplate. To preside over the macabre spectacle, Mélac has chosen to wear his attire as general-in-chief of the Magna Vampyria.

The masses are not the only ones to witness this show of force. Other spectators arrive of their own free will by the dozens. These are the Parisian vampyres who've come from their private mansions aboard draft-proof carriages. As night falls, they take their places in the grandstand, markedly lowering the already glacial temperature with their presence. Clothed in fabrics and outfits just as lavish as those worn in Versailles, they sit on velvet-upholstered chairs that have been brought here especially for them. Noble ladies in sable coats take out opera glasses to get a better look at the details of the hanging. Gentlemen in richly brocaded jackets empty flasks of fresh blood by way of breakfast. All of them bow and curtsy before Mélac, who represents the royal authority.

In the midst of this torrent of sickening obsequiousness, one immortal attracts attention: a silent young man who must have been around twenty years old when he was transmuted. His charcoal-gray wool coat stands out from the shimmering velvets of the other guests. But it's really his hair, so unlike the long curled styles that are popular in Versailles, that strikes me. His is black and spiked into a crest above the closely shaved sides of his head.

A little baffled, I notice he's observing me, too, his dark eyes piercing right through me in the crowd. I can't be the one who looks away first—I'm supposed to be the king's proud squire, not a shy commoner.

I let him come over as I continue to stare.

As he gets closer, I notice his amber complexion, his high cheekbones, and the tapered shape of his eyes. The last seem underlined with a black pencil, something only female courtiers do, which only reinforces the intensity of his expression. The flickering torches cast a shine on a loop that he wears in his left ear. At first, I think it's an iron ring . . . then I see that it's a safety pin. And in his closed mouth, he's holding a thin wooden stick—a toothpick. Nothing is more absurd for a bloodsucker who hasn't eaten a solid meal in eons. Obviously, he's an eccentric.

"Mademoiselle de Gastefriche, I presume," he says in an accent I instantly recognize as being the same English one as Proserpina's.

"How did you know?"

"Your reputation precedes you," he replies, barely parting his lips.

His toothpick gives his mouth an undefined expression, neither a smile nor a frown.

"Not only did you save the king in Versailles, but you're his representative here in Paris tonight," he adds.

I gesture in Mélac's direction, where he and his horde of flatterers are engaged in social chatter.

"I'm not the king's representative this evening. That would be the Marquis de Mélac."

"Really? Then why did the Immutable dispatch not one but three of his squires, in addition to his minister of the armies?" He glances at Suraj and Hélénaïs, who are busy talking to the courtiers. "Something tells me that you're here about the Lady of Miracles, whose name is on everyone's lips since this morning, am I right?"

I now have the feeling that this strange individual is trying to get information out of me. I notice flashes of gold in the depths of his black eyes, as if each color is trying to deceive me.

"And you are?" I say, avoiding the question.

"Lord Sterling Raindust, attaché to the embassy of England, at your service. Let me take the opportunity to thank you for recommending to the king that he include my compatriot, Proserpina Castlecliff, among his squires. I'm told you're the one who urged him to accept her candidacy."

I smile, a little awkwardly. I did indeed plead with the Immutable to accept Proserpina as a squire, because there was a time when she and I had been friends and I had called her Poppy. The Sip of the King was the only way to cure her chronic tuberculosis. It was also a way of making me feel less guilty about having revealed her condition to the entire court, something I did during my frantic race to become a squire.

"Having an Englishwoman among the king's bodyguards also contributes to the rapprochement of our two countries," the lord says.

In one swift motion, he removes the toothpick from his mouth and sticks it behind one of his ears. Then he leans toward me.

Whereas Raoul de Montfaucon's hand-kiss made me bristle with disgust, Lord Raindust's only makes me shiver.

A voice comes from behind me. "Don't listen to that smooth talker, Diane. Never trust the English."

I turn around. It's Alexandre de Mortange, looking dashing in a midnight-blue velvet coat on which rests his resplendent red hair.

"Alex, you're here," I say, put out by the presence of my embarrassing protector.

"I had my coffin brought to Paris early this morning. I wanted to be sure I'd be present for you this evening," he says proudly. "And from what I see, I was right to make haste in order to save you from dubious encounters."

He looks at the vampyre stranger suspiciously.

"According to my sources, this Raindust is new in town. Avoid him as you would the plague."

"You, Mortange, have only recently returned to Paris after a long absence, so they say," Lord Raindust counters. He gestures toward the crowd. "Tonight, *Hell is empty, and all the devils are here.*"

"What's that gibberish?"

"Shakespeare's *The Tempest*," the curt Englishman replies. "I imagine that being exiled in the Auvergne must have been hell for a devil of a socialite like you."

I think I see Alexandre's marble cheeks flush. If there's one thing he hates, it's to be reminded of his banishment from Versailles these last twenty years by order of the king. Taking part in killing my family of rebels is what allowed him to return.

"Here in Paris we quote Molière, France's greatest playwright, not Shakespeare, monsieur," he says, losing his temper. "Devil or not, I'm a loyal French subject. Not a punk anarchist, a spy in the pocket of treacherous Albion."

It's public knowledge that the vice-queen Anne isn't held in high esteem at the court. But she's never dared defy the Immutable as openly as the Lady of Miracles. The split between France and England isn't a done deal yet—as Poppy's selection to be a squire attests, along with Lord Raindust's attendance at tonight's reception.

"Punk anarchist or spy in the service of power, you must choose one, Viscount," the lord says calmly. "My role as attaché to the embassy of England is official and aboveboard. As for my intentions, they're quite honorable. I'm working toward the rapprochement of our two peoples, nothing more."

He's about to kiss my hand again, thus giving an ambiguous and very personal meaning to his last words.

Alexandre steps between us, mad with jealousy.

"Stop right there, you jackal. Diane, listen to me, you must be careful. The capital is full of scoundrels with ill intentions. Especially when it concerns a young lady as pure and innocent as yourself."

Just like every time my white knight pretends to be "protecting" me, I fight against the urge to slap him and make him swallow back his words.

Drums start beating from somewhere, signaling that the execution is about to get underway.

"According to rumors, the viscount knows firsthand of what he speaks," Lord Raindust says, still calm, cool, and collected—the opposite of Alexandre's display of fervor.

Alexandre places a hand on the finely crafted sword hanging from his belt.

"How dare you say that I frequent unsavory social circles, Monsieur Brit!"

"You misunderstood me, I—"

"Now, that's better."

"I meant that you're an expert when it comes to pure and innocent young ladies."

Alexandre's face turns white under his tawny hair.

It's not the first time others have alluded to the bevy of mortals he fell in love with before I came along . . . whose fate ended tragically under his jaws. Right up to the last one, someone named Aneta, who was also one of the king's squires and who perished from Alexandre's excess of "love," hence his banishment to the Auvergne.

The cruel Don Juan opens his mouth to defend himself, but loud clapping puts an end to the altercation. It's Mélac. He's clapping his hands at the front of the grandstand.

"Let us proceed with the hanging," he orders, smiling.

The drums double their intense beating.

Trumpets blare, echoing off the high Paris walls that surround us.

Straightaway, a sinister choreography is set in motion to the rhythm of the invisible drums. A dozen executioners, hooded in the same manner as the royal executioner, approach in procession from each side of the gallows. Behind them they drag a string of bound prisoners, forcing them to climb the stone steps that lead to the crossbeams. One by one, the executioners slip ropes around the necks of the condemned until one hundred and ten alcoves are occupied.

It's horrible to see these figures shivering from cold, their feet bare, balanced on frozen planks. They already look like ghosts as the evening air lifts their shirts like phantom sheets.

Only one alcove is occupied on the uppermost level, the one that's also the most visible to the people. The attitude of the condemned leads me to guess it's Blanche de La Roncière, regal to the end. Instinctively, I raise my hand to my head, where she tore a chunk of my hair earlier.

At that exact moment, Mélac lifts his armor-clad arm, a delicately laced sleeve dangling from it—and, like a Roman emperor in an amphitheater, turns his thumb and its pointy fingernail downward.

It's the signal.

Abruptly, the drums stop beating.

Driven by a hidden mechanism in the depths of the gallows, the planks give way in unison under the prisoners' feet. All one hundred and ten bodies fall into the void, emitting a horrible concert of cracking sounds: the dislocation of vertebrae—necks that snapped. For some dreadful seconds, the bodies are riddled with nervous spasms that resemble a frenzied jig. Then the bodies go still.

I look away, disgusted by this grisly scene and even more so by the cheerful comments of the courtiers reveling in the spectacle. The people below erupt in a savage joy that pains me, as if the downfall of a handful of those who wielded power can improve their miserable fate.

"Justice is served!" Mélac shouts. "Let the ravens and vultures pick at these bodies right down to the bone. Let their skeletons be removed and crushed so nothing remains of these wretches, not even their names."

He's barely finished speaking when a thunderous roar reverberates. At first, I think the drums have started up again, but no, the thunder is coming from above, not from the ground.

An explosion of white light sprays the sky over the gallows.

"Fireworks," Suraj says.

"To celebrate the Immutable?" Hélénaïs asks the grand equerry, who's standing by our sides.

Montfaucon doesn't answer. The bones of his austere face seem sculpted by the successive detonations. Since my arrival at Versailles, I've attended several nighttime festivities. I know the king's pyrotechnicians use many colors to dazzle the courtiers. But tonight, only dreary bursts tear at the night sky.

At the front of the grandstand, Mélac is livid. The glimmering splashes that bounce against the heavenly sky reflect on his armor, a useless shell to fight against an invisible enemy.

At the bottom of the hill, the people fan out in shouts of bewilderment . . . in cries of terror.

Coming out of his stupor, Mélac yells orders.

"What are you waiting for, you imbecile, find the troublemakers!" he hollers at L'Esquille, who's trembling beneath his wig. "Evacuate the mob! Enforce the curfew! Now! Do it now!"

An unspeakable chaos takes over.

A crowning explosion lights up the sky.

Phosphoric sparks rain down and latch onto the beams where the hanged bodies dangle.

The dry wood catches fire.

The flames engulf the shirts of the executed.

The whole of the gallows becomes a blazing inferno.

6

ESCORT

I'm walking into pitch darkness, black as ink.

Under my feet, the spongy ground makes squishy sighing sounds.

My fingers grope the void, meeting up with slippery stones that feel unpleasantly slimy, as if covered in half-frozen moss.

The air, too, is foul, with a stench that's coming from the invisible ground, a putrid vapor in the chilled air.

Am I on the right path?

I've barely asked myself this question when the sky cracks open and a pale light rains down on the world.

And there, in the center of the forest of motionless rocks, lies a body.

It's a girl with gray hair, her neck savagely slashed.

I wake up with a jolt, breathless, my eyes wide open in a darkened room.

Another nightmare.

Another vision of death—*my death.*

Blanche de La Roncière's final threat comes back to me like a slap: *"May my last words be stamped on your brain: I curse you, and Tristan will come back to avenge me."*

Her curse must have shaken me more than I thought. It must have brought on the weird dream. I slit Tristan's throat; now I saw myself with a sliced throat too.

I shake myself to chase away the horrible image that's already beginning to clear. Tristan de La Roncière is no more, and neither is his mother. I saw her body catch fire when the gallows went up in flames.

The memory of the previous evening replaces the last hazy bit of my dream.

I remember the panic, the flames, the screams.

Mélac, who had come to take credit for a successful hanging, returned to Versailles with his tail between his legs, forced to report on the fiasco to the king. As for us, the three squires, L'Esquille made us evacuate to the center of Paris under heavy guard. That's how we made our way through the darkened capital, whose outline I could barely distinguish in the black night. I understood why Paris is called the City of Shadows—nearly all of it is just one big pool of darkness. Only the lanterns brandished by the soldiers of the Royal Watch lit the cobblestones in front of us. That's how we arrived at the Grand Châtelet, a lugubrious medieval citadel that rises on the right bank of the Seine. It's been the police headquarters since ancestral times. The building looked like a beleaguered fortress, flanked by legions of armored soldiers who were guarding it throughout the night against any attacks by ghouls. Here, in this place that's even more closely guarded than a prison, L'Esquille assigned us rooms that could be mistaken for cells. It didn't take long for me to fall asleep . . . until my abrupt awakening.

As I throw off my sweat-drenched sheets, my hand comes into contact with the mother-of-pearl handle of my squire's sword. After the incident at the palace two nights ago, I decided to never again sleep unarmed. I grab hold of the sword, get up and walk to the window, and pull the curtains aside in one swift motion. No surprise: the window is protected by iron bars. Beyond them, the morning light reveals the rooftops of Paris. A panorama even vaster than anything I imagined in yesterday's twilight spreads out before me.

Clusters of shacks jammed together like dull insect colonies, dozens of pointed bell towers misted in morning fog, a tangle of streets unraveling in all directions—it isn't a city that spreads out in front of me; it's a labyrinth without beginning or end.

And I'm supposed to find the Lady of Miracles in this chaos?

Where to begin?

I take a deep breath, gathering my thoughts. I had to learn how to play a duplicitous game when I slipped into the courtiers' rituals at the Palace of Versailles. But in this unfamiliar city, so close to those I'm supposed to deceive, it's a whole other story.

As I mull things over, I anxiously stroke the onyx stone that adorns my ring. I'll have to proceed methodically. This investigation will start off like a long-distance race before it turns into a sprint. First, I'll have to join my teammates and investigate alongside them; working as a trio, we'll have a much better chance of finding a lead. Then, in the final stretch, I'll have to accelerate and pass them by in order to eliminate the lady before they can capture her. Blinded by the burst of light from the *essence de jour*, they may not even see me drive a stake through her heart.

"The Lady of Miracles is behind the destruction of the Gibbet of Montfaucon," L'Esquille announces.

After a light breakfast, the police lieutenant general gathered us—Hélénaïs, Suraj, and me—in one of the vaulted rooms at the Grand Châtelet. He seemed tired yesterday, but this morning he looks positively exhausted. There are deep circles under his worried eyes, and no amount of concealer can hide them. On the table sit pitchers filled with steaming black coffee, no doubt the fuel that keeps him going.

"When my men were finally able to determine from which sewer holes the incendiary fireworks were set off, the pyrotechnicians were long gone," he says. "We found only powder, rocket casings, a mixture of Greek fire . . . and this."

His hand shaking, he brandishes a bundle of papers that he lets fall onto the center of the table as if it were burning his fingers.

It's a leaflet that has been reproduced in multiple copies.

I instantly recognize the etching decorating the printout. It represents the seal of the Lady of Miracles, even more menacing than on yesterday's envelope. The lunar face of the goddess Hecate now eclipses the sun mask of the god Apollo.

The illustration is coupled with a poem in an alexandrine meter.

To Louis

We offered you a most timely understanding.
You chose to embrace war, you belligerent king.
Yet no need to get completely down and dirty.
Just withdraw your armies and give us the city.
If you have not ceded by the Night of Shadows
We'll unleash a fury of quick, staggering blows.
Abominations and ghouls out of the abyss
Will ring the death knell and plunder all of Paris.
Louis, get a grip and avoid a debacle.
Come, partner up with the Lady of Miracles.

"These vile leaflets have also been handed out to the people, spit from manholes to the four corners of the capital," L'Esquille goes on, his voice quivering. "This morning, the entire city is buzzing with the rumor that the Lady of Miracles burned the gallows of the kings of France to ashes. And now she's threatening the Immutable with chaos if he doesn't officially acknowledge her as vice-queen of Paris before the Night of Shadows. It's already November thirtieth . . . the deadline is just three short weeks away."

Like every inhabitant of the Magna Vampyria, I know the Night of Shadows falls each year on December 21, on the winter solstice, the longest night of the year. According to the Hematics' liturgical calendar, it's also the most sacred night. The night that celebrates the transmutation of vampyres and the advent of the era of Shadows.

Hélénaïs bangs her fist on the table, rattling our coffee cups.

"What are we waiting for to start hunting that renegade?" she asks.

L'Esquille shakes his head, agitating the curls of his wig.

"Well, we . . . we don't know where she's hiding," he confesses, his fingertips fiddling with his thin mustache. "For months, every police resource has been mobilized, day and night. All in vain."

Mélac may have pretended that the rumors about the Lady of Miracles were just gossip, but he obviously lent them some credibility, since he made them the priority of his police lieutenant general. Now I understand why L'Esquille looks so haggard. In his relentless quest to find the Lady of Miracles, he can't sleep. He's probably afraid of losing his job, maybe even his life. The King of Shadows isn't a patient sovereign, and his anger is deadly. L'Esquille's head will be the first to roll if the search doesn't succeed.

"By the grace of the Shadows, and with the help of the royal squires, the police will finally be able to apprehend this dangerous criminal," he says.

"Start by helping us so that we can help you," I tell him, taking advantage of his distress. "Tell us everything you know about the Lady of Miracles. When did she come on the scene? And how?"

The lieutenant general's shoulders sag a little more under his brown velvet jacket, as if all these questions overwhelm him. He shrivels up in his chair and helps himself to another cup of coffee to muster some courage.

"The rumor mill started last summer, without us being able to trace the exact source," he says. "In the wake of attacks by ghouls that grew increasingly frequent and increasingly violent, the squares and alleyways began to swirl with talk of the Lady of Miracles. In the past, these monsters always acted alone, or in small groups, but now hordes of them rise from the sewers and underground quarries where they hole up during the day." L'Esquille sighs. "It takes every available police force to protect official state and Faculty buildings at night. That leaves the commoners' neighborhoods at the mercy of those flocks. They devour anyone or anything in their path before returning to their lairs. Every single one of their unpredictable appearances ends in total carnage. And that's not all. They take off with the reserves of flour and wheat, the stocks of bread and wine, the slightest foodstuffs they come across."

Suraj raises his eyes, knitting together his thick black brows.

"Strange . . . from what I know, the ghouls are scavengers who feed exclusively on human remains."

"Ever since the Lady of Miracles showed up, their appetite knows no bounds," L'Esquille says. "The ghouls have . . . evolved. From opportunistic vultures, they've become aggressive predators. They ravage everything."

Unable to hold back any longer, I weigh in on the conversation.

"Excuse me, monsieur, I don't know anything about ghouls, and I've never seen one in my life. I thought they were simply wild beasts."

"Beasts? Not really. They're not born from an animal womb. For all we know, they form directly in the bowels of the earth, generating spontaneously under the influence of the Shadows."

I remain quiet, thinking back to what Montfaucon said when he explained that ghouls were "children of the Shadows" of a different kind than vampyres. Since the Sip of the King, I, too, have a little bit of the Shadows in my veins, a few drops of royal blood saturated with shadowessence, that fifth humor recognized by the Faculty. Even darker than black bile, a substance about which we still really know nothing.

"You say the ghouls have evolved," Suraj picks up. "To the point that they would plaster an envelope on the king's mortuary chamber and set fire to the Gibbet of Montfaucon?"

L'Esquille turns pale.

"Probably not," he admits. "The ghouls can't manipulate tools, most likely because they don't have thumbs."

I think back to the exposed appendages in Montfaucon's jars. It's true: those "hands" only had four fingers, similar to animal paws.

"The Lady of Miracles, whoever she is, must have powerful supporters," L'Esquille says with a groan. "Until the letter she left yesterday, we didn't know she was a vampyre. Maybe she's not the only immortal hiding out in the Court of Miracles."

I exchange a look with the other two squires.

We came to the capital thinking we were dealing with a solitary vampyre. But if there's more than one, as L'Esquille believes, it changes everything.

"What makes you think other vampyres are hiding out in the Court of Miracles?" Hélénaïs asks him with a hint of aggression that does little to mask her worry.

"After each of the ghouls' bloody attacks, people go missing."

"You already told us that those horrid creatures gnawed on lowlifes right on the spot," Hélénaïs says impatiently.

"Those unfortunate enough to fall between the jaws of the ghouls don't vanish *entirely*," the lieutenant general corrects himself. "Usually, the ghouls leave half-devoured bits behind. But now it seems they also capture live prey to take back deep down." L'Esquille swallows, white as a sheet. "An idea has been haunting me since yesterday, driving me to the point of sleeplessness . . . What if the Court of Miracles welcomed a large number of unrecorded vampyres that the so-called *missing* feed with their fresh blood?"

"How many?" Suraj asks.

"Impossible to say. No police officer has ever set foot inside the Court of Miracles."

"Let me rephrase the question: How many have vanished without a trace?"

L'Esquille's shoulders hunch a bit more, as if the question was the coup de grâce.

"The census that the Hematic Faculty of Paris carries out each month is indisputable," he says. "Since the summer, three thousand Parisians have simply disappeared."

"What?" Hélénaïs hiccups into her coffee cup.

"The doctors of the Faculty keep very strict records on the number of commoners who have their blood drawn every month to pay the tithe," L'Esquille explains. "Since summer, three thousand have gone missing from today's roll call. We haven't been able to identify their remains in the carnage left by the ghouls. And that number keeps growing each night."

A cold sweat trickles down my spine. I understand now why the grand equerry is so set on having me eliminate the Lady of Miracles before the Immutable can wrench the secret of the ghouls out of her. Command over the ghouls offers unlimited power to the one who wields it. For six months, it seems she's allowed dozens of illegal vampyres to feed with impunity in the bowels of Paris.

"Do we have any clue as to where the Court of Miracles is to be found?" I ask.

With difficulty, L'Esquille gets out of his chair and walks over to one of the decrepit walls of the room. A large map hangs there, a map of Paris.

"The Court of Miracles . . . ," he mumbles. "No one is certain where this lawless enclave is, exactly. On the right bank or on the left? In the center or in the outskirts?"

He sweeps an unsure hand across the map. The maze of streets that were laid out slowly over the course of centuries seems even more impenetrable on paper than it looked from my bedroom window this morning.

"Nearly three hundred years ago, my distant predecessor managed to locate the old Court of Miracles," says L'Esquille. "It was situated here, not far from Les Halles, Paris's main food market." He points to a spot on the map. "A place known today as Rue de la Grande-Truanderie—the street of high crime—for all the cons, panhandlers, and cutthroats who used to populate that street and rough area."

L'Esquille heaves a sigh of nostalgia, visibly longing for the time when police lieutenants were up against more conventional criminals.

"We have no way of knowing where the new Court of Miracles is to be found," he laments. "We only know one thing for sure: it's located in the depths of the city. Paris is like swiss cheese, with an underground system of tunnels that was dug throughout the ages. An impossible labyrinth to map out. This city is peppered with so many drainage holes, hidden caves, and subterranean tunnels that we never know where the ghouls will strike next."

"Why don't you follow the trail of their carnage?" I ask.

"They do hit-and-run attacks, and my men usually arrive after the fact at the scene of the crimes. The soldiers that Mélac sent me as reinforcement didn't fare any better. The few times they were able to chase the ghouls underground, the wind below snuffed out their torches. Ghouls are scared of light, of course, but how can you keep a flame going where it's humid and the air is scarce? We never saw those unfortunate souls again." L'Esquille sighs once more. "The most powerful army in the world can't do a thing against a guerrilla force that lies in wait in unknown territory. What we need to do is strike at the top. We need to capture the vampyre who's magically coordinating the ghouls. With no general at the helm, those legions of abominations will disband."

"Surely you have a slight idea of their whereabouts, monsieur," I insist. "Tell us where to begin our search. We must start somewhere."

The lieutenant general lets out a long helpless groan.

"Where to begin? Where to begin?" he repeats. "I was hoping you'd tell me, since you're the Immutable's squires. Don't they say that the sovereign's blood pulses through your veins, thus enhancing your senses and intuition?"

"Is that your plan, to use us like vulgar hunting dogs?" Hélénaïs says. "Were you appointed police lieutenant by sheer luck of the draw?"

While she fulminates, Suraj keeps his cool.

"Diane is right, we need to start somewhere," he says. "When and where did the last ghoul attack take place?"

"All the way south of Paris, near Mont Parnasse, just three days ago."

Suraj gets up, his hand on the strange dagger that's lodged in the sheath at his belt. It's got two curved blades that deploy, one on each side of the horned handle. A weapon that has come all the way from India, just as he has.

"So, what are we waiting for?" he asks. "Let's get moving."

Perched atop Typhon, I start across the Pont au Change, which straddles the Seine, leading from the Grand Châtelet and heading south of Paris. Actually, it's hard to make out that it's a bridge. The houses lining each side are so packed together that it's impossible to see the river that flows behind them. The rich facades, adorned with large windows filled with jewels and crowned by fine gold-lettered signs, impress me nearly as much as the splendors of Versailles. Fragrant scents waft out of them. Most passersby are as richly attired as the mortal courtiers at the palace. Some gentlemen tip their hats as we go by, saluting the king's squires, who are recognizable by the engraved sun on our leather breastplates. Onlookers linger over Suraj's turban, something I notice because his horse walks next to mine.

"Who lives in these houses?" I ask him, remembering that he knows Paris.

"Wealthy merchants," he answers. "The ground floors are filled with the shops of jewelers, gold- and silversmiths, and money changers, hence the name of the bridge. There are also many glove makers and perfumers."

"What a nice change from the squalid outskirts of Montfaucon," Hélénaïs says from high atop her chestnut sorrel. "I feel more in my element here."

"That's the paradox of Paris," Suraj says. "A city that shelters the wealthiest as well as those in abject misery."

But Hélénaïs isn't listening to him.

"Look at the magnificent diamond necklace in that window!" she gushes. "It would look dazzling around my throat during the soirées at Versailles. I must send the jeweler's name to my father. My birthday's coming up soon."

She gives me a pointed look to emphasize her words. It's as if I can read her resentment in her golden-brown eyes: *You might have seen some harsh words in my father's letter, you little snoop, but he loves me unconditionally. He's always willing to spend a fortune on me.*

"Speaking of jewelry, I noticed that you got yourself a new ring with your wages," she says, eyeing the onyx on my left hand. "A little rustic, I'd say. I imagine it's the style in the Auvergne."

"That's because I have neither your ample means nor your good taste," I reply, hurrying to divert Hélénaïs from the forbidden ring.

I force myself to refocus her attention on her own jewelry.

"The pendant around your neck is beautiful," I rave as I gesture toward the blue gem that pops out against the black of her breastplate. "Is it an aquamarine?"

"No, a sapphire. I don't do things halfway. I don't wear semiprecious stones."

"Of course, what am I thinking? And I suppose the charming bracelet on your wrist is made of solid white gold."

"Platinum, the first among metals, for the one who'll be first to capture the Lady of Miracles."

The roman numeral *I* is engraved on the surface of the bracelet, as if proclaiming to the world that Hélénaïs aspires to be number one in all things . . .

Escorted by the six horsemen of the Royal Watch that L'Esquille assigned to us, we stay on the path toward the Île de la Cité. Dead in the center, the silhouette of a colossal cathedral rises up.

"It used to be called Notre-Dame de Paris," Suraj explains to me. "The biggest Catholic church in the kingdom of France. Today, it's the tallest cathedral belonging to the Hematic Faculty, as well as the headquarters of the archiater of Paris. It was rebaptized Notre-Damn, not referencing the Virgin Mary anymore but the mystic damnation that unleashed the era of the Shadows. A damnation that the lords of the night are so proud of and owe their eternal life to." He points toward the vampyric statues filling the niches of the facade. "The saints of yesterday were replaced by *sanguine* statues. Effigies that correspond to different neighborhoods in Paris: Sang-Michel, Sang-Germain, Sang-Honoré, and countless others. Rumor has it that the gigantic tanks on the twin towers of Notre-Damn hold enough blood to fill all the ponds in the parks of Paris."

I can't help but shiver as I pass by the shadows of the sinister towers. In times past, I imagine they were decorated with Christian crosses. But three hundred years ago, the crucifixes gave way to metallic bats, their wings outstretched, the emblem of the new state religion imposed by the immortals. And so a portion of the blood collected from the tithe is warehoused in these vast tanks.

"I don't dare imagine the number of Parisian vampyres who drink from such a large reservoir . . . ," I say, thinking out loud.

"The *numerus clausus* applies to the capital just as it does to the rest of the Magna Vampyria," Suraj explains. "A hundred commoners for one courtier. That's the ratio imposed by the Faculty. Which means there are around ten thousand immortals in Paris proper. But the bulk of the liquid in the towers of Notre-Damn only constitutes table blood for daily consumption. The rest of the cathedral serves as blood cellars where the doctors of the Faculty produce the best vintages from each neighborhood. Alcoholized blood of Sorbonne students from Sang-Michel, full-bodied blood from the workers at Les Halles, and so on."

"And the massive palace behind us on the right bank?" I ask, eager to look away from the cheerless cathedral.

I point toward an immense gray facade pierced with thousands of windows.

"That's the Louvre Palace," Suraj explains. "It's been the residence of the kings of France for centuries, up until Louis XIV decided to move his court to Versailles. Nowadays, it isn't used much, only for meetings or royal visits."

As we arrive on the left bank, the streets quickly become narrower, the buildings less opulent. Cut stone gives way to wood and plaster. The compact and unembellished structures look as if they're holding each other up precariously, like a house of cards. The tops rise ever higher and more uneven, in order to house more and more inhabitants. The clothes of the bystanders change, too, slowly losing their vivid hues for gray tones that blend in with the facades. Without red lipsticks and rosy cheek blushes, the faces themselves blend in with the pallid colors. Surprised by our presence, the onlookers seem hostile and unsettled. Here, people go bareheaded, without hats to tip and salute us. In fact, wobbly doors shut and frayed curtains are drawn as we pass by. Police officers are not welcome, and the king's squires even less so. My heart is gripped by the thought that these thousands of people have been born and will die in the confines of this place. Not only have they never ventured beyond the city walls of Paris, but most of them have never left their immediate vicinity. In the capital, the law of the sequester is enforced neighborhood by neighborhood, and one must get special authorization to travel from one to another. At least in my village in the Auvergne, I could get away during daylight hours to go hunting in the woods; the commoners of Paris won't ever experience that luxury.

After a long way, we plunge into a maze of streets that are so narrow we're forced to make our horses walk single file. The sophisticated fragrances of the Pont au Change are replaced by a bitter, persistent stench. We proceed one after the other, still closely bookended by the horsemen of the Royal Watch. The sky is now just a pale strip above our heads, its luminosity lessened by the many clotheslines filled with tattered rags that run the length of one facade to another. It's like entering a gigantic spider's web . . .

"Here we are. Mont Parnasse," says the Royal Watch captain, a gruff man who was instructed not to leave our sides.

We've just emerged onto a large spot, open to the sky, much like an unexpected clearing in the middle of an urban forest.

There's a hill made of rubble here, with dilapidated shacks spreading out on its sides.

"It's a lot different than Ovid's Mount Parnassus," Hélénaïs says, sounding stuffed up. Ever since we crossed the Seine, she's been holding her lace handkerchief pressed against her nose to protect herself from the stench.

Like her and every student at the Grande Écurie, I've read Ovid's *Metamorphoses*. In ancient mythology, Mount Parnassus referred to the most beautiful mountain in Greece. The heavenly residence of the muses themselves.

"Ovid?" says the Royal Watch captain. "Never heard of him. The immortals of the affluent neighborhoods are the ones who named this slum Mont Parnasse."

I grit my teeth, taking in the contemptuous irony of the bloodsuckers. Not only do they cram commoners together in slums, but on top of that they joke about their misery.

"Actually, it's not much like a hill," the obtuse captain goes on. "The loose rocks are debris from the excavated catacombs."

"Cata—what?" Hélénaïs says.

"The catacombs are the vast underground quarries where the stones to build the city were excavated," the captain explains. "If our ancestors had only known that by digging those thousands of tunnels, they were preparing a choice burrow for those damned ghouls." At the mention of the despised creatures, the captain spits on the ground from atop his horse. "The digging stopped a long time ago, and we've been trying to seal off the entrances. But they're too many, and so every night the ground vomits batches of abominations. Some are deadlier than others . . . like the one that came up three days ago, which ravaged this place."

I pay closer attention to the dwellings adjoining the hill and see that they're in ruins. Busted doors and broken shutters—as if a hurricane swept through here. In the middle of this disaster, somewhere in the distance, I can hear the shouts of children playing. It's like life is already trying to reclaim its rights.

We dismount and tie our horses up so that we can meet the survivors in their battered homes.

"Listen up, people, by order of the police, come out of your ratholes!" the captain shouts.

The children's cries stop, like a frightened flock of birds has suddenly flown off. Hunched figures emerge from the hovels, mouths shut, shifty eyed, shivering from the cold in their tattered rags. It's heartrending to see these poor people whose blood and misery nourish the prosperity of the vampyres. They're the exact opposite of all the gilt at Versailles.

"Mind your manners," the captain scolds them. "The king's squires are paying you a visit."

Every command coming from the police captain only serves to shut down the faces even more.

He stuffs his hand in the pocket of his jerkin and takes out a piece of paper with scribbling.

"Of the four thousand three hundred inhabitants of Mont Parnasse, we've counted one hundred and seven dead and fifty-two missing," he reads. "There are also twenty-two severely wounded who were taken to the Hospice of the Incurables. The other inhabitants fled like rats when the ghouls arrived, returning only in the early morning." Once again, he admonishes the crowd, "Yes, you fled in contempt of the law of the curfew, you scoundrels. Instead of staying home to defend the wheat given to you by the king!"

Hearing this, an old lady with eyes red from weeping now steps forward from the silent crowd and throws herself at Hélénaïs's feet.

"Have pity on us, beautiful lady, you, who look like an angel! Have pity on a poor widow. The ghouls snatched my boy, his wife, and their son. They devoured all our stockpiles, and our larders are empty. Tell the king to give us more flour. Tell him to free us from the Lady of Miracles!"

"I . . . uh . . . ," Hélénaïs stammers, caught off guard.

"Rumor says this demon will ruin Paris during the Night of Shadows," the widow wails as she sheds tears all over the squire's boots. "Our lords and masters have to protect us. Me, Mère Mahaut, I can't read, but it's written in the laws, isn't it? It's written in the Mortal Code that the doctors of the Faculty preach to us every Sunday at the hematic church." She starts a religious chant: "Oboedientia—*From cradle to grave, commoners remain under the protection of the vampyres, in return for which they owe total submission.*"

I'm overwhelmed by the way this poor woman clings to the Mortal Code, the unfair edict that sequesters the fourth estate in exchange for the so-called protection of the vampyres. In Paris, the destitute give their blood and get nothing in return, only despair. Right until the end, they're swindled.

Already, the soldiers of the Royal Watch rush to push back the unwelcome woman, but Suraj raises his arm to hold them at bay.

"Leave her be."

He takes a step forward and offers his gloved hand to help the old woman up.

"We are precisely here in the king's name to stop the Lady of Miracles and to protect the people," he tells her gently. "The massacre on the Night of Shadows will not happen. And we'll do all we can to bring back the remains of your dear ones so that you may offer them a burial."

I'm torn between Suraj's show of humanity and the reality of our mission. The Immutable never dispatched us to Paris to "protect the people." He asked us to find the Lady of Miracles so that he could appropriate her army of ghouls. And I don't doubt that if he succeeds, he'll use this army against the fourth estate at the first opportunity.

"As for the flour, I'm sure we'll be able to get some bags delivered to you," Suraj promises.

"But—" the Royal Watch captain starts to object.

"By order of the king!" the squire cuts him off in a tone that brooks no argument. "And now, let us investigate *our way*—that, too, is the king's order."

The captain frowns. He takes a few steps back as he gives us a dismissive look.

"My men and I will wait for you here with the horses. But I doubt you'll find anything. The police already scoured the area with a fine-tooth comb."

Suraj ignores the veteran's sarcasm and offers his arm to the old woman.

"You are good, Monsieur Ottoman," she says, lifting her wrinkled eyes toward the squire's turban.

"I'm Indian."

"Indian . . . ," she repeats, her voice quivering.

"Lead us to the spot where you last saw your son and his family, Mère Mahaut."

He gestures for us to follow him, and we head into the maze of the hill. It's a tangle of slender alleyways and obscure dead ends, rendered all the more chaotic by the devastation wrought by the ghouls. The unpaved ground is littered with a debris of tiles that crunches under our boots.

We finally arrive in front of a shack with a busted door. The wind makes the flap clap mournfully. It's a complete disarray of toppled tables inside. The doors of the larder gape open, revealing empty shelves. The iron trapdoor at the back of the room is also open, with a ladder plunging down to the cellar.

"For a long time, my son feared there would be a massive onslaught by the ghouls," Mère Mahaut explains. "He fortified the cellar so that he could take refuge there with his wife, his son, and his food supplies in case of a surprise attack. But his efforts were useless against those monsters."

While the widow bursts into sobs, Suraj kneels down to examine the trapdoor more closely.

"I don't think the ghouls had anything to do with this," Suraj announces.

"Wha—what?" the old lady sputters.

"Ghouls have sharp claws to tear at flesh and powerful jaws to break bones. But neither their nails nor their fangs can twist metal this way."

He points to the jagged iron lock that was supposed to protect the family. He traces its edges with his index finger and wipes a residue of fine black powder.

"This trap door was blown up," he says. "And ghouls can't handle cannon powder."

"Which means that somebody came after the ghouls left and forced open the door that resisted the ghouls' attack," I say, completing Suraj's reasoning.

The old woman dries her tears with her apron and raises hopeful, moist eyes toward me.

"You mean that human hands kidnapped my son, his Claudine, and their little Martin? The ghouls didn't devour them? So maybe they're still alive! Oh, I beg you, please find them!"

Sadness overwhelms me as I think about the fate that must have befallen Mère Mahaut's loved ones. The hands that kidnapped them might have been human, but my guess is that they were also as cold as death . . . the hands of vampyres. Ending up under the fangs of the unrecorded at the Court of Miracles isn't in any way more desirable than being a snack for the ghouls.

To avoid looking at the old widow's hopeful eyes, I start to inspect the frame of the trapdoor, too, as if I'm searching for clues. I notice a shiny glare on the cracked floor tiles.

"All right, can we get going?" Hélénaïs says. She's clearly in a rush to leave this place where the specter of death hovers.

"Wait," I tell her. "There are glass fragments on the ground."

Hélénaïs shrugs. "So what? Don't start thinking you're a hotshot detective just because you're poking around." That's a new allusion to the letter I read. She gives me a pointed look. "I don't find that surprising. The ghouls broke everything, glass included."

"Except that there wasn't any glass in this house. The neighborhood is too poor to have glass-paned windows or delicate dishware in the sideboards."

Hélénaïs widens her eyes as she realizes that the windows only have broken shutters to close, and that the bowls and flatware strewed on the ground are made of either iron or wood. Having been raised in the lap of luxury, she can't imagine a home with no glass windows or fine china. But in the countryside where I grew up, most of the homes were without. You only found glass at the tavern, to preserve wine in bottles, and at the apothecary, to collect the blood tithe in vials.

"We drink from goblets here at home," Mère Mahaut says as she wraps her old shawl snugly around her shivering shoulders.

Just as I suspected.

Gingerly, I gather some broken glass pieces. The fragments are crystal clear, perfectly curved, far more transparent than the receptacles that my father used for his pharmacopoeia. A first-rate material, out of reach for a simple country apothecary.

I wrap the fragments in a lace handkerchief that I carefully slide into my small leather shoulder bag.

It's time to take our leave of the widow.

Hélénaïs heaves a sigh of relief as we emerge outside.

She's already hurrying into the alley to get back to the clearing, but Suraj grabs her by the arm.

"Not that way," he tells her.

"But . . . that's how we came, and the Royal Watch is waiting for us."

"Exactly. Let them wait some more. Long enough so we can put some distance between us."

Hélénaïs looks at Suraj as if he's lost his marbles.

"There's no way we can investigate things if we're flanked by escorts who are easy to spot from a mile off," he tells her. "We've learned a lot more in ten minutes on our own than the police have in weeks. We now know the ghouls don't act alone. L'Esquille just had a hypothesis; now we have proof. The Lady of Miracles is surrounded by accomplices, mortal or immortal, but definitely human. They come out of the bowels of Paris with its monsters to kidnap people. And the glass fragments Diane retrieved probably have some significance that eludes us . . . but that we'll end up finding out."

Suraj fingers the pocket of his breastplate.

"We don't need the police to continue our investigation. If needed, the royal passes the king gave us will open every door. My instincts tell me to go now to the Hospice of the Incurables, where the wounded of Mont Parnasse were taken. Maybe they'll have something to tell us, and they'll speak a lot more freely if they don't have to suffer the insults of the Royal Watch captain. And for tonight, I know a modest inn where we can stay in the university neighborhood of Sang-Michel. It'll be a much more discreet home base than the Grand Châtelet."

"A *modest* inn?" Hélénaïs says with a frown, as if she were uttering a dirty word. "We already abandoned our apartments at Versailles for the tiny rooms at the Grand Châtelet, but at least the view of the Seine is breathtaking. I'm not sure I want to get bitten by bedbugs on a mattress that peasants have slept on."

"You're free to go back to L'Esquille's boors and spend the next three weeks before the Night of Shadows sightseeing in Paris. As for me, I have a mission to accomplish on behalf of the king."

Suraj's last words shut her up. After all, she's a good little soldier of the Magna Vampyria. And as a faithful death-licker, she'd never want to demean herself in the sovereign's eyes. As for me, I'm not scared off by bedbugs; Butte-aux-Rats had its share of harmful pests, and their bites never killed me.

"What about our horses?" I ask.

"We won't need them while we investigate aboveground. Even less so when the time comes to descend into the depths of subterranean Paris. So, are you following me, yes or no?"

Hélénaïs gives me a look. I can tell she's filled with the same burning sense of competition that consumed her at the Grande Écurie.

"No way I'm letting you capture the Lady of Miracles first, little mouse," she tosses out at me. "And you, too, Suraj. You're not beating me to the punch. Like I told you, the king's blood sharpened my reflexes. They're supernaturally amazing. No one is faster than I am now. So it'll be *me* who brings the renegade and her army of ghouls to the Immutable."

You won't be the fastest if I incapacitate you, I think to myself, vowing to stop Hélénaïs if she comes between me and my target.

I'll send the lady to her ultimate death before my teammates can capture her—so that the Fronde can live, and so that tomorrow the Light can be reborn.

We head west of the hill, with no escort and no safety net, toward the unknown.

7
INCURABLES

While our equestrian procession drew a lot of attention earlier, now no one is paying us any heed in the teeming city streets.

To be fair, I admit that in exchange for a few pennies, we procured three long, thick gray-hooded capes that conceal our faces and leather breastplates. That's how we thread our way between washerwomen with arms full of laundry, chimney sweepers covered in soot, porters conveying construction materials on the backs of donkeys, and merchants selling off meager fish that were caught in the Seine to supplement the everyday food. Next to me, I hear Hélénaïs's wheezy breathing from under her hood. She tied her silk handkerchief over her face after announcing that she was on the verge of passing out. I have to admit that the odor we're surrounded by is persistent: greasy food, whiffs of urine, the sweat of men and beasts, and aromatic herbs to mask everything; it all blends together to create a dense, stale smell that becomes almost palpable despite the cold temperature.

"Here we are. The Hospice of the Incurables," Suraj finally announces.

I raise my eyes from under the brim of my hood and see a large stone enclosure emerge between the buildings. Same as at the Grand Châtelet, numerous men are guarding the premises. Not only soldiers of the Royal Watch, but also the king's dragoons, identifiable by their pointy gray hats. They're the kingdom's elite fighters, the same regiment that murdered my family in the Auvergne.

At this hour of the day, most of these ferocious combatants are napping in the camps erected around the enclosure. It's at night that they must increase their vigilance, when the nocturnal abominations come out and the Lady of Miracles is likely to strike.

We clear a path between the bivouacs and firepits until we reach a gate crowned with a large cast-iron bat covered in frost. It's holding a snake in its claws, the animal that's the symbol of apothecaries, the symbol that was etched into the door of my family's small shop in Butte-aux-Rats.

My heart tightens as I remember the happy times before the vampyric inquisition came and destroyed my family . . .

Suraj lifts the bronze bat-shaped door knocker.

A peephole opens in the thick nail-studded wood panel, and two suspicious eyes glisten behind it.

"Who goes there?"

"Let us enter, by order of the king!" Suraj says.

He takes a card out of his cape pocket, his pass signed by the royal hand.

The door opens with a squeak, revealing an imposing nun from the Hematic Faculty. She's wearing a full-length gray robe and a veil of the same color.

"I'm Sister Purpurine, the doorkeeper," she says gruffly, introducing herself.

"Our visit is confidential," Suraj hurries to tell her.

"And we, humble servants of the Shadows, aren't in the habit of spreading gossip. What brings you here?"

"We'd like to see some of your patients," Hélénaïs says.

"All visitation requests must be cleared by the Reverend Mother," the nun tells us. "Follow me."

She shuts the door behind us, quelling the noise from the streets. Then she motions for us to follow her across a large courtyard until we reach a main building shaped like a U, capped by a triangular chapel with bloodred stained glass.

A stifling atmosphere prevails in the hallways of the building.

The hospital nuns tend to their tasks without saying anything as they go by us. Some of them carry linen baskets to dress wounds, others trays of syringes to draw blood. Even behind the walls of hospices, the cruel tithe extends to commoners of the fourth estate.

Shattering the nuns' silence, a few sudden rattling dry coughs can be heard between cracks in the thick walls.

"Those are the tuberculosis patients," our guide explains. "The cold of the slack season doesn't bode well for their damaged lungs."

With emotion, I remember the coughing fits Poppy had before the Sip of the King cured her. I can only imagine how much she must have suffered . . . and how countless others are suffering now.

But already the racking coughs are replaced by moans and groans. Of pain? Of despair?

"Don't pay attention to those cries," Sister Purpurine says as if by rote. "We're heading down the right wing, where the insane are kept. Most of them are harmless. But this evening will be a full moon, and it agitates the lunatics. We'll have to bleed them to calm them."

We finally reach the director's office. It's in the heart of the hospice, behind an iron door as thick as the one to the room where the crown jewels of Versailles are kept. That one also has multiple locks. This room is austere, with no windows, the walls lined with cracked leather-bound volumes. The sole piece of furniture is a large dark wooden desk. Documents are spread out on top of it, lit by a massive bronze candelabra. The Reverend Mother rises from her chair, unbending her long body. She's as lean as she is tall, enveloped in an all-black robe. A pendant shaped like a bat glistens over it.

A pair of spectacles sits perched at the tip of her pointy nose, reflecting the light from the candelabra.

"Mother Incarnadine, reverend in charge of the Incurables," she says, introducing herself after Sister Purpurine leaves and shuts the heavy door with a dull clicking sound.

"Mademoiselle de Plumigny, heiress to the Plumigny estate," Hélénaïs says proudly. "I'm accompanied by Monsieur de Jaipur, Knight of India . . ." She shoots me a side glance, reluctantly adding, ". . . and Gastefriche."

The reverend stares at Hélénaïs from above her iron-framed specs. Her pale-blue eyes are so cold and so hard that I think I see frosty splinters shoot out of them.

"To what do we owe the honor of a visit from the king's squires?" she asks, her courteous voice in stark contrast with her expression.

"Take us to the survivors of the Mont Parnasse attack, if you please."

"I fear that's impossible, mademoiselle."

"What do you mean, *impossible*?" Hélénaïs asks. "You said it yourself, we are the king's squires. And we know that twenty-two of the wounded were brought here. We demand to speak to them immediately."

"You can talk to them all you like, they won't respond."

"Is that so? Did they take the veil and vows of silence?"

"The only veil they took is a shroud," the reverend answers. "They're dead."

Hélénaïs is rendered speechless.

"Dead?" I repeat. "You mean all twenty-two who arrived here barely three days ago?"

The reverend turns to me, her expression inscrutable.

"In the majority of cases, ghoul venom takes less than a day to kill its victims," she says. "Just one claw scratch infects a healthy person. Why do you think that among the dozens of hospices run by the Faculty of Paris, the police brought the wounded here?"

"Because they were . . . incurable," I whisper.

The reverend nods gravely, moving the folds of her black veil.

"Here, we welcome desperate cases, the sick who have no hope of recovery—lepers, syphilitics, final-stage tuberculosis patients, delirious lunatics . . . and victims of the ghouls. That's how those repugnant creatures hunt in their natural environment—they lie in ambush in dark nooks when night falls, slash their prey as the latter wander too close, then patiently track it until the toxin has spread its poison. They're vicious creatures who prefer to avoid confrontation."

"Except for recent attacks, would you agree?" Suraj pipes up. "When I went to confront the ghouls in the cemeteries of Paris on orders of the king last spring, I had to flush them out and provoke fights. But they've changed tactics recently, attacking the population head-on. From scavenging opportunists, they've become ferocious predators who serve under the command of the Lady of Miracles."

The name falls like a ton of bricks in the silence of the office, its walls covered with austere shelves.

"May the Shadows get rid of this abomination of abominations!" the reverend says.

Joining her index finger to her middle one, she traces the triple sign of the Blood over her body, just like Dr. Boniface did at church before the Sunday sermon in Buttes-aux-Rats. First she touches her mortal beating heart, then her left jugular, followed by her right one, the exact spot where the lords of the night like to plant their fangs.

"That's the reason you're here, isn't it?" she goes on. "To eradicate this . . . this scourge that the police have been unable to deal with for months?"

Suraj nods. "Precisely. And we'd be grateful if you didn't mention our visit to the police. We prefer to carry out the investigation our way."

"Of course. But as I said, you came here for nothing. The ones you wanted to question are not of this world anymore."

The reverend opens her arms to accompany us to the exit.

"Leave me now. I have work to do, a hospice to run, and quotas of blood to collect for the Faculty. The Incurables has always been a top-rated establishment in that regard."

But I'm determined to stay on the premises until I've gathered as much information as possible.

"Wait, Mother Incarnadine," I quickly say. "The souls of the Mont Parnasse victims may have left this world, but what's become of their bodies?"

"Their bodies? They're resting in the hospice's morgue. I don't see what you could get out of seeing them."

"Maybe nothing. Or maybe a kernel of truth."

"My name is Vermillonne. I'm the Sister of Final Care," an elderly nun says, greeting us at the entrance to the morgue.

We had to go all the way down to the basement of the hospice, into caves where the temperature is consistently low so as to preserve the corpses. Purpurin is an orangey red, incarnadine a pinkish red, and now vermilion, the brightest of all. The nuns we crossed paths with all bear names that describe a shade of human blood. That's the custom for those who enter the order of the Hematic Faculty.

"So you've come to see the ones who died at Mont Parnasse?" Sister Vermillonne says. "Follow me."

She walks off, a slight limp in her gait, shedding light with her lantern. The halo illuminates gaping vaults on the wall to the right, an alignment of cold rooms. A pungent odor of aromatic herbs fills the air; it helps to slow down the decomposition of corpses and prevents possible contamination. Rosemary, everlasting flower, medicinal mint . . . as these familiar scents invade my nostrils, I'm flooded with memories. Images of Papa's apothecary rush by, catching me completely by surprise. It takes my breath away. The wooden counter where I helped Maman grind herbs in the mortar . . . the little table next to it, where Bastien painstakingly painted the names of the healing potions onto clay jars . . . the reprimands of my other, older brother, Valère, when he caught us playing with the paints instead of working . . . so many quarrels, reconciliations, and bursts of laughter echoed in that narrow shop, now forever silent.

"This is a transit point for the deceased before their final resting place," our guide explains, snapping me back to the present.

"You mean before being buried?" Hélénaïs asks, clearly not reassured.

The Sister of Final Care stops and raises the lantern near her head. Her face is furrowed with wrinkles.

"The poor don't receive individual burials," she says. "Their bodies are thrown into mass graves. It's kind of a tacit ancestral pact with the ghouls. The hospices of Paris provide them with enough remains to gnaw on to keep them quiet. At least, it was that way for centuries, until the Lady of Miracles came on the scene." The nun starts walking again. "Only the aristocratic mortals and the rich bourgeois can afford an armored vault in the cemeteries of Paris. A vault that can't be desecrated by ghouls. As for crypts in places of worship, those are reserved for members of the Hematic Faculty."

Sister Vermillonne lifts her lantern again, revealing multiple niches in the wall that faces the cold rooms. Each one holds a coffin.

"Here are the graves of nuns who for centuries have cared for the incurables." She stops in front of the last occupied niche, which is followed by a series of empty cells. "Some, like Sister Amarante, ended up just like their patients."

"What do you mean?" I ask.

"Sister Amarante was an exemplary nun, sparing no effort with her studies or her work."

I detect a tremor of emotion in the Sister of Final Care's gruff voice.

"She had no equal when it came to helping the Reverend Mother organize her library. She also spent a good deal of time with the lunatics of the asylum. Out of solidarity with the crazies who are confined there, she never left the hospice." Sister Vermillonne heaves a disenchanted sigh. "That dear soul must have been too fragile for the harshness of the world. The one time she did leave these walls, she paid with her life. Two and a half years ago, in July, she accompanied the cart that was going to toss the remains of the dead into the mass grave at the Place du

Trône. She must have lingered a little too long, because one of the first ghouls to emerge at dusk clawed her. She was rushed back here, to the Incurables. But in vain. She was infected. She died less than twenty-four hours after being wounded."

Sister Vermillonne gently places her hand on the coffin, as if she wants to communicate with the nun who once walked these premises.

"Enough talk," she says as she gets going again. "We've come now to the room where the dead of Mont Parnasse lie."

She makes her way under a vault and ignites the oil lamp on the ceiling.

A dim light spreads over stone beds where twenty or so bodies have been laid out. The scent of aromatic herbs is even stronger here.

The nuns took care to arrange the torn clothing of the dead and to place the bodies in serene postures, arms folded over chests. It's a last show of respect before the great plunge into the mass grave. I feel my heart drop, torn between resentment for these nuns who participate in the bloodsuckers' reign and admiration for the care they dispense to society's outcasts. At the end of the day, they're human beings, full of paradoxes like everyone else . . . most of the ones who took their vows are probably trying to do good, however small the extent, like beloved Sister Amarante. They allow a bit of humanity to shine through in a world obscured by vampyres, a world filled with evil and the Shadows.

"Look at their skin," I whisper as I step closer to the corpses. "It's ashen, as if necrosis set in. And it's cracked like bark."

"Ghoul venom is one of the most virulent," Sister Vermillonne says. "Gangrene quickly spreads to the entire body of those who succumb. We can only alleviate their suffering with a lot of white willow."

Yet again memories of the past overwhelm me. My herbalist mother also used white willow to treat the patients who came to the apothecary . . . and to help with my headaches.

I feel black bile rush to my brain, bringing on melancholy and a migraine.

Suddenly, the air in the basement feels too thin, the scent of the aromatic herbs too powerful.

"I . . . I don't feel well," I say quickly. "Let's go back up."

Hélénaïs seizes my moment of weakness to taunt me.

"Well, little hick, what's wrong? Are you missing the country air? You're so pale."

"There's nothing to learn here," I say, gripping a wall. "We came to the Incurables in the hope of gathering clues, but it looks like it's a bust. There are no Mont Parnasse survivors and so no one to bear witness to the Lady of Miracles' presence."

Suraj nods. Sister Vermillonne snuffs out the ceiling lamp and takes hold of the lantern again to guide us toward the exit.

"True and false," she says as she sets off.

"Pardon?" I pant.

"True, all the wounded from Mont Parnasse died. False, their testimony didn't vanish with them."

Suraj, Hélénaïs, and I exchange a quizzical glance in the dim hallway where the remains of generations of nuns who died at the Incurables are resting.

"Young people, do you think Final Care is limited to handing out white willow herbal tea to the dying?" Sister Vermillonne says, her worn shoes striking the damp paving stones. "It's just as important to offer words of comfort and a kind ear."

In the glow of the lantern, the nun smiles with sadness, deepening the grooves of her many wrinkles. In that instant, she has never looked more exhausted and worn out—or more beautiful. Her compassionate smile, humble in the face of death, is the same as my father's when he tended to the dying in their final hours.

"In the days when kings and queens still passed away, history books noted their last edifying words, dictated for posterity," the nun says. "But the final words of the humble aren't written down anywhere, and to my eyes, these are far more precious. They speak about the nitty-gritty of life itself, words of love for those left behind, and regrets for not having spent more time close to them."

I'm deeply moved by the old nun's compassion. She lives in her crypt like Orfeo lives in his cave, two solitary, taciturn individuals. And yet both are overflowing with humanity, a lot more so than people who walk about in broad daylight. The Sister of Final Care gathers the words of the dying; the recluse at the Grande Écurie listens to the songs of the dead. The beauty of their calling brings a lump to my throat and makes my eyes water.

With the back of my sleeve, I pretend to wipe away the basement dust from my eyes, but I'm wiping away tears. I don't want my teammates to see me crying.

"And so I gathered the testimony of the poor souls of Mont Parnasse," the nun says as she starts up the staircase that leads aboveground. "I also heard the accounts from the victims of La Madeleine last week, from Sang-Lazare last month, and so on since the Lady of Miracles began her attacks. Oh, it was often just endless babble, without heads or tails, because ghoul venom targets the brain in the same way it does the other organs. Still, in all their delirium, certain things kept coming back with troubling regularity. These individuals came from totally different neighborhoods of Paris and had never met in their lives, yet, strangely, they muttered very similar things on their deathbeds."

"What things?" Hélénaïs demands as she grabs the nun by her sleeve. "Tell us."

The old woman freezes on the stairs. She gives a witheringly cold look, and the squire lets go of her robe.

"They spoke about a terrifying and pale celestial body that came up from the depths of the earth," she says softly. "They described a gigantic moon rising from the abyss right after the ghouls."

"The occult moon from the depths . . . ," I whisper, remembering what Exili said in front of the mortuary chamber. "It's the goddess Hecate, mother of monsters, nightmares, and sorcery. The alchemical symbol of the ghouls."

The nun nods gravely.

"Indeed, my child. Elders observed that the ghouls' migrations were dictated by the nocturnal orb. They noticed that every night the ghouls rose from the abyss like tides, according to the phases of the moon. And they'd dive back come sunrise. Nights of a full moon coincided with the largest upswells. That's how the popular dictum *'Full is the moon, out come the ghouls'* came about." Sister Vermillonne lowers her voice. "In the past, the distant moon in the sky influenced the ghouls' movements; it was like clockwork, and therefore easy to predict their arrival. There were even almanacs devoted to this. Now, an underground moon seems to control them in a way that we don't understand. The Lady of Miracles may be a virtuoso alchemist . . . or maybe she's Hecate herself. I'm afraid the tidal wave she's threatening Paris with on the Night of Shadows will wipe out everything in its path."

In silence, we climb the last steps of the stairs, ruminating over the image of an apocalyptic Paris submerged under a deluge of abominations.

Once we surface from the basement, the light of the winter day seems fainter than when we went below earlier. Behind the grayish sky, the sun is nothing more than a waning dot. Like the small flame of a candle going out.

Sister Vermillonne turns her furrowed face toward us.

"The fourth estate has been subjected to the blood tithe for three centuries, a price it has paid with great difficulty. But the new mortal tax imposed by the nocturnal abominations is unbearable. The mistress of the ghouls won't stop until she's crowned vice-queen. A title that the Immutable will never bestow upon her. The people of Paris are not strong enough to endure both the King of Shadows *and* the Lady of Miracles at the same time. One of them has to disappear."

Quick as lightning, Suraj swings open his cape and pulls out his double-bladed dagger.

"Don't blaspheme, Sister!" he berates her. "Don't forget you're speaking to the squires of Louis the Immutable, representative of the

Shadows on earth, absolute monarch, anointed by the Hematic Faculty on which you depend."

As with Hélénaïs earlier, the nun looks at Suraj with tired eyes—eyes that have seen a lot of misery over the years, as well as, I think, a lot of human goodness.

"I'm not forgetting, and I remain the most humble of the Immutable's servants," she says softly. "But if the people die and disappear, on whom will the vampyres feed? The way things are going, the king will end up ruling over a dead city—even if the Faculty anointed him."

Suraj puts his dagger away. "The Lady of Miracles' reign is coming to an end," he assures her. "Before the dawn of December twenty-first, I promise you."

He raises his face skyward, looking serious and resolute. Yesterday with Montfaucon, Suraj declared that he was guided by a sense of duty, and that's exactly what he resembles at this instant: a bronze statue of duty incarnate.

"In her leaflets, the renegade threatens the king with an eclipse, but such a phenomenon is short lived," he says. "The sun always ends up shining bright again, sending the moon that briefly hid it back into the void."

With an abrupt gesture, he pulls the large hood of his cape down over his head and leads us toward the exit of the hospice.

8

INNOCENTS

The Yellow Cat Inn isn't much to look at.

It's a crumbling house wedged at the back of a dark impasse.

To get there, Suraj made us navigate a labyrinth of alleys crammed with taverns and gambling dens, seedy places where students from the Sorbonne congregate after classes. The Sang-Michel neighborhood resembles a human anthill where drunken young people, beggars in rags, and prostitutes abound. There's nothing like being in a crowd to go unnoticed. When we paid the innkeeper for our overnight stay, we didn't even have to say who we were. No one asks traveling guests questions in places of ill repute.

We requested the entire uppermost floor, where a narrow landing opens onto three dormered rooms at the top of a rickety staircase. There, away from prying eyes, we finally removed our hoods. Suraj asked that a servant leave us a light meal in front of his room. All three of us are gathered there now, having a bite to eat on a small wobbly table.

"What is this broth made of?" Hélénaïs asks, complaining. "The smell alone turns my stomach."

She lifts her spoon from the greasy broth, stretching strands of brown cheese that smell particularly strong. From the bottom of her bowl, she fishes out a viscous glob.

"Pee-*ew*, it looks like a ghoul's eyeball," she says, letting the glob fall back into her bowl.

"It's an onion caramelized in butter," Suraj corrects her. "Onion soup is a typical Parisian dish made to invigorate the warehouse workers at Les Halles. It sticks to the ribs for hours and lets you brave the cold."

Unconvinced, Hélénaïs grabs a slice of bread with her fingertips.

"This stale bread is hard as a rock," she whines. "I can't eat it."

"Aren't you the one who suggested giving Parisians bread with gravel?" I snap at her, tired of her recriminations. "Just dunk it in your broth to soften it."

She frowns. "Dunk it in the soup? Pfft, those are the manners of a commoner."

"Well, that's good, since that's what we're pretending to be."

"A role that suits you to a T, you're so true to life," she shoots back.

Again, Suraj raises his eyes from his bowl, which he's half emptied. The weak flames flickering in the fireplace with the cracked lintel cast a dubious light on his face.

"Diane's right, you have to eat," he says. "We need energy before we head out to the Innocents."

That's his plan. Since we don't know where the Lady of Miracles will strike next, he proposed that we go to the spot where he hunted ghouls last spring. The Cemetery of the Innocents is the largest in Paris. It's also the one where the nocturnal abominations appear the most frequently to feed.

"Tonight there'll be a full moon," the squire adds.

"How could I forget?" Hélénaïs whines. "I can still hear those lunatics shouting at the hospice."

"It's also an auspicious night for the ghouls to appear."

"If we capture one, will we be able to make it talk?" I ask as I crumble my hunk of bread over my soup.

"Unfortunately, no. Ghouls aren't gifted with speech or intelligence. But maybe we'll be able to glean an additional clue from one of them so that we can pinpoint the Court of Miracles."

I think about what Suraj said, my gaze wandering to the dirty dormer window of the small room as I try to visualize the creatures that are terrorizing Paris.

But I can't.

"Suraj, what do the ghouls look like?"

"They're odious hybrids. Some move around on all fours, others walk on two legs, like we do. Their repulsive faces hover between animal and human. And their horrible eyes are even better than a vampyre's at seeing in total darkness. Ghouls are all different, but each one is a gruesome human imitation, an insult to nature."

A gust of icy wind whistles its way through the frame of the dormer window. It's as if evoking the ghouls is enough to bring on the cold that accompanies all abominations.

I can't help but think of the jars displayed in Montfaucon's office.

"Like the grand equerry's collection of ghoul paws," I say. "They look like deformed human hands made monstrous by I don't know what kind of sorcery." The insignificance of our team suddenly hits me. "How can the Immutable imagine we'll defeat the Lady of Miracles? We're just three young people, barely adults, against an army of abominations."

Suraj gives me a dark stare.

He's never looked at me in such an intense, almost painful way.

"The blood!" he says. "*That's* our asset. The Sip of the King that runs in our veins will make all the difference when we come face to face with the ghouls."

Suraj's words are in sync with Montfaucon's. The grand equerry seemed convinced that the king had chosen me to bring him the lady because he believed I was endowed with some sort of supernatural power or other.

I'd like to reply that I haven't felt any stronger since I imbibed a sip of royal blood, contrary to Hélénaïs, who is faster, and Suraj, who is stronger. But Hélénaïs speaks up first.

"Personally, I also have another advantage that the ghouls will appreciate," she says boastfully.

She places her shoulder bag on the table and takes out a large piece of metal with sharp cutting edges—a hand equipped with claws.

"Lucrèce's iron gauntlet!" I say.

Lucrèce du Crèvecœur was the king's fiercest squire before she died during the La Roncière plot. Only Suraj survived. Lucrèce was also Hélénaïs's role model while the latter was a mere student at the Grande Écurie.

"The Immutable gave me this gauntlet," she says, glowing with pride. "Believe it or not, it isn't made of ordinary iron, Diane, but of death-silver—to better stab the nocturnal abominations."

"Death-silver? Don't you mean quicksilver, like what's used to treat syphilitics?"

I bite my lips, afraid I've said too much. As the daughter of an apothecary, I know the medicinal uses of quicksilver, which also goes by the name mercury. But is the daughter of a baron supposed to know such things?

Fortunately, Hélénaïs doesn't notice. She's too happy to lecture me.

"Ah, which proves you don't know everything," she says with relish, only too glad to get payback for all the times I got the better of her during our art-of-conversation lessons at the Grande Écurie. "Death-silver is a very rare alchemical alloy made of steel and silver. It was created by the Faculty to forge the strongest, the sharpest . . . the *deadliest* weapons."

"But I—I thought silver was forbidden in all the Magna Vampyria," I stammer. "Vampyres are vulnerable to it, aren't they?"

"In fact, they are," Suraj confirms. "But so are the ghouls, same as all creatures of the Shadows. Only a few select mortals have the right to use silver and its alloys: archiaters, the Faculty's inquisitors . . . and us, the king's squires, in whom he has placed his implicit trust." Suraj fingers the curved double-bladed dagger hanging from his belt. "When I entered His Majesty's service, the two steel blades of my haladie were replaced with two death-silver blades. If only the trade secret of the alloy could be revealed to the warriors of the maharaja of Jaipur. It would help them combat the stryges of the Thar Desert . . ."

Suraj's black eyes mist over as he speaks. He doesn't usually talk about his past, and this is the first time he's said anything about his faraway country in my presence. All I know is that he came to Versailles in the hopes of forging an alliance with the King of Shadows in order to defend his small kingdom from the menacing stryges. Those creatures have the reputation of being the fiercest among the nocturnal abominations, defying all imagination. In truth, no one in the kingdom of France has ever seen one. For centuries, the Immutable's armies confined the stryges to the eastern borders of the Magna Vampyria, in a cursed region that bears no other name than Terra Abominanda: Abominable Land.

"Your sword is made of death-silver too," Suraj says, tearing me from my thoughts.

I glance at my belt, which I placed on the back of my chair when we sat down to eat. It has two sheaths attached to it. From one extends the sword with the mother-of-pearl handle that was given to me at the beginning of my service; from the other, a piece of sharpened wood. Montfaucon gave each of us a stake specifically for this mission.

"Our stakes are made of applewood," Suraj says. "It's the most effective natural essence for immobilizing immortals. The Faculty authorized its use strictly against unrecorded vampyres. It might come in handy against the Lady of Miracles' followers."

And against the lady herself, as Montfaucon asked me! I think as I place my finger on the sharpened tip of the stake.

My black onyx ring makes a dull sound as it comes into contact with the wood. In addition to the stake and the sword, here is a third weapon that my teammates don't possess: my secret weapon.

The squire is about to finish his bowl of onion soup, but Hélénaïs places her delicate hand on his muscular arm.

"By the way, Suraj, do you mind if I use Lucrèce's gauntlet in combat?" she asks, batting the long lashes of her golden-brown eyes.

"No, why?" he asks, startled.

"You and Lucrèce were very close. If the conspirators hadn't killed her, I'm certain the king would have married the two of you within the year."

A nearly imperceptible tremor perturbs Suraj's thick brows. It was public knowledge that Lucrèce had her heart set on him. Only Naoko and I know a secret that Hélénaïs and all Versailles are in the dark about: cruel Lucrèce's passion for the aloof warrior wasn't reciprocal. His heart was already spoken for. In fact, it still is, by someone whose name he can't reveal. Suraj de Jaipur's forbidden love is Rafael de Montesueño. Theirs is a scandalous passion in a court with rigid codes where all unions must be sanctified by the Immutable himself, starting with those of his squires.

"Lucrèce would have wanted her gauntlet to be used again," Suraj says, obviously in a hurry to change the subject.

"Are you really sure it doesn't bother you?" Hélénaïs insists.

"That hand belongs to you now."

"And if I'm correct, your own hand is free again," she responds, smiling with her perfectly aligned, pearly-white teeth. "You deserve to find a wife who's your equal. A warrior as brave as you are."

I . . . I can't believe it. Hélénaïs is hitting on him.

She's the kind of girl who's always gotten what she wants, and now it looks like her sights are set on our fellow knight. I'd noticed that he turned quite a few heads in the halls of the palace, what with his proud allure and entrancing aura. Not to mention that he comes with a vast fortune from the maharaja of Jaipur so that he can sumptuously represent his country at the court. That's probably all it took to awaken Hélénaïs's interest. Suraj must have caught her eye the same way the diamond necklace in the jeweler's window did this morning on the Pont au Change.

"I . . . uh . . . let's focus on the mission the king entrusted us with," he stammers.

He gives me a side glance, as if he fears I'll reveal the nature of his attractions to Hélénaïs.

I give him a reassuring nod. His secret is safe with me. I won't ever use it against him . . . unless it's my last recourse to snatch the Lady of Miracles from him when the time comes.

The sun has almost set when we depart from the inn, our faces hidden under our hoods.

We leave Sang-Michel and cross the Seine again, clearing a path among the crowd of commoners who are rushing home before the start of the curfew. We cut through the shadow of the Grand Châtelet where, at this hour, L'Esquille must be biting his nails over losing our trace. On the right bank, the merchant neighborhood of Les Halles is just as inextricable as the students' area on the left bank. The shop fronts of butchers and vegetable sellers are closing behind iron curtains that have somehow been patched up in the hopes of protecting them against the monsters who roam at night. My stomach tenses as the light dims and the temperature plunges below zero. I may be clothed in the finery of the king's noble squires under my breastplate, but I'm still a commoner who was taught to fear the twilight. My parents inculcated me with the Mortal Code—not out of respect for the lords of the night but to protect me from their cruelty. For vampyres have the right to feed at will on whoever goes out after the sun sets. *Ignitegium.* After listening to frightening stories and terrifying children's fairy tales, I've been imprinted with the law of the curfew since childhood.

Suddenly, at the bend of an almost deserted crossroad, we stumble upon a little boy clothed in rags, his cheeks blue from the cold, his shoes full of holes. He's a young street singer, his clear voice rising in the twilight.

"By light of the moon,
Firmly shut your doors.
When descends the gloom,
Vampyres will soar."

My heart bleeds to see that this child is still outside at this hour. Totally at the mercy of the bloodsuckers he's singing about.

"Poor homeless Pierrot,
His blood they will steal.
Leaving just marrow,
A grim ghoulish meal."

Slipping away from the other two squires, I rush over to the small boy. "Quickly, go home, little one!"

His big sickly eyes overwhelm his gaunt face, looking at me intently, full of distrust. I gather that under the large hood that hides my face, I'm probably not the most reassuring sight.

"Don't you have a home to go to?" I ask him in the softest voice possible.

"Yes, m'dame. But Papa told me not to come back until I earned at least a penny," he answers, wiping his runny nose with the back of his patched sleeve.

I see that the cap at his feet is empty. I dig into my shoulder bag to find a coin and place it in his freezing hand.

His eyes widen in disbelief.

"Hurry, go on home and warm up!" I say, as worried for him as if he was my little brother, Bastien.

He gathers the cap and scampers off like a rabbit, disappearing around the corner of the street.

"A gold crown?!" Hélénaïs says. "Are you crazy?"

"It's the first coin I got my hands on."

"Might as well take off your hood and tell him who you are. We're not going to stay incognito if you keep giving out money hand over fist to commoners."

Not knowing what to say, I follow my companions, and we make our way through the last streets that separate us from the Innocents.

The church bell starts ringing at the precise instant that we arrive in front of the cemetery. It's a large area surrounded by high archways. Curiously, the cemetery is elevated above street level by several yards.

"Is this another Parisian hill, like Montmartre and Mont Parnasse?" Hélénaïs inquires.

"In a way," Suraj answers. "The millions of dead buried here over the centuries have little by little bloated the cemetery with their remains, until the earth cracked open and disgorged the bones into the cellars of every neighboring house. This overflow led to the creation of the catacombs before they were themselves replaced by the communal graves of the outlying areas."

I shiver in horror at that description. For the first time, I realize the true nature of Paris, where a thin surface layer of the living covers up innumerable strata of the dead.

Suraj pushes the gate of the cemetery, which opens onto a steep embankment.

"Nowadays, only rich bougies are interred at the Innocents, into niches sealed with mortar," he explains, gesturing toward the archways that surround the area. "But the ground is still stuffed with the bones of hundreds of generations of Parisians. This manna continues to attract ghouls to this very day."

At the top of the embankment, a strong smell of humus nourished by centuries of decomposition fills my nostrils.

The cemetery itself resembles a vast wasteland crushed by silence, upon which the light of the full moon rains down. This sole source of light drapes everything in a ghostly aspect. A forest of headstones, most of them invaded by brambles and ferns, marks this surreal place. The stone crosses that had been atop the headstones were wrenched off three hundred years ago when the Hematic Faculty became the state religion.

Here and there, structures rise between the tombs—short, turreted, made of stone, and completely walled in. No doors, no windows.

"What are those?" I ask reluctantly. "Ossuaries?"

"No," Suraj answers. "Reclusories. Hermit cells, forever sealed."

His cold breath escapes from his mouth, adding to the impression of the surreal. In the twilight, his hooded outline looks like that of the grim reaper himself.

"It's a relic from the Middle Ages," he explains. "At that time, penitents asked to be sealed into these cells in order to expiate their sins and go to heaven. Today, there aren't any priests to bless these voluntary reclusions . . . and who knows if there's still a heaven?"

Suraj doesn't say any more. All the dogmas of ancient religions were banned by the Faculty. It's forbidden to invoke the possibility of an afterlife for mortals. According to the credo preached by the archiaters, only vampyres are privileged with an eternal existence after their transmutation.

"And now?" Hélénaïs wants to know, clicking the articulations of her gauntlet with impatience.

"Without the Lady of Miracles' magic to command them, ghouls don't appear in droves," Suraj answers. "If we're lucky, some will simply come to feed discreetly on the bones in solitary fashion, so we'll have to flush them out. Let's go separate ways. And whoever spots a ghoul first should shout out." He removes his double-bladed dagger from his belt. "Listen closely, for at night you hear the abominations before you see them."

As Suraj and Hélénaïs move off, I pull my sword from its sheath. It's a weapon I learned how to use recently, during the art-of-weaponry lessons taught by the Knight of Saint-Loup.

Back in my forests in the Auvergne, I was used to hunting with a sling . . . but I doubt that a simple stone would be enough to take down a ghoul.

My hands clenched around the mother-of-pearl handle, I advance slowly into the dim light. The moonbeams splash onto the headstones and the mostly eroded engravings worn away by the centuries. With each step, it seems the eternal silence of the dead is answered by a minute quiver of life. Behind gloomy archways as black as chasms, the city still shakes itself off: last locks being bolted; shutters clacking closed; and the occasional distant, muffled cry, signaling that an unfortunate vagabond has fallen prey to the fangs of an early-rising vampyre.

Closer to me, I also hear the whoosh of the breeze in the ferns, the soft patter of rodents in the thickets, the flapping wings of an owl.

Yet although I prick up my ears, I can't make out any sounds of claws digging at the ground or teeth crushing bones.

Will the ghouls come out tonight?

Or are they busy destroying a neighborhood at the other end of Paris under orders of their mistress, a massacre we'll learn about only tomorrow at dawn?

Suddenly, I hear a whistling sound coming from behind my shoulder, cutting short my thoughts.

I turn around swiftly, brandishing my sword, my heart racing so fast I think my chest is going to explode.

But there's nothing behind me, only the dense night, the unmoving graves, and the dark outline of a reclusory a few steps away from me.

"*Pssst!*"

The reclusory. It's as if the sound is coming from over there.

I'm about to shout out to warn my teammates and alert them that I've found a ghoul, but the humanlike whisper that escapes from the turreted cell stops me.

"*Pssst*, over here. Do you have alms for a wretch like me?"

Squinting, I notice a crack in the bricks, a narrow opening about fifteen inches high. The voice inside sounds like it's coming from beyond the grave.

"You who are here to visit the dead, come closer to my little window," a quivering voice invites me.

"The dead don't speak," I answer.

I hear a scraping noise in the night, the same hard sound as a flint lighter. It takes me an instant to realize it's snickering.

"Well, I'm half-dead. But the other half of my old carcass is still alive, and it's got to eat. So give me some alms, I tell you."

Slowly, I approach the cell. It looks like it's less than two yards wide. I'm astounded that a human being can survive within such a narrow space.

When Suraj told us that reclusories date back to the Middle Ages, I assumed they had been deserted a long time ago. Never would I have imagined that a penitent could still be shut inside.

"Who are you?" I whisper.

"The alms!" demands the voice in a dreadful croaking. "If you've come to the Innocents so late in the day, after the curfew, you can't be a commoner. Which means you're a noble lady with deep pockets."

I dig into my shoulder bag and take out a coin. A copper coin this time.

But just as I'm about to toss it into the small opening, the voice stops me.

"Do you really think I can chew on metal? Do you want me to break the last of my old, rotting teeth? Give me something to eat instead."

Again, I plunge a hand into my bag, and this time I take out one of the two hunks of bread I saved for the trip.

"I warn you, this bread isn't the fresh—" I start to say.

But before I can finish my sentence, a hand lunges from the small window and snatches the chunk of bread. I have barely enough time to notice the bony fingers and their incredibly long nails before they disappear into the slit, like an eel darting behind a rock.

I hear a chewing noise coming from within the cell, punctuated by muffled cursing.

"*Owww* . . . my poor teeth! . . . this bread is as hard as a gargoyle's rump."

I wait until the litany of oaths has died down to repeat my question.

"Who are you? What's your name?"

"My name? I left it behind, along with all my possessions, ages ago. Was it Jean or Jacques? Maybe Jules? I don't know . . . the Eye of the Innocents is what they call me now, for I never get any shut-eye. I watch everything from behind my small window. *Everything*, do you hear me?"

"But . . . but how long have you been locked in there?"

"Don't remember that either."

In vain, I try to see through the dark of the slit. If the recluse can see me, bathed as I am in the moonlight, I can't make him out at all.

"Enough questions about *me*," he says, annoyed. "Usually those who come here ask questions about *themselves*."

"What do you mean?"

"The Eye of the Innocents doesn't simply watch over the cemetery paths. He also sees the paths of the future."

A part of me would like to put an end to this nonsensical conversation. The recluse has clearly lost his mind as well as his memory over the course of his confinement.

I search for Suraj and Hélénaïs in the rustling darkness, but no one is there. It's as if the night has closed in on me and this strange creature.

Despite a vague apprehension, something is making me stay.

"If, as you say, you really see everything that happens here, then you must have witnessed the ghouls in action, correct?"

"The Shadows protect me from their nasty claws. I'm safe tucked in my cell."

"Perhaps you have information about the Lady of Miracles?"

The Eye of the Innocents suddenly goes silent, walling up in muteness as impenetrable as his prison.

"Speak," I whisper as I come closer to the slit. "Speak without fear." I take out the second hunk of bread from my shoulder bag and wave it in front of the opening. "If you tell me what you know, you'll get this . . . *ohhhhh!*"

Quick as lightning, the hand lunges again from its lair, not to grab the food but to seize my wrist.

I've been sucked in by a force I would never have expected from the frail cell dweller. My arm is lodged in the slit all the way up to my elbow.

"Let go of me!" I shout, scared out of my wits. "I order you to release me!"

But the recluse holds on tight.

"Your hand . . . ," he croaks. "It bears the lines of a great destiny."

"Wha—what?" I sputter.

I can feel the recluse's sharp fingernail graze my palm, tracing a groove . . . or rather, following the ones etched there at birth.

"Your lifeline is remarkable . . . ," he mumbles. "So is your death line."

"My death line? What are you talking about? You're the half-dead one who's going to get a final taste of mortality if you don't let go of me."

With my free hand, I draw my sword and thrust the tip into the cell. I want to scare the recluse, not spear him.

It seems to be working. He lets go of my wrist . . . but only so that he can grab my blade. At least that's what it feels like as my arm is given a violent pull.

Taken by surprise, I release the handle. The entire sword disappears into the cell like a dragonfly swallowed whole by a frog.

"Give me back your hand!" the recluse barks. "Let me read your future. Let me show you what you don't want to see and tell you what you don't want to hear."

I'm overwhelmed by a sense of panic that's welling up from deep within me. I was wrong to listen to that nutcase, and now my gut tells me to flee before his evil words poison my mind.

"Death, darkness, and desolation!" he shouts in a dreadful hoarse voice that sounds like raspy croaking.

I take off running. I want to get as far away as possible from his horrible predictions.

"Ruin!"

I weave in and out of the chipped tombstones.

"Bereavement!"

I jump over gnarled tree roots.

". . . and tor . . . ment!"

The curses trail off into the night, disappearing behind my own panting.

I lean back onto a funereal column to catch my breath, exhaling small clouds of fog as I massage my sore wrist. Where are the other two squires? It's pitch black around me. A cloud has just passed over the moon, plunging the cemetery into complete darkness.

"Suraj . . . ?" I whisper. "Hélénaïs . . . ?"

I grope my way forward, leaning on the icy tombstones.

Am I heading toward the exit?

I've barely asked myself the question when I'm gripped by a dizzying sense of having already seen, thought, and imagined this.

The squishy sounds of the spongy ground under my feet are the ones from my nightmare last night.

The cold, slimy stones under my fingers are like the ones I felt in my dream.

And just like in my dream, the clouds obstructing the sky suddenly tear apart to allow a white light to rain down.

The pale moonbeams rest on the nearest headstone, which has been ripped open. A debris of bones spews out of it. A creature is kneeling in the middle of the remains, hunched over itself.

A ghoul.

In a flash, I take in its emaciated limbs, its protruding ribs, and its stooped, spiky-pointed spine. Its claws, which are dug into the rotting earth, seem incredibly long, as if they've grown ten times faster than the rest of its skinny body. But more than anything, it's the ghoul's eyes that mesmerize me: two enormous milk-white globes without pupils—just like Suraj said, day-blind eyes that are capable of seeing in the most obscure darkness.

Instinctively, I bring my hand to my belt, searching for my sword. I forgot that it's not there.

At the same time, the ghoul springs back on its thighs, activating a horrible mass of muscles and tendons under its naked, disgustingly shiny skin.

I lost my weapon to the recluse, and the creature is already on me, leaving me no time to unsheathe my wooden stake.

Its noxious breath reeks of the stench from its grisly meal, burning my nostrils. I just have time to cross my arms over my chest to form a shield. If, like Suraj said, the Immutable's blood endowed me with any supernatural abilities, now would be the moment for them to manifest themselves.

But nothing happens. My poor mortal muscles start to shake.

I know that it's too late for me to even unscrew the onyx from my ring and liberate the *essence de jour*.

The ghoul's jaws snap just inches from my forehead, two rows of crooked fangs that spread across a "face" that is neither human nor animal but a hideous hybrid of the two.

"Help . . . help," I gasp, trying not to breathe so that I don't inhale a poisoned whiff.

A cold aura emanates from the abomination, a telltale sign of the Shadows.

But there's something even more chilling—the recollection of having seen the ultimate image of this confrontation in my dream. My body, throat slit, lying out among the stones.

Overcome with horror and disgust, I start to feel faint in the face of the inevitable.

My arms weaken.

The ghoul's claws converge on my pulsing carotid.

It's over.

My horrifying premonition is about to unfold.

An unspeakable pain pierces my throat.

A silver bolt of lightning cuts through the night.

Everything goes dark.

9

ARCANA

I open my eyes onto the dark night.

I'm stretched out, seemingly paralyzed.

As my nerve endings regain feeling, I sense the pebbly cemetery ground digging into my spine . . .

. . . as well as the pain from the scratch that chills my neck.

"She's awake now," a voice says.

Slowly, I turn my head. Hélénaïs is bent over me, her long, coiled chestnut hair falling on my face.

"The . . . the ghoul," I whisper, each word scraping my dry throat. "Beware of the ghoul."

"That ghoul won't be bothering anyone else," someone else replies.

A second face enters my field of vision. Suraj's.

"Hélénaïs killed the creature before it could finish you off," he says.

Little by little, I start to remember the moonbeams on the abomination, the monster's deadly grasp, its claws piercing the base of my neck, the lightning that tore through the night.

But it wasn't a bolt of lightning after all. It was Hélénaïs's death-silver gauntlet.

"You've been sleeping for two days," Suraj says.

Two days?

Slowly, I realize that the moonless, starless night above me isn't the sky. It's a ceiling covered in soot from the thousands of candles that have burned here over the years. As for the irregular surface under my back, it's not the cemetery ground but a bad mattress with tired springs. The Innocents has been replaced by a small dark room, all curtains drawn.

"We carried you to the Yellow Cat," Suraj explains. "In the first twenty-four hours, your fever was so high we were sure we'd lose you. But it fell this morning." He takes a fresh compress from a basin at my bedside and lays it across my forehead with a gentleness unexpected from such a fierce warrior. "Remember what Sister Vermillonne told us. The great majority of victims clawed by ghouls die in less than a day. You, I believe, will survive."

I turn my cheek against my sweat-drenched pillow to face Hélénaïs. "Thank you," I whisper, uttering words I never thought I'd say to her.

She shrugs. "You should thank the Immutable's blood. Thanks to him, you're still alive."

"Hélénaïs was right when she said the Sip of the King developed her superhuman reflexes," Suraj acknowledges. "It seems it gave you enhanced resistance . . . same as for me."

He pulls up the sleeves of his shirt. His forearms are furrowed with hairline scars, remnants of battles waged against the abominations, wounds that the royal blood magically healed.

"This is why the king sent me to battle the ghouls last spring," he explains. "His blood boosts the vitality of all his squires, but it gave me a particularly amazing regenerative ability. Such is my dark gift. Perhaps it's yours as well, even if I've never been laid low more than an hour after being clawed by a ghoul, and my wounds have never taken long to close up."

I raise a trembling hand to my neck, to the spot where the pain continues to throb. My fingers connect with a thick bandage.

Hélénaïs gives a sarcastic laugh as she plays with her platinum bracelet.

"Under your tough airs, could it be you're nothing more than a *little* lightweight, *little* mouse?" she says. "It's about time the king realized you're not so extraordinary and that you don't deserve pride of place in his heart. In the meantime, you'll be kind enough to let him know that I saved the life of his *little chérie*."

I nod, having no illusions. It may be that Hélénaïs came to my rescue only so she could assure her promotion at the court. That would be just like her.

"I'm not the little lightweight that you think," I tell her. "I'm better now. Let's go off in search of the Lady of Miracles again."

I attempt to sit up, but I wobble and fall back with a thud onto the mattress, making it squeak.

"You're far from fully recovered," Suraj says gravely. "You must stay in bed. We had a broth brought up; it's here on the bedside table. Now rest, and whatever you do, don't draw attention to yourself. The inn-keeper doesn't know about your accident, so in his eyes you're still just a customer who's passing through."

"What about you?" I whine, furious that my body is failing me when I need it to be fit.

"There was a new attack by the Lady of Miracles last night, on the Boulevard de Clichy, in northern Paris. Hélénaïs and I are headed there to investigate. So rest up. Drink the broth while it's still hot. We'll be back before nightfall."

The two squires get up and leave the room.

The lock turns twice in the door.

The footsteps grow fainter in the hallway.

I'm alone and shut in.

Confined as I am to my room, the hours go by painfully slow.

My weakened body marinates in the sheets. But even though I'm pinned to the bed, nothing keeps my mind from racing, prey to a whirl-wind of agonizing questions.

What if Hélénaïs and Suraj find the Lady of Miracles before I do?

What if they deliver her to the King of Shadows?

What if he appropriates her army?

I find myself copying Montfaucon's nervous habit, he who always fiddles with his many rings whenever something preoccupies his thoughts. I do the same with my onyx ring, turning it round and round my middle finger, as the grand equerry's warnings reverberate in my head: *"You must find the Lady of Miracles before the royal armies do, Jeanne. You must destroy her before she reveals to the Immutable by what diabolic means she controls the ghouls. The future of the Fronde is at stake."*

The features of the creature who attacked me at the Innocents come back to me. The enormous whitish eyes and sharp teeth are etched in my memory, but everything else happened so fast that I only have a vague recollection. I think the ghoul resembled a hairless hyena, hideously naked.

Flabby jowls instead of lips. Translucent, pointy ears that framed a bald head. But the nose looked human—or, more precisely, it was truncated like a skeleton's.

I shiver under the sheets as the horrible memory mingles with my lingering fever. Two days ago, I came face to face with a wandering ghoul and nearly died; last night a horde of them swarmed onto another neighborhood in Paris. What can the poor people possibly do against hundreds of those creatures when it took only one to get the better of me?

I feel so weak, so alone. The loss of my family weighs heavier than ever. I would give anything to see my dear Bastien again, the brother I spent so much time dreaming about foreign lands with during our childhood in Butte-aux-Rats. He would call me his weasel and tousle my gray hair. My father would know how to make me better and get me back on my feet in no time. My eldest brother, serious Valère, would no doubt scold me for being imprudent, and I'd poke fun at him until he smiled. As for my mother . . . I've never needed her wise counsel more than I do now. What would she do in my place?

I remember the strange vision that came to me in the king's mortuary chamber the night I killed Tristan and foiled the La Roncière conspiracy. There, in that room that exists outside of time, I thought I saw my mother more alive than ever. I thought I was home once again in Butte-aux-Rats, at the same time that I was elsewhere. I thought I was in a world where the light was brighter and lighter, as if cleansed of the Shadows. Of course, it was a dream, a mere mirage, for the Shadows are everywhere.

With a heavy heart, I stick my hand into the pocket of my blouse to take out my mother's watch. But there's nothing there. I remember that I gave it to Orfeo back at the Grande Écurie.

As I think about the living dead with the big heart, my own heart melts a little more. I can see his wan smile when I gave him the watch, making my eyes tear up. In turn, I'm reminded of Naoko. Before I knew her, I'd never had a true friend. The cocoon of my family was all I needed. Now I realize how much I missed out on friendship. And how much I miss Naoko. Someone I can confide in about my doubts, fears, and personal failures without holding back or pretending. Instead, I'm stuck in this unfamiliar city, crushed by fatigue in a hovel, tasked with a mission that seems beyond my abilities, and two companions I have to perpetually lie to.

Night has fallen when they finally return.

"So?" I ask.

"So, nothing," Hélénaïs answers. "Nothing but devastation and sobbing peasants. The ghouls obliterated everything on the Boulevard de Clichy, worse even than at Mont Parnasse." She takes out a printed gazette from her shoulder bag. "I got hold of the latest issue of *Le Mercure Galant* on the way back, something to take my mind off things."

She plops down in a chair and buries her head in the pages of the gazette. It's a publication that all the courtiers at Versailles vie to get their hands on because it reproduces etchings of the latest fashion styles and dishes on the juiciest gossip.

"I'm afraid that these killing sprees are just a foretaste of things to come on the Night of Shadows," Suraj says gloomily. "It's already December third. Only eighteen days till the big day."

"Eighteen days gives us plenty of time to find the Lady of Miracles," I shout.

My sudden outcry leaves me breathless.

"Calm down," Suraj orders me. "You haven't fully recovered. And it isn't certain that the king will wait eighteen days before he cuts off food supplies to Paris."

"Wha . . . what?" I gasp, struggling to get my breath back.

"A crow came to me from Versailles. The Immutable views the attack on the Boulevard de Clichy as yet another personal affront. Since the ghouls are stealing his wheat, he's threatening to halt provisions to the capital until the Lady of Miracles is caught."

I don't know what shocks me more, the sovereign's cruelty or the fact that he communicates directly with Suraj.

Yet nothing should surprise me, not coming from a Machiavellian tyrant who's been holding everyone in the palm of his hand these past three centuries. True to habit, he divides to better rule. On one hand, he orders Mélac to find the renegade using every resource at the disposal of the police; on the other, he entrusts the same mission to his squires. Among our team, he keeps in touch with only one, without bothering to let the two others know. To think that Hélénaïs called me a *little chérie*. Like her, I'm just a novice at the court, while Suraj has already served the king for nearly a year.

"If wheat supplies stop arriving before winter sets in, it'll be a total disaster," I say. "The children, the sick, and the elderly will be the first to die. The king . . . the king can't do such a thing."

"The king does what he pleases," Suraj says, his face clamping down like a trap. "Whatever he desires, we must comply. In the same mail, he announces his decision to hold a grand ball at the Louvre Palace on December twentieth."

Hélénaïs lifts her nose out of the pages of *Le Mercure Galant*, a wide smile accentuating her dimples.

"A ball?" she says. "What a marvelous idea! But that's right on the eve of the Night of Shadows, isn't it?"

"Correct, and the liturgical celebration of the Night of Shadows will take place in the royal chapel at the Palace of Versailles, as it does every year," Suraj reminds us. "But on the night preceding the winter solstice, the king will throw a grand party in Paris to show he doesn't fear the Lady of Miracles. Everyone at court is invited, including us."

Is this the same young man I saw comforting old Mère Mahaut?

Can his loyalty to the monarch so easily erase all his humanity?

"Doesn't it bother you to live it up while the people starve?" I toss out at him, gathering my strength to raise my voice. "And what about the flour that you promised the inhabitants of Mont Parnasse?"

"That flour belongs to the Immutable, as do the Parisians . . . as do we, Diane."

A harsh furrow wrinkles his smooth forehead under his ocher turban. His thick brows scrunch above his black eyes—from fatigue, from frustration. Suraj may have an answer for everything, but the truth is that he's just as helpless as I am.

The investigation is at a dead end. I can't count on the other two squires to find the Lady of Miracles. I have to take matters into my own hands, starting by shaking off this damned weakness that's keeping me pinned to the bed.

Time passes tediously as my body keeps fighting the ghoulish venom.

I've never slept so much in my life, even if my nights bring me little rest. Every morning I wake up a little before noon, completely exhausted, as if I've run an entire mile.

I spend the daylight hours trying to regain control over my body. But my sheets feel like lead when I lift them; three steps around the bed and I'm dead tired. I lie down again, short of breath, my limbs overcome with cramps.

In the evenings, Suraj and Hélénaïs return empty handed from their search. They head back out after a light meal and wander through the night, hoping to find the path that leads to the Court of Miracles. Suraj forbids me from joining them, claiming I'm still on the mend.

Each time, their steps lead them to the deserted streets of Paris after the curfew, and only after the fact do they learn about the latest neighborhood that the ghouls destroyed. The city is so spread out, so full of tunnels, that it's impossible to predict where the enemy will strike next.

"I feel much better now," I say on the morning of the eighth day since I was wounded. "Let me come with you today."

Suraj looks me over from head to toe. "You still look a little pale," he says.

"That's because I'm stuck inside this blasted room. I'm suffocating!"

"You don't have a sword to defend yourself with since you lost yours at the Innocents. We'll buy you one in the city today, and tomorrow we'll see if you're really better enough to use it." He turns toward Hélénaïs. "While we're at it, maybe you could also get Diane a dress for the grand ball at the Louvre?"

The squire pouts. "If someone had told me I'd be shopping for Diane de Gastefriche one day, I wouldn't have believed it," she says. She sizes me up for measurements, all wrinkled as I am in bedsheets that haven't been changed in days. Her eyes linger on my tangled hair, then on the rustic onyx ring on my finger. "Do you have a favorite color? Gray, I would think, and more likely drab? Wait, don't tell me, I'll see what I find. I can't guarantee it'll be the latest style from *Le Mercure Galant*."

Once again, the two squires abandon me and head out to spend the day in remote areas of Paris.

They're not aware that I didn't lose my precious death-silver sword during my fight with the ghoul, like I told them I did, but that it was snatched into the recluse's slit. I didn't breathe a word about the Eye of the Innocents. The incident seemed too absurd to mention. And probably too scary as well. *"Let me read your future!"* the madman had shouted, walled up alive in his stone tomb. *"Let me show you what you don't want to see and tell you what you don't want to hear!"*

At the time, his words filled me with disgust and dread. But now that I think about them with a clear mind, I wonder if they meant something. Can that man really see the future, like he pretended? All prospects seem bleak. I'm in profound need of direction. Right now, there's no sign that I don't want to see, no oracle that I don't want to hear.

At last, the time has come for me to leave this room and lead the investigation my way.

I have to go back to the Innocents.

I have to consult the seer.

Because he's my only recourse, however crazy he may be.

By day, the enclosure of the cemetery seems smaller than at night, when the darkness elongated distances and deformed perspectives.

The surrounding areas are a lot more populated, too, packed with curious strollers and street peddlers.

In my long and hooded cape, I have no problem blending into the crowd. Escaping from the inn earlier, however, was a lot harder. Since the lock to my room was bolted from the outside, I had to climb out the window facing the rear courtyard. I often took to the rooftops when I studied at the Grande Écurie, but today, still weak from the ghoulish venom, I don't have my past agility. I nearly broke my neck more than once as I made my way down the gutter.

"How about a charm to ward off the Lady of Miracles, my friend?" a peddler shouts as I walk by. "Only ten copper pennies to protect your home and your life."

The peddler addresses me with a semitoothless smile. With my cape and leather shoes, he takes me for a man.

"These are real moon pearls," he assures me, brandishing a necklace in front of my hood. "Nail it to your door, and the ghouls will spare your home."

The necklace of "moon pearls" is in fact just three misshapen rocks, probably gathered on the banks of the Seine, a coarse thread of hemp wound around them.

"Go on now, make up your mind, there won't be enough for everyone," the peddler insists.

I realize that all around me many inhabitants have come to buy similar amulets from the charlatans who congregate near the cemetery. In desperation, these men and women are ready to believe anything to protect their families. Already overwhelmed by the destruction wrought by the Lady of Miracles, they're unaware that the Immutable is about to cut off their food supply.

"I'll take my chances," I say, fleeing the peddler to climb the slope that leads to the cemetery.

Here again, in broad daylight, everything looks less mysterious than at night but also more desolate. The chaos of the tombstones is sad to see; they look like worn stumps planted every which way. The barren ground, so repeatedly upturned over many generations to bury cartloads of corpses, seems out of breath, incapable of producing even one blade of grass. It's now covered by a film of ice; winter truly arrived during my convalescence at the inn, enveloping the city in its frosted claws.

I cut through the gloomy landscape, the ice cracking under my feet, until I reach the last reclusory.

A long line of shivering people has formed in front of the window slit. Some are dressed only in rags, others in more bougie attire. My guess is that this is everyone who's come to consult the seer, looking for guidance in these uncertain times. There are so many people that my turn won't come before nightfall, when Suraj and Hélénaïs will be returning to the inn.

THE COURT OF MIRACLES

As I rack my brain for a way to cut the line, a quivering voice suddenly reverberates. It's the same voice that eight nights ago predicted my ruin.

"That's enough for today!" the Eye of the Innocents yells from his slit.

A concert of protests mounts from those waiting in line.

"Enough, I say," the seer adds. "I feel evil spirits rising at this very minute from the cemetery ground to gnaw on the soles of your shoes. Those of you who stay will end up with peeling feet and frozen guts, I tell you."

It doesn't take more for the crowd to disperse, everyone running toward the archways, toward the nearest exits. As for me, I don't believe in the seer's evil spirits any more than I do in the peddlers' moon pearls.

I hurry over to the window slit.

"It's me, the girl who came to the cemetery at night just eight days a—" I start to say.

"I know, little ignoramus," the recluse cuts me off. "I saw you arrive at the end of the line, and I recognized your cape. Why do you think I made up that story about peeling feet to scare off the simpletons?"

"Because you want to help me?" I venture, touched by his unexpected attention.

"Because your last visit plunged me into a state of complete anguish, you wretched girl! Because I lost sleep over it. Because I want to carry on with what I started to see in the lines of your hand."

I stuff said hand into my shoulder bag, hiding the palm where the seer claims he glimpsed the worst.

I take out a small bundle that I swiftly slip into the window slit.

"Those are fresh bread rolls that I bought on the way here. You won't break your teeth on them like last time."

My gift vanishes through the slit without a thank-you.

"Last time I was here, you told me that people come to you with questions," I say. "That's why I'm here today. If I show you my hand, do you promise not to grab it violently again . . . and to answer my questions?"

"Your hand won't suffice to answer my questions, nor yours, you belligerent girl," the seer snaps back shrilly. "What I glimpsed requires a very different tool than palm reading, coffee grounds, or any of the other methods of simple divination that I use for regular readings. We must consult the tarot cards."

"Tarot cards?"

By way of response, a small table springs out from the window slit, creating an improvised counter between me and the occupant of the cell.

Then the hands of the walled-up recluse wriggle through the slit. In broad daylight, they look even more wizened than I remembered. The flesh is so emaciated, the bones so visible, they resemble the hands of a skeleton. As for the long yellow nails, they can't have been trimmed in eons, to the point that those of his two thumbs stick up hideously.

I shiver as I recall the way the recluse introduced himself when we first met, pretending he was already half-dead.

The frail, bony fingers spread a deck of cards out onto the dry wood. These are large cards whose black backsides are engraved with entangled arabesques, totally different from the cards that my brothers and I killed time with playing *brelan* during the long winter evenings in Butte-aux-Rats.

I don't know if it's the sight of this old, yellowed deck, the last of my fever, or the icy wind, but I'm trembling so hard that I nearly hear my spine rattle.

"Arcana, blades, the cards of the Forbidden Tarot go by many names," the seer says. "But come closer to the slit, and hide the table in the shadow of your cape. No one else must see this deck."

I glance over my shoulder. The area is completely deserted.

"No one's here," I say.

"Scoot closer. In what language do I have to tell you that? Aramaic?" the seer says, all worked up. "I'm not going to eat you. You're far too tough for the few stubs I've got left!" Laughter escapes from the window slit. "If I ask you to come nearer, it's so you can hide my precious tarot, my most treasured friend. I took it with me without anyone knowing when I became a recluse a long time ago. In one lifetime, I still haven't deciphered the cards' complete meaning, for they hold more knowledge than all the books in the world combined."

I sense madness in the words of this man who's sacrificed his life to seal himself off with his obsession, this deck of cards that he calls "his treasured friend." I'm now plagued with doubt. Was I right to come here?

"I risk my life by taking out the Forbidden Tarot in daylight," he whispers. "It's strictly banned by the Hematic Faculty. But it's the only way to unscramble a future as complicated as yours."

I force myself to swallow my fear. I came all this way to the Innocents, and I'm not about to back away from the last inches that separate me from the reclusory. Besides, I still have the sharpened stake at my belt. If the seer attacks me like last time, I'll be ready.

I plaster myself against the cell and try to glimpse the speaker's features through the slit. But I can't see much. The daylight doesn't penetrate farther than the small table, casting light on the dark cards, their corners all dog eared from decades of use.

"Why is this tarot forbidden?"

"Because it allows one to reveal things that are hidden. Because it allows one to break through the Shadows and illuminate what's invisible."

"Like shed light on the Lady of Miracles?" I ask, hopeful.

The furious clacking of a tongue reverberates through the dark slit, behind which is the sealed-off recluse.

"Here you go again. You already questioned me about her last week."

"And you never answered me. But I need to know where she's hiding. My . . . my life depends on it."

In reality, it's the survival of the Fronde that depends on it, but I can't, of course, say so out loud.

Once more, the recluse makes his tongue clack.

"Hmmm . . . if your life is really tied to the Lady of Miracles, the arcana will tell us so," he says. "And if your paths are meant to cross, the cards will show that too."

As he says this, he places his shaking hands on the cards, spreading them in a large fanlike pattern.

"Let's start with a simple draw, the Small Path," the Eye of the Innocents says. "Choose four arcana."

"Choose them how?"

A whistling sigh escapes from the window slit.

"Trust your instincts, little goose. I can tell you're not lacking in that department, even if you've hit the brakes lately, like most people do. Let your intuition take over, same as you would in a dream."

The seer's words trouble me. I remember my recent nightmares— the one that preceded Paulin's intrusion into my bedchamber, followed by the one I had the night before the ghoul's attack at the Innocents. Each time, I saw myself dead. Like a warning sent by . . . my intuition?

I let my eyes wander across the strange patterns that decorate the backs of the cards' mesmerizing interlacings. Feeling overcome with dizziness, I quickly select four.

The skeletal hand snatches them and places three of them in front of me, backsides up in a row.

"Here is your past, present, and future." His hand puts the fourth card on top of the card for the present, right in the middle, as if to block it. "And here is the obstacle on your path."

Before I can even ask a question, the long bony fingers turn over the first card in the row, the one for the past. I see an etching of a girl in breeches and leather boots. She's leaning on a walking stick and staring into the distance, her lantern raised to light the way at dusk.

"Guide of the Stake," the Eye of the Innocents declares.

A stake? Actually, as I take a closer look, the tip of the stick is dangerously sharp. I'm starting to see why this tarot is banned by the Faculty.

"Energy and vitality," the seer interprets. "And maybe even a little temerity. I see you surrounded by woods, by deep, dense forests."

"I grew up in the forests of the Auvergne," I blabber. As I remember the baronette I'm supposed to be now, I instantly add, "In a manor on the edges of the forests."

Is this card really . . . me? I eye the pattern, which is both primitive and complex. The figure's momentum, the confident smile on her lips, right down to the breeches hugging her body—all of it reminds me of the carefree times of the past when I went poaching in the woods, in defiance of the sequester. Reckless? Yes, undoubtedly, and my mother berated me each time I came home with a partridge. But this risk-taking now seems so paltry compared to the dangers I've put myself in since leaving my beloved, vampyre-free countryside to come to the city, where they're everywhere.

Already the seer is turning over the second card—the present. An equestrian appears, long sword in hand, atop a black steed that reminds me of Typhon.

"The little demoiselle of childhood has grown into an adolescent horsewoman," the seer mumbles. "Equestrian of the Sword, to be precise. Spirited warrior, impulsive, uncompromising . . . maybe even obstinate?"

Once again, the words hit home. I'd never held a sword in my life before coming up to Versailles. Since then, I've lived solely for my obsessions. First, avenging the murder of my loved ones, by hook or by crook. And now, eliminating the Lady of Miracles, no matter what the cost.

Unable to wait anymore, I turn over the third card in the row, following the past and the present—the card of the future.

I gasp. The card shows a full moon with a vampyric face, similar to the one on the leaflet distributed in Paris after the fire at Montfaucon. Below the lugubrious orb are two howling creatures that resemble dogs . . . or ghouls.

"It's her!" I say so excitedly that I nearly topple the little table. "It's the Lady of Miracles, right here in my future."

"The Moon is a major arcana, one of the most difficult to interpret . . ."

"Tell me where I can find her. Make the tarot speak."

"You interpret things too literally, clouded as you are by your obsessions and certainties," the seer says. "The Moon, quite the contrary, reflects *un*certainty, confusion, and fluctuation. There's something amorphous within you, something still gestating. And this card invites you to question yourself."

"That doesn't help me. I didn't come here to be told I have self-doubts. I already know that."

"There is none so deaf as the one who will not hear, and none so blind as the one who will not see."

"Let me draw a new card, and maybe I'll see more clearly!"

The scrawny arm shoots through the slit and raises its index finger in front of my lips to silence me.

"Wait. Before you choose another arcana, there's one more to reveal. The obstacle—what's holding you back in the present and preventing you from reaching your future. For each one of us on earth wages a secret battle within our hearts."

He turns the card that covered the one in the center.

I shudder as I see what it represents: a skeleton armed with a scythe, harvesting a wasteland sowed with human remains.

"Death," I gasp, suddenly short of breath under the rim of my hood.

"It's also called the Arcana with No Name," the Eye of the Innocents corrects me. "Here again, interpretation is a delicate matter."

He grows suddenly quiet.

A moment ago he accused me of not wanting to hear, but now I have the feeling he no longer wants to speak.

Why?

"Stop squirming and tell me," I beg him, my stomach knotted in fear. "Does this card mean I'm going to die before I find the lady? Or am I not supposed to interpret this one literally either? Yet the first time I came to the cemetery, you predicted death, darkness, and desolation."

The pale hands start to shake, due to old age . . . or genuine fear? It's all the more chilling because I don't know the reason.

"In your palm, I read an endless death line, I won't deny it," the seer admits in a whisper. "And the Arcana with No Name comes up in a contrary position that worries me. I have . . . I have to think and make sense of it all. In any case, you're not receptive today, you're not listening to anything. Come back tomorrow."

Already the fingers move like long whitish spider legs to gather the scattered cards.

"No!" I cry out. "You can't leave me hanging!"

"Be quiet, you chatterbox, you'll wake up the entire neighbor—"

"I need to know where to find the Lady of Miracles—not tomorrow but tonight!"

I grab one of the last cards still spread out, before the seer gathers them all, and quickly turn it over.

It depicts a high tower struck by a destructive bolt of lightning.

"Give it back, you thief!" the old man yelps.

He tries to grab the arcana from my frozen hands.

The ancient card, which held up through I don't know how many centuries, tears in my fingers.

An inhuman wail comes from within the window slit, as if I'd just yanked off one of the occupant's limbs.

"Damn! Damn you!"

I stagger backward, my head ringing like a warning bell, my feet striking the icy pebbles of the cemetery. I came to the Innocents seeking answers, but I'm leaving with more fear and confusion than when I entered.

Now I'm three times damned. First by Blanche de La Roncière, next by the Forbidden Tarot, and last by the cards' owner.

10

TOWER

"Is there a tower in Paris?" I ask.

Suraj and Hélénaïs exchange a startled glance in my bedroom doorway.

Just before they returned and came to check on me, I made my way back to the inn unobtrusively, pretending I'd spent the entire day sitting by the fire. During the entire walk, I couldn't get the image of the fifth arcana out of my mind. The first four seemed so . . . so on target, strangely resonating with my life. Maybe there was a meaning to extract from the last card, literal or not.

"Paris has many towers," Suraj answers, closing the door behind him. "Sang-Jacques Tower, Jean-sans-Peur Tower, the towers of Notre-Damn that you saw for yourself, and many others, without counting the ones that stand erect along the outer ramparts."

"You'll have to get used to it, little mouse," Hélénaïs says, snickering. "Hope you won't get vertigo. Remember that you're in the city now, not in your countryside." She glances at the hearth that I didn't have time to rekindle after rushing back. "You're so lazy you let the fire die out."

She takes off her cape, all stiff from the cold, and throws it on the back of a chair. Then she puts logs in the fireplace and stirs the embers with a poker to get the flames going again.

"What I mean is, is there a tower that's different from the others?" I persist, turning toward Suraj.

"Different?" he repeats.

At a loss for words, I look out the dirty dormer window, where the light is going down. But I don't see any tower, only flat rooftops with shapes elongated by the low winter sun.

The images of the arcana dance in my head, superimposing themselves onto the dirty windowpane. When I grabbed that card at random, I was obsessed with the need to know where to look for the Lady of Miracles. Yes, I was burning with an ardent desire to find her this *very* evening. And what if the mysterious tarot heard my question? What if it answered me through this card?

If only I had taken it with me instead of letting the seer recover the two torn halves. Now, I can rely only on my memory to try and decipher the hypothetical message. If I remember correctly, the windows of the tower were up in flames, and small figures were jumping into the void to escape the blaze.

"A tower struck by a bolt of lightning . . . ," I say, lost in thought. "A terrible fire . . ."

"Lightning often strikes bell towers in Paris," Suraj says. "But tell us, Diane, why all the questions?"

"It's . . . uh . . . it's just an intuition," I say, tearing my gaze away from the dormer window.

Hélénaïs turns from the hearth, where she's kneeling, and gives Suraj a look laden with unspoken meaning.

"Do you think it's the ghoul venom that's making her delirious? Maybe we should send her back to Versailles, right beside the king."

As I hear the king mentioned, I recall something clearly. At the top of the card, the decapitated tower was topped with crenellations in the shape of a crown.

"A royal tower!" I shout. "We have to look for a royal tower. The tallest in Paris. A tower with sealed doors, where the only way out is by jumping from the windows." I grab Suraj's wrist. "Answer me: Does that mean anything to you, Suraj?"

He seems struck by my determination.

"The description might correspond to the Temple Tower," he says. "It's a royal prison, north of the Marais, formerly built by the Knights Templars. The dark dungeon overlooks the surrounding rooftops. I'm guessing the only way out is through the windows . . . at the risk of breaking one's neck."

I let go of Suraj's wrist, my heart racing, my throat dry.

"We have to go there tonight. I told you . . . I have an intuition."

"Out of the question," Hélénaïs objects, brandishing the poker under my nose. "First off, you're not fully back on your feet, what with your delirious visions. Secondly, Suraj and I were going to explore the cemetery at the Invalides."

But Suraj raises his hand to tamp down his colleague's zeal.

"Hold off, Hélénaïs. For starters, Diane does look better. She got out of bed and got dressed. Also, you and I visited the cemetery of Sang-Eustache last night, the one at Vaugirard the night before, and so on, without finding any hint of a trace that could lead us to the Court of Miracles. The few ghouls we could lay a hand on were only able to utter inarticulate grumblings. The Lady of Miracles is never where we are. So instead of just mindlessly scrolling through our list of Parisian cemeteries, maybe we should go with Diane's intuition, at least for tonight."

"But it's absurd," Hélénaïs insists.

"Maybe . . . or maybe not. What if the king's blood enhanced Diane's perception beyond that of regular humans? And what if, ultimately, that's her dark gift?"

Hélénaïs grumbles but doesn't dare contradict her partner, no doubt fearing she might say something blasphemous. The king's blood is sacred, like the powers it bestows.

Suraj takes the opportunity to unfurl the folds of his cape and removes a brand-new sword. He hands it to me.

"A gift to replace the one you lost," he says. "It's made only of steel, not death-silver, but it's better than nothing."

"Your dress, on the other hand, isn't free," Hélénaïs snaps. "I ordered it from a seamstress on the Rue Dauphine. It'll be ready in time for the grand ball at the Louvre. Five gold crowns, to be paid in full. I'm not running a charity!"

To reach the Temple area, we cut across the Marais, one of the toniest neighborhoods of Paris.

Magnificent town houses line the streets, their bright-white facades popping out all the more in the twilight. Through the high windows, I can see servants lighting gigantic chandeliers and pouring a red liquid into decanters. The domestics are bustling in anticipation of the imminent awakening of their vampyre masters. Melodies drift down from these rich dwellings, so as to make the lords of the night's rising all the more pleasant. Notes from harpsichords blend with the soft gurgling of the nearly frozen fountains. In the street, workers are rushing to light the wicks of large iron lanterns; public lighting exists here, unlike most areas of the city, which are populated by commoners subjected to the curfew. That's because, in the Marais, the lords of the night coexist with mortal nobles who are allowed to go out after dusk.

But beyond the Rue des Gravilliers, the public lanterns suddenly disappear, and the architecture changes dramatically. The alabaster town houses are replaced by dark shacks that tumble onto one another. The old medieval city reclaims its rights. Here, there are no brightly lit windows: shutters are tightly closed. No chamber music: a deathly silence weighs down on streets drowned in the cold night. Once again Paris becomes the City of Shadows.

Suddenly, it appears—the Temple Tower. It's a grim dungeon over fifty yards high, flanked by four small corner turrets. Unlike at the Grand Châtelet or the Incurables, no guards of the Royal Watch or dragoons are present. The Temple may be a royal building, but it doesn't welcome any prominent citizens of the regime or any nuns of the Faculty. Only prisoners. So it wasn't deemed necessary to accord it any particular protection.

"I suggest we find shelter and wait for nightfall," Suraj says. "If Diane's intuition firms up and the lady appears, better to be under cover when the first ghouls show themselves."

He heads toward a building bearing an iron sign dripping with icicles. Peeling letters sprawl across a thin layer of ice: THE TEMPLAR TAVERN. Here, too, the shutters are closed since bars shut at twilight.

With his gloved hand, Suraj knocks three times on the panel.

The door opens partway, releasing a blast of warmth into the cold.

A pair of suspicious eyes blinks in the gap.

"What do you want?"

"Open up, tavern keeper."

"We're closed. This isn't the poorhouse!"

Already the door is shutting, but Suraj slides his boot in to block it. The tavern keeper's chubby face goes from wariness to vague unease.

"If this is about the protection tax, I already paid it this month and—"

"We haven't come to ask for money but rather to offer you some," Suraj cuts him off. "We need shelter for the night and can pay adequately."

He takes a coin from his purse.

The tavern keeper eyes the money greedily. But just then, the strident warning bells ring from the towers of Paris. Fear of the night wins out over the lure of financial gain.

"It's too late, I told you."

"It's never too late for the king, you churl," Hélénaïs pipes up, enraged. She brandishes her pass.

The royal seal sweeps away the tavern keeper's reluctance. The door opens on a robust man, bundled in a thick nightgown, a sleeping bonnet plunked halfway down his forehead.

"I . . . I welcome you into my humble establishment," he stammers. "But all my bedrooms are already occupied by the roofers who've come to repair the tiles of the Temple Tower."

I shiver under my hood. "The roof of the tower, you say?"

"Yes, lightning fell on the temple last week."

I do my best not to burst out with nervous, jubilant laughter. The tower was hit by lightning, just like on the arcana. The tarot told the truth. We've come to the right place.

"We'll be content in your cellar, friend," Suraj assures him, slipping the coin into the tavern keeper's palm.

"But there aren't any beds in the cellar. And it's too humid to be fit for the king's envoys."

"It's perfectly fine, especially as we don't intend to get much shut-eye," Suraj replies. "And I advise you not to sleep too soundly, either, tonight."

"You shouldn't have told the tavern keeper that we're the king's envoys, Hélénaïs," Suraj says.

"But you saw how that lout wouldn't let us in," she counters, losing her temper.

We're sitting on uncomfortable stools around an oil lamp. The flame projects the squire's quivering shadow onto the brick cellar walls. Her silhouette is weirdly deformed by the worm-eaten wooden shelves where coarse glass bottles are stored, along with clay amphora jars.

"All the same, it was hardly discreet," Suraj reproaches her. "You didn't have to show him your royal pass."

"What about you, telling him to sleep with one eye open? Do you think it was discreet to imply that a surge of ghouls is imminent?"

"Hey!" I pipe up. "Seems to me you're now giving my intuition some credit, Hélénaïs."

She gives me an outraged glance, as if she suddenly remembers I'm here as she argues with the squire whose heart she'd like to win over.

"I believe only what I see," she shoots back haughtily. "This story of lightning that struck the Temple Tower is probably nothing more than coincidence. You must have overheard a snippet of conversation about it when we wandered through Paris on our first day, and the ghoul venom dredged it up into your foggy brain. Big deal. That would explain this 'intuition' that leads nowhere except to a damp cellar where we're freezing our butt cheeks off."

"This cellar isn't the worst place to wait," Suraj points out. "The walls are solidly cemented, and the trap door is bolted from within. We're safe here. If the ghouls show up aboveground, we're well placed to ambush them and strike when we deem the time is right."

Hélénaïs heaves an exasperated sigh, releasing a cloud of vapor in the halo of the oil lamp.

"Whatever . . . I'll say it again, I don't think we'll catch the Lady of Miracles tonight. On the other hand, thanks to Diane, we'll probably catch our deaths."

Hélénaïs's words make me shiver more that the surrounding cold. *Catch our deaths* . . . I think back to the Arcana with No Name, the one that hampered my reading. And what if it's Death with a capital *D* that's coming for me tonight, mowing me down with its long scythe? Unless that card is meaningless. Unless the fact that we're here at the Temple is the result of pure coincidences and dubious interpretations, just as Hélénaïs claims.

"I have no intention of catching a cruel death just before the grand ball," she grumbles. "I admit I eagerly await the big event. Ah, to be among civilized society for one night. To converse with beautiful people who smell good rather than inhale the foul breath of peasants in rags. To savor refined dishes instead of the greasy gruel at the Yellow Cat. To dance on the arm of a proud gentleman and dazzle everyone around."

She glances quickly at Suraj, whose gaze in no way encourages flirting. "In short, to live again!"

The hours go by in the silence of the cellar, disturbed only by Hélénaïs's insufferable comments.

Despite my cape, my fur-lined boots, and my gloves, little by little, I feel my body stiffen and become encrusted on the icy stool. The oil lamp casts swirls on the moldy walls in a strange, hypnotic ballet.

My mind also goes numb.

My senses grow dull.

My thoughts slow down.

Stay awake . . .

I have to fight against falling asleep . . .

Suddenly, the ground starts to shake under the soles of my boots, a shaking caused by a jolt coming from deep inside the earth.

The bottles on the shelves clatter against each other.

A furious drumming echoes against the walls and ceiling, producing a rain of saltpeter on our heads . . .

"The ghouls!" I shout.

The two other squires and I leap to our feet, our eyes riveted to the bolted trap door above our heads . . .

. . . but the danger is coming from behind us.

The shelves and their dozens of bottles topple in a loud crash of broken glass.

A draft of polar air penetrates the cellar, blowing out the flame of the oil lamp.

The total darkness swallows us in its howling throat, bristling with fangs.

"Aaaaaah!"

All of a sudden, I open my eyes, my heart thumping.

"What's wrong with you? You're howling like a lunatic!" Hélénaïs tosses out at me.

The lamp, still lit, illuminates her angry face. Behind her, the wall isn't smashed, and the bottles are neatly lined up on the shelves.

"Calm down," Suraj tells the squire. "Diane must have had a nightmare, that's all."

A nightmare?

Yes, it's coming back to me. I just dozed off for a second on my stool and imagined the rest.

Only here's the thing: I realize that ever since I drank the Sip of the King, my dreams have an unfortunate tendency to be premonitory. Each time I've glimpsed my own death in my dreams, I've then brushed against death in real life.

"I . . . I think the ghouls are about to arrive," I stammer.

"Another one of your dubious intuitions?" Hélénaïs says mockingly. "Keep them to yourself. Even if the ghouls were to show up, we're safe in this shelter, like Suraj said. We'll only leave the cellar after the onslaught of those horrors, so we can pluck the Lady of Miracles like a flower."

She points toward the heavy lock that bolts the trap door.

"The ghouls won't be coming through there," I say.

"What you mean is that they won't be coming at all!"

Ignoring the squire's taunts, I hurry over to the shelves and start removing bottles and their half-frozen contents.

"Help me," I yell, bending over to roll a heavy barrel.

"Help you do what? Empty the cellar? You're already crazy enough without having to get drunk like a . . ."

Hélénaïs doesn't finish her sentence. Behind the shelves, she's just seen the same thing I have: the bricks are coming loose. There's a narrow passageway, one that the bottles, barrels, and amphora jars hid—a jumble of stuff that's been piled up for years.

"How did you know there was a corridor here?" she asks me, flabbergasted.

"The question isn't finding out how Diane knew but how to get out of this mess," Suraj says. "I thought this cellar was safe, but I was wrong. If the enemy attacks us from that tunnel, we're trapped like rats."

He takes out the key the tavern keeper gave him and rushes over to unbolt the trap door.

Just then, the bottles that remain on the wooden planks start to vibrate . . . to rattle, just like in my dream.

I unsheathe my new sword.

Hélénaïs hurries to strap on her death-silver gauntlet.

A distant roar can be heard through the black hole of the passageway, like a hunting horn announcing a kill. A horrible feeling of cold penetrates the marrow of my bones. The ghouls are coming.

"Hurry!" Suraj yells as he pops the lock.

We dash up the wobbly steps and emerge onto the ground floor. The common room is lit by a single lantern that rests on the fireplace mantel, serving as a night-light.

Beyond the tavern walls, the night is filled with shrill howls, some distant and muffled, others frighteningly close.

Drowsy men in long nightshirts, candles in hand, are clumsily coming down the upper-floor staircase. I'm guessing these are the roofers who've been jolted awake by the noise. The tavern keeper shoves them aside to get to the exit door. He's fully clothed from head to toe, having obviously taken Suraj's earlier warning seriously, and I'll wager he's removing his most precious valuables in the big bag strapped to his back.

"No!" Suraj shouts at him. "The slaughter has already started outside! This structure seems solid. It's safer to stay put."

Livid, the tavern keeper freezes on the doorstep.

"The rest of you, help us to block the cellar!" the squire yells.

The frantic workers hurry to help us hoist the tavern's heaviest table over the trap door. But despite all the chairs and stools we pile on to consolidate this makeshift barricade, the sound coming from the depths of the earth is too powerful. The improvised tower shakes, and the pile collapses in a loud splintering of wood.

With horror, I see the trap door fly open into pieces.

Long, hairless limbs emerge.

Suraj pounces onto the opening, whirling his dagger. The double blade easily slices the monstrous fingers that grip the edges, the death-silver cutting through the ghoulish flesh.

Hélénaïs goes over to give him a helping hand with her fearsome gauntlet. The metallic claws slice through the air with such incredible speed, multiplied tenfold by the Immutable's blood, that I can't follow their movement. But I see shreds of pale flesh fly all around as the squire mows down the abominations.

I let out a hoarse shout and throw myself into the fight, ramming my sword into the dark hole.

Between the three of us, we may just succeed in containing the invisible pack that's trying to open a path.

I've barely formulated this crazy hope when I feel a brisk wind hit the back of my neck. The gust is coming from the front door. Giving in to panic, the tavern keeper has fled into the night. He can't have gotten far, the poor fellow—already, I hear his screams of terror, which don't take long to turn into a death rattle.

A dark, howling swarm rushes through the open door.

We're forced to turn away from the trap door and face the tidal wave coming from the outside. The workers let go of their candles, which snuff out as they hit the floor. I swing wildly into the obscurity with my sword, where dozens of milky ghoul eyes glow.

"This way!" comes Suraj's voice from somewhere in the chaos.

I hear a shutter banging, then the loud sound of breaking glass. Suraj just smashed one of the windowpanes to give us a way out.

A pale moonbeam falls into the dark tavern, illuminating a scene straight out of the bowels of hell.

The ghouls are so abundant, so dense, that it's impossible to see the ground. They form a shapeless mass, like some whitish larva spiked with a multitude of limbs—a deadly centipede made to eviscerate and shred. The unfortunate workers have completely vanished under this maelstrom from which emanates a stomach-churning stench of putrefaction.

I'm sorely tempted to unscrew the bezel of my onyx ring, a little bit of light to pierce through these Shadows of death.

No, Jeanne.

Not now.

You only have one chance to use the ring!

Hélénaïs is the first to hurl herself through the broken window. I gather my momentum and follow behind her, landing on the street's ice-covered paving stones.

The Temple neighborhood, which was so calm and quiet when we arrived, has become total pandemonium. Hordes cleave the darkness, chasing hundreds of terrified inhabitants. Those unlucky enough to stumble are instantly caught, trampled, and slashed to bits. The sound of cracking beams blends with the more subtle crushing of bones. At times, the call of an invisible hunting horn engulfs everything. High above this devastation stands the gutted roof of the Temple Tower, surrounded by the halo of an impassive quarter moon.

"We have to retreat!" Suraj yells. "We're not up to the task!"

As strong as my desire may be to kill the Lady of Miracles, I know he's right. The ghouls will get us before their mistress appears.

But Hélénaïs doesn't see it that way.

"No way we're leaving before we capture the lady," she wails, her beautiful face torn between the instinct to survive and the need to satisfy the king.

Her indecisiveness blunts her supernatural speed and makes her vulnerable. She doesn't see the dark, huddled shape on the gutter just above her head, like a gargoyle ready to pounce.

"Careful!" I shout.

The ghoul, twice as large as the one I confronted at the Innocents, leaps down onto the squire. Hélénaïs rolls to the ground. Crushed under this mass of gleaming muscle, every advantage of her extraordinary reflexes is neutralized, and there's no way she can use her gauntlet.

Suraj rushes to help her, but three other ghouls appear from behind the tavern, barring the way.

Clamping my clammy hands around the hilt of my weapon, I hurry to aid my fellow squire. In vain. My sword may be new, but it's made only of steel and not death-silver. The blade glides over the ghoul's thick spine, barely piercing the viscous flesh.

The creature turns its repulsive mug toward me. Its truncated nose quivers, inhaling my scent through the skeletal holes that serve as nostrils. Its huge pale eyes stare at me. They look like the fish eyes at the merchants' stalls: dead, glassy orbs. And yet they aren't completely empty. Even without pupils, I can tell they see me in their own way, and through them, I have the dizzying feeling the abyss is looking right at me.

"Let her go!" I scream, raising my pathetic sword.

The ghoul draws back its drooling chops, revealing two nightmarish rows of teeth massive enough to snap femurs, a real hyena jaw. It lets out a roar, along with a killer breath that sweeps the strands on my forehead and brings tears to my eyes.

"I . . . I told you to let her go!" I shout, squinting, bringing my weapon down again and again.

With each blow against the rough skin, the edge of my blade blunts, hardly able to make a scratch.

The creature rises in one leap.

Standing firm, I brandish the edge of my sword in front of me like a ridiculous shield.

The ghoul's chest smacks against the blade, sending painful vibrations deep inside me. The sword starts to tremble between my tight fists; my frozen muscles start to flinch. Within seconds, the hellish face comes closer to my own . . .

An impossibly long tongue now flicks out from between the yellow teeth and stretches toward me. Threads of saliva spatter into the air, all sticky under the moon. The spongy tongue smacks onto my cheek with a horrible sucking noise—the very organ that last night was no doubt winding its way into the hollows of a tibia to extract the putrid marrow.

As I'm about to faint from horror and disgust, and as the last of my strength is about to give out, the horrid tongue detaches itself from my cheek.

And a growl gushes out from the monster's face, mere inches from me.

"Who are you?"

A terror-filled panic grips my heart, more absolute even than the fear of being devoured. This chthonic voice sounds as deep as the bowels of the earth, where ghouls are born out of thin air.

But, most of all, this is impossible. *These things aren't supposed to talk.*

Before I can react, a shape appears above the ghoul.

A short blade comes down on the creature's bald head, without slipping. This dagger is forged from death-silver, and it pierces the top of my adversary's skull right through to the hilt.

The jaw dislocates.

The tongue falls limply to the side.

Suraj grabs my arm. Behind him, Hélénaïs gets up, panting.

No need to confer to know we're about to be overwhelmed. We flee through the dark, ice-covered alleyways, as far as possible from the Temple area.

11

WHO ARE YOU?

The ghoul spoke to me.

"Who are you?" Those three hollow syllables went round in my head all night long, back at the Yellow Cat Inn, where we took refuge after the debacle at the Temple.

This morning, after sleepless hours spent wallowing in my thoughts and in black bile, a raging migraine drills into my skull.

I get up, get dressed, and do a bit of grooming in front of the chipped mirror that hangs on the wall above a cold basin of water. *"Who are you?"* As I look at my reflection, I think about the real baronette, the one whose identity I usurped. Because she imprudently welcomed my brother to her home, then was too cowardly to warn us that the inquisitors were going to strike, she caused Bastien's death and that of my entire family. When her father, the baron, tried to skewer me with his rapier, I used her like a shield—me, the last Froidelac still alive. I would have liked for things to unfold differently. After all, if Bastien loved the real Diane de Gastefriche, maybe she wasn't entirely bad. Maybe in her own way she, too, was a victim: of her rigid education, her tyrannical father, and the horrible circumstances of the Magna Vampyria.

Someone knocks at my door.

I tamp down my melancholy.

"Come in."

It's Suraj and Hélénaïs. As usual, they're joining me in my room for a small breakfast of dry bread and watered-down coffee. Judging by how weary they look, they must've had as restless a night as I did.

"I was so close to capturing the Lady of Miracles," Hélénaïs says, her nose buried in her bowl of coffee. "It would have been perfect to deliver her to the king, feet and wrists bound, before the grand ball at the Louvre on December twentieth. If Diane hadn't stopped me, I would have done it."

Her bad faith leaves me breathless.

"Stopped you?" I choke out. "Don't you mean that I saved your life? We're even now."

Testily, Hélénaïs lowers her bowl.

"No, we are not even!" she says, raising her voice. "Far from it. You're hiding something from us. How did you know the ghouls would attack the Temple last night?"

"I already explained about my intuition."

"Easy to blame it on that. Are you also going to pretend it's thanks to your intuition that you discovered the hidden passageway behind the archways of the cellar?"

I don't know how to answer. I don't want to open up about my strange premonitory dreams to my teammates. They're too personal, too dangerous; they touch a part of me that I don't understand and escapes me completely.

"I simply detected a draft that alerted me, is all," I lie. "Nothing more."

"Oh, I think there's a great deal more to it. I'm increasingly convinced that you aren't who you pretend to be."

I place my hands on either side of my bowl to stop them from shaking.

Suraj, who's usually quick to moderate Hélénaïs's heated fervor, doesn't intervene. He's looking at me suspiciously too.

"What are you talking about?" I say, defensively. "Of course you know who I am. I'm an unsophisticated baronette from the countryside, just like you take pleasure in reminding me. A squire intent on capturing the Lady of Miracles before you do, so I can gain the king's favor."

In truth, under all my sarcasm, do I really know who I am? I can't deny anymore that there's a whole part of me I know nothing about. The Sip of the King seems to have carved out a black hole within me. A bottomless well from which shadowy premonitions and hidden talents rise up, like being able to understand the language of the ghouls.

"Who are you?" The rumbling voice in my memory reverberates again.

If only I knew.

"I . . . I think the ghoul venom is still affecting me a little," I say. "I have a terrible migraine. I'd better stay in bed today."

"That's probably a good idea," Suraj agrees. "Hélénaïs and I are going back to the Temple area to try and gather some clues. We'll meet up with you tonight, after our rounds."

The two squires finish their breakfast in silence, then leave my room without a word.

Buried under the hood of my cape, I rush through the cold streets in long strides.

I quit the inn as soon as my teammates left. This time, I simply picked my door lock without losing time going over the rooftops. I have only one goal in mind: return to the Innocents to question the seer again. He has to draw the cards one last time. He has to help me understand what happened at the Temple yesterday—and even more, what the Sip of the King awakened in me.

As I head up toward the area of Les Halles, I can't shake the feeling that I'm being followed. I look over my shoulder at every street crossing, expecting to see Suraj and Hélénaïs on my heels. But no, there are only bystanders in rags going about their business, oblivious to my presence. I don't know if I can trust my instincts anymore. Everything is a jumble of confusion in my head.

Arriving at the Innocents, I climb the slope, pass through the archways, and cross the cemetery on the double toward the reclusory.

Unlike yesterday, there's no line, no one waiting for a consultation with the Eye of the Innocents. I'm in luck! I rush over to the slit . . . but as I near the turret, I freeze. A fault line has split the side of the cell, and the stones have exploded, leaving a gap a few inches wide.

"Monsieur Seer?" I call out.

No response.

My hand on the hilt of my sword, I twist my body to slip through the gap.

First, a stale smell mixed with organic mustiness assaults my nostrils, the scent of an entire life lived in this narrow cell, no bigger than a cage. Then my eyes adjust to the dimness, and I can make out the pitiful furnishings. A dried-out straw mattress takes up nearly the entire ground, barely large enough to lie on, all curled up. Next to it, there's just enough room for a chipped chamber pot. Last, a shallow niche welcomes a jumble of gnawed chicken bones and bits of candles given by passersby.

A metallic object lies among the scattered bricks. I bend over to examine it, knocking my ribs against the narrow walls. It's my court sword. Did the seer use it to loosen the walls of his prison? I have a hard time imagining his frail, scrawny hands wielding my weapon like an ice pick . . . but at the same time, I underestimated their strength when they grabbed onto me the first night.

The result is that the one who said he'd been a recluse for too many years to keep count has disappeared. He took his precious tarot cards and all hope of uncovering the secret that's eating me up inside.

As I grab the handle of my sword, I notice a piece of paper jammed underneath. It's wrapping paper, torn and sticky, that probably enclosed a beignet or some other offering brought to the seer by one of his admirers. A strange handwriting—shaky like an old person's and arduous like a child's—runs between the grease stains.

I'm suddenly dizzy at the idea that the seer anticipated my visit. After I'd been here twice to question him about the Court of Miracles, did he foresee that I'd come back a third time? Or did he read it in his cards? Are they the ones that led him to the gloomy prophecy?

Distraught, I stuff the paper in my pocket and slip through the cell with my reclaimed sword. The light outside is blinding.

"That's a sign of great misfortune," a voice close at hand groans.

Blinking, I make out a small woman standing there, bundled in layers of rags, looking lost in thought.

"When those who are walled up start abandoning their cells, the apocalypse isn't far behind," she laments. "The Night of Shadows is near, and with it the evening when the Lady of Miracles will destroy Paris for good."

You will never find the Court of Miracles.

But perhaps the Court of Miracles will find you, once you've lost all hope.

The most marvelous dreams come true there. And the most frightening nightmares too.

"Do you know where the Eye of the Innocents went to?" I ask.

"Who can say? To hell, maybe!" she yells, twisting her patch-work-mittened hands.

Realizing I won't be getting any information out of her, I quickly take off.

All along the way back, I can't shake the same unpleasant feeling of being followed. And what if the Eye of the Innocents is trailing me? I never saw his face, so every elderly person I cross paths with arouses my suspicion.

I hoped to find relief at the Yellow Cat, so that I could think with a clear head, but it's not to be. Even behind the walls of the inn, I still have the impression I'm being watched. I climb to my room and shut myself in, closing the shutters.

Maybe this is my last recourse: sleep. To plunge into the dark abyss of my dreams and try to bring back pearls of premonitions, just like I did, without meaning to, several times before.

"I'd like this to last forever . . . but you'll catch cold," Tristan says softly into my ear.

Through the exposed neckline of his shirt, my cheek resting against his soft skin, I can hear his heart beating.

The wind rustles the tall grasses of the clearing that surround our entwined bodies.

"I'll never catch cold in your arms," I say, pressing myself closer to his chest.

"My arms won't be able to warm you against the arriving winter."

I raise my eyes toward Tristan's face to snuff out his tender words with a kiss.

But above his torso, there's no ash-blond hair tousled by the breeze, no loving eyes the color of the summer sky. There's only a severed neck.

The sound of the warning bell tears me from my sleep.

I emerge out of a dark, day-long slumber. Instead of a premonitory dream, I've only brought back a memory—the first kiss Tristan and I shared, clashing with the last stroke of the blade that separated us forever . . .

It seems one can't dream on command. The hours I spent sleeping fully dressed in my bed didn't bring any sudden insights, just this strange memory of the past, coupled with a pounding headache.

As I get up to go find some white willow pills in my shoulder bag, there are three knocks at my door. Suraj and Hélénaïs must be back from their wanderings.

"Come in!" I shout after stuffing my mouth with a handful of pills.

The door opens on a hooded figure. One quick look and I can tell that it's not the cape worn by my fellow squires.

I grab hold of my recently recovered court sword, ready to slay the intruder who's come to grab hold of me just as I wake up, much like Paulin did in my room at Versailles.

"I'm here as a friend," declares the figure in a familiar English accent.

He lowers his hood, revealing the high cheekbones of Lord Sterling Raindust.

His black head of hair, thick and lustrous, immediately straightens up above his perfectly proportioned skull. Vampyre hair is endowed with a supernatural, magical vitality.

"How did you know I was staying here?" I toss out at him, not letting my guard down.

"I conducted an investigation, Mademoiselle de Gastefriche," he answers with his cold half smile, punctuated by the toothpick that never seems to leave his mouth. "Your admirer, Mortange, was right to say that I'm a bit of a spy."

"He also told me to be wary of you."

The vampyre looks at me with his dark eyes contoured by black pencil. His amber complexion glistens almost supernaturally in the diffuse light of the ceiling oil lamp. The flickering flame reflects off the safety pin that pierces one of his ears.

"The viscount was wrong on that score," he says. "On the contrary, I'm not the one you should be careful of. I came to warn you of an imminent danger. Allow me to close the door so that we can talk quietly."

Without waiting for my response, he gently shuts the panel at his back.

The bolt locks with a tiny click.

"I warn you that my sword is made of death-silver," I tell him. "And my companions-in-arms will be back any second."

"I don't think so. I sent them clear across Paris, to the Chaussée-d'Antin, so that you and I could speak in peace."

A cold sweat trickles down my spine. The temperature in the room is several degrees lower since the vampyre entered, cooling the embers in the fireplace.

"What do you mean you 'sent' them clear across Paris?"

"Oh, nothing more than that," he says as he sits down at the small table where I usually dine with my teammates. "I paid one of the street urchins, the ones who go from neighborhood to neighborhood in contempt of the sequester. I asked the child to pretend the Lady of Miracles had left a trail at the Chaussée-d'Antin. Your friends quickly decided to go look for clues before the police got there first—as I do believe you aren't working hand in hand with L'Esquille on this matter, am I right?"

I clamp my lips, troubled by the fact that he knows so much about a mission that's supposed to be secret.

"As for how I found you, I simply had to follow the crows that the king sends to Suraj. You see, they communicate every night."

"I know that. We squires hold no secrets from one another."

It's a lie. Even if Suraj acknowledged having received one of the king's crows, I didn't know they corresponded on a daily basis.

Sterling Raindust stops fiddling with his toothpick and sticks it behind one of his ears. At present, all his attention is focused on me. He stares at me as if he wanted to read my thoughts.

"Are you also aware that a large part of this correspondence concerns you?" he asks.

"How so?" I choke out.

"I've intercepted several of these crows before letting them complete their route. You see, my transmutation is recent, going back only to the year 296 of the Shadows, when I was twenty years old. But during my three years of immortality, I've developed a special bond with the birds of the night."

I mull his words over, slowly lowering the tip of my sword. The problem with vampyres is that you can never gauge their real age—hence Alexandre seems to be eternally nineteen, even though he's plagued the earth for decades, if not centuries. This Sterling Raindust, however, is close in years to what he appears to be: he's only twenty-three on the clock. Which means he was mortal during the greater part of his life, until that day. That makes him a little more . . . human to me. As for his "close bond" with the crows that he speaks of, I've heard rumors that certain lords of the night can control nocturnal animals.

"To read the king's personal correspondence constitutes a crime of treason," I warn him halfheartedly as I sit down facing him. "If word got out, you'd end up impaled on the Hunting Wall."

"As you say, if word got out," he replies tersely. "But it won't."

I laugh nervously. "I've heard of the English composure, which you evidently lack," I tell him. "You border on recklessness. Don't forget you're addressing the king's favorite squire. One word from me is all it would take to have you condemned."

"I don't believe you'd utter that word," he answers, as calm as can be. "In regard to the king's favor, everyone knows it's ever fluid. Funny way to treat a favorite, using her as bait."

I can't hide my surprise.

"Bait?"

"You heard me. It's the term used in the messages. By saving the king from ultimate death, you didn't just make friends. All those who, for one reason or another, are opposed to the crown resent you. In the standoff that pits her against Louis for the control of Paris, the Lady of Miracles would gain by capturing you. You're a symbol." Sterling leans forward, the better to read the expression on my face. "That's the Immutable's strategy: let his enemy come to you, like a fish nips at bait."

"I don't understand . . ."

"A little of the king's blood runs through your veins. And that blood is a mystical magnet unlike any other. If the Lady of Miracles takes you hostage and drags you into her underground lair, the Immutable will come to Paris. From the surface, he'll use the blood link that unites you to him to locate you, as long as you're alive . . . and to strike the Court of Miracles with precision."

The English vampyre's words make my head spin. Ever since the Sip of the King, I've tried to forget that my body contains a little of the monarch's shadowessence. Sterling Raindust just reminded me of it in the cruelest way.

"In his letters, the king tells Suraj to expose you without scruples," he says. "So that the Lady of Miracles and her henchmen can easily abduct you."

The memory of my first visit to the Innocents rushes back like a slap in the face. I ended up alone when a ghoul attacked me. Now that I think about it, Suraj's instructions to separate in order to flush out the abominations were likely for no other reason than to leave me out in the open. He let me wander off through the cemetery like a fly-fisher casting a lure to reel in a big catch.

I think back to what he said when he assured me that the Immutable's blood constituted our advantage against the ghouls. He didn't mean that the Sip would develop in me a skill to render me invincible. Quite the opposite: he knew the cursed blood would transform me into a sacrificial victim in his quest to find the Court of Miracles!

"The king himself suggested to his squire that you all sleep in the city, in this unsafe inn, rather than under heavy guard at the Grand Châtelet," Sterling goes on. "In fact, weren't you surprised that L'Esquille didn't rush to find you?"

"But . . . but we're here incognito," I stammer, holding on to the last of my beliefs.

An ambiguous emotion comes over the vampyre's smooth face. It's the first time I've seen him truly smile, revealing his white teeth. And yet his expression is even colder than the one he displayed when his toothpick prevented him from completely stretching his lips. There's something wobbly about his smile . . . something profoundly melancholic.

"That may be what Jaipur led you to believe," he says, dealing the final blow. "In reality, the backstreets of Paris are buzzing with the news that the king's squires are staying at the Yellow Cat. In truth, no need to be a spy to find you. One just needs to know whom to ask."

I swallow without managing to wash down the bitter taste that's invaded my mouth. All these days and nights of convalescence, when Suraj asked me to stay in bed while he and Hélénaïs went out . . . it wasn't just so that I would get better. It was also—primarily!—to put me in reach of the Lady of Miracles. Alone at the inn, shut inside my room, without even my death-silver sword, I was sitting prey.

To think that only minutes ago I was boasting to Sterling about being the king's favorite squire. Now I'm so ashamed. In my weakness, I realize I attributed human feelings to the king, believing that he had some sort of affection for me. What a mistake. Montfaucon was right to speak of the tyrant's *malicious wisdom*," one honed over the centuries. I'm merely a tool in his hands, a *"little gray mouse"* to whet the appetite of the she-cat Hecate.

"Why?" I ask, my fists clenched under the table.

"I already told you: to lure the enemy."

"I mean why are you telling me all this? Why the interest?"

The lord's strange smile widens without becoming any warmer.

"My interest concerns the Crown of England, of course," he states in his flat, monotone voice. "Our sovereign, Anne Stuart, isn't keen on seeing the Immutable appropriate the legions of ghouls that proliferate in the bowels of Paris. The balance of power between the vampyric nations of Europe is already very fragile. May the Shadows save the queen."

"The *vice-queen*," I correct him. "As for the European nations, England included, they're vassals to the King of Shadows."

"Of course, vassals. Just as you are. But being a vassal doesn't mean total servitude. Same for vice-kingdoms as for courtiers: it's advisable to submit before the sovereign, all the while keeping assets in one's pocket, just in case. That's the secret to surviving, to advancing, and to enduring."

The parallel between the court of Versailles and the concert of nations stuns me. I realize that in spite of his recent transmutation and eccentric bearing, the young lord is well schooled in the diplomatic game.

"Now that you know how the Immutable is using you, you're free to act accordingly," he continues. "Not to save London, no, Diane de Gastefriche, but to save yourself. Be on guard. For if you're captured and, by a miracle—pun not intended—you reach the bowels alive, it would be only a reprieve. Once the Court of Miracles is located, the king will be pitiless. He'll unleash the full force of his army to crush it without discernment. The only prisoner he wants is the Lady of Miracles herself, not you. You won't survive a battle waged between the ghouls and the royal army." The lord slightly squints his black-contoured eyelids, as if to better stare at me. "Diane de Gastefriche, at our first encounter I sensed a remarkable vital force within you. You don't give me the impression of someone who accepts dying easily, even to serve her sovereign."

The vampyre's dark eyes give off a mysterious gleam, like the last red embers in the hearth. Suddenly, I wonder if he knows the reason for my "*vital force*," the thirst for justice that I inherited from my parents, one that burns even stronger since their murder . . . but no, it's impossible. Montfaucon is far too cautious to send crows in all directions. The Englishman has no means to know my real identity.

"I thank you for alerting me," I say. "I'll be on guard, because you're right, I'm not ready to die. But the king is resolute. You must have read in his letters that he's about to cut off food supplies to Paris. As for us, his squires, he won't be calling us back to Versailles until we've brought him his enemy."

"Unless this enemy disappears."

Sterling opens the folds of his cape and takes out a velvet pouch that he places on the table.

He unties the fabric with his pale fingers and takes out a shiny pistol.

"Do you know how to shoot?" he asks me, point blank.

"At the Grande Écurie, the art-of-weaponry class was largely focused around bladed weapons, but we were taught the rudiments of firearms. And when I lived in the Auvergne, I learned how to wield a sling."

Sterling raises his black brows. The sling isn't commonly used by noble young ladies, even those who hail from the most out-of-the-way provinces.

"You have hidden talents" is all he says. "When you arrive in the bowels, whether of your own doing or after being abducted by the Lady of Miracles' henchmen, you'll need to kill her with one shot to the heart. Once she's destroyed, her army of ghouls will disband, for these monsters were never able to organize themselves before the lady appeared. The coordinated attacks will cease. And maybe you'll have a chance to get back to the surface alive."

I graze the pistol with my fingertips. The iron of my onyx ring makes a slight grating sound as it brushes against the steel barrel. Sterling doesn't know that I already possess a secret weapon, the one the Fronde gave me. And now the Crown of England is giving me a second one.

By strange coincidence, the objective from London meshes with my secret goal: eliminate the Lady of Miracles so that the Immutable can't seize her powers.

"I thought only a wooden stake could end the lives of you immortals," I tell him. "Followed by a proper decapitation."

"That is in fact the traditional method. The stake paralyzes the vampyre and stops their regenerative ability before the sword serves its function. But such a technique to deliver ultimate death requires hand-to-hand combat, and I doubt the Lady of Miracles will let anyone come close enough." He turns over the gun's velvet pouch: the reverse side has half a dozen small pockets sewn into it, each one holding a silvery bullet. "These ammunitions are made of death-silver, a metal as formidable as the blade you threatened me with before. What am I saying: even fiercer! For this is *enchanted* death-silver, something achieved by a very complex alchemical process, one that's officially banned by the Faculty on the Continent. Vice-Queen Anne's silversmiths were able to modify the properties of the metal. Each of these bullets involved thousands of hours of alchemical work in the secret cellars of Kensington Palace in London to make sure they liquefy upon reaching their target. Once lodged in a vampyre's heart, the projectile releases its death-silver, which enters the veins of the victim, neutralizing the shadowessence."

Shadowessence . . . the mystical humor that runs through the bodies of vampyres and gives them eternal life.

Lord Raindust lowers his voice before continuing his explanations. The subject he's addressing, so he said, is blacklisted by the Faculty. The very act of talking about it constitutes a terrible blasphemy.

"Without shadowessence to give it supernatural force, a vampyre's body inevitably withers," he says. "The Lady of Miracles will lose her immortality and at the same time succumb to the bullet's perforation. But don't forget that you must aim for the heart, or the enchanted death-silver won't spread throughout her body. You have six bullets, six tries—plus the one I already placed in the gun chamber."

I nod and take the weapon . . . and quickly point the barrel toward my visitor, straight at his chest.

"Everything you've just told me is a matter of high treason," I say, my heart racing. "I could test out this pistol on you, right here, right now, and deliver your corpse to the king."

Held at arm's length, the vampyre doesn't budge one iota. His face doesn't betray alarm or even the least bit of worry, as if the prospect of his own death doesn't rattle him.

"You could, in fact," he says. "But I don't think you'll do so."

"You don't think I have it in me?"

"I believe you're far too intelligent for that."

Deep flashes glisten in his black eyes, golden specks that I'd already glimpsed when we first met.

"All the world's a stage, and all the men and women merely players."

"Let me guess: Shakespeare?"

He nods, gravely. "The Immutable is the great director of the Magna Vampyria Theater. He assigns roles as he pleases, to individuals as well as to the people. In his eyes, you're a bit player he's decided to sacrifice to capture the lady. But, more than anything, he detests when actors veer off script and start improvising their own lines."

Sterling Raindust doesn't have to say anything more for me to get the message. By giving me all this information, he's also buying my silence. If I tell the king that I learned he's using me, I run the risk of losing his favor.

I lower the barrel of the pistol.

"If I reach the Court of Miracles, you said the king will have to come to Paris to sniff my trail," I say. "Can't he do that from Versailles?"

"The blood link is proportional to the quantity. The lords of the night can get a whiff of their progeny from miles away since a new immortal is created by filling a body with several gallons of vampyric blood. But you're only the king's squire, not his creation. Only a few ounces of blood course through your veins, sending a weak signal. If necessary, he'll have to be on the spot to pinpoint you in the depths."

The young lord dusts off his long cape, made to help him blend into the gloom of the city. "Destroy the Lady of Miracles, and leave her body to rot in the subterranean tunnels from which she'll never be exhumed. The Immutable will have no one to blame. Maybe he'll conclude that the ghoul tamer, having exhausted her alchemical powers, ended up being devoured by her own abominations. The army of ghouls will dissolve on its own, and you'll return to Versailles safe and sound, where you'll pursue your career as a courtier as you await your transmutation."

Given what he says, I gather Sterling hasn't stumbled onto who I really am. So after weighing everything, I don't see any downside to the pact he's offering me.

I put the pistol and precious bullets away at the bottom of my shoulder bag.

"Understood," I say.

"Good. I need to go now," he says as he gets to his feet. "I need to be gone before your dear *companions-in-arms* return." He emphasizes the phrase I used, one that rings awfully hollow now that I know the content of the correspondence between Suraj and the king. "It goes without saying that you and I never saw each other this evening. Hide the pistol well until you use it. In any case, should a third party learn of its existence, there's nothing linking it to me or to England."

He readies to leave, but I get up, too, spurred by a need to know more. "Wait."

I grab his wrist, which I let go of immediately. It's as cold as marble.

"What is it?" the vampyre asks, his black eyes gleaming mere inches away from mine.

"The other day, at the Gibbet of Montfaucon, Alexandre de Mortange called you an anarchist. He also insulted you using a term I've never heard: *punk*."

No emotion crosses the lord's face as I repeat the word Alexandre tossed out as an insult.

"The Court of London is not as stiff as that of Versailles," he explains, his dark-contoured eyes not blinking for an instant. "In

England, the Faculty is far less uptight than on the Continent, and the *numerus clausus* far less severe. We transmute left and right—not only nobles with ten quarters of nobility but also lesser knights, and mere gentlemen with no fortune or title . . . like me."

I don't believe my ears.

A nontitled aristocrat as lord or vampyre?

I had heard that Vice-Queen Anne was mad, but this goes beyond anything I had imagined. A country where even small-time squires can access immortality reminds me of the dreams of the La Roncière conspirators—and of the nightmare for the people. This explains why England has its eye on the mortal population of the Continent. Without a strict *numerus clausus*, the number of bloodsuckers must have exploded.

Sterling seems to see how stunned I am.

"Those in the House of Lords look at us in the same way you do tonight, Diane," he says, addressing me with the informality of my given name. "With a great deal of contempt."

"You . . . you're mistaken . . . ," I start to say.

"No use denying it, baronette. I don't hide the fact that I'm of common birth. My parents didn't have three pennies to their name to fix the roof of their old country house. The ancestral home of the Raindusts still leaks as we speak . . . at least, I believe so, as I severed all ties with my family the day I left the place and went up to London to chart my path. Over there, flat-out broke, I lived like a commoner indeed. Yes, you heard me, baronette: I ate, drank, slept, and loved like a beggar. Right up until I met the woman who transmuted me in the backstreets where mortals and vampyres mingle in endless debauchery."

He no doubt thinks he's shocking me by tossing all this in my face.

The safety pin dangling from his ear moves with his heated declaration, and he stops it with his finger.

"I've kept this trinket from my years in London. To remind me that before I was employed by the Crown, I wore only rags held together by safety pins. And my habit of chewing on a toothpick comes from the theaters at Covent Garden, where I worked as a stagehand to make ends meet. I've kept up the habit even if nothing gets stuck between my choppers anymore. A way for me to remember I was still mortal not that long ago." His mouth twists in a half-bitter, half-triumphant smirk, exposing the tips of his pointy canines for the first time. "I know the polite society of the Magna Vampyria finds these manners crass, but it's who I am, baronette, whether it pleases you or not."

For the first time, the sophisticated demeanor of the diplomat cracks, revealing a wilder nature. Even his language is coarser. He looks me up and down in defiance, searching for the impact of his words, not knowing that I come from the very people he rubbed shoulders with.

"The peers from the high aristocracy of historic vampyres found a tainted word to refer to the newly transmuted, those who were penniless and slumming it with commoners: *punks*, wretches, good-for-nothings. But we're still worth something. Who better than a punk to blend into the backstreets of a foreign capital? That must have been what the vice-queen thought when she dispatched me to the embassy in Paris."

He takes the toothpick from behind his ear and slips it into a corner of his mouth, as if to seal it. His lips close in the same impenetrable expression that I just discovered hides a magma of concealed anger. He's decidedly an odd diplomat, just like the strange country that's supposedly consumed in madness.

"Who knows, little Baronne de Gastefriche," he says sarcastically. "You might just get tired of competing with the other death-lickers at Versailles. Maybe one night, if your transmutation takes too long to come by on French soil, you'll cross the Channel to hasten it along? On that night, in some obscure ally in Soho, as guitars hurl their chords and beer flows freely, I'll take pleasure in draining you of your blood to fill you with mine."

And thus he pulls his hood over his head of black hair, hiding his face, piercing eyes, toothpick, and earring. Then he turns on his heel and vanishes into the darkness of the hallway.

12

DREAD

"Sorry to come back so late," Suraj says as he opens the door to my room, Hélénaïs right behind him. "We were sent on a wild-goose chase."

"A wild-goose chase?" I repeat, feigning surprise.

"We heard a rumor claiming that the Lady of Miracles had shown up at the Chaussée-d'Antin, but we found no trace of her. No more than at the Temple this afternoon. The area was destroyed. Many inhabitants have vanished, many dwellings are deserted, and we couldn't find any interesting clues . . . other than this."

His cheeks blue from the cold, he takes out a handkerchief from his pocket and unfolds it on the table. I see long glass fragments, like at Mont Parnasse. Nothing similar to the coarse, nearly opaque glass from the bottles at the Templar Tavern. This glass is sublimely pure and transparent, worthy of the china seen on only the most beautiful table settings.

"And you, how are you doing?" Suraj asks me as he removes his cape. "Do you still feel the effects of the ghoulish venom?"

I force myself to smile calmly, even though I'm steaming inside. How dare he pretend to be concerned about my health when he didn't hesitate one second to use me as bait?

"I'm better," I whisper. "Much better, even. So much so that this afternoon I went back to the Innocents to look for my lost sword."

A disapproving look comes over Suraj's face.

"But your door was locked."

"I picked the lock."

"You shouldn't have left the inn without telling us!"

"No? And why not?"

"Because we have to look out for each other."

What you need to look out for is that the bait doesn't get off the hook and swim away, I snap back in my head. *You backstabbing slug.*

"I told you to be careful of her," Hélénaïs scoffs. "Today she picked the lock to her room; yesterday it was the one to my closet at the Grande Écurie. We can't trust her. Diane and team spirit, it's like oil and water."

"Speaking of team spirit, seems to me I'm like a third wheel," I say softly. "You make such a perfect tandem, a truly organic couple."

At the mention of *couple*, Hélénaïs blushes with pleasure, while Suraj turns a little pale.

"Honestly, these last few days, I've felt like a tagalong," I go on, knowing full well that my words are like torture for the Indian squire. "I don't really feel like I belong with the two of you. I only slow you down. Maybe I should just continue on my own and let you carry on together."

"That . . . that's not a good idea, Diane," Suraj stammers.

"On the contrary, it's an excellent one," Hélénaïs says. "If we lead the investigation on two fronts, we multiply the chances of finding the Lady of Miracles. Besides, Diane is right: she's not playing on the same field." The squire's golden-brown eyes look deep into Suraj's. "You and I were made to be allies. Your endurance, my speed: we're elite warriors, whereas Diane is a dreamer with a delicate constitution, not really cut out for the battlefield. Let's leave her to her foggy visions and investigate, just you and me."

She rummages through her shoulder bag and takes out a quill-written note that she stuffs into my hand.

"The receipt for your dress. Rosine Couture, 25 bis Rue Dauphine. The order will be ready on Tuesday. You can see about alterations then." She turns again toward Suraj. "My dress will be finished in one week, in time for the grand ball at the Louvre. We'll enter together, arm in arm. In tandem, like Diane said. I already see us splashed on the cover of *Le Mercure Galant*: 'Hélénaïs and Suraj, the Most Beautiful Couple of the Evening.'"

Suraj opens his mouth to respond, but I silence him with a dagger-like stare: *"If you protest, I'll tell her everything about you and Rafael."* Not that I would, if only out of regard for Rafael. But the timing couldn't be better to remind him of the trump card in my hand.

Just then, someone knocks three times at the door. It's the servant bringing our dinner, which she's been instructed to leave outside.

Hélénaïs waits until the footsteps grow faint on the creaky staircase before she collects the steaming bowls and bread. All during the meal, she elaborates on her plans for the following day without a word from Suraj.

Then it's time to turn in. The two others head to their respective rooms. They're barely gone when I lace up my boots, put on my cape, and gather my things into my shoulder bag. It's out of the question for me to spend another night under this roof, where the Lady of Miracles' henchmen can come and pluck me from the bed at any second. Besides, I slept most of the afternoon, so I'm not tired. It's time for me to set sail and navigate solo. To find the enemy on my own terms.

But just as I place my hand on the doorknob, it turns under my fingertips. Suraj is back.

"You're not sleeping?" I say. "What do you want?"

"I already told you," he whispers, taking great care to shut the door behind him soundlessly. "I want you to stay with us."

I'm gripped by a burning desire to shout in his face. To shout that I know all about his schemes. I grit my teeth to suppress my rage. I have nothing to gain by Suraj knowing that I learned the truth.

"I've made up my mind," I tell him. "As of tonight, I'm going my own way."

"Where will you sleep?"

"Probably at the Grand Châtelet."

In your dreams. If you come looking for me at the Grand Châtelet tomorrow, you won't find me. With my purse full and the royal pass in my pocket, I'm sure I'll be able to find a place to stay. A place where I won't have to answer to anyone. Not Suraj, not the police, not even the king. From Versailles, the Immutable can't use the blood link to isolate my whereabouts. And I doubt he'll come to Paris before he's been officially informed that I've been abducted by the Lady of Miracles. That's the reason Suraj is insisting I remain at the inn. For days now, he's been hoping the lady will come and kidnap me, and, as witness to my abduction, he can then alert the palace. But if I'm out of sight, he won't know if I've been captured or if I've just run off.

Resolute, I hold my ground. "Get out of the way now."

But Suraj doesn't budge.

"Why do you want to leave, Diane? I don't understand." He lowers his voice. "I don't know where you got it into your head that Hélénaïs and I are a couple. You know that . . . that I love someone else."

"What I know is that I'm fed up with your constant bullying and bossing around. I want to conduct the investigation on my terms, without the two of you breathing down my neck."

He continues to bar the door, his powerful arms crossed over his chest.

"I can't allow it."

"That's what I mean about you being high and mighty. I don't need your permission, Jaipur. You're not my father. I answer only to the king."

"The king would be displeased to learn that you bailed on us."

"He'd be even more displeased if he knew that two boys belonging to his personal guards were fooling around together behind his back. Rumor has it that he doesn't appreciate romances that deviate from the norm."

Under his ocher turban, Suraj's face freezes.

"Lower . . . lower your voice," he whispers, as if he's suddenly afraid the walls will hear us.

This sudden distress, from someone usually so stoic, tears at my heart. Ever since I met brooding Suraj, I've known he's tormented by his love for Rafael. A burning love that he wants to hide at all costs but that devours him from within. Right now, I'm sure I'll never betray his secret. But he can't know how far I'm willing to go.

"If you don't let me by, I'll spill everything to Hélénaïs tomorrow," I threaten. "Seeing as how she's so infatuated with you, she'll be bitter. And knowing her, the rumor will spread like wildfire throughout Paris, up to Versailles, right to the king."

A tiny tremor crosses Suraj's brows.

"The . . . the king must never learn of it," Suraj stammers. "I . . . I don't have the right to disappoint him. The salvation of the kingdom of Jaipur depends on it."

In spite of his betrayal, I'm suddenly overcome by a surge of empathy for this boy caught in the cross fire, between his duty toward his native land and his all-consuming passion. He believes that if the king learns of his romance with Rafael, he'll fall into disgrace—and he's probably right. But he's wrong in thinking that if he stays devoted to the monarch, he'll finally obtain the necessary backing to combat the stryges threatening the kingdom of Jaipur. In truth, my sense is that the King of Shadows will never send his troops as reinforcement; he'll never reveal the secret of the death-silver process to a country outside of the Magna Vamypria. I presently know the Immutable well enough to understand that he benefits by dividing and weakening those around him. Sterling was right to say that all his subjects are mere players in his eyes.

"If your irreproachable reputation as squire is so dear to you, get out of the way," I tell him. "It's my last warning."

His face tormented by doubt, Suraj steps aside.

I pass by him without so much as a glance and take off down the hallway.

I walk through the icy streets in long strides. The sheaths that house my wooden stake and my death-silver sword flap against my side; the strap of my bag digs into my shoulder, weighed down by the pistol Sterling gave me; then I touch the precious onyx ring on my finger. These weapons reassure me on this dark night lined by closed shutters and doors.

All of a sudden, I hear a cracking sound at my back.

I turn around, expecting to see Suraj trailing me—ready to confront him.

But no, the street is deserted; the icy cobblestones glisten under the waning moon. The pale orb was full when we first came to the Innocents and has since dwindled inexorably each night, dispensing an ever-rarer light.

I shiver as I think about the fact that December 21, the Night of Shadows, is only ten days away. I pull the hood more snugly around my head. Then I continue to head north. I've decided to take refuge at the Temple. As Suraj said, the area is destroyed, and many dwellings are empty. Thanks to the nighttime, I'll be able to make my way there with no trouble, and I'll devise a plan with a clear head. Maybe I'll dream new dreams that will show me the path to follow. We'll see.

A second cracking sound, closer this time.

Again, I turn on my heel.

I already had the unpleasant feeling of being followed earlier in the day when I went to the cemetery. The same feeling is back, in the dead of night, more alarming than ever.

"Who's there?" I ask.

My voice collides against the deaf and blind facades.

Because I avoided the main roads to get to the Temple neighborhood as inconspicuously as possible, I'm now embedded in a labyrinth of narrow alleyways. I'm not going to cross the Seine at the Pont au Change but farther to the east, across one of the small bridges that straddles the river. Nervously, I finger the royal pass in my shoulder bag, ready to pull it out if any guards of the Royal Watch come to check whether I'm allowed to run around the streets after the curfew. But there's no one about. No armed mortals looking to uphold the law, no immortals hunting down the miserable wretches without shelter.

Still, if I'm really all alone, where is this ominous feeling of dread coming from, this obsessive fear that has only increased since this morning and has now reached its peak?

Maybe I've finally drawn the attention of the Lady of Miracles . . .

Maybe she's come to kidnap me at last, fulfilling the king's wishes . . .

"If you're here, Lady of Miracles, show yourself!" I shout.

Once again my voice resonates in the void. The darkness is so dense in this interlacing of alleyways that I can't make out the cobblestones anymore. The glimmer of the waning moon doesn't descend farther than the icicles hanging from the uneven gutters. Below that, it's pitch black.

I slip my hand into my pocket and take out my tinderbox lighter. I rub it once . . .

Twice . . .

Three times . . .

A flame flickers in the palm of my hand, projecting a trembling halo.

I let out a stifled cry. Here, just yards away from me, stands a man wearing a long black leather coat, his head under a hood.

"Stay back!" I warn him, brandishing the lighter in my left hand and pulling out my sword with my right one.

The man takes a step in my direction, making the same sound that I've already heard several times coming from behind me—the sound of cracking ice.

"Stay back, I said, or I won't hesitate to strike!"

The stranger takes another step forward, loud and determined—mechanical—without an ounce of hesitation.

My breathing speeds up; the cold burns my lungs. Who is this person? A mortal? A vampyre?

As he takes a third step, a supernatural wave of cold seeps through my clothes and answers my question. This icy aura belongs to the Shadows.

"I'm warning you, my sword is made of death-silver."

He continues to advance, stepping over a frozen puddle of water.

"You're asking for it."

I thrust my blade toward the tip of his hood to whisk it off and see the face hiding in that black hole.

Pinned to my sword, the leather hood falls back.

Underneath . . . there's . . . nothing.

The coat's stiff high collar simply stops, with no neck, no head above.

And yet, by some evil spell, the headless body continues to come closer.

I quickly pull the sword from the hood so that I can plant it into the creature's chest.

But the tip collides against a mass as hard as a rock, sending vibrations up to my elbow.

The headless body holds out its black-gloved hands toward me.

"No!" I scream, slashing its chest with the edge of my sword.

Why is the blade only cutting the leather of the coat and not the flesh underneath? I'm dealing with an abomination, after all. The death-silver should go through.

The arms clamp down on my shoulders like a vise, preventing me from wielding my sword.

I'm irresistibly clasped against the chest that I tried to wound, without inflicting any harm.

My face is crushed against the tattered leather, against skin as cold as a statue. The contact is surprisingly soft under my cheek, almost velvety. But the most astonishing thing is the thumping sound against my ear—a throbbing pulsates in this cadaver, not like the beating of an organic heart but mechanical, similar to the gears of a clock.

Quickly, I realize that it's *him*.

Him, the one Blanche de La Roncière promised me would get vengeance when she was in the cart taking her to the gallows.

Him, the one I dreamed about this afternoon, in the secluded clearing of happier days.

"Tristan, I . . . I . . . it's impossible," I stammer. "I saw your body impaled on the Hunting Wall. There was almost nothing left of you but the bones."

In response, the arms clasp me tighter, in a loving . . . deadly . . . embrace.

I once told Tristan that I wanted to stay in the haven of his embrace forever. Now that winter is nearly here, he squeezes me against him, but not to warm me.

To crush me.

"You don't exist anymore, Tristan," I say, gasping for air. "You . . . you're dead."

An echo pierces the silence. It's the sound of my sword and shoulder bag falling onto the cobblestones.

My limbs are so compressed that I almost don't feel them anymore.

The revenant's supernatural heart beats louder and louder against my skull, like an infernal machine, as my own heartbeats begin to slow down.

The fourth card from my tarot reading flashes in my mind—the obstacle card with the grinning skeleton.

The tarot was right. My future will never come to pass, and I'll never reach the Court of Miracles, because Death blocks my path.

Everything's going to end.

Right here in this sordid alleyway.

Forgive me, Paulin; your rebellion was in vain . . .

Forgive me, Bastien; your weasel will not avenge you . . .

Forgive me, Maman; I don't measure up to the hopes you placed in me . . .

"Liberty or death, Jeanne." My dear mother's soft voice resonates deep in my conscience. *"Liberty or death."*

Above my torturer's shoulder, among the immobile constellations, a tiny shooting star whizzes by. A free spark in the middle of this dead sky—small and furtive, just like me.

It's the ultimate trigger, my last chance. I can still regain freedom.

I make myself smaller than ever, completely weasellike, contorting myself enough to pull my shoulders out and slide free of the cape. My battered body falls to the ground, leaving the empty coat in the revenant's arms.

In one leap, I get to my feet. I grab the strap of my shoulder bag and take off like the wind into the urban maze.

"Open up!" I shout, my throat burning.

My cries are lost in the indifferent night.

Behind me, Tristan's footsteps crunch the ice and make the ground shake. He's running too.

I bump against street corners, unable to clearly distinguish my way in the darkness.

The doors against which I pound my fists stay hermetically shut.

"Please, someone open up! I'm one of the king's squires!"

My lungs burning, I tumble onto a long, narrow quay that looks bluish in the moonlight. It's a spot where the bank of the Seine is irregular, with a sheer drop into water as black as that of the Styx.

With one glance, I dash toward the nearest bridge. It seems terribly far away, resembling a mere twig in the night, several hundred yards from the chasm that cuts off my escape. At my back, Tristan's dreaded footsteps seem amplified by an echo, as if there were suddenly several revenants chasing me.

Wild with fear, I spin around, rummaging feverishly in my shoulder bag for the pistol. But my fingers are shaking too much, and the headless body is already on the quay. He's coming straight at me.

I realize now that he's not alone. Four dark silhouettes break through the night. It's the hammering of their boots that I was hearing, not an echo.

Just when Tristan is almost upon me, the four masked figures catch up to him and pull out their daggers. The blades rain down again and again on the revenant's back without slashing him any more than my sword did earlier. But he staggers under the quadruple attack, the soles of his boots slipping on the icy quay . . . until he's at the edge.

The headless body, deprived of a mouth with which to scream, topples into the abyss without a peep. I hear only a brief crash as he hits the dark icy water, before it carries him off in silence.

My heart racing, I turn to face my mysterious saviors.

"Thank you from the bottom of—"

Before I can finish my sentence, a big sack falls over my head, and a heavy weight comes down on the back of my neck.

13

TEARS

I wake up with a horrible headache.

For once, no need to blame it on black bile. I distinctly remember getting whacked, which caused this pounding migraine.

I sit up on the straw mat where I was laid down. As my eyes adjust to the dark, little by little I start to make out my surroundings. I'm in a small windowless room, lit only by a lantern with an anemic flame.

I try to raise my hands to massage my aching neck, but I can't. My wrists are bound.

I'm a prisoner.

The Lady of Miracles has finally captured me, just when I'd decided to escape the Yellow Cat and regain the upper hand so that I could deal with her in my own way. My shoulder bag was removed, along with the pistol I would have used to kill my enemy. Worse: the onyx ring Montfaucon gave me isn't on my finger anymore. I've arrived at the Court of Miracles under the worst circumstances, completely vulnerable and disarmed, my wrists tied. A dreadful sense of failure overwhelms me, even more crushing than the bludgeon that knocked me down earlier.

The door to the cell suddenly squeaks open.

Instinctively, I curl up on the straw mat, expecting to see a grimacing ghoul come in . . .

But it's a man dressed in black who enters the room. Probably one of the lady's henchmen.

"So, you're awake," he states with a slight foreign accent I can't place.

"Who are you? What are you going to do with me? And where is your mistress?"

He doesn't answer. In the dimness of the doorway, I have a hard time distinguishing his features. The only thing I see is the scar that runs across his forehead.

He shuts the door with a bang.

Left alone again, I plunge back into my dark thoughts. The king's plan is unfolding exactly as he foresaw. I played my part as bait to perfection, and the enemy swallowed the lure. I'll have a hard time concealing my identity as a squire. For one thing, I shouted it plenty loud in the streets when the revenant was chasing after me; for another, the royal pass sits in the pocket of the shoulder bag that was taken from me. The Lady of Miracles will probably boast that she caught the Immutable's favorite squire, the one who saved him from ultimate death, in her next leaflet. Maybe she'll try to use me as a hostage to negotiate her crown as vice-queen of Paris. But the king will use me as well, both to locate the precise spot where I am so that he can send in his troops and to capture his rival.

There are only two ways to prevent Louis from getting his hands on the Lady of Miracles' formidable army. I have to escape or die. The first option seems unrealistic, given the situation I'm in. That leaves the second. Sterling implied that the blood link uniting me to the sovereign would extinguish if I perished—and with it, any possibility of tracking me down.

I'm consumed with anxiety when the man in black returns to the room. He helps me to get up and pushes me ahead of him into a dark corridor that I imagine is buried deep in the bowels of Paris. The smell of saltpeter coming off the walls reminds me of the odor in the basement of the Grande Écurie. Here, just as there, total silence. Are we one yard underground or a hundred? Impossible to tell.

We emerge onto a circular room not much bigger than my cell, lit by tall candles planted on iron candelabras. Men dressed in the same pantaloons and black doublet as my jailer stand all around, rooted like statues.

Only one person is seated, on a large chest covered with a tiger pelt. A solemn woman, shrouded in a long dark velvet gown, her face hidden by a black lace veil. Except for the opulent gold jewelry that gleams at her neck and wrists, her attire reminds me of a widow's.

The lady.

It's her.

The one who's terrorized hundreds of thousands of people for weeks now.

The one who named herself after the goddess Hecate, mother of monsters and sorcery.

I'm now just yards away from her, and yet hidden as she is behind her veil, like the moon behind a cloud, she still eludes me.

"My respects, madame," I say hoarsely, trying to buy enough time to find a possible means of escape.

My words reverberate like a lugubrious echo against the walls of the small subterranean room.

The motionless henchmen standing at attention leave me no hope of escape. Are they unrecorded vampyres, ready to bleed me on their mistress's orders? Is the cold of the room due to their presence or just to the season? I don't know how to interpret what my senses perceive anymore.

"Do you plan on sending my head to the Immutable?" I ask, my stomach contracting.

"Nothing of the sort, Diane de Gastefriche," says the voice that filters through the veil, both suave and hoarse, like flowing honey mixed with crushed glass. "You're worth far more alive than dead."

My stomach clenches a little more. I was right to be scared. She wants to use me as leverage. I can't risk having the king exploit our blood link. The lord of the Magna Vampyria must *never ever* become master of the ghouls as well. Montfaucon told me that such power concentrated in his evil hands would ruin the Fronde's chances forever.

Maybe that's what the Arcana with No Name was all about. Having failed to eliminate the lady, I have to die to stop the worst from happening.

"You've already killed thousands of Parisians, so why spare me?" I argue, my throat tight, advocating for my own execution for the sake of the rebels who'll take up the torch. "The king will see this as a sign of weakness in the war you're waging against him. But he'll understand your true power if you send him my head . . . and he'll finally crown yours."

"It's out of the question to send him anything," the lady answers, her uniquely raspy voice bearing a melodious accent. "I'm not stupid enough to risk dealing with the Immutable. Actually, certain mortals are prepared to pay dearly for you."

My lips start to tremble. "Mortals? Which mortals? Am I . . . am I not at the Court of Miracles?"

The woman raises her ring-laden fingers and lifts her veil, revealing a middle-aged face. Her olive complexion doesn't have the spectral whiteness of immortals. The fine crow's-feet around her large black shadowed eyes show that she's still in the grips of time.

"No, you're not at the Court of Miracles," she answers me.

"But where am I, then?"

She shrugs. "Here, there, what does it matter? The Lachryma gather wherever they please, and never twice in the same place."

As she says *Lachryma* . . . I realize there's a teardrop by the woman's right eye. Not a real one but a tattooed motif, inked onto her skin. The same symbol appears on my jailer's face, and, as I suddenly notice, on everyone in the room. I remember that I've already seen this strange tattoo: Orfeo has the same one at the corner of his right eye.

"You . . . you aren't a vampyre," I stammer. "And you're not the Lady of Miracles."

"Perish the thought!" the woman says, grinning. She uses her index and pinkie finger to make the sign of the devil, the same one some villagers at Butte-aux-Rats made to ward off the evil eye. "I'm Ravenna de Tarella, godmother of the Lachryma, the most powerful organized crime syndicate in Paris."

I remember my conversations with Montfaucon when he explained that Orfeo's head must have once belonged to a Neapolitan bandit . . . just like the ones who surround me. I'm not at all where I thought I was, which totally upends my resolutions. No more asking to die. The hope of getting out alive is reborn from its ashes.

I look around at the room more closely. As small as it is, it's set up like a throne room, and the godmother has the bearing of a queen as she sits on the chest. As for the name she mentioned, Tarella, I've already heard it at the Court of Shadows. It belongs to the Marquise de Vauvalon's lover, the very marquise for whom I was forced to puncture poor Toinette.

"Are you by any chance related to Count Marcantonio de Tarella?" I ask.

"He's my great-great-great-uncle," the woman answers.

"Oh, what a strange coincidence," I say, forcing myself to smile as I take a huge gamble. "The count and I get along wonderfully well."

It's a big lie. The first time I crossed paths with the Italian courtier was at the end of summer, during the gallant hunt in the gardens of Versailles. He and Edmée de Vauvalon had tried to bleed me on the spot. I survived thanks to Alexandre de Mortange's unexpected intervention, as well as the king's when he came on the scene. But the godmother doesn't have to know all that, does she?

"Well, I detest him, that *bastardo!*" she says, dashing my hopes of using the count's name to my advantage. "The plague be on that ancestor. As for that noble title he's appropriated, it's a vile fraud, for he was born a commoner just like me, in the village of Tarella, in Sicily."

Anxious not to worsen my predicament, I hurry to change the subject.

"Please excuse my faux pas. And also for having confused you with the Lady of Miracles. I was mixed up. I thought I had landed at her court."

The Sicilian's brows, accentuated by a dark pencil line, go up disdainfully.

"For your information, the real Court of Miracles disappeared centuries ago. It's precisely in this vacant space that we, the Lachryma, have rushed into—in the obscure impasses, in the heart of forgotten alleys, through cracks in the walls. The only court of bandits that resides in Paris is ours. An exiled court, always on the move, always elusive. An international brotherhood made up of members from Naples and Sicily but also many other vice-kingdoms of the Magna Vampyria: Savoy, Austria, Portugal, Prussia, the United Provinces, France of course—Guzeppi, who led you to me, is even Maltese! For generations, we've collected ransom money, looted, and killed in the background."

As the godmother speaks, I realize that the outlaws surrounding me present all kinds of costumes and hairstyles, mirroring the rich diversity of the European continent. Behind the name of the Magna Vampyria, giving the illusion of one single empire, there is a myriad of peoples and cultures, held together by the iron yoke of Versailles.

That being said, the godmother may boast that her cosmopolitan court has replaced the old Court of Miracles, but I bet that she must have been just as surprised as the police and the honest people when the lady mysteriously regrouped in the depths of Paris, centuries after the historic court disbanded. This unexpected competition in the area of criminal activity and terror surely caught her off guard.

"When it comes to ransoms, lootings, and killings, it seems to me that the Lady of Miracles doesn't pull any punches," I point out.

The godmother's face twists in fury. I hit a nerve.

"May the Shadows swallow that demon," she swears. "Ever since she showed up, the tavern- and innkeepers balk at paying the protection money we're due. Even the Grand Châtelet doesn't fork over its tribute."

I remember the Templar tavern keeper. At first, he mistook us for tax collectors who'd come to get the "protection money." At the time, I thought it meant yet another tax requested by the Faculty, but that's not the case. It's the price to be paid in exchange for not being hassled by the bandits.

As for the godmother's claims about the police, I'm confused.

"The Grand Châtelet pays you protection money?"

"Of course! Every job deserves compensation, including keeping the slums under the regime's heel." The godmother sizes me up from under the heavy makeup of her lids. "We, the Lachryma, do the dirty work for the Royal Guards. We slice the throats of the miserable wretches who shout a little too loudly about their rebellion against the Magna Vampyria. We bring back ladies of the night who try to flee from their brothels. Sometimes, we eliminate unrecorded vampyres who loiter in the streets, and we fulfill contracts placed on the heads of the overly ambitious."

I can't believe my ears. When he greeted us at the Grand Châtelet, L'Esquille was careful not to breathe a word about consorting with this pack of scoundrels. I bet the king is clueless as to how his capital is being "run." Without a doubt, Paris is rotten to the core, and whether it's because of the claws of power or because of the gangsters, it's always the commoners who bear the brunt of it.

The woman slips her long purple-polished fingernails into the pocket of her gown and takes out a cigar.

So that's the reason for her hoarse voice. It's raspy from tobacco.

One of her lieutenants, a tall blond fellow, slavishly hurries over to activate a lighter under her red lips.

"Thank you, Wilfried." The tip of the cigar reddens, releasing an acrid smoke that quickly saturates the confined air of the room. "Where were we? Ah yes, the Lady of Miracles . . . you, Gastefriche, squire to the king, must have realized that fear brings order. That's how your master has been able to reign for three centuries, *vero o no?* What works for an empire is just as efficient for a city. A healthy dose of fear assures lasting stability, and that's the precise specialty of the Lachryma."

Greedily, she draws on her cigar. It's like she's inhaling the resources of the people with as much avarice as the vampyres swill their blood.

"Fear keeps a society in step," she goes on. "But terror, on the other hand, only brings chaos and disorder. These last few months have been a pitiful example. The city dwellers ruined by the ghoul attacks no longer pay our tax. They spend the little money they have left on worthless amulets. That inept L'Esquille is totally in over his head. The confrontation between the King of Shadows and the Lady of Miracles will end up consuming all of Paris!"

She rounds her lips into an O and exhales a series of smoke rings. The circles rise to the ceiling, where they unravel, foreshadowing the smoke of the impending disaster.

"It's time for our clan to find new digs," she concludes. "I've thought about relocating to Madrid; there is a lot of gold there coming from the Americas, and several of my men speak Spanish. We've always been nomads, so we're used to moving around and taking our treasure with us."

She places a hand on the chest and caresses it lovingly. She may have said "*our treasure*," but her possessive voice implied "*my* treasure."

"The gold of the Lachryma follows me everywhere," she whispers. "It will leave this city with me, before the Night of Shadows, without waiting for Paris to be reduced to ashes."

I ponder her words, which taste more bitter than the suffocating smell from the cigar. Until now, I considered the fourth estate as an entity, the solid mass of the oppressed. Now I realize that some commoners managed to turn the laws of the Magna Vampyria to their advantage, like these gangsters who deal with the royal police and scorn the sequester. Born of commoners, these parasites now attack their own. When a city ceases to feed them, they head to another, like fleas that jump from one dog to the next.

"Why have you abducted me if you can't be bothered with Paris anymore and if you're getting ready to leave?" I toss out.

"Oh, simple, because you represent a situation that's far too lucrative to pass up. There's always room for a few more gold bars in my coffer. I told you, some are prepared to pay a handsome price for your head. You see, the key conspirators of the La Roncière plot may have been cremated at the Gibbet of Montfaucon, but lots of rich, powerful lords are left who'll never forgive you for thwarting their scheme."

Hearing the La Roncière name instantly reminds me of the headless body. A long shiver runs down my spine as I picture the revenant's black coat crashing into the icy water of the Seine.

"Are you the one who brought Tristan de La Roncière's decapitated body back from the dead to torture me?" I ask.

Again, Ravenna makes a conjuring gesture, her countless bracelets jangling.

"Never! The Lachryma don't fool around with alchemy and even less with necromancy. In case you hadn't noticed, my men saved you from that creature who came from who knows where. You say it was Tristan de La Roncière? Your imagination may be playing tricks on you, for I was told it was only a nocturnal abomination, like the ones that pop up with increased frequency in this damned city."

I grit my teeth, certain that I didn't imagine anything. I recognized Tristan's embrace, so similar to the one in my dream . . . it was him, I'm sure of it.

"We didn't need any magic to find you," the godmother says. "Your presence at the Yellow Cat Inn wasn't a secret. I simply had you followed until the moment to kidnap you was right."

Once again, I taste the bitter irony of the situation. It's no wonder I had the impression I was being followed those last hours. And this is what the king's wangling has led to. By using me as bait, by spreading the name of the place where I was lodging, he'll only have succeeded in delivering me to the latest conspirators who want him destroyed.

"Who?" I ask. "Who's buying my head?"

"I haven't decided yet, *cara mia*. I'm going to let the bids go higher. That's why I've been talking to you. Tell me, what price do you think your family is ready to pay for your life?"

I suddenly realize the godmother's long monologue was aimed at showing me that my future rests in her hands and to pressure me to extort money from what she imagines is my family.

"Since you're so well informed, you must know I'm an orphan," I tell her.

"I do, but don't you have close relatives who'd be ready to cough up?"

"Sorry to disappoint you; the barony of Gastefriche is among the poorest."

And poorer still, the village of Butte-aux-Rats, where I'm actually from, you old buzzard! I think.

The pack leader pouts, obviously disappointed.

"*Che peccato*, that's too bad . . . I should have known better just by looking at the only pieces of jewelry you were wearing, that plated signet ring and the cheap onyx one. They landed in my chest, but they're just droplets of water in the Lachryma fortune." She sighs. "Which means I'll have to turn you over to your worst enemies. Take comfort; while you wait you'll get a taste of the Lachryma's legendary hospitality."

She snaps her fingers, her bracelets jingling.

"Guzeppi, take her back to her cell!"

Scar-face takes my arm and drags me out of the room.

In the depths of my strange imprisonment, I start to lose track of time.

Now and then, the godmother's men put a sack over my head and lead me through corridors and alleyways. I see nothing. I only regain my sight once I've arrived in a new cell, the walls sometimes made of lime, sometimes stone, sometimes just hard clay. There are never any windows, nothing that allows me to determine if it's day or night. As for the meals, I don't know if I'm having lunch or dinner anymore: a hunk of bread topped with cheese is what I get every time. I'm bound to the Lachryma's daily cycle of migrations, this group of exiled bandits who, generation upon generation, have never slept twice in the same spot.

Sleep is my only escape. I'm desperately waiting for some premonition, some sign that will point me toward a hypothetical salvation. But nothing comes to me other than amorphous dreams where my family's smiling faces merge with those of grimacing ghouls.

Often, I wonder how far Suraj and Hélénaïs are in their investigation. Did they end up finding conclusive clues? And have the police under L'Esquille found a lead? I hope not.

"Here's your food, chestnut-flour gruel," Guzeppi tells me as he slides a bowl full of unappetizing glop in front of me. "You'll have to make do. The king stopped the wheat supply to Paris."

"What day are we?"

My jailer gives me a sidelong glance.

Under his scar and sinister appearance, he's younger than I first thought. He must be about twenty-five years old, even if life has aged him beyond his years. He exudes a rude charm with his black eyes and dark hair. In spite of his crude manners, he's treated me with a certain respect since my capture.

"Well, I guess I can bring you up to speed since you won't be with us anymore after tomorrow," he says. "Today is December fifteenth."

He closes the door and double-locks it.

The gruel is insipid, and yet it leaves a sour taste in my mouth as I think about what I've just learned. It seems the Immutable made good on his threat. One week before the Night of Shadows, he's stopped food supplies to the capital. As a way to dismiss the Lady of Miracles' demands for elevation. As a final declaration of war against his enemy. Ravenna of Sicily's prediction is about to come true: Paris and her people will be crushed, caught between two megalomaniac immortals, each ready to do anything to supplant the other. As for me, I probably won't be alive to witness the cataclysm.

If Guzeppi told me the truth, I'll be handed over to those who want to see me defeated as soon as tomorrow.

"Who bought my head?" I ask him when he comes back to take my empty bowl.

"I can't tell you that. I swore on my tear."

Instinctively, he touches the tattoo at the corner of his right eye. The gesture reminds me of the godmother's bizarre conjurations. These gangsters who live on the razor's edge, in defiance of governments and their laws, are strangely superstitious.

"What does the tear represent?" I ask softly.

Guzeppi raises his black eyes toward me, and for the first time, I believe I detect a glimmer of emotion.

"It's the tattoo every Lachryma receives during his baptism of tears. It marks entry into the brotherhood," he explains. "We have to swear never to cry again, no matter what hardships we go through . . . no matter what crimes we commit." The young Maltese's face, which had softened for an instant, hardens again. "Our loyalty is to the godmother and her alone, with no regrets and no remorse."

I think about Orfeo, who also bears this tattoo. In another life, he probably swore the same allegiance.

"And what happens to those who break the oath?" I ask reluctantly.

"We chop off their tongue and decapitate them. Then we toss everything into a mass grave," Guzeppi says.

I shiver as I think about the suture marks around Orfeo's neck, about his inability to say a single word. It seems the Lachryma threw his head into one of the communal graves in Paris, just because he wanted to leave them. But those who defy sorcery and alchemy are no doubt clueless that their victim rose from the dead, brought back to life by unknown hands in an assemblage of body parts stitched together . . .

"In the long history of the Lachryma, there's been only one traitor who's managed to flee in one piece," Guzeppi mumbles, echoing my thoughts.

A scowl deforms his face, a mixture of hate and contempt.

"That would be your friend, Marcantonio de Tarella. Since the century that he was transmuted, that silk-stockinged piece of garbage has escaped our vendetta."

14

TRANSACTION

I'm perspiring buckets under the sack that covers my head.

Unlike all the other times combined, today I've been dragged a longer distance. The Lachryma must have chosen a remote and secret place to carry out the transaction that concerns me. Judging by the hammering of boots around me, the godmother has flanked me with a sizable escort. Guzeppi guides me, holding my arm.

"Don't make any noise," he suddenly whispers in my ear.

"Why?"

"We're about to go through an underground passage only known to us. Even if it's daylight outside, when ghouls are supposed to be sleeping in their lairs, better not to wake them."

As he says this, his hand reaches under the sack to gag my mouth with a scarf, as a precaution. He himself stays silent, leaving my imagination to wander as we move forward. Where are they taking me? To the outer edges of Paris? I tried to sleep as much as possible to gather all my strength. Whoever it is I'm being brought to, I'm determined to give them a hard time, even if my wrists are bound and the outcome doesn't look promising.

As we leave the underground depths, a cool breeze rushes under the edge of the sack that blinds me. When I think we've finally reached our destination, we start walking again.

I prick my ears and listen for the noises of the city. The sounds seem softened, muffled. I only hear the whistling of the cold wind. Its frosted breath slips right through the moth-eaten coat the bandits tossed over my shoulders, seeping into the core of my bones.

Under the soles of my boots, cobblestone streets give way to loose, crunching soil. Several times, I trip on obstacles that feel like roots and I have to grab hold of Guzeppi's arm so I don't tumble.

"We're here," he suddenly says.

He removes the sack that covers my head, then the gag.

After my long confinement, I'm inebriated by the fresh air and blinded by the daylight.

My eyes take several seconds to adjust to the dazzling white. The landscape around me is completely immaculate, and the crunching I heard under my footsteps was that of freshly fallen snow.

We find ourselves at a crossroads in the middle of a forest. I count eight paths that fan out in a star-shaped configuration, white furrows visible between the frost-covered tree trunks. In the middle of the junction stands a stone obelisk topped with a vulture statue, its wings frosted in ice. Fog clings to the naked branches weighed down by snow. Even though it's impossible to determine the position of the sun in the clouded sky, my rural instincts tell me the fog is morning mist. There's not a soul in sight. In this cottony silence, the bustling city seems to have disappeared, as if it never existed.

"We've crossed over to the other side of the outer ramparts," I whisper.

"Our client prefers to do business here, in the Bois de Boulogne, without needing to engage in small talk with the border-customs officers," Guzeppi says.

I notice he's wearing a black scarf, hiding the upper half of his face, same as the other six bandits accompanying us.

As for the client he's referring to . . . I see him arriving in the distance, aboard a four-horse-drawn carriage that cuts through the fog of the center path. As the vehicle approaches, I realize the two coachmen are also masked, along with the four armed men standing on the foot-board at the rear. Unlike the Lachryma, these men aren't wearing the same simple cotton scarves with holes for the eyes but custom-made velvet masks. As the sacrificial lamb, I'm the only one whose face is exposed. So be it: I won't lower my head. I raise my chin, letting the wind tousle my gray hair at the back of my neck and the snowflakes cover my head.

Oh, Maman, lend me your courage, for I need it more than ever.

The horses stop at the end of the path, fifteen yards away from us, their hooves jammed into the snow up to their pasterns. Their nostrils let out long jets of vapor into the frosty air.

A gloved hand parts the thick velvet curtain hanging from the pan-eless carriage window. The person inside is dressed in a rich dark-green leather coat lined with mink, a plumed hat on his head. The top of his face is also hidden behind a velvet half mask, revealing only his narrow, smooth chin.

"That's her!" he says. "I wanted to come and make sure for myself."

"Delighted that you know me," I say loudly. "But I, monsieur, cannot place you."

The thin-lipped mouth scowls under the mask in a hideous grin.

"Impertinent child, if you only knew who you're talking to."

"Well, you've hit the nail on the head. I don't know."

"Just because you have a few drops of the Immutable's blood run-ning in your veins doesn't make you superior to me. My quarters of nobility go back three times as far as yours."

"No need to have quarters of nobility reaching who knows how far back to grasp the basic rules of courtesy. A gentleman worthy of that name is supposed to remove his hat in front of a lady. With your hat *and* your mask, you're doubly rude. How terribly uncouth."

"I . . . I'll make you swallow your insolence," the mysterious lord chokes out.

His four henchmen jump to the ground, their boots kicking up snow powder.

They draw their rifles and point them in my direction.

"*Lentamente!*" Guzeppi intervenes. "No one touches the merchandise before paying for it. Show us the gold first, then we'll hand over the girl."

The five other Lachrymas pull guns out of their coats and aim them at their counterparts.

The two parties hold each other at gunpoint under the inert eye of the vulture affixed to the top of the obelisk.

"Have one of your men bring the payment to the middle of the junction," Guzeppi orders. "And one of us will bring the hostage."

From the safe haven of his carriage, the lord gestures with his gloved hand.

The strongest of his henchmen takes out a burlap bag from the luggage hold and brings it to the middle of the star, at the foot of the obelisk. He drops it with a thud in the snow, then unties the knot to expose its contents. Bars of gold glisten weakly in the morning fog.

"No dirty tricks. The full amount better be there," Guzeppi warns nervously.

As the henchman takes out the gold bars to count them one by one, I take his master to task again.

"I'm flattered you're paying such a high price for me," I say, my breath giving off a cloud of mist into the icy air. "But it's unfortunate you have to fork over so much money. It would have cost you a lot less had Tristan de La Roncière settled the score, free of charge, a few nights ago."

In my dire circumstances, the least bit of information I can extract may help me to negotiate for my life or, at least, find out in whose name I'm dying.

His lips widen in a cruel smile that confirms he's totally aware of my misadventures.

"You crossed paths with the revenant and managed to get away?" he says. "Witch that you are. But you'll get what you deserve. I'll see to it you don't escape from him a second time. I'll bring you to him, feet and wrists bound. You won't perish by my hand but by his. Tristan de La Roncière will strangle you, do you hear?"

My heart speeds up as I remember the deadly embrace on the quays of the Seine. The prospect of being in the revenant's monstrous grip again tears my soul. Oh, the unnatural combination of desire and death . . .

"I'm sorry to dash your hopes, but you're too late," I say, wanting to sound confident, but with a trembling voice. "Tristan sank straight to the bottom of the Seine."

The lord's smile changes to dry laughter, sounding like a rattle.

"You poor, ignorant girl. Thinking you could get rid of him so easily. You'll see Tristan again, I assure you, for that's the nature of revenants— they return, again and again, until they've gotten their revenge. This one has a lock of your hair in his chest, sewn right into his alchemical heart. He'll find you wherever you are."

I'm abruptly reminded of Blanche de La Roncière and how she bit into my scalp, yanking strands of hair with her teeth. That attack had nothing to do with desperate rage, as I had thought. It was a cold, calculated move, intended to gather a key ingredient for the ritual that bestowed a monstrous kind of life into Tristan's body.

"Who . . . who are you?" I stammer, the wind whipping my hair against my cheeks. The very hair that binds me to the revenant and he to me, a diabolical love token. "Are you the one who brought Tristan back from the dead? What did you do with his corpse? Last time I saw him on the Hunting Wall, there was nothing left of him but his skeletal remains."

The lord keeps his lips sealed. All my previous prodding forced his back to the wall, but now he's pulled himself together again. He's said enough.

"Twelve gold bars. It's all here," Guzeppi says behind me. "Let's do the exchange. But careful, no hasty gestures. My men are trigger happy."

Someone pushes me forward.

Try as I may to pull on the bindings that hinder my wrists, they're too tight. I lock my knees, but my boots still slip in the snow. With each step, I get closer to the obelisk, to the mound of gold, and to the masked thug waiting for me on the other side.

"Hand her over," he orders Guzeppi.

He gets ready to receive me.

At that exact moment, an explosion pierces the silence. A red hole spreads on the large hand the man extended toward me, and he shrieks in pain.

And then everything happens quickly. Guzeppi gives me a big shove and hits the ground. His men shoot their guns. The lord's men respond with heavy fire.

Sick with fear, I start to crawl, my elbows covered in bruises under the sleeves of my shirtfront, my hindered palms scraping the frozen roots. The snow gets into my eyes, the shouts of the combatants drill into my ears, the pungent scent of gunpowder burns my nostrils.

The edge of the forest is just yards away . . .

"Diane, over here," a clear voice says, filtering through the tree trunks, almost inaudible in the middle of the pandemonium.

I raise my head, scared by this voice that's come out of nowhere and that I would recognize anywhere.

"Naoko?"

I blink furiously to chase away the snowflakes that are blinding me and can just make out a small horse hidden behind some trees at the edge of the nearest path. The mount is just a few yards off from me, but its dappled gray coat blends so well with the snow and fog that no one saw it. It's Calypso, Naoko's mare. Naoko is perched on its back, wrapped in a long light-beige hooded coat. She's holding a pistol in one hand, the one I'm guessing she used to set off the hostilities when she shot the bearer of gold. She reaches out to me with her other hand.

I get to my feet in one leap as the firestorm of bullets continues behind me, and I run toward Naoko to grab her extended arm with my two bound hands. I may be petite, but Naoko isn't much larger.

She groans as she helps me up, holding fast to Calypso's mane so she doesn't topple.

I'm barely positioned behind Naoko when she spurs her horse. Since my bound wrists prevent me from holding on to anything, I compensate by squeezing my thighs against the mare's pulsating flanks. The snowy ground on the path is slippery beneath us. The tree branches fuse above our heads.

The echoing gunfire subsides with each stride that heads toward freedom, toward life, toward . . .

Suddenly, the whistling of a bullet reverberates behind me.

Calypso whinnies in howling pain.

I feel the mare's body collapse under me.

Hurtled forward, Naoko and I tumble in a somersault.

It feels like all my bones are breaking as I fall, the snow doing little to soften the impact. Stunned, my eyes and mouth full of powdery snow, I don't have time to gather my wits when a set of hands brutally grabs the back of my neck.

"No more running, *cagna*," Guzeppi whispers, his warm breath against my frozen ear.

He forces me to my feet.

A few yards behind me, the mare's body rests on its quivering flank, losing blood from the bullet hole. Guzeppi points his gun toward the horse and puts an end to its life with a shot to the head.

Farther off, at the foot of the obelisk, the bodies of five men struck down by the gunfire lie in the snow. As for the carriage, it's gone, having disappeared into the fog.

I blink to clear my tears, along with the melted snowflakes, and lower my eyes.

Only then do I see Naoko's lifeless body, twisted awkwardly, resting on winter's shroud. Her fallen hood exposes her porcelain face, frozen, whiter than snow.

"No!" I scream.

A sack descends over my head, stifling my cries and blocking my sight.

If the trip over seemed long, the trip back is interminable. On the way here, all my senses were alert under the hood as I tried to figure out the itinerary that my jailers were taking me on. I steeled my will as we moved forward, prepping to save my skin.

Now all my courage has drained. Knowing I'm to blame for Naoko's death kills me. The Eye of the Innocents was right: I'm damned. Death imprinted my palm with its hallmark at birth; Death manifested itself in my tarot reading as an obstacle that I would never clear. Wherever I go, it extends its shadow all around me. In the past, in the Auvergne, it mowed down all those I loved. Not long ago, it gave me a weapon to kill a boy I loved in spite of myself. Today, it's taken my only friend at Versailles.

I'm the one who should have died this morning, not Naoko.

Sister Vermillonne taught me that what we regret most when we take stock of our lives is not having spent enough time with those we love. Naoko was the sister I never had. Orfeo could have become a new brother. These flesh and blood human beings were my treasure, and I let them down. To serve the abstract ideal of the Fronde, I abandoned them and threw myself headlong into a vile city. How I regret it all now.

"Back to square one," Guzeppi says, removing the sack.

Is it the same cell?

Is it another?

I don't want to know.

My hair damp with melted snow, I collapse on the straw mat, imploring sleep to spirit me away.

15

CONTRACT

"Jeanne?"

I turn around on my moldy straw mat.

I don't want any dreams, any visions of the past or future.

I want only to burrow into the dark ocean of forgetfulness.

"Jeanne, it's me."

I groan, half-drowsy, wanting to chase away this female voice that's pestering me. It sounds like Naoko, but she's gone forever. Tristan already haunts me, and I don't need the ghost of my best friend coming back to twist the knife of guilt into my fresh open wound.

"Jeanne, do you hear me?"

I quickly open my eyes onto the dark, narrow cell where Guzeppi left me without even a candle for a light.

This tenuous voice isn't coming from inside my head but from the wall next to me.

Feverishly, I touch the rough wall, pushing my cheek against it so I can better hear.

There, between two disjointed bricks, my bound hands meet up with a gap.

"Naoko?" I say softly.

"Oh, Jeanne," a whisper comes from the crack. "I'm so sorry."

Sorry? My heart explodes from joy. I can barely refrain from shouting.

"You . . . you aren't dead!" I stammer, my eyes welling with tears.

"I think I just fainted, then I came to in this unlit room. Honestly, I wish I'd slept a little longer. Waking up is rough." She laughs softly, but I'm guessing it's to tamp down the pain she's feeling. "I . . . I didn't break anything. At least, I don't think so. How are you doing?"

I place my palms on the cold bricks. I so wish I could hug Naoko to comfort her.

"I feel a thousand times better now that I hear your voice. I was afraid I'd lost you in the Bois de Boulogne."

"What happened?"

"A bullet struck down Calypso."

A whimper comes from the crack. Naoko was as attached to her mare as I am to Typhon.

"She didn't suffer," I assure her, my heart heavy as I think about the bullet that finished off the mare. "But tell me, how did you track me down?"

Naoko swallows back her tears. Everything is completely silent and dark around me. We only have to whisper to communicate, so it's easy to imagine that my friend is right beside me, no wall separating us.

"Orfeo alerted me," she explains.

"Orfeo?"

"Ever since you left Versailles, he and I have become . . . friends. The grand equerry is so busy running the school and attending meetings at the palace that I spend all my time in Orfeo's company. We've learned to communicate using his slate board and chalk. He took me to the farthest corners of the Grande Écurie's basement so I could stretch my legs. And he played me magnificent tunes on his harmonica so I wasn't sad about not hearing the birds sing in the sky."

Naoko's words are full of tenderness, just like the gentle sensitivity that unknowingly nestles in Orfeo's monstrous body. Not long ago, I was also moved by the melodies he played on his harmonica. They give voice to a sensitivity that he can't express with words.

"I recognized Italian operatic arias," Naoko says stirringly, as if she were hearing the tunes. "Monteverdi . . . Cavalli . . . Vivaldi . . . what symphonies he's able to create with such a small instrument."

Those names don't mean anything to me, the commoner who has never set foot in the opera. But the way Naoko speaks about it is moving.

"Did you know that Orfeo can escape at will from the Grande Écurie whenever he wants?" she asks. "He just goes up the chimney flues."

"That's where I met him for the first time," I say, remembering. "Up on the school roof."

"Well, as it happens, he was on the rooftop two weeks ago, soon after you left. He saw two Swiss Guards take down Tristan de La Roncière's body from the Hunting Wall. Nothing unusual so far, especially since the corpse was long frozen and the ravens couldn't peck away at it anymore. But instead of tossing his remains into the communal grave, as usual, the Swiss Guards discreetly transferred them into a ragman's cart, which hurried off. Orfeo's curiosity was piqued, so he followed the cart for miles and miles. He's swift as a deer, endowed with supernatural strength, as you yourself know. Eventually he reached the junction with the vulture obelisk, in the heart of the Bois de Boulogne, where the so-called ragman met up with the masked occupants of a carriage. He gave them the corpse. Orfeo didn't see anything more since it was nearly dawn and he had to return to the depths of the Grande Écurie. Once back, he told me everything with the help of his slate board."

I ponder these words. Although Orfeo strikes a chord in me more than most human beings, he's still a nocturnal abomination governed by the power of the Shadows. He fears daylight the same way vampyres and ghouls do. As for the mysterious carriage that collected Tristan's body, no need to be a genius to know it was the same carriage we encountered this morning.

VICTOR DIXEN

"I immediately suspected the nostalgic La Roncière conspirators were behind this bizarre fetishism," Naoko continues. "I warned the grand equerry. But he gruffly dismissed my worries, as he does so well, barking that the conspiracy was foiled and that he had more pressing matters to deal with. He's got a lot on his plate, what with the preparations to attack the Lady of Miracles. As I said, the king requests his presence at the palace every night since he's an expert ghoul hunter and can assess the situation. He often ends up sleeping at the palace during the day, after the Hunting Wall is closed. So I was condemned to languish in my cell with my dreadful premonition."

"Your premonition was right, Naoko," I say, shivering. "By whatever means of sorcery, Tristan's remains were brought back to life. I confronted him on the quays of Paris, before the bandits captured me."

A few seconds in silence go by in the heavy, sticky darkness. I shiver as I think about Tristan's embrace. The masked lord's prediction frightens me even more: *Revenants—they return, again and again, until they've gotten their revenge.*

"I also had a premonition you'd be kidnapped," Naoko goes on. "Five days ago, when Montfaucon breezed into the Grande Écurie, he told me they'd lost track of you in Paris. He got the information from the king himself, who got it from Suraj."

"Those two correspond every night by way of a crow," I say bitterly. "Suraj accused me of having deserted the team, is that it?"

"He just wrote that you wished to continue the investigation on your own. The grand equerry was fine with the explanation." Naoko heaves a worried sigh. "It filled me with anxiety to know you were alone in an unfamiliar city while conspirators were still prowling in the area. What if something happened to you? I asked Orfeo to return to the vulture junction to try and gather information. But every night, the woods were empty . . . until the other evening, when the carriage appeared again. Men on foot, also masked, came to meet the vehicle. Orfeo overheard their conversation from his perch in a tree. He heard the name *Diane de Gastefriche* and the sum of twelve gold bars in exchange for

206

your head. The name *Lord Serpent* was also mentioned, the alias for the person who ordered the abduction and who would collect the hostage himself. The transaction was supposed to take place a few hours later, in the morning. Orfeo barely had time to return to Versailles to tell me, scribbling like mad on his slate board. I had no one to warn. The grand equerry was spending yet another day at the palace, behind the closed wall. As for Orfeo, despite all his goodwill, he was physically unable to brave the daylight. I could rely only on myself. Orfeo went against his master's orders to keep me locked up. He gave me a pistol and let me come aboveground. The school was just coming awake, so I discreetly saddled Calypso and set out at full speed toward the Bois de Boulogne. The rest, you already know."

My heart breaks between gratitude for Naoko, who didn't hesitate one second to come to my rescue, and guilt at having dragged her, in spite of myself, into this inescapable trap.

"You shouldn't have," I say.

"Hush. You'd have done the same for me. That's what friends do."

Even if Naoko can't see me, I nod, my chest swelling with almost painful appreciation. As a solitary hunter, I've long believed that I could count only on myself. Now I know how wrong I was. Friendship can move mountains. I'll do everything in my power to be deserving of Naoko's.

"If you only knew how much I've missed you," I say, mostly at a loss for words.

"You, too, Jeanne. Now we're reunited, which makes me happy even if I thought that would happen in Versailles instead of . . ." She pauses. ". . . uh, where are we, exactly?"

"Somewhere in Paris, I fear. The Lachryma are constantly on the move, going from hideout to hideout."

"The Lachryma? Is that what your kidnappers call themselves? Why such a strange name?"

"Because they all have a teardrop tattoo at the corner of their right eye . . . like Orfeo."

I clamp my hand over my mouth, scared that I've suddenly spoken too loudly, but no one opens the door to see what's going on in my cell.

"Orfeo was once a Lachryma," I continue, lowering my voice. "Or at least, his head belonged to a member of the gang." I have a sudden flicker of hope. "The Lachryma use a secret passageway to cross under the outer ramparts. Maybe Orfeo will use it, too, and track us down?"

Naoko gives a resigned sigh. "His head may have belonged to one of those bandits, but it doesn't remember anything, I tell you."

"It remembers the operatic arias you told me about, though."

"Those notes aren't etched in his head but in his soul, which will always be Italian."

I ponder what Naoko just said. She's right. It's delusional to expect Orfeo's help. In going from life to death, he lost not only the ability to speak but probably the memory of the Lachryma and their ways as well.

Now I detect a clicking sound coming from behind the wall. The door to the adjoining cell was just flung open.

"Naoko!" I yell. "Don't touch her!"

In response, the door to my own cell opens with a din.

"After what happened this morning, you still dare to order us around?" Guzeppi says. "You've got a lot of nerve."

"Do whatever you want to me, but leave my friend out of it."

"That'll be up to the godmother to decide."

He grabs my arm and drags me out of the cell.

Naoko's waiting for us in the doorway, hands bound like mine, a man also standing guard by her side. There are long scratches on her porcelain cheeks and a big black-and-blue bruise on her forehead. But her bun is intact, solidly locked by an intricate array of hairpins.

Our guards push us down some unfamiliar corridors until we reach a new, improvised throne room.

The godmother of the Lachryma presides here, dressed in her Sicilian mourning attire, seated on top of her tiger-skin-covered treasure chest. As with the first time she granted me an audience, her lieutenants stand at attention along the walls.

"Here they are, *Madrina*," Guzeppi says. "The ones responsible for Gigi's and Cesare's deaths."

The godmother lifts her veil to size us up with her somber, impenetrable, heavily made-up eyes.

"Which one of you fired the gun?" she asks.

"I did, madame," Naoko says, bravely stepping forward.

"She fired, yes, but not on your men," I speak up. "The people from the other party killed them, Lord Serpent's followers. My friend isn't guilty. She didn't shed a drop of the Lachrymas' blood."

The gang leader raises her gold-ringed hands to stop me from speaking.

"*Taci*! I was asking to offer congratulations. One must be mighty accurate to hit a target in such fog."

My protests die in my throat. Adept as she is in meditation and martial arts, Naoko is an amazing shot. I'd already noticed her sharp reflexes at the Grande Écurie, under the guise of her porcelain-doll looks.

"As for Gigi and Cesare, it's unfortunate," the godmother says. "But those are the risks of the trade, and they knew that. We won't shed tears for them."

I nod, remembering the Lachryma's harsh code of honor that Guzeppi told me about. Around us, none of the faces betray any sadness, as if the single tattooed tear was enough to express all the mourning and sorrow.

"Besides, our brothers didn't die in vain," the godmother continues. "During the skirmish, the client took off without his gold. I requisitioned it in the name of the Lachryma, the price for the blood of our own."

She gestures toward the burlap bag at her feet, where gold bars glisten. Some of them still have dried brown bloodstains.

"We've nabbed a fortune without having to hand over the hostage," the godmother says gleefully. "Even better, we captured a second girl." She observes Naoko, lingering on the precious mother-of-pearl hairpins decorating her bun and the fine silk dress peeking from under her coat. "You, the Asian beauty, look like you're worth your weight in gold. Tell me, who are you? Do you have family ready to open its coffers?"

"My name is Naoko Takagari. I'm the daughter of the daytime ambassador from Japan at Versailles." Naoko lowers her eyes beneath her bangs. "But I don't know how much my father would be willing to pay."

My friend told me about her detached father. Ever since her mother died in childbirth, he's never paid her much attention. Throughout her childhood and adolescence, the secret of the evilmouth prevented Naoko from getting close to anyone, even her own progenitor. In many ways, she's really just an orphan like me.

The godmother scowls. "Everyone knows diplomats are the stingiest. I hate doing business with them. It's always a series of never-ending hassles. The less I deal with Versailles, the happier I am. Which is why I don't intend to negotiate for his squire's head with the king. We'll have to do something else with the two of you."

She rises from her makeshift throne, unfolding a much taller body than I had expected, and walks up to us. A sensuous perfume precedes her, a heady blend of tuberose essence and stale cigar.

"Hmmm . . . ," she says, eyeing Naoko more closely. "You've got a certain . . . shall we say, *unique* appeal. I know a high-end brothel in Nice that would pay me a handsome price to add you to their stable."

"Don't think of it!" I yell.

"For you, no. Even though you're pretty, your rebellious personality would scare off customers, not to mention your nasty history of killing your lover." She squints, like an old snake leers at its prey. "Still, there are masochists who might enjoy your insolence. It takes all kinds."

A rush of anger comes over me as I listen to this madam talking about human beings like they were livestock. Despite her pious gestures to ward off abominations, her soul is as dark as a vampyre's.

"As for those mother-of-pearl ornaments, they're worthy of being added to my treasure," she says, her long polished nails reaching for the pins and sticks that hold Naoko's bun firmly in place.

"No!" Naoko yells.

She jumps back, knocking into the bandit escorting her.

I know Naoko isn't reacting like this to save a few barrettes. She wants to hide the abomination that burrows under her hair. If the Lachryma were to discover it, superstitious as they are, they wouldn't be sending Naoko to the high-end brothel but to the slaughterhouse.

"Well, well, you're more wild than you look too," the godmother says. "I guess those decorations are part of your charm. I'll include them in the package and ask the people in Nice for an even better price." She snaps her fingers. "Wilfried, take her back to her cell and go find a midwife to draw up a formal certificate of virginity. That'll certainly help raise the bidding."

The bandit doesn't need to be told twice. He grabs Naoko's arm as she gives me a desperate look under her black bangs.

It's the same heartrending expression I saw on Bastien's face before the old Baron de Gastefriche's sword ended his life. At the time, I couldn't do anything to save my beloved brother.

"Wait!" I yell. "Don't take her away. I . . . I'll do anything you ask."

I can feel Guzeppi's hands tighten around my waist while his mistress assesses me scornfully.

"Anything I want? I'm afraid you don't have a lot more to offer."

"Yes," I reply hoarsely. "Count Marcantonio of Tarella."

A look of surprise comes over the godmother's usually blasé expression.

"I know your great-great-great-uncle betrayed the Lachryma a century ago," I say. "Guzeppi told me. I also know you can't stand the fact that he continues to live since leaving the brotherhood."

"He didn't just *leave the brotherhood*," Ravenna says hoarsely. "He fled long before I was born, when our little gang was not yet the international organization it has since become, taking the family treasure of the

Lachryma with him. Which is how he built his fortune and reputation at the court. That first-rate death-licker went so far as to be transmuted! He bought his title of count from the Faculty at a steep price so he could escape the vendetta of his former brothers-in-arms. Ever since, he's stuck a beauty mark at the corner of his eye to hide his tattoo and all trace of his previous life. My ancestors put out a contract on his powdered head. Ah, how I long to chop it off his shoulders and make him suffer the punishment given to traitors. But it's impossible to get near him at the Palace of Versailles, where he hides among the other bloodsuckers."

She makes one of her superstitious hand gestures, her anger causing her gold bracelets to jingle loudly.

"Let me make good on the contract and fulfill your vendetta," I tell her.

"Don't take me for a fool. You really think I'm going to send you back to Versailles without guarantees?"

"No, not to Versailles. Here, to Paris." I stare the godmother down. "Surely you're aware that the Immutable organized a grand ball at the Louvre for December twentieth, on the eve of the Night of Shadows. The entire court will be there, including Marcantonio. As a squire to the king, I'm also expected to attend. I'll be able to approach your enemy and eliminate him there. I offer you his head in exchange for Naoko's freedom."

A nearly religious silence greets my proposition. Not only do I have the gang leader's full attention, but all of her lieutenants' too. These gangsters renounced all human values when they were baptized with the tear, except for one value that they've taken to a new height: loyalty. In their eyes, there's no worse sin than betraying the brotherhood. And no greater duty than to punish traitors.

"I have to say, it would be quite a coup before leaving Paris," the godmother says. "It was my great-great-grandfather, Godfather Celestino, who led the Lachryma when his brother Marcantonio swooped off with the treasure. Vengeance is a dish best served cold . . . after one century, it's time to come to the table." Her lips widen in an ambiguous smile, revealing several gold teeth. "But tell me, Gastefriche, even if you manage to eliminate that *bastardo*, it's unlikely you'll get out alive."

"It's a risk I'm willing to take."

Naoko groans. "No, I beg you, Diane."

She's using my alias, but it's the real friend she's imploring with her vibrant eyes.

"I've made my decision, Naoko."

I give her my most reassuring look. She's truly a member of my family. Not the one that was ripped away from me and that will always remain in my heart, but the one this tumultuous life gave me. Naoko, Montfaucon, and Orfeo: a battered, patched-up family made up of damaged beings like me. A gift from life, more precious than anything. A family that I'll fight for till the end.

I look at the godmother again, my heart resolute.

"I need three things from you for my plan to succeed."

"Three things?" she says, laughing. "You drive a hard bargain. If by some miracle you come out alive, you'll have a spot among the Lachryma. Go on, what are your terms?"

"First, you have to swear that Naoko will be freed as soon as you learn that Marcantonio is dead."

"Granted. Ravenna of Sicily keeps her promises. I swear it on the vault of the Tarellas, where the bones of my ancestors rest. Next?"

"Give me back my gun, the one that was in my shoulder bag when your men captured me. It's loaded with death-silver bullets. Once I'm at the Louvre, I'll find a way to lodge one of them into Marcantonio's heart."

The godmother nods. "Agreed. Your last request?"

"I'd also like to retrieve my royal pass, as well as my signet and onyx rings. The document may help me reach the count. And the jewelry is two-bit junk, like you said, but it's all I have left of my father, the Baron de Gastefriche. It has sentimental value."

The godmother acquiesces again. "Your trinkets will be returned to you," she says. "Now it's my turn to impose a condition. If we don't have formal proof that the traitor is destroyed by noon on December twenty-first, we'll take your dear Naoko with us when we leave Paris for Nice. You'll never see her again."

Marcantonio de Tarella's great-great-grand-niece extends her arm to seal the contract.

She crushes my hand in hers in a cold, hard shake, much like the solid gold around her fingers.

16

EXHUMATION

"For the hundredth time, you don't have to sacrifice yourself on my account," Naoko pleads.

"For the hundredth and first time, my mind's made up. Don't forget what you called me: *a stubborn mule.*"

We're both sitting on the straw mat of my cell, my friend brushing my hair like she used to at the Grande Écurie.

Ever since I struck a deal with the godmother, she's tolerated that Naoko and I spend a few hours together daily. Today is day four of our detention and my last. It's been agreed that I'll leave this lair in less than an hour and return to the Yellow Cat Inn. There, I'll be reunited with Suraj and Hélénaïs and pretend that I used the last week to crisscross Paris in search of clues. Without success, of course. And tonight, I'll attend the grand ball at the Louvre with my two fellow squires to fulfill my contract.

"I'll find a way to survive at the brothel," Naoko insists as she puts the finishing touch on the silver braid she's artistically woven around my head.

"That's out of the question," I say. "Do you really see yourself disrobing for strangers? Letting them put their filthy paws on you? Allowing them to undo your bun?"

Naoko's fingers freeze in my hair. I know I'm being cruel, but she has to see reason. She has to accept my decision. And she has to run away to freedom without me in case I lose my life trying to eliminate Marcantonio.

"I . . . I can't allow you to die on my behalf," she stammers.

"Let me repeat that I have no intention of dying. Jeanne Froidelac was already pretty tough skinned, but Gastefriche has an even coarser hide. That baronette surprises me. She survived a tidal wave of ghouls at the Temple, no less. So a lone bloodsucker isn't about to do her in. He's the one who'll probably break a few sharp canines."

I pretend to bite my arm and hurt my teeth, just to get a smile out of Naoko.

"You're so silly!" she huffs.

"Don't forget that I also have my pistol, loaded with death-silver bullets. It's a big advantage. Between us, my gut tells me it's not the end for me."

Naoko's smile turns to confusion. "Gut?"

"Yes, Naoko. I think the Immutable's blood developed a sort of . . . how shall I say? . . . a gift of *premonition* in me. Each time I'm faced with a mortal danger, I dream about it a few hours before. But I've been sleeping like a log lately. So I'm convinced nothing is going to happen to me."

Naoko doesn't look convinced. "What about the Lady of Miracles?" she asks.

"I've done everything I can to find her, and up till now, I've failed. I'm not giving up, but what's most important at this point is making sure you get away from Paris before the Night of Shadows. Promise me that you'll flee the city, with or without me, if the Lachryma release you."

I take her hands and stare deep into her eyes, determined not to let go of her until she agrees to my demand.

Finally, she nods. "I promise."

Right then, someone knocks three times on my cell door.

Guzeppi enters the room, carrying a tray. It's our breakfast. Nothing like the chestnut-flour gruel he brought me in the days before the Lord Serpent incident. This tray holds slices of hot toasted bread and pieces of fried lard. A second plate is heaped with boiled vegetables, in keeping with Naoko's vegetarian diet. The Lachryma get all this foodstuff on the black market, which has been thriving since the Immutable cut off provisions to the capital. Now that Ravenna of Sicily appointed me her instrument of vengeance, it's like I'm her guest instead of her prisoner. I've even been allowed to wash and given scented bath salts to perfume my skin in anticipation of the ball at the Louvre. It's agreed that I'll go fetch the dress that Hélénaïs ordered for me.

"*Buon appetito!*" Guzeppi says, placing the tray at the foot of the straw mat.

His attitude has changed. He's back to his thoughtful manners of my early confinement and more. As if I were part of the brotherhood.

"The godmother's right," he says. "You could really join us if you survive the Louvre. A teardrop by your eye would go well with your mischievous look."

He blushes slightly as he utters this compliment but doesn't move. I guess I don't leave him indifferent, and he obviously wants to talk some more before I go. I don't reciprocate his feelings. When it comes to handsome scarred boys, I've had my fill. Tristan had a bad-boy scar, too, and I'm not about to fall into that trap again.

Yet I force myself to smile amiably at the Maltese. Even if the thought of joining his gang of swindlers repulses me, I can't show it. I have to play the game as long as Naoko isn't free.

"Why not?" I simper. "I don't see myself going back to the court after I've settled accounts with the count."

I emphasize my wordplay with a knowing wink. Guzeppi answers with a love-struck smile.

"Oh, not only are you pretty, you've also got a big brain, using language like the powdered folks at Versailles," he says awkwardly. "Believe me, you belong here with us a lot more than with those flunky squires. Why serve a king when you can serve yourself?"

"You're right. No king, no master," I say.

I refrain from reminding him how servile he is in front of his gang leader, in spite of his invincible swagger. As for my life away from the court, if I'm able to escape, I'll live it by Montfaucon's side, working on a cause that's way bigger than me—the one my parents were a part of. The Fronde of the people. I'm not about to join up with a bunch of gangsters who act only for their own selfish interests.

"Speaking of squires, that reminds me of Plumigny and what that swine Tarella put her through," Guzeppi says, guffawing.

I exchange a questioning glance with Naoko.

"Plumigny?" she says. "I don't understand. Is there a link between the count of Tarella and Hélénaïs?"

"Oh, I'm not talking about the second Plumigny daughter but the first, Iphigénie."

The name hits me like a bullet.

I don't know anything about Hélénaïs's mysterious sister, except for a few sentences I read on the sly in a letter. Lord Anacréon of Plumigny had written how disappointed he was in his eldest child. He ordered his younger daughter to restore the family's prestige at the court.

"What happened?" I ask lightheartedly, trying to hide my curiosity.

"Didn't your colleague tell you? I thought you squires didn't keep any secrets from each other. The gossip mill says you share everything: meals, spare time . . ." A devilish smile spreads across his roguish face. ". . . even your beds."

"Don't believe all the rumors. Hélénaïs never mentioned her sister to me."

Guzeppi sits down beside me on the mat, obviously eager to establish with me the same personal bond that he believes exists between the king's squires.

"Three years ago, that lady-in-waiting to the Marquise de Vauvalon was seduced by the count of Tarella," he explains. "Iphigénie de

Plumigny was just a death-licker, ready to offer herself to the first blood-sucker who came along, like hundreds of others at Versailles. Tarella must have promised the moon to that young twenty-two-year-old goose for her to let him drink from her neck over the course of many months. All in secret, of course. But word of their affair got back to the king. During a private audience, the Immutable ordered the culprit to leave the court and enter a convent. My guess is that Vauvalon demanded the girl's banishment. After all, she's Tarella's longtime mistress, and I'm sure she didn't appreciate being cheated on with a mortal. As for the young girl's father, he disowned and disinherited her. He used her dowry to squelch the scandal and muzzle the press. Not one mention of it in *Le Mercure Galant*. But the Lachryma don't need those grubby journalists to know the gossip. Hahaha!"

Naoko ignores Guzeppi's laughter and touches my hand. She's obviously as startled as I am by this unexpected bit of information.

"That must be why Hélénaïs clung so hard during the competition for the Sip of the King," she reasons, thinking out loud. "It wasn't only to bask in glory but also to clear her family's honor."

"Right. And I bet her father put a lot of pressure on her."

"What happened to Iphigénie is unfair," Naoko says. "Why is it that in those situations the man always continues to strut around while the woman heads to a convent?"

Guzeppi deems it a good time to give us his opinion.

"Well, I think it's normal. Men have needs. Women who deserve to be called *ladies* should know how to stay virtuous."

I clench my jaw behind my frozen smile and plaster my hands against the straw mat so I don't slap this idiot hoodlum's face. That's *my* need, and I have a hard time not hitting him.

"Besides, in Plumigny's case, she didn't end up at a convent," he says. "She went to the Hospice of the Incurables."

As I hear him mention the hospice, my heart skips a beat. The Incurables—I was there only three weeks ago. Maybe I crossed paths with Iphigénie. Like me, she's a victim of the vampyres' tyranny. An orphan by force of circumstance. The fact that I might have grazed her veil stirs me with emotion.

"I visited that hospice with Hélénaïs," I say. "She didn't seem to know her sister was there."

Guzeppi shrugs. "Well, that's not surprising. The place where Iphigénie took her vows was secret. I already told you how the lord of Plumigny cut off ties with his eldest daughter." He snorts disdainfully. "Those high-society folks give themselves grand airs and look down on us, but they're just as ferocious as we are when it comes to defending their honor."

"And somehow, despite all the secrecy, the Lachryma knew Iphigénie was at the Incurables? How?"

"One year after the girl was banished, we followed Marcantonio when he went to abduct her like a lovesick puppy. That slimeball may be a cold-blooded vampyre, but he's still the same old hot-blooded Marcantonio." Another fiery wink in my direction. "For once, he'd left the protection of Versailles, and we pounced on the opportunity. We had the chance to finish him off. He was so close to death when he transmuted Iphigénie."

Hélénaïs's sister was transmuted?

My head spins as I hear all this.

I reach for the straw mat again so I have something to hold on to. Unfortunately, my fingers accidentally come to rest on Guzeppi's thigh. He thinks it's an invitation and immediately scoots closer.

"Yes, he transmuted her, and I swear it wasn't pretty to see," he says cheerfully. "Bloodsuckers have really unappealing habits. He bled her like a piglet in a room at the Pandemonium, the fanciest hotel in Paris. But like everywhere, we have connections there. His body was being drained of blood to fill Plumigny's when we attacked. I was within a whisker, one whisker, of planting my stake into his heart. But somehow that swine got away."

"And Iphigénie?" I ask, softly.

He brushes off my question with a sweep of his hand and takes the opportunity to let his palm fall on my thigh.

"The transmuted? We left her there and chased after Marcantonio. That pauper probably went off to swell the herd of unrecorded bloodsuckers. Most of them don't survive more than a few months. The Faculty tracks them down like rats. She must be a pile of ashes by now, and everyone's already forgotten the name Iphigénie de Plumigny, or Sister Amarante, the name she was called at the Incurables."

I jump up, tearing myself from Guzeppi's invasive grip.

I have a hard time slowing my racing breath and stopping my limbs from trembling.

"What's the matter?" Guzeppi asks, confused. "Excuse me if I put the moves on you too soon. I just wanted to give you a little human warmth before you get down to business."

"I'm all warmed up now," I say, gritting my teeth. "And ready to brave the cold. It's time for me to head to the ball at the Louvre."

I rush through the snow-laden streets of Paris.

The Lachryma released me somewhere north of the city, after making me travel through a maze of corridors with a sack over my head, as is their way. They gave me a heavy coat to replace the cape I left in Tristan's hands and returned my shoulder bag.

Instead of going directly to the Yellow Cat Inn to join the two other squires and get ready for the ball this evening, I decide to swing by the Incurables.

When Sister Vermillonne told us about Sister Amarante and how she occupied the most recent coffin in the crypt, I thought she was referring to an older nun like herself. I never imagined that it could be a young woman barely older than me and, even less, Hélénaïs's sister. I *must* learn why Vermillonne said the deceased succumbed to an attack by ghouls when she really disappeared after being transmuted. Did the

Sister of Final Care truly believe that story? Did she lie to us on purpose about Sister Amarante's death? If so, why did she conceal the truth? The hospice is hiding a dark mystery—I can feel it so acutely that it's hard for me to breathe. Does this secret have something to do with the Lady of Miracles? Three weeks ago, we started our investigation at the Incurables, where dozens of her army's victims end up each day. We left empty handed. The time has come for me to go back so that I can be sure, once and for all, before the Night of Shadows.

Still, I have to be quick because a second, even more pressing deadline weighs on me: Naoko's fate. It's already almost noon. I have only half a day ahead of me before the grand ball where I must destroy the count of Tarella, the very person who transmuted Iphigénie. The number of challenges I face makes me dizzy, the Louvre colliding into the Incurables at breathtaking speed.

Out of breath, my head a beehive of questions, I finally emerge onto the square of the hospice. The soldiers' and dragoons' bivouacs in the area seem denser than last time, with a cloud of smoke coming from a campfire. I push my way toward the door knocker.

Just like three weeks ago, the peephole opens onto Sister Purpurine's baggy eyes. She's the doorkeeper.

"Ah, it's you again?" she says, squinting to see me better under the hood of my coat.

"Open up! I must speak to the Reverend Mother."

The hefty woman has to muster all her strength to push the door blocked by the snow. Her face looks even wearier than I'd estimated through the peephole. By the looks of her gray vestment, smudged with melted snow and slush, she must not have changed in several days.

"Now's not a good time to visit," she says. "The Incurables is overflowing with patients since food supplies to the city were stopped."

It's true. The hospice courtyard is full of poor people waiting in front of makeshift tents heated by braseros with dying embers. Some nuns are ladling scoopfuls of steaming soup from large tubs, pouring them into the bowls of the frozen wretches.

"We're overwhelmed," Sister Purpurine grumbles. "So much so that we're forced to stuff patients two to a bed in the disabled ward and cram the insane in groups of four to one cell in the lunatic ward. And our food cellars aren't inexhaustible. They'll soon be as empty as the wheat lofts at Montmartre. All on orders of the king."

She gives me a furious look, as if she holds me personally responsible for the Immutable's drastic decision. Just because I'm his squire.

"I'm very busy," she says, lashing out. "You know the way to the Reverend Mother's office."

And with that, she quickly turns her back to me and goes off to help at the soup tents.

The hallways of the hospice are even more miserable than the courtyard. The poor who huddle here, looking for a little heat, are even frailer than the ones lined up outside. The old, wounded, sick—these are all the people for whom one day without food can mean death. Their moans blend with the cries of the insane coming from behind the walls of the asylum.

I shiver in my coat as I weave through these unhappy souls and the nuns trying to organize the chaos. Even with a hunk of bread in their hands, most of the needy refuse to leave.

"For pity's sake, Sister!" an old man cries, his eyes rolling back as he hangs on to one of the nun's vestments. "The Night of Shadows will be upon us tomorrow evening. My mud shack in Vaugirard is as run down as my old bones. It won't stand up to the ghouls sent by the Lady of Miracles. Let me stay here! Maybe I'll survive behind these solid stone walls."

"These walls are too narrow to accommodate all the poor of Paris," the nun replies, her voice hoarse from fatigue. "Now that you're fed, you need to let others have their turn."

The old man lifts his tattered sleeve, revealing his scrawny, black-and-blue arm.

"Is it blood you need? You can draw as much as you like, but let me take shelter here, for the love of the Shadows!"

"One puncture too many would kill you faster than a ghoul attack, old man. And the shelter you'd find is in our morgue."

The morgue? That's where Sister Amarante's mortal remains are supposedly kept. What if I paid the morgue a visit before going to see the Reverend Mother?

I veer off at the end of the hallway, and instead of climbing the stairs, I enter the narrow corridor under the main staircase. There's no one around, no nuns, no patients. It's completely dark.

I rub my tinderbox lighter, which gives me a weak light, and dash down the slippery steps where old Sister Vermillonne guided us not that long ago. In the silence of the crypt, the moans and pleas from above can't be heard. It's dead silent. I hurry under the ancient vaults, inhaling the damp, herb-scented air. The cold rooms that open on the right-hand side of the wall look a lot more cramped than the first time I was here. A combination of the lady's attacks and the king's food restrictions. The niches on the left wall seem to observe this slaughter, like so many black, impassive eyes, each welcoming the coffin of a former nun.

Finally, I come to the last occupied niche. I bring the flame of the lighter closer. A small bronze plaque is screwed into the oak coffin.

SISTER AMARANTE

274–297

It's easy to do the math. The nun was laid in the coffin when she was twenty-three, the exact age of the older Plumigny sister when she was transmuted, at least according to Guzeppi.

I take a deep breath. It's time to exhume the past . . . and, more literally, the body of Iphigénie de Plumigny. I close my lighter, grab hold of the metal handles on each side of the coffin, and pull with all my might.

Blast it. If Hélénaïs's sister is inside this box, she weighs as much as a dead horse.

Unable to support the weight of the coffin that's now halfway out of the niche, I let it slip and jump to the side so it doesn't come crashing down on my feet. The planks break in a deafening din, echoing farther and farther down the vaults of the crypt.

In haste, I relight my lighter to assess the damage. In the trembling halo, I see wooden fragments and torn cloth bags from which flows a white powder. It looks like . . . salt. But there's no body, not even the smallest bone. Sister Amarante's coffin only contained ballast, to give the impression of being filled.

"Goodness, what's all this noise?" a voice scolds behind me.

I turn around, panicked. The halo of a lantern comes limping closer.

"Patients aren't allowed in the crypt. But . . . what happened here?" Sister Vermillonne's angry face appears from the shadows.

"Desecration!" she hoots. "Woe on whoever's come to disturb the eternal rest of the hospital nuns!"

She raises her lantern above the broken coffin, and her curses instantly die in her throat. Her mouth forms an astonished O, the contours of her lips full of fine wrinkles. By her expression, I can tell she's even more surprised than I am.

"By the Shadows," she says.

"It's me, Diane de Gastefriche, squire to the king," I whisper as I remove my hood so she can recognize me.

"What are you doing here?" she chokes out.

"I'm looking for the truth about Sister Amarante. As you can see, she's not in this coffin."

"But . . . but . . . ," the old nun stammers. "I saw her drag herself into the hospice one night in July, two and a half years ago. After the ghouls attacked the Barrière du Trône. She went and took refuge in the Reverend Mother's apartments, the latter personally tending to Sister Amarante during her final hours, until the night she died."

"You mean, the night that her death was *faked*," I correct her. "Who put her in the coffin?"

"I did, since I'm the Sister of Final Care. When a nun passes, the custom is to expose her body in one of the cold rooms of the crypt for an entire night, so the other nuns can mourn for her." Sister Vermillonne frowns as she tries to remember. "Usually, the wake takes place with an open casket. But this time the Reverend Mother asked me to close it right after the corpse was laid out. She feared that the scratch, which was infected by an especially virulent strain of ghoul venom, might leak its noxious properties into the air."

I grab the nun's wrist and stare into her eyes, prodding her to remember more.

"The scratch, did you see it?"

"I . . . huh . . . no. The reverend ordered me not to wash the body because it was too severely infected. I put Sister Amarante into the coffin in her bloodstained vestment where the ghoul scratched her on her chest."

I take a deep breath.

The stale air in the crypt feels more suffocating than ever.

"So to summarize, the reverend is the last person who witnessed Sister Amarante's supposed demise. And it's also the reverend who insisted her coffin be sealed as soon as possible."

"Yes, that's what I told you," Sister Vermillonne says, her voice trembling. "So as not to poison the air."

"Or maybe to avoid having anyone find out that the deceased wasn't really dead," I say. "You see, reliable sources tell me that Sister Amarante didn't die because ghouls got to her. She was illegally transmuted."

The old nun's lantern starts to shake in her hand, making her shadow and mine dance on the walls of the crypt.

"That's . . . that's impossible . . . ," she stammers. "Every illegal transmutation is blasphemous. A nun belonging to the Faculty would never do such a thing."

"Someone dared for her. And your reverend did everything to hide it. The next question, Sister Vermillonne, is, Don't you want to know why?"

The old nun nods, her eyes gleaming in the half light. She takes my hand in her emaciated fingers and squeezes it warmly.

"From the day you first visited, I could tell you were different from the other squires. Closer to the people. More sensitive. I saw your eyes mist up when I was talking about the last hours of the ghouls' poor victims."

I'm dying to tell her who I really am, but I don't. I'm content letting my eyes communicate with this old, wise, kind woman. I'd like to believe that my mother would have grown old just like her if the king's dragoons hadn't abruptly snipped the thread of her life.

Sister Vermillonne knocks three times on the heavy iron-fortified door to the reverend's office. Then she states her name, shouting loudly to make sure her voice is heard through the thick panel.

One by one, three huge metal locks turn, making clicking sounds, and the door squeaks open onto Mother Incarnadine.

"What's the meaning of this intrusion?" the reverend objects as Sister Vermillonne and I enter the room.

As on my first visit, the writing desk behind her is covered with books and documents lit by a huge candelabra. We've interrupted her studies. But why does she need to be behind a triple-locked door to work?

"Vermillonne, don't you have your hands full at the morgue?" she scolds. "And you, young lady, I recognize you. You're one of the king's squires." She shoots daggers at me above her spectacles. "Seems your investigation hasn't gone anywhere in nearly a month. The Lady of Miracles is still on the rampage, and the result is that the hospice is overflowing with patients. We don't know where to put them."

"Good news, Mother Incarnadine, a niche just opened up in the crypt," I reply, not missing a beat. "Sister Amarante's."

The reverend's stern face goes pale between the folds of her black veil.

"A niche?" she says softly. "Sister Amarante's? I don't understand what you mean."

"Oh, I think you understand all too well," I say as I close the door behind Sister Vermillonne and me. "We opened the coffin. It's empty."

The director of the establishment turns toward her subordinate so abruptly that the bat medallion around her neck jumps on her vestment. The fiery flames in the fireplace send feverish reflections on her angry face.

"Vermillonne, how did you dare commit such blasphemy?"

"With all due respect, Mother, it's you who blasphemed first," the Sister of Final Care shoots back. Her face turns crimson, veering toward the vermilion red she owes her religious name to. "You were the last person to stay with Amarante's coffin after the wake," she says. "I remember clearly how you insisted on being alone with her in the crypt, because she was your protégée." She squints, a tangle of wrinkles forming at the corners of her eyes, eyes still bright despite her advanced age. "The other nuns and I never knew who that young recruit was before she took the veil. We assumed she came from a noble family, what with her good manners and her level of education. She was so curious and full of life. She was also one of the few who could read Latin and Greek, which is why you assigned her to organize the library. We could tell she was of special worth to you. So much so you kept her cloistered within these walls as if she were a lunatic during the long year she lived among us. And why you kept the last watch by her bedside. You had plenty of time to open the coffin, remove the body, and stuff it with the bags of salt we use to help preserve corpses. There were lots of bags in the room."

Mother Incarnadine shivers in indignation . . . and, it seems, from anxiety.

"Remove Amarante from the coffin?" she says, shrilly. "You've lost your mind! What in the world would I have done with a body infested with ghoul venom?"

"It wasn't ghoul venom running through that body. It was vampyre blood," I reply coldly.

The reverend's authoritarian polish cracks. She starts to tremble so hard that her spectacles begin to move at the tip of her nose.

"How do you know that? Has Amarante come back? Oh, may the Shadows come to my aid and get me through the night!"

"Leave the Shadows out of it and assume responsibility," I tell her. "It certainly seems as if you covered up an illegal transmutation. And I know who performed it: Count Marcantonio of Tarella. I also know the victim's real name: Iphigénie de Plumigny. I remember the harsh look you cast on Hélénaïs when we came to see you at the end of November. A look of hate, I now realize. She was completely unaware that her sister had lived inside your walls, under the name Sister Amarante. But you, why have you let everyone believe the nun was dead and buried? Answer, in the name of the king!"

Mother Incarnadine steps back toward her writing desk and falls into her chair, overwhelmed.

"Because . . . because I didn't know what to do," she stammers. "Sister Amarante was never supposed to leave the enclosure of the hospice. When she disappeared on the evening of July 297, I was so disappointed that she broke her vow of confinement."

"She didn't leave of her own will, she was abducted by a vampyre."

"Yes, she was abducted, not far from the mass grave at the Barrière du Trône, where she went without my authorization," the reverend says. "If she'd stayed at the hospice, none of that would have happened. In fact, who's to say she didn't consent to the transmutation? Maybe she got scared once she became an unrecorded. Maybe she realized she'd become a criminal, doomed to be destroyed under the wrath of the Inquisition. When she came to find me the following night, in tears, her vestment full of bloodstains, I was unprepared. A nun from my hospice had broken the Faculty's most sacred law. What infamy! And what's more, my most precious resident whose father paid a handsome sum each month so his daughter would stay cloistered. I felt betrayed by this young, reckless girl. The thought of the impending scandal made . . . made me lose reason." With a trembling hand, the reverend opens one of the desk drawers and takes out a small wooden handle. "When that abomination with a human face sought solace in my arms, I grabbed a quill pen similar to this one and . . . and I used all my strength to plant it right through her heart."

The reverend's cruelty toward a nun in her care, one who was evidently devoted to her, shocks me. The rage she must have felt to stab the miserable girl with a simple quill pen fills me with terror.

"How could you?" I say.

"I know I should have called an inquisitor from the Faculty to deal with that unrecorded, per protocol," she mumbles, her eyes fixed to the ground so as not to meet mine. "But I preferred to resolve things myself. I didn't want to attract further attention on this unfortunate incident. With the quill pen firmly planted in her chest, Amarante was paralyzed and could pass for dead, as long as no one looked too closely."

"You made up that story about her being scratched by a ghoul and her body being infected so that I wouldn't look under her vestment," Sister Vermillonne cries out.

"Yes, and it worked," the reverend replies, raising her head. "Your old, nearly myopic eyes were fooled. Once I was alone with the coffin, I opened it to finish what needed to be done—decapitating Amarante with a saw I borrowed from the workshop of the nun who handles maintenance repairs. Unfortunately, Amarante lunged at my throat. That blasted quill pen got dislodged from her heart when she was in the coffin."

A horrified scowl deforms Mother Incarnadine's pale features as she remembers that night, a night she hasn't spoken to anyone about until now.

"Maybe the wooden handle was too thin, or the essence wasn't potent enough," she says, like a crazy person rehashing obsessive thoughts. "Fruit trees are the most effective for paralyzing the non-dead, for their branches bear life. If my quill pen had been made from apple or walnut wood instead of a pine, things would have turned out differently and—"

"Stop your complaining," I break in. "Just tell us what really happened."

She jumps, torn from her ruminations. "Everything happened very quickly. I tried to cut her with my saw. But she got away. She fled out of the crypt and up the stairs, where the other nuns were already fast asleep after the wake. The sun was just rising, so I knew that miserable, unnatural being would soon sizzle up somewhere in the city. I filled the empty coffin with bags of salt and closed it, making sure to turn the screws tightly so that the sordid secret would never be revealed . . . until today."

Mother Incarnadine raises her pale eyes toward me. Now that she's no longer panicked, her icy expression is back.

"You know everything now," she says drily, her voice used to giving orders, indicating the end of the discussion. "If you decide to inform the king of this incident, I'll tell him the truth. Everything I did was to preserve the reputation of this hospice. I have nothing to feel ashamed of."

"Indeed, you didn't blush when you asked me if Amarante had come back, you turned pale," I respond. "You claim the sun did her in, but deep down you aren't sure . . . and you're scared she could return and take vengeance."

"That's ridiculous," the prelate chokes out. "A Reverend Mother belonging to the Faculty isn't afraid of an ordinary unrecorded. Anyway, I don't see how she could reach me behind these walls. Not to mention getting past all the soldiers standing watch outside, night and day."

Sister Vermillonne clears her throat behind me.

"Now I understand why you had all the locks at the hospice changed at the end of 297."

"I did so because of the lunatics who escaped," the reverend says defensively. "At your advanced age, memory doesn't serve you well, but maybe you recall that some lunatics escaped two years ago, in

December, looting the library on the way out. It was my duty to secure the hospice."

"I'll have you know that I'm not senile yet, and my memory isn't deficient," the nun of Final Care answers, not allowing herself to be intimidated. "I remember very well that someone let the lunatics out from the outside. Someone who had the keys to the asylum. When she was alive, Sister Amarante had a set of those keys. She also spent a lot of time with the insane. She's the one who let them out, isn't she? And that terrifies you."

"That . . . that's merely a wild theory with no proof," Mother Incarnadine says.

"You haven't left the walls of the hospice in two years. You exchanged your office, which used to look out on the courtyard, for this windowless room. You ordered the steel reinforcement of the door, and you shut yourself in as soon as the warning bell rings, triple-locking the door." The nun of Final Care points her gnarled finger at a curtain-covered alcove next to the fireplace, between bookcases full of theological treatises. "You even had a bed brought into this windowless strong room. And you asked the Faculty to double the number of soldiers and dragoons outside on the pretext that the nuns needed protection. But in fact, you're in fear for your own life."

The reverend cowers in her chair, as if Sister Amarante was about to come and take her revenge, right here on the spot. The panic she'd managed to suppress has her back in its grip. Terrified, she gasps for breath as her eyes dart with paranoia under the edge of her veil.

"You say you didn't alert your supervisors about Sister Amarante's transmutation to preserve the reputation of the Incurables," I assail her. "But seeing the state you're in, it's clear something else changed your mind. A compelling reason, strong enough for you to resolve to live in fear, alone with your secret." I lean my face close to hers. "What's the reason, Mother Incarnadine?"

"I . . . I . . ."

"Speak up if you don't want me to denounce you to the king's royal executioner, Raoul de Montfaucon. He'll know how to get a confession out of you."

A feverish glimmer passes over the reverend's pale eyes, as if the fire of the gallows was reflecting there.

"Aside from me, Sister Amarante was the only one who had a key to the asylum and to the library," she admits hoarsely. "Many of the books stolen from the shelves on the night the lunatics escaped dealt with nocturnal abominations, specifically ghouls. A year and a half later, the first coordinated attacks of those monsters began in Paris."

The reverend, this harsh and pitiless woman, starts to stammer like a child begging to be forgiven for a mistake that overpowers her.

"If the Faculty were to learn what monster left my hospice, I . . . I can't imagine the punishment I'd receive. For the love of the Shadows, don't breathe a word to the archiaters . . . don't . . . don't tell the king."

She grabs my hand and clamps onto it, looking at me despairingly.

"I . . . I think Sister Amarante and the Lady of Miracles are one and the same."

17

TRIUMPH

I quicken my pace along the twilit streets.

The setting sun casts red gleams on the snow, evoking long streaks of blood. As if the mirage of an upcoming slaughter was being projected onto the whole city.

Mother Incarnadine's words still reverberate in my head. When the last barriers of her lies gave way, she literally collapsed, breaking down into tearful terror and guilt. If her theory is correct, by trying to hide that one of her nuns was transmuted instead of straightaway denouncing her to the Faculty, she unknowingly facilitated the emergence of the Lady of Miracles—the King of Shadows' major rival. It's an unforgivable crime, which explains why she shrouded herself in silence all this time.

But these crucial answers raise many other questions. If Iphigénie de Plumigny is in fact the Lady of Miracles, how did she acquire the power to control the ghouls? Did she draw this forbidden know-how from the books stolen from the hospice library? What exactly did she hope to gain by freeing the lunatics? And, most of all, how does setting the city on fire help her?

Deep down, I think I know the answer to the last question. Not long ago, I was also consumed and obsessed with vengeance, whatever the cost and the number of victims I left in my wake. And Iphigénie de Plumigny has every reason to seek vengeance from a world that didn't do her any favors. I totally understand why she would want to snatch one of the sovereign's crowns, since he forced her to take the veil. Maybe this obsessive need for revenge pushed her over the edge.

The doleful warning bell echoes on the Paris rooftops when I finally reach the Yellow Cat. I dash inside, the innkeeper looking at me in alarm, as if I were a ghost. I climb the stairs four at a time, until I reach the landing . . . where I run smack into Hélénaïs.

She's busy pacing the hallway to loosen the folds of her new ball gown, a magnificent bright-yellow silk dress embellished with exquisite lace and delicate trim. Her hair is artfully braided into a bun and studded with matching silk flowers, and her face is delicately made up.

"You're here!" she says. "Where have you been?"

"I was conducting a search on my own, as you know."

She flutters her mascara-lengthened lashes. "And I imagine you didn't find anything."

I shake my head. In a way, even if Hélénaïs has never been kind to me, I feel that she deserves the truth. But I can't allow myself to tell her that the Lady of Miracles, who she's been chasing for a month, is very likely her own sister. The information might give her an advantage in tracking her down before I do. And once I've saved Naoko, my priority is still to eliminate the mistress of the ghouls.

Overhearing our conversation, Suraj comes out of his room. He's already dressed for the ball as well, sporting a long light-green velvet Indian waistcoat with a stand-up collar. It's a bespoke garment, tailored to his athletic body. His absinthe-colored turban is decorated with an emerald.

"Diane!" he says.

"In the flesh. I see I've come just in time to get ready." I gesture to the large sack hanging next to my shoulder bag. "I stopped by Rosine Couture just before closing time and picked up my dress. I can't wait to drink a piping-hot onion soup. I'm really hungry! Is the ball still starting at ten o'clock?"

Hélénaïs rolls her eyes and sighs, as if I'm a half-wit.

Suraj shows more patience. "There's been a change during your absence, Diane. We're expected at the Louvre at eight o'clock, to await the king's triumphant arrival."

"The king's triumphant arrival?" I repeat, my temples buzzing as I hear this troubling news. I didn't think the Immutable would come to Paris, especially since he never leaves Versailles.

"Yes. His Majesty decided to honor the ball with his presence, to show that he doesn't fear his enemy. He'll enter Paris through the Porte de L'Étoile and make his way triumphantly down the Avenue des Champs-Élysées to the Louvre Palace. His squires are to accompany him, and we have to meet up with the rest of them at the Tuileries Gardens."

The dress Hélénaïs picked out for me is a far cry from the luxurious, refined gown she chose for herself. As she said, she selected the most ordinary flannel, in a particularly dull shade of gray. Just as well. It'll be that much easier for me to go unnoticed as I inch my way closer to Marcantonio to carry out the Lachryma's vendetta.

As for the bustle that Hélénaïs requested, I suspect it was meant to ruin my silhouette. But it's an accessory that will serve me well. During the art-of-weaponry classes at the Grande Écurie, the Knight of Saint-Loup, who taught our class, explained that bustles were ideal for concealing a weapon. It's a lesson I haven't forgotten, and it'll be the perfect spot to hide my pistol with the death-silver bullets.

Last detail: my onyx ring. With its dull iron band and somber lackluster stone, it pairs really well with my grayish attire. I'm ready for the night ahead of me, the one that will determine Naoko's future as well as the Fronde's, and mine.

Soon the three of us set off wrapped in full-length coats over our ceremonial dress. In the sky, the moon is nearly round; it'll be completely full tomorrow again, for the Night of Shadows. Exactly twenty-one days since the start of our investigation. With each breath I take, the biting cold fills my lungs with frost. As we walk, I learn that my teammates didn't make much progress with their search. In fact, the massacres orchestrated by the lady only multiplied exponentially, resulting in yet more deaths, fires, and kidnappings, be they at the Parc Monceau, at the Rue de Charonne, at Ménilmontant . . .

"Will the rest of the court arrive together with the king?" I ask innocently as we chat, anxious to know where and when to strike Marcantonio de Tarella.

"Some courtiers are already in Paris," Suraj answers. "Many of them own town houses in the capital and so came early to get ready for the festivities."

Hard to tell if the count of Tarella is among these early arrivals. I guess I'll have to wait until I'm in the Louvre to find him.

The Rue Sang-Honoré, where we're walking, is lined with the type of beautiful residences that Suraj just alluded to. The imposing facades are lit with gleaming lanterns. The sidewalks were salted to prevent dresses from getting smudged with snow and slush. Noble mortals, all decked out, along with immortals in full regalia are heading in the same direction we are. Everyone wants to see the king arrive.

"I can't wait to see the familiar faces of the court," Hélénaïs says, hurrying forward.

"Neither can I," I reply, agreeing wholeheartedly. "Poppy, Rafael, and Zacharie. I have to admit I've even missed the most irritating courtiers, like the Marquise de Vauvalon and Count Tarella."

From under the brim of my hood, I glance at Hélénaïs. Her face froze when I mentioned the count. Her expression, a mix of horror and anger, betrays her. She obviously knows who's responsible for her sister's downfall, even if she's oblivious of where her sister was cloistered.

This could be an opportunity to find out more about Iphigénie's character, and any information that could help me corner the Lady of Miracles is worth getting.

"I hear Count Tarella is a dangerous skirt chaser," I continue to banter. "Probably better to steer clear of him at the ball tonight."

Hélénaïs suddenly stops to face me, blocking my way with the width of her pannier dress.

"Shut up, Gastefriche," she says.

"What's the matter?" I ask, feigning surprise at her violent reaction.

"Don't play innocent, you little snoop. You read my letters at the Grande Écurie, so you know perfectly well what happened between my sister, Iphigénie, and Tarella."

"I read only *one* of your letters, and it didn't say much," I say defensively.

She grabs my wrist and squeezes it hard. "Well, let me summarize the rest. That stupid Iphigénie was weak enough to fall for Tarella. She paid a heavy price and ended up in a damp convent deep in the backwoods of Brittany, where my father banished her. She died of sorrow in less than a year."

Hélénaïs spit all this in my face, as if she were coughing up phlegm. But the words that came out of her mouth aren't hers. I recognize the harsh and emotionless tone that I read in the letters from Anacréon de Plumigny, her father. Hélénaïs's face, on the other hand, twisted in pain at the mention of her sister, whom she never saw again after the latter was exiled from Versailles. A sister she believes died in some unknown convent at the other end of France.

More than ever, I have an acute sense of the terror with which the lord of Plumigny has kept a grip on his daughters. After Iphigénie, it's Hélénaïs who's paying the price. She'll never be free as long as her father keeps her under his thumb. In her own way, she's as much a prisoner as any commoner. The only difference: in her case the law of the sequester erects gilded bars. Everything in her life exploits her, even the gifts she receives, like the bracelet engraved with the number *I*, a reminder that she must always be first. I feel a surge of compassion for her. It's a lot harder for me to peg her as a pampered, capricious poodle born in silks now that I'm getting a glimpse of what her life has been like. A relentless, merciless pressure to shine.

"If you thought you could torment me by bringing up memories of my sister, you're mistaken," she says. "My sister is dead and buried, and so is her memory."

"Hélénaïs—" Suraj tries to intervene.

"Don't butt in. Diane needs to hear a few home truths." She pulls me toward her and whispers, her bronze eyes staring into mine, "The hope of the Plumignys at the court rests on me now. Nothing is going to get in my way, least of all a miserable little gray mouse."

She finally lets go of my wrist and pushes me away. We spend the rest of the walk in tense silence until we reach a large esplanade, the Tuileries Gardens.

The park is lit up with numerous torches. The ground has been completely cleared of snow, showcasing the parterres and their geometrically designed beds. The trees and trimmed bushes, clipped à la française, are strewn with thousands of garlands and paper lanterns shaped like shimmering flowers. It's as if this parcel of nature in the center of Paris has been torn away from a mortal winter and hurled into an artificial spring. I can't imagine the cost of this one-night extravaganza, done while the rest of the city is dying of hunger.

Behind us, at the other end of the gardens and courtyard beyond, stands the imposing facade of the Louvre. The palace is covered in frost and lit by a thousand lights; it's as if it's made of crystal.

A large avenue faces it, making its way west in the frigid night, as far as the eye can see, heading toward the Place de L'Étoile and beyond, up to the outer ramparts. A formidable procession makes its way down the avenue, with twenty horses walking abreast. The riders in gleaming armor are accompanied by foot soldiers decked out with plumes—legions of soldiers descending the Champs-Élysées, a veritable army ready for battle. Countless nobles follow on horseback, lords attired in long fur coats and ladies riding sidesaddle. In the middle of this throng, a sunlike figure stands out, brilliantly illuminated by Swiss Guards carrying torches—the king, atop a huge white steed, far taller than the other horses, its nostrils blowing out jets of steam.

The monarch wears a huge, spotless ermine coat, its train covering the entire backside of his formidable mount. A tall ostrich-feathered hat crowns the abundant head of hair above his golden mask, which reflects the bright torches. A crushing magnificence emanates from this procession, underscored by drumrolls that match the horses' steps. Now I know why Suraj referred to a "triumphant arrival." Louis enters Paris like a war general of antiquity entered a conquered city, signifying that the Lady of Miracles is already defeated.

I squint, anxiously searching for Count Tarella among the oncoming procession. But most of the courtiers are hooded, as are the majority of guests already present in the gardens. Where is Marcantonio? Is the mysterious Lord Serpent also in the crowd? I doubt he'll try to do anything to me if he recognizes who I am. Conspirators like him only act in dim light.

The procession comes to a stop in the middle of the gardens.

The soldiers go take their positions around the Louvre, while hundreds of courtiers dismount. Straightaway, grooms spring out from behind the garlanded trees, hurrying toward the horses to lead them off to the stable. The court continues on foot, guided by the king, whose long white train glides on the lawn like the coat of the war god of winter himself. A wave of cold a thousand times more intense than the biting December wind washes over me, preceding this tide of mortals and vampyres.

The most powerful among them stops a few yards from Suraj, Hélénaïs, and me.

Thus majestically attired, resplendent in all his military glory, the Immutable appears more invincible than ever.

"Jaipur, Plumigny, walk with us," he invites them, his hollow voice escaping from his immobile lips.

"Sire," they respond.

They bow deeply, then join the three other squires near the king.

Not knowing whether I should follow them, I stay frozen in place, under the sovereign's inscrutable gaze. I also feel the eyes of his closest ministers and advisers staring at me: Exili, Mélac, the Princess des Ursins, all of them wearing sumptuous furs. Montfaucon is here, too, standing several steps back from the highest dignitaries of the regime.

"As for you, Gastefriche, are you done being the lone rider?" the Immutable asks me. "Do you deign to grace our modest ball with your invaluable presence? You do us too great an honor."

The monarch's sarcasm mortifies me. He doesn't need to raise his voice to let the court know how much my solitary escapade has displeased him.

I curtsy in turn, which makes my bustle stick out ridiculously, eliciting stifled laughter from the courtiers.

"I . . . I am your humble servant, sire," I stammer.

"Humble indeed. We would even say you are at the bottom of the heap. You are stripped of your duties as squire. We no longer desire your presence among us."

Already, the sovereign is walking off, without saying another word. I'm the only one of the six squires he hasn't publicly invited to follow him.

"Courage," the grand equerry whispers as he passes in front of me along with the rest of the personal guards.

He gives me an apologetic look between the curls of his wig. He can't afford to stop and talk to me, so I can't let him know what I found out about the Lady of Miracles. Nothing can slow down the royal procession.

I'm not a squire anymore.

Stunned by the sudden turn of events, I'm about to join the moving crowd when two Swiss Guards block my path with their halberds.

"The king stripped you of your privileges," one of them tells me. "You can't enter the Louvre with the members of the court. You'll be allowed in last of all, along with the lowly landowners."

This time my disgrace is absolute, my dishonor complete. I'm forced to stay on the sidelines, in the cold, with small-time Parisian nobles who have neither prestige nor the means to keep an apartment in Versailles.

The courtiers look at me disdainfully as they pass by. Among the petty games at the court, nothing makes them happier than to see others humiliated. I'm sure they think my cheeks are flushed from shame, but it's only frustration at having to wait a little longer to fulfill the contract that will free Naoko.

"Mademoiselle de Gastefriche?" someone says behind me.

I turn to find a short, bewigged man, wrapped in a mink coat, perched on high heels.

He's a noble mortal.

"Narcisse du Sérail, journalist at *Le Mercure Galant*," he says, introducing himself as he smooths his waxed mustache. "Your first reactions after the royal disgrace?"

He takes out a notebook and an ink-filled quill from his pocket so he can record my thoughts.

"I have nothing to say."

He pouts, obviously annoyed. "Now, now, just a few words for our faithful readers. Will you be taking refuge in a convent?"

I was stunned; now I'm angry.

"That practice of shutting away young girls for no good reason?" I lash out. "Take a hike!"

"I see . . . ," the journalist says, scribbling in his notebook. "And how do you plan on winning back the king's favor? By bringing him the Lady of Miracles? Do you have a lead?"

"If anyone asks you, tell them you don't know."

I ditch him and go off to join the rear of the procession. Now that the upper crust has entered the Louvre, it's finally the turn of the low nobility, whose ranks I've been relegated to.

I cross the immense palace courtyard framed by ancient wings with hundreds of frost-paned windows, right up to the main entrance flanked by two dozen Swiss Guards.

I've barely passed through the wide door when my cheeks heat up. There's a soft warmth here, maintained by blazing fireplaces. Pleasant chamber music flows under the high painted ceilings. The melody blends with the olfactory notes wafting from the large vases where magnificent bouquets of flowers are in full bloom despite the season.

Some uniformed servants rush over to remove my coat and put it in the cloakroom. As the noble ladies around me take off their wraps and capes, I notice they're all wearing yellow or orange dresses embellished with gold ribbons. Sun motifs are sewn onto the decorated bustiers, and jewels shaped like sunrays dangle from bare necks. Evidently, the theme of the ball is the sun—the Immutable's emblem par excellence, for him who sports the mask of Apollo and presents himself as the star of kings. Everyone knows he wants to reconquer daylight in order to extend his empire onto the twenty-four hours of the dial. The alchemical work he engages in with Exili hasn't allowed him to realize this despicable goal, fortunately so. I can't imagine a world where vampyres reign supreme without any rest. But this evening, he's determined to reaffirm that he's the one and only master of the night.

Hélénaïs was careful not to clue me in on the evening's dress code. I really stand out like a somber cloud in a sunny sky in the gray flannel dress she ordered for me.

"Well, now, you never do anything like everyone else, Gastefriche," someone says behind me. "And neither do I."

I turn around. It's Poppy.

She sticks out among all the sunny finery as well. She's wearing a pale-blue dress cut from that inexpensive fabric she's particularly fond of—denim. And as usual, she's pulled her thick black hair into a bun and studded it with ribbons from the same material. But her face is far less pale than I remember. Since I left Versailles, the regenerating power of the royal blood has continued to heal her lungs of tuberculosis and bring color to her cheeks. Unless her rosy glow is due to the glass of wine she's holding in her hand?

"I admit that fashion and I are like oil and water," I say, a little surprised. It's the first time Poppy has spoken to me since the tests for the Sip of the King, where I betrayed her trust. "I'm not about to be splashed on the style section of *Le Mercure Galant*."

"You'll make it into the Rumor Has It pages, you'll see. I saw that journalist accost you earlier. A real hawk." She leans closer. "In fact, he's right here as we speak."

She quickly turns around and pretends to bump into the small man spying on us.

Her glass of red wine spills onto Narcisse du Sérail, splattering his frilled shirt and drowning his notes.

"Oh gosh, dreadfully sorry!" she says.

The indiscreet man's face turns as crimson as the stain on his shirt. He takes off among the courtiers, grumbling.

"The tabloids wreak havoc on the other side of the Channel too," Poppy says with a wink. "And that's the best way to treat them."

"*Merci*, Poppy," I say, touched. "You . . . you aren't mad at me anymore?"

She shrugs. "Well, I do owe you for getting me my spot among the squires, *and* my brand-new lungs. Without the Sip of the King, I'd probably be pushing up daisies today. So it's my turn to help if I can. I'll try to plead your case to the king. He isn't easy, but I'll do my best to come up with reasons why he needs a brat like you among his personal guards." She smirks, her lips smeared with dark lipstick. "Truth be told, the more I get to know the courtiers at Versailles, the more I like you, flaws and all. Even if you're a bitch, I like you a lot, darling."

Poppy's words, both rough and tender, warm my heart.

"Speaking of bitches, it must have been hard to put up with Plumigny these last few weeks," she continues. "Is that why you took off? Or did you want to give the two lovebirds some privacy?"

She points with her chin to the other end of the hallway, where couples are dancing to the sounds of a minuet. Hélénaïs, looking radiant, is hanging on to Suraj's arm. He forces himself to smile at the courtiers streaming by them while holding back from glancing at Rafael, who's alone on the other side of the room. Over these past weeks spent with my teammates, I've identified their vulnerabilities. Even if circumstances have kept me locked in a double identity, I'm not the only one who's torn up inside. As the Eye of the Innocents told me, each one of us here below wages a secret battle in our hearts. Their fights are as important to them as mine is to me.

"You know, I'm a little envious of Hélénaïs's gumption," Poppy says. "She's direct. She goes after what she wants, while I still haven't breathed a word of my feelings to Zach."

From under her smoky eyeshadow, she glances toward the sixth squire, the most enigmatic one: Zacharie de Grand-Domaine. The handsome half-African, half-French squire from Louisiana is talking to stern-looking vampyres. I think some are His Majesty's advisers.

"Zach is always busy chatting up boring old fogies," Poppy says with a sigh. "About what? And about whom? A mystery. He's brought a lot of worries with him from Louisiana, worries that I can tell are eating away at him. I wish he'd share them with me . . . but I bet in a few minutes, he'll vanish from the ballroom and shut himself in the office where the king retired with the grand equerry and his ministers."

I bite the inside of my cheeks. Montfaucon is with the king? I won't be able to tell him what's happened to me over these last weeks, or to Naoko.

Thinking of my friend, I'm stung with urgency. Where is Marcantonio?

As I look around at the socialites and dancers, a servant comes over with an ornate pewter tray.

"A refreshment, mesdemoiselles?"

Half of the glass flutes on the tray are filled with a bubbly pink beverage, the other half with a pale-red liquid topped with a thin purplish foam.

"Tonight we're offering two aperitifs, both specialties of the House of Merceaugnac. A semidry rosé champagne. And a champagne-style foamy blood drawn from students at Sang-Michel."

"Impossible to refuse," Poppy says, depositing her empty glass on the tray and grabbing a flute of champagne.

"And for you, mademoiselle?" the servant asks me.

"*Merci*, but I'm not thirsty," I reply, eager to hurry off in search of my target.

The words are barely out of my mouth when two long white hands slip in beside me to take one flute each.

"Come on, Diane, no need to be thirsty to party," says a cheerful voice.

I raise my eyes and see the last person I needed to cross paths with tonight. Alexandre de Mortange is here, looking more radiant than ever in his gold-threaded waistcoat. The fit of the garment, snug around his torso, is like a warrior's antique breastplate. A wreath of golden laurels rests atop his magnificent head of loose red hair.

"Well, I see I'm the only squire without a beau," Poppy whispers in my ear, totally misconstruing the feelings Alexandre inspires in me. "I'll leave you. Have fun, and don't get carried away."

As she disappears into the crowd, Alexandre hands me the flute of pink champagne and clinks it with the other, full of human blood.

"*Tchin-tchin*, my dear, and may the festivities begin."

18

BALL

"How do you like my Alexander the Great attire?"

"It's magnificent," I answer.

The Great? The Great Fool, yes: that's who is in front of me, greatest of them all!

"On this triumphant evening, I thought what better way to pay homage to our noble king than by dressing after my illustrious namesake."

As he lifts his chin, the chandeliers make his laurel wreath sparkle with gold tints and give his hair coppery highlights.

"For Louis, I'd be ready to conquer half the globe, from Europe to Asia, like Alexander of Macedonia," he brags. A smile appears on his lips. "But for you, Diane, I'd conquer the entire world."

"That's nice of you, Alex. But I get completely lost in the hallways at the Palace of Versailles as it is, so imagine the entire world . . ."

He bursts out laughing, displaying his pearly teeth, canines carefully retracted in his gums. Tonight, he's here to seduce, not frighten me.

"You truly combine great wit with a lovely face," he compliments me. "I love that you're a nonconformist. Showing up wearing such foggy gray on a night we're celebrating the triumphant sun is truly sassy, and, dare I say, quite smashing."

"Glad you like my sense of humor. The king doesn't seem to appreciate it."

"Forget that," he says, sweeping my words away with the back of his hand. "I know all too well that every disgrace is temporary. And charming as you are, it won't take you the twenty years it took me to regain your standing." He gives me a knowing wink. "Come on, don't worry about it. Let's drink to your ascension at the court."

Without taking his deep-blue eyes off me, he sips his beverage. I feel like a gazelle, frozen under the stare of a panther who's come to quench its thirst from the same river.

"Hmmm, this bubbly from Sang-Michel is definitely strong," he says. "The students are known to get hammered in the taverns near the Sorbonne, and let me tell you that you can taste it on the tongue."

I bring my glass to my lips, so that there's something between us, and finish it off in one gulp.

"Bottoms up! I expected no less of you," he says, wiping his bloody lips with his fingertip. "But you need to eat something, otherwise you'll be tipsy."

He leads me toward a sumptuous buffet laid out on a table covered with a white tablecloth. Exotic fruits, glazed roasts, and powdered cakes are artistically arranged on porcelain platters, all on different tiers, under a giant gold-leaf cornucopia. The mortal guests help themselves while servants replenish the buffet as needed. Any dish that's been dug into and looks less than presentable is quickly whisked away and replaced by another. This bounty of refined offerings, while commoners are starving, makes me ill.

"A croissant, mademoiselle?" a valet asks as he offers me a basket full of small pastries shaped like crescent moons. "It's a specialty from Vienna that the royal kitchens have adapted to current tastes and to commemorate the sun's victory over the moon."

Around me, courtiers are taking big bites of this new treat, as if the war were already won.

"Something tells me that this delightful pastry will become a symbol of French gastronomy," Alexandre says as he stuffs a croissant into my hand. "Hmmm, smells like fresh butter, which reminds me of when I was mortal." His deep-blue eyes widen with pleasure. "Oh! And do you also remember the breakfasts that were prepared for you in the carriage bringing us from the Auvergne to Versailles? If I dared, I'd say it was our honeymoon, but the word *moon* is out of place tonight."

Remembering our time together, those long hours we spent in his carriage, seems to enchant him. My own recollections are nothing short of abhorrent. It was the day after my family had been killed, and this monster had given the last stroke of death to my dear mother. The baskets of bread, butter, and jam that Alexandre's men left for me each morning as he slept in the baggage hold tasted like ash. Every turn of the wheels took me a little farther from Butte-aux-Rats and a past forever shattered.

"Ah, those were memorable nights, the two of us getting to know one another," he says dreamily. "It was just a prelude to eternity." He brings his velvety lips to my ear and whispers a few words, his silky hair brushing my neck. "If your bad luck persists and the king refuses to transmute you, you can count on me to give you my blood despite the *numerus clausus*. For you, Diane with the silver hair, I'll defy the Faculty and every law. And we'll take off together again like two lovers, just like the first time."

I shiver in horror, which, given Alexandre's widening smile, he probably interprets as a shiver of pleasure. His amorous ardor petrifies me . . . and gives me a sudden idea.

"Do you happen to know where Marcantonio de Tarella might be?" I ask him.

"Tarella?" he says, his face darkening. "That fop? Why?"

The enmity between Alexandre and Marcantonio is nothing new. It worsened in September, when the latter tried to bleed me during the gallant hunt.

"I confess that ever since his abuse last summer, he terrifies me," I pretend. "Before I left for Paris, he was constantly ogling me in the hallways at Versailles. I know he's waiting for the first chance he gets to finish what he started in the royal gardens. I'm worried he'll take advantage of the fact that the sovereign has shunned me." I snuggle against Alexandre's cold chest and look at him with fearful eyes. "Earlier, in the procession, he smiled at me, showing off his canines, as if saying that I'll get what's coming to me. I'd like to make him understand, once and for all, that I'm under your protection."

The words sting my lips. I'll never be under the protection of any man, let alone a vampyre. But I'm ready to say anything if it flatters Alexandre's ego and helps me eliminate Marcantonio as quickly as possible.

"He dared to show his canines, the cad!" Alexandre says. "He's going to get a taste of mine."

"Do you know where he is?"

"Hard to miss him, what with his extravagant getup, that peacock," Alexandre says, carried away, as if forgetting he's also decked out in shimmering finery. "At this hour, he must be swaggering in the foundations with his companion, Vauvalon."

"The foundations?" I ask.

Before I can get any more information, Alexandre takes my hand and pulls me behind him through the tall, paneled hallways.

We cut through hoop dresses and jostle servants, awakening a concert of protests in our wake. I don't know if it's the champagne or the mad dash, but my head is spinning. Perfumes, colors, and music blend together in a frantic whirlwind.

We hurtle down a wide staircase and arrive in front of a double door guarded by butlers in uniform.

"The prey have already started to be released," one of them says.

"Make way, or I'll prey on you," Alexandre says angrily.

The butlers open the doors, muttering excuses, and we enter what Alexandre calls the foundations.

Here, no precious gilded halls, no elaborate moldings or crystal chandeliers. Only bare stone lit with weak torches. It's a lot colder than above.

"You dragged me underground," I say, panting.

I try to catch my breath, but my heart beats wildly. In Paris, at night, the underground is the most dangerous place to be, for it opens directly onto hell.

"These are the foundations of the old medieval castle, before successive architects changed it into a palace," Alexandre explains. "We're walking in what used to be the castle moat."

Indeed, the wide hallway curves in front of us and heads off into the darkness, like the bottom of a moat hugs the contours of a dungeon. Furtive silhouettes run here and there, laughing savagely. I can hardly make them out in the dim light. But each time one of them brushes against us, I shiver.

I'm sure the ambient cold isn't just due to a lack of a fireplace. If I hardly crossed paths with immortals in the hallways leading here, in contrast, the foundations are swarming with them. These moving silhouettes belong to dozens of bloodsuckers intoxicated by the excitement of the hunt.

"We're in the middle of a gallant hunt," I say in horror, only now realizing what the butler meant by "the prey has already started to be released."

"Indeed," Alexandre replies. "And tonight, the game is suited to the theme of the evening. Be careful!"

He jumps to the side. But I don't possess his supernatural reflexes or his keen nocturnal eyesight, and one of the silhouettes shoots forward into the half light, crashing right into me.

"I . . . I'm sorry," I stammer, blinking so I can make out the vampyre who just collided into me in his pursuit.

But it's not a vampyre.

That pale skin, bald head, and sharp claws that tore my dress . . .

It looks like . . . a ghoul.

I scream as I try to push the ghoul away. But it clings all the harder, looking at me imploringly. The flicker of a faraway torch reveals two trembling eyes, unlike the empty eye sockets of all the other ghouls I've encountered thus far.

"Mademoiselle, spare me! I have a wife and two children."

A man's voice comes out of this humanlike mouth, very different from the jaws of scavenging ghouls. Frightened and wide eyed, I stare at the creature in spite of the weak light . . . and I realize that I'm looking at a human made to resemble a ghoul. His head was shaved and his seminaked body coated with a white paste. Smeared ashes deepen the lines of his face, giving the illusion that his nose is truncated like a skeleton's. Tufts of hair are glued to his ears to make them look pointy, and his fingers are elongated with fake claws.

"If I stole a loaf of bread at the market, it's only because I needed to feed my little ones," the man cries. He's in the prime of life yet reduced to a weeping puppet for the amusement of the lords of the night. "With the blockade, my family is starving. But . . . but I swear I won't do it again."

"Step back, commoner," Alexandre says, coming to my rescue.

He snatches the poor man from my arms, revealing his long, protruding canines in a hoarse howl.

"Pity, monsieur!" the terrorized victim yells. "Don't bleed me!"

"Not a chance," Alexandre growls, his smooth features wrinkled in disgust. "I find that disguise in the worst possible taste. That over-the-top clownish farce may be appetizing to some courtiers, but it makes me ill. I'm a lover of beauty; ugliness repulses me. Scram, buzz off, little puppet ghoul."

The poor man clears out without another word. I watch him disappear into the shadows of the moat, heartbroken by the certitude that his escape is a lost cause. Inevitably, it won't be long before a less delicate bloodsucker than my host will capture and drain him of his blood.

"I'm sorry you had to be subjected to that grotesque spectacle," Alexandre says. "The stewards of the royal amusements came up with the idea as a way to humiliate the Lady of Miracles. Tonight, mortals eat croissants in her image, and immortals drink from beggars disguised as her vile soldiers. The gallant hunt is being held in the foundations precisely to mimic the underground corridors at the Court of Miracles." He touches the bodice of my dress with his tapered pianist's fingers. "Oh, that lout damaged your lovely dress."

My throat is too tight for me to utter a response.

No need to possess the eyes of a vampyre to guess that all around me, other unfortunate commoners, male and female, made up to look like ghouls, are fleeing as fast as they can. Their cries of terror are enough to let me imagine what's going on, just as I can imagine the aristocrats pursuing them by their gleeful whoops.

"Well, look who's here," a voice says, punctuated by a crystal-clear laugh I'd recognize anywhere. It's the same laughter that chilled my blood last summer during the gallant hunt in the gardens at Versailles.

The tall silhouette of a woman emerges from the shadows, topped by a bun studded with diamonds that catch the gleams of light from the few torches.

A large collar, with sundry points resembling the rays of the sun, frames her opalescent face. It's the Marquise de Vauvalon.

"Mademoiselle de Gastefriche is with me," Alexandre warns.

"And that's exactly what's most surprising, Mortange—that you haven't bled her yet. Did you bring her here to the foundations so you could do precisely that at your ease?"

With one hand, the marquise adjusts a strand of hair that escaped from her bun during the chase, and with the other, she wipes the corners of her mouth. Despite the dim light, I know that her lips are stained red not only from lipstick but also from human blood.

"Don't forget you're speaking about one of the king's squires, marquise," Alexandre says.

"Squire? Didn't you hear the king's decree? She's been stripped of her position. She's no more a squire than I am queen of Sheba. What do you think, my friend?"

A second silhouette appears from the semidarkness, a courtier dressed in a shirt with an open jabot that shows his hairless chest, his sleeves rolled up on pale, muscular arms. Those sensual lips and the single fake beauty spot next to his right eye . . . Count Tarella.

"I believe this wench arrives just in time for our dessert, my dear," he says with a grin. "Tonight, we'll be able to finish what we started a few months ago. This time the king won't come to her rescue. He may even thank us for getting rid of the *last of his servants*, as they say he called her. Everyone knows he hates being ill served."

He gives a wide smile, revealing his reddened jaw, still dripping with the blood of a "ghoul" that fell under his canines. Tonight he's wearing golden ribbons in his brown lion's mane of hair, his way of paying homage to the royal sun. He reaches out to me with a hand bedecked in rings—also made of gold, reminding me of those worn by the godmother.

"Hands off!" Alexandre intervenes. "That's precisely why I came down here, to order you to never even lay your eyes on her."

"Is that so? Or else, what?"

"The Shadows are my witness, I'll make you taste true death, you and your marquise!"

I hesitate to pull my pistol out of its hiding place while the three vampyres clash. Exposing my weapon in front of the other bloodsuckers doesn't scare me if it's to save Naoko. But am I close enough to Marcantonio to aim at his chest without missing? I only have one chance to shoot because I won't have time to reload if I miss.

"Make us taste true death, you say?" he says, laughing. "Oh, I'm just quaking in my boots. Edmée and I weren't born yesterday. We each have close to one century of immortality and the power that goes along with that."

"And I'm older than the two of you combined!" Alexandre roars.

The two other vampyres freeze in an instant, no doubt as surprised as I am. Until now, Alexandre kept his real age a secret, bragging that he was "always nineteen in his head." Is he bluffing? Or has he really infested the world for more than two hundred years? It doesn't matter. The only thing that matters now is to shoot a magical death-silver bullet into the count's ribcage.

The dimness works against me. I have to get closer to my target . . . or let him get closer to me.

"It's hard to believe that a pipsqueak like you could really be two hundred years old," the marquise says, forgetting I'm there.

"It must indeed be hard for an old bag who's twice as young but three times as wrinkled," Alexandre shoots back.

Edmée's face twists in anger. Alexandre definitely spoke in bad faith. For even though she's furious, the marquise's vampyric skin is perfectly smooth. Still, his insult struck a nerve.

"I'll make you eat your words," she howls as she leaps on him, her canines all out.

Now's the time.

I rush into the depths of the moat as fast as I can. No need to turn around to know that Marcantonio is on my heels. I know his predator instinct took over like a cat after a furtive mouse. I run until I'm breathless, not really seeing where I'm going.

It won't be long until the vampyre is on me . . .

Just a few more yards . . .

Just a . . .

My heart freezes the second his icy hand closes around my arm. Roughly, he drags me away from the main moat into a recess lit by a vacillating torch. The large curls of his hair submerge me, as if animated by a supernatural force, like the tentacles of a sea monster drawing me closer.

"Wait!" I say, panting, my back against the raw stone.

Frantically, I slide my free hand into the fold of my dress, feeling around the padding of my bustle until my fingers meet up with the pistol grip.

Marcantonio laughs. "I'm not the type who waits to pluck the fruit that whets my appetite."

"And yet you courted Iphigénie de Plumigny before you bled her."

In the glow of the torch, I can see the vampyre's powdered face frown in shock.

"Don't remind me of the time I wasted on that scatterbrained girl," he says. "She fought like a little devil when I tried to give her the ultimate gift—eternal life. The thought of becoming an unrecorded must have frightened her. Too bad. I ditched her on the spot, and she must have gone off to croak in some filthy alley." A contemptuous snarl deforms his lips. "If you think invoking Iphigénie's name will help get you transmuted, not a chance. I'm going to drain you of your blood, you strumpet, and not give you one drop of mine."

I wasn't requesting anything, only trying to get one last scrap of information about Iphigénie . . . it seems her executioner thinks she's dead because of the fiasco that took place at the Pandemonium Hotel, when he was forced to abandon his victim to escape the Lachryma. Convinced that the transmutation failed, he doesn't know Iphigénie became immortal, returned to visit the Incurables, and that ever since then, she haunts the depths of Paris.

"It's just you and me, *ragazza*!" he howls.

His huge gaping jaw blocks my field of vision. Strands of blood from his previous prey stretch between his oversize canines. As soon as he bends down to plaster his body against mine, I take the pistol out from the folds of my skirt.

My hand clammy with sweat, I press the barrel of the gun to his chest.

My trembling finger searches for the trigger . . .

. . . finds it . . .

. . . and . . .

"Ahhhhhh!" I cry, as I feel the pain from canines piercing my jugular.

Bang!

The deafening blast of the pistol shatters my eardrums.

The grip that was cutting off my breath suddenly loosens. My eyes clouded with tears, I blink repeatedly. Only inches from my face, Marcantonio's is frozen in a grotesque expression, his bloody mouth rounded in surprise. His skin, until now marble-like, swells, little by little, with bluish veins in the half dark. I assume the London alchemists' magical death-silver liquefied and spread quickly throughout his body to neutralize the shadowessence.

"Ma . . . ma che . . . ?" he stammers, bringing his hand to his chest.

A ring spreads on his silk shirt, not bright red and viscous, like the human blood he's spilled so much of, but dark and sooty from the evaporating shadowessence.

The corner of his eye has acquired a grungy stain too. The teardrop tattoo has started to run, releasing its ink beyond the beauty spot meant to conceal it. After all this time, it's as if the Lachryma's vengeance is catching hold of the traitor.

He falls to his knees.

My heart races, wavering between horror and ecstasy, like an out-of-control metronome.

I . . . I destroyed him.

The first vampyre I've inflicted ultimate death on.

I'd like to stay until the end, even to take the torch from the wall to get a better look at this monster's agony.

But already, from the main moat where the hunt continues despite the gunshot, an echo of footsteps gets louder. My survival instinct takes over. Now that I've saved Naoko from the brothel, do I still have a chance to save my own skin?

I slide my hand under the folds of my dress to look for a new death-silver bullet. Before I can find one, fingers quick as lightning grab the pistol from my hands.

"Enough."

Scared, I turn around and discover Lord Raindust, his safety pin earring gleaming in the weak light.

"This isn't why I gave you that weapon," he whispers, glaring at me with his dark eyes.

On the ground, Marcantonio lies motionless, his groans growing weaker and weaker. A puddle of liquid darker than the obscurity spreads under his paralyzed body while his flesh dries up and shrivels horribly. Deprived of the evil power of the shadowessence, he seems to mummify in front of my eyes.

"I . . . I can explain," I stammer, vaguely aware of the approaching footsteps that are increasingly louder.

"Not here," Sterling orders.

I grab one of the gold rings from Tarella's rigid hands, now as brittle as those of a hundred-year-old skeleton. The signet ring glides from his pinky, bearing the coat of arms he bought at a steep price one century ago. I barely have time to place it on my left index finger before Sterling grasps me firmly. At a run, he drags me through the semidarkness, leaving the wizened corpse behind us, the corpse of the one who in former times betrayed the great-great-grandfather of Ravenna of Sicily.

19

RETRIBUTION

"Where . . . where are you taking me?" I stammer.

"As far away from here as possible."

We run off at full speed.

Muffled cries resonate behind us in the darkness. Not the savage joy of vampyres out hunting but panic at having found one of their own reduced to ultimate death, especially as they assumed they were spared forever. Back there, in the recesses of the moat, Marcantonio's unrecognizable body was just discovered.

But Sterling is already dragging me up a narrow staircase at the end opposite to the one I arrived from earlier with Alexandre. I climb the steps four at a time behind him, my hand on my punctured and painfully throbbing neck. I'm breathless, about to pass out.

At the top, no staid butlers. Only a simple exit door that opens onto a remote wing of the Louvre. We emerge into a dark hallway, far from the rooms where the celebration is in full swing. The sounds of the violins barely reach us.

"Follow me," Sterling orders.

His cold hand still gripping mine, he leads me to a door guarded by a drowsy soldier leaning heavily on his halberd. By the way the man jumps, I assume he wasn't expecting to see any courtiers appear in this part of the palace.

"Uh, my . . . my compliments, mam'zelle," he stammers, staring at my sweaty face and the hand I've clamped to my neck.

"Let us by, my good man," Sterling requests. "This young feather-brain danced the never-ending jig and got hurt when she fell. She needs fresh air."

The man steps aside, and we find ourselves out in the night. We pass through two more checkpoints manned by soldiers—I shiver as I recognize the tall, pointy hats of the king's dragoons—all of them trying to keep warm near braseros.

Without letting me catch my breath, Sterling drags me several hundred yards away from the palace, alongside the snowy bank of the Seine. When the last sounds of music have totally disappeared behind the silence of the night, he finally stops and grabs me by the shoulders.

"What were you thinking?" he growls. "I didn't give you this gun so that you could slaughter courtiers at the king's ball." His black eyes, the pupils so dilated by the darkness they devour all the white, shoot lightning bolts. "All you deserve is for me to put an end to you and toss your body into the Seine. That would wipe away any lingering evidence of this fiasco!"

I'm aware now of my vulnerable position, shivering as I am in my flannel dress on the deserted riverbank, my neck dripping with blood.

Never mind. I carried out the mission I set out to accomplish at the Louvre.

"Bleed me if that makes you happy; finish what Tarella started," I tell him. "But I warn you, I taste bitter, and I'm not easy to digest."

Sterling opens his mouth, displaying his white teeth.

I feel his icy lips land on my neck, right on the spot where Marcantonio bit me a few minutes ago . . .

. . . but instead of a crucifying puncture from his canines, his soft, cold tongue meets my lacerated flesh.

He's . . . licking my wound?

Little by little, the pain subsides, as if each lick of his tongue was spiriting it away. When Sterling finally raises his head, my neck doesn't hurt anymore.

"Vampyric saliva possesses healing properties," he explains in a whisper.

"Glad to know it. You called me a death-licker the other night at the inn, so should I call you a life-licker?"

He glares at me with his black-underlined eyes, but I'm not about to cower.

"Let's get away from here," he says. "We got by all the soldiers posted on the ground, but the ones up on the roof of the Louvre can still spot us. Better to leave before news of Tarella's demise spreads." He gestures toward the immense looming shape of the palace, bathed in moonlight. In between the chimneys glistening with frost, I notice dozens of half-hidden dark figures. "It's not only the royal guard of Versailles that came up to Paris tonight, but all the manpower of the capital police is also mobilized to secure the Louvre. Including Mélac's special forces, as you saw from all the dragoons. Nothing was over-looked to try and set a foolproof trap for the Lady of Miracles. Come, let's hurry and find shelter where you can tell me what went through your head, and where I'll have the leisure to decide whether or not to bleed you."

He's ready to set off, but I grab him by his jacket sleeve.

"Wait! If the entire police force is at the Louvre tonight, does that mean the rest of Paris isn't protected?"

"Like I said, through this carnival that pokes fun at the Lady of Miracles every which way, the king seeks to provoke and lead her right into the wolf's jaws. He's pushing her to make a move at the Louvre, where all his armed forces are assembled. Tonight, the rest of Paris doesn't count. Only the Immutable's plan does."

An idea explodes in my head.

Because of his obsessive nature, Louis's focus on vengeance may have allowed a second retaliation to take place. Not at the Louvre but on the other side of the Seine.

"The Incurables," I say in a whisper.

Sterling looks at me, perplexed. "Excuse me?"

"The Hospice of the Incurables, that's where we have to go." I look at him, inhaling long breaths of icy air so that I don't suffocate in the black abyss of his eyes. "We may still have a chance to use your pistol the way you intended. There are six death-silver bullets left to pierce the Lady of Miracles' heart. That's London's objective. There's still time to make it happen. Quick, let's go! I'll tell you everything on the way."

We've been on the other side of the Seine some time before I finish my story. Tristan's decapitated return, being kidnapped by the Lachryma, Naoko's failed rescue, and, finally, my impromptu visit with Mother Incarnadine. I spilled everything to Sterling as we hurried through the maze of streets on the left bank. The only thing I kept from him was my real identity; he still thinks I'm the baronette I pretend to be.

"There, now you know everything," I say, breathless, my lungs on fire.

"You're one tough cookie," he says. "But you're still a mortal, and your flame can be snuffed out by the slightest gust of wind that proves too strong."

He takes his charcoal velvet jacket off and throws it over my shoulders.

"I'll grant you a reprieve because you might still be useful to the English crown," he says coldly. "We'll see if your input leads us to the Lady of Miracles."

A short while later, we arrive in front of the Hospice of the Incurables.

The scene is vastly different from on my previous visits. The encampments around the building are completely deserted, void of any military troops. All around the square, the hermetically sealed shutters blend into the night. The only source of light comes from the nearly full moon that bathes the intertwined-bat-and-snake-shaped wrought iron sign. Everything is at a total standstill, as motionless as a frozen painting.

"Do you really think the Lady of Miracles could come knocking here tonight?" Sterling asks doubtfully.

In the cozy calm of the square, such a thing seems impossible. But the Temple neighborhood was just as quiet only minutes before the ghouls unleashed their destruction.

"All I'm sure about is that she won't strike at the Louvre the way the king thinks she will," I say. "From the beginning, she's been sly enough to show up where she's not expected. And if she didn't take the bait I was meant to be, she's not about to fall for an even more blatant trap. On the other hand, tonight is her golden opportunity to avenge herself on her executioner. Mother Incarnadine must have known the hospice would be left defenseless when she begged the Shadows to help her get through the night earlier."

The lord nods. The nocturnal wind puffs out his cotton shirttails without making him shiver, while I'm dying of cold under his thick velvet jacket.

We head toward the gate in silence, stepping over icy patches and snow mounds blackened by ashes from the abandoned braseros. A sign is posted on the heavy, studded wooden door panel, just under the peephole. Shaky handwriting discourages visitors from going any farther.

Hospice closed from dusk to dawn

"I doubt anyone will come open the door at this hour," I say. "But we can always knock."

"Who's knocking?" Sterling says.

He raises his eyes to the sky and lets out a hoarse cry, a croaking sound that gushes out of his throat. For a second, against the strange light of the moon, his crested hair and dilated pupils make him look like a man-bird hybrid. Yes, he resembles a dark angel with chopped wings, calling out to the sky from where he's fallen.

Shadows pass in front of the pale orb and cross high over the surrounding wall of the hospice. Their shrill croaking seems to answer Sterling.

"You spoke to them?" I ask, remembering the Englishman is imbued with shadowessence that developed the special affinity he has with the birds of the night.

As if in response, a clicking sound can be heard in the middle of the silence. It's the lock opening on the other side of the gate.

Sterling brushes snow aside with the heel of his boot and pulls on the doorknob. The heavy panel opens with a creak that makes the ravens fly off from the other side.

"How did they do that?" I ask, dumbfounded. "With their beaks and legs?"

"You may hail from the countryside, baronette, but you wear blinkers, like every mortal. Your perception is as closed off as the narrow walls of your country manor."

"I didn't wait around for you to escape from those walls and hunt in the forests," I whisper, cutting to the quick, dying to tell him that I was poaching on the lands of the real baron.

"You think a few hunting parties with hounds make you different than the courtiers in the cities? You're just another arrogant aristocrat who's sure that everything is yours for the taking. If there's one lesson our impious existence should have taught you mortals, it's that a new predator can always emerge at the top of the food chain. You know nothing about the unfathomable mysteries of nature."

He looks me up and down from his full height, and though he's right next to me, it's as if he's infinitely far away, as immortals always stand vastly apart from mortals. But that's not the only thing: his cold amber complexion, high cheekbones, elongated eyes, both intense and detached . . . his cold handsome features evoke a place far more distant than the shores of England.

Who is Lord Raindust, really?

Where does he come from?

And why did he use the word *impious* when he referred to the vampyric condition that the Faculty, quite the contrary, celebrates as sacred?

"Before we enter the hospice, I have something to ask you," I tell him. "Do you have a quill pen on you?"

His jet-black brows shoot up. "Of course I do. As a diplomat I'm never without one. Why the question? You don't really want me to sign a contract promising I'll let you go, do you?"

I let out a pained laugh. "I've no faith in the words of a vampyre, even less in those of a spy. It definitely has to do with a contract, but one that I've already fulfilled—killing Tarella. All of Paris needs to hear about it, and the news must reach the ears of the Lachryma as soon as possible. My friend Naoko's life is at stake." I stare deep into his eyes. "I would think that someone who whispers into the ears of birds wouldn't have any trouble sending a carrier crow to the editorial offices of *Le Mercure Galant*, am I right?"

Sterling nods. "The quill pen is in the pocket of the jacket that's over your shoulders. You'll also find paper there."

I scribble a quick statement. Then, using wax from a candle that's abandoned in one of the braseros, I create a makeshift seal. I press the coat of arms from Tarella's signet ring onto the wax as proof. A few minutes later, a black bird flies off into the night with my message in its claws.

"Now, to the hospice!" Sterling says. "Let's see if your intuition is right or if you're just trying to buy time before I finish you off."

He takes his toothpick from behind his ear and slides it between his lips, putting an end to the discussion.

The hospice courtyard is empty of beggars now, and we cross it in silence. Only the tents where the nuns ladled out soup remain; the burlap tarps, stiff from frost, flap in the icy wind.

With a silent gesture, I point toward the nearest entrance. We enter the cold stone hallway on tiptoes. The moonbeams raining down through the thick windowpanes cast pale diamonds on the floor tiles where the miserable commoners were huddled together only hours ago. Only the muffled wails coming from the lunatic ward disturb the tranquility.

Sterling and I continue into the heart of the hospice, so far from any windows that I have to use my tinderbox lighter in order to see anything.

"Here," I say, stopping in front of the Reverend Mother's office, which, in her paranoia, doubles as her cell. "There are no windows in that strong room. I don't think your winged friends will be able to come and turn the lock from the other side."

Sterling rolls the toothpick between his lips.

"Why go in? If the Lady of Miracles is Sister Amarante and she shows up tonight to seek retribution, she'll have to come this way to get to the reverend." He pats the butt of the pistol at his belt. "I'll make good use of this weapon."

"That's right, William Tell, the Lady of Miracles will probably turn up with an apple on her head and strike a pose so you can shoot."

Sterling looks upset.

"I've already survived an attack of ghouls," I say. "Believe me, it's like a hurricane. If the lady comes, better to wait for her behind this door and draw the gun at the right time."

I bang my fist on the thick panel.

Immediately, an anxious voice filters through, proof that the occupant of the room wasn't sleeping, probably too panicked to drift off.

"Sister Garance? Is it already dawn? I didn't hear the morning bells ring."

"Dawn's still a long ways off, and the morning bells won't be ringing anytime soon, Mother Incarnadine," I respond, my lips glued to the door. "It isn't Sister Garance. It's Diane de Gastefriche."

A dull groan can be heard through the studded wood.

"You again. Why have you come back to torment me?"

"I'm not here to torment you but to protect you. I know the soldiers and dragoons have left."

"You may be a squire, but I don't think you can take on Sister Amarante and her ghouls, should they decide to kill me."

"Maybe. But I'm not alone. I've got a lord of the night with me."

A second of silence, then obvious distress.

"An inquisitor-vampyre from the Faculty . . . damn you, you reported me!"

"No. This immortal has nothing to do with the Faculty. Open up now, or I can in fact go knock on the gates at Notre-Damn and spill the beans to the archiater of Paris."

The multiple locks unclick; then the door opens onto the reverend's tall silhouette as it pops out against the fire burning in the hearth.

"Come in quick," she pleads, eager to barricade herself again.

When the last lock is bolted, she turns her pale face toward us, framed by her black veil.

"Who are you, monsieur?" she asks Sterling.

Her small eyes blink with suspicion behind her spectacles as she scrutinizes the vampyre's crested hair, the safety pin in his ear, and the toothpick between his lips.

"I'm a mere shadow, one that you'll never see again once this night is over," he answers.

Relief washes over the nun's drawn face. The mere assumption that she might survive the night seems to reassure her. She doesn't need to know more.

"Praise the Shadows, mysterious lord. With your help, I'll live to see the dawn."

"You, maybe." He gives me a dark look. "Her, maybe not."

I sense the menace in Sterling's voice. He didn't hide that he was going to finish me off if the lady didn't show, and despite his promises to the reverend, he could eliminate her as well if necessary, the better to erase any trace of his time here. He's a spy, first and foremost, and as he told me, his loyalty is to the vice-queen of England.

"And now?" he asks after dragging me close to the fire, away from the nun. "Are we going to kill time chatting about the theology of the Shadows with our hostess? I'm warning you that I've never been interested in the Faculty's made-up poppycock."

Once again, the lord's words clash with those of ordinary courtiers who are completely devoted when it comes to flattering Exili and the big shots of the official religion.

"No need to talk to anyone," I reply. "I prefer silence to your conversation. If tonight is to be my last night, I want to spend it as I wish. By taking a little nap."

His mouth twists into his inimitable half smile.

"Spend your last hours sleeping: now, that's such a mortal weakness."

"Don't forget that this mortal has some of the Immutable's blood in her veins. You're not the only one who developed a dark gift. I have a power too. I don't mean jabbering with birds. It's more like . . . premonitions. I could try and see where and how the Lady of Miracles will turn up. But my visions only appear in my dreams."

Sterling moves the toothpick from one corner of his mouth to the other without looking away.

"Very well, sleep to your heart's content if it pleases you. But I'm warning you, the only visions you'll likely have are those of my next embrace. I accept the role of *life-licker*, as you say—and the sample taste I got of you wasn't as bitter as you claimed. Your flavor is definitely strange, different from all the other blood I've drunk up to now. It's more . . . How shall I say? . . . Complex. Unexpected, a little like the color of your hair."

The way this bloodsucker talks about my *flavor* gives me goose bumps.

"I don't see why my blood would be different than another's," I say. "Or why what it tastes like has to do with my hair color. You probably just got a hint of the Sip of the King that got diluted in my veins."

"Doesn't matter, you worked up my appetite. My second kiss won't heal your wounds. It'll open them up wide again and let your life flow into my mouth."

I shrug and head toward the alcove at the other end of the office, where the reverend's bed is.

Behind the heavy curtain, the sheets aren't undone. I curl up, fully clothed, on the narrow mattress, Sterling's jacket serving as a blanket. On four different occasions now, my dreams have warned me of impending death: before Paulin burst into my room at Versailles; the night before I encountered a ghoul at the Innocents; a few minutes before the army from the depths destroyed the Temple neighborhood; and before Tristan returned from the dead. Tonight again, I want sleep to bring me a vision about the mortal danger that awaits me, whether it be between the claws of the Lady of Miracles or at the hands of Lord Raindust.

The alcove is too cramped.

The mattress too narrow.

The curtain too heavy.

I feel claustrophobic in this tiny space. I can't sleep. It's like I'm suffocating!

I try to get up to leave the nook, but my back collides with the ceiling.

I extend a hand to push the curtain aside, but my fingers meet a stiff wall instead of fabric.

As for the soft mattress under my body, it's now a hard rock.

I become aware that I'm no longer in the alcove or at the Incurables. I'm in a dark, subterranean tunnel, barely large enough for me to crawl through. The silence of the reverend's office has given way to deafening groans . . . coming from behind me, closer and closer.

My heart starts beating wildly. I'm on the run!

Who's pursuing me?

Stuck in this shaft, I can't turn around and see who my attackers are.

So I crawl faster, scraping my knees and elbows, fighting against the paralyzing sensation of being buried alive.

But the slimy stone is slippery under my limbs.

The air, saturated with the stench of musty moss and rot, is scarce.

I . . . I'm suffocating.

I scream when I feel a clammy hand close around my bare ankle.

I have to wake up.

Now!

But no. The nightmare continues, and I have the horrible impression of being imprisoned in my own dream.

Other hands grip my feet, calves, and thighs—so many that I stop counting. I feel lots of claws digging into my flesh, infecting me with their lethal venom.

No!

I can't die in my dream.

But as much as I twist and turn, scream and kick, my efforts are pathetic.

In a last-ditch attempt at survival, I reach for the index finger of my left hand so that I can unscrew the onyx stone and liberate the essence de jour . . . but my finger is bare. The ring is gone.

Greedy mouths close in on my legs.

Ferocious jaws tear at my flesh.

I sense the dreadful cracking of a tibia—my own.

The ghouls . . . the ghouls . . . are devouring me alive.

Quickly, I open my eyes, my lids brimming with tears, my airway blocked. My heart beating savagely, I frantically touch my legs under my flannel dress to make sure they're still there. But even as I pat them, the nauseous feeling of having them torn from my body lingers.

The alcove curtain suddenly opens, spreading the trembling light of the fireplace onto the mattress.

"What's going on, Diane?" Sterling asks. "Why did you scream like that?"

"A . . . a nightmare," I stammer.

Nervously, I fiddle with the onyx ring on my finger.

Its presence barely reassures me.

"A nightmare?" Mother Incarnadine repeats, coming up behind Sterling's shoulder. "What do you mean? What did you see?"

"Nothing specific," I say, even though my vision seemed terribly real.

Sterling makes his toothpick go in circles between his lips.

"Hello, premonition, I'm impressed," he mocks, sounding as ironic as ever. "It seems we came for nothing."

He's barely uttered these words when a muffled cry can be heard coming from far behind the thick walls of the strong room.

The reverend freezes, livid.

"It's probably just one of the lunatics in the asylum," she mumbles, as if to convince herself. "They're light sleepers when the moon is almost full."

A second wail quickly resonates, then a third. Within seconds, a veritable concert of screams rises up from the depths of the hospice.

Mother Incarnadine is seized by a long shiver.

"Oh, the Shadows have pity on me! It's . . . it's starting. My nuns are abandoning me and fleeing like rats."

"And so they should, for it's you and you alone that hell is coming for," I spit out in one breath.

The old woman's hand trembles so badly she barely makes the triple sign of the Blood over her vestment. The call of a hunting horn pierces the walls—the same doleful, deep sound I heard at the Temple seconds before chaos was unleashed.

Already, the ground is shaking under our feet. The papers and books piled on the reverend's desk start to get furiously jostled.

Sterling shoots me a feverish glare. He draws his pistol and points it at the armored door as it starts to shake on its steel hinges.

Is it going to give way?

Will the lord be able to aim accurately enough to kill the Lady of Miracles?

I touch the onyx ring on my finger, ready to unscrew the stone at the opportune moment.

It's one of two things: If Sterling destroys the lady, I'll use the *essence de jour* to blind him and the ghouls while I save myself; if he misses his shot, the blinding glare will allow me to take his pistol and try my own luck.

20

MIRACLES

"I . . . I had the door reinforced by the best workers, the very ones who fortified the Royal Bank of Paris," Mother Incarnadine stammers. "The ghouls' claws will never be able to pierce it, isn't that right?"

"Maybe not the ghouls' claws," I reply between clenched teeth. "But the lady's pyrotechnics certainly will."

The reverend lets out a groan. "The pyrotechnics . . . ?"

"Remember the fireworks that engulfed the Gibbet of Montfaucon? The lady used explosives at Mont Parnasse, too, and many other sites to draw out the people who were holed up in their homes."

The racket in the hallway behind the door is now so thunderous that we don't even hear the screams of the nuns and patients fleeing the hospice. I think about Sister Vermillonne and hope with all my heart that she's among the survivors. For us, however, there's no escape.

The drumming of clawed fists on the door makes the entire room vibrate. The reverend's theological treatises tumble from the shelves and crash onto the floor tiles. A shower of stinging dust descends from the ceiling beams.

Suddenly, silence.

After such a terrible ruckus, this absolute calm petrifies me.

I hear my own labored breathing, as well as Mother Incarnadine's anxious wheezing. Sterling, on the other hand, makes no sound.

Readying myself for the attack, I slowly turn the onyx stone of my ring, per Montfaucon's instructions.

Three turns to the left . . .

Two turns to the right . . .

That leaves me one last rotation before it completely unscrews and I liberate its contents.

The sound of boots can be heard. Not the monstrous stomping of ghouls but hushed, measured treads. Those of killers taking their time, confident that their victims have no way of escaping. The light tapping against the door is more frightening than the drumming was earlier. It's the sound of the inevitable.

When it stops, I assume the assailants are done setting the explosives.

Sterling, Mother Incarnadine, and I back away instinctively, toward the rear of the room.

The reverend trembles so badly that the iron pendant around her neck jumps on her vestment.

The lord's outstretched arm doesn't move one iota, the barrel pointed at the door.

And swiftly, the dreaded explosion goes off.

The blast tears my eardrums, and my head starts to ring like the peal of a bell. I keep my eyes wide open, riveted on the smoking door-knob, my fingers clasped around the bezel of my ring. The door half opens without a noise, unless the bang left me completely deaf.

What's that stream of light spilling into the room?

Is it coming from the door's debris burning in the hallway?

No, no fire is capable of diffusing such a white, blinding light.

I suddenly remember the last words Sister Vermillonne gathered from the Lady of Miracles' victims: *"A terrifying and pale celestial body that came up from the depths of the earth. A gigantic moon rising from the abyss right after the ghouls."*

My lips tremble. "It's . . . it's her. It's the occult moon of the goddess Hecate."

The light burns my retinas so badly I have a hard time keeping my eyes open. And I thought I could just fend off the Lady of Miracles and her army with a little *essence de jour*. My onyx ring seems totally useless now.

A hushed yelping comes from beside me. It's Mother Incarnadine's voice, barely audible in my ringing ears.

"Shoot! Shoot now!"

I can't see the reverend anymore, or the lord.

I hear only a muffled blast.

Did Sterling pull the trigger?

Did he hit the lady?

I widen my burning eyes to try and see something, all in vain. A pitch-black night abruptly descends on me.

I have the devastating impression that I've gone back several days in time, to when the Lachrymas were dragging me through Paris with a sack over my head.

This time, it's a blindfold that deprives me of sight. Bindings tie my wrists, and a tight gag silences me. I've lost hope that Sterling struck the lady. His bullet must have gotten lost in the light.

Disarmed, completely vulnerable, I let myself be dragged into the depths by brutal hands along a slope that keeps descending lower and lower. My morale also plummets with each step. Often, an arm lifts me up when I stumble; sometimes I'm forced to lower my head so it doesn't hit an obstacle. I have no doubts that I left the surface a long time ago. Even if I don't see anything, I inhale the smell of damp rocks, putrid moss, and muddy soil. I hear the hollow echoes of my footsteps and those of my mysterious kidnappers. I can also make out the far-away groans of ghouls and the deafening bellowing of hunting horns.

The lady's people must be using those instruments to direct the abominations that continue to destroy the neighborhood of the Incurables, without anything or anyone standing in the way.

As dark as my despair may be, I also sense the tingle of morbid excitement in the pit of my stomach. A painful mix of terror and impatience. My gut tells me I'm finally about to reach the place I've been searching for these last weeks—the Court of Miracles! I'm certain that's where I'm being taken. Didn't the Eye of the Innocents tell me so in the only legacy he handed me? *"You will never find the Court of Miracles. But perhaps the Court of Miracles will find you, once you've lost all hope."*

After what seems like an eternity, the ground under my feet becomes more or less flat again. A rhythmic noise joins the thumping of boots, like wheels creaking on their axles.

Are there carriages this deep down?

But what kind of vehicle and horses could possibly wind their way through the narrow corridors we just came from?

Unless the perpetual rumbling is coming from the Gehenna, the torture chamber of hell, where the damned are attached to studded wheels and suffer eternal agony. The gag stops me from asking the questions I'm dying to get answers to; the blindfold stops me from seeing the surroundings that mess with my mind. Until I'm forced to stop. Only then does one of my abductors rip off the blindfold, in a snap.

Wonderment.

I don't see another way of describing the emotion that overwhelms me. I was ready to discover a magma of fire, blood, and Shadows. But it's the exact opposite.

Instead of the hell of humanity's former religion, it's a paradise that opens in front of me, as depicted in the old illuminated books. A celestial vault lit with a myriad of dazzling stars. They're so near, as if I've been thrust into the heart of paradise. It's . . . it's a miracle.

Eyes wide, I turn my head to feast on this surreal panorama. That's when I see Sterling, to my right. His mouth is also gagged, but not by a cloth rag. A sparkling chain spreads his jaw apart, his canines protruding and dripping with saliva. The way his pale cheeks have darkened from contact with the chain links, I assume the latter are made of silver. The cuffs binding his wrists are made of silver, too, as evidenced by his swollen skin. Next to him, Mother Incarnadine, also bound and gagged, blinks frantically behind her thick, cracked spectacles.

A strange welcome indeed to paradise . . .

My heart thumps as I look again at what I took to be constellations. Now that I focus more, the glittering orbs aren't stars. I think I can make out glass spheres, in the center of which shine white lights. Yes, there are hundreds of spheres for sure, containing starbursts plucked from space by means of who knows what sorcery and cast into the depths of the ground.

For that's precisely where I am: not in the sky but in the bowels of Paris.

I remember the Eye of the Innocents also wrote the following lines about the Court of Miracles: *The most marvelous dreams come true there. And the most frightening nightmares too.*

I grow aware of the steep walls behind the lights. I'm at the entrance of a subterranean grotto. Long mineral stalactites dangle from the irregular vault. In the hollow of this rocky valley flows a deep river where several large waterwheels are installed. That's what I heard turning: the wooden paddles activated by the flow of underground water. Maybe the wheels are destined to grind the wheat to make contraband flour?

Finally, when my eyes adjust to the ambient light, I'm able to distinguish who brought us here.

There are adults, but children too. Scars mark most of the faces, many jaws are semitoothless, here and there a punctured eye or a torn ear. In contrast to these worn faces, our abductors' clothes seem to be of top quality, and their boots brand new. They all sport a dagger at their belts and also an odd metal tube. A musical instrument, perhaps. Could it be the horn they use to accompany the ghoul attacks? No, going by the sound I heard, that horn should be a lot larger.

One of them, a one-eyed male, neither young nor old, approaches Mother Incarnadine. His good eye blinks uncontrollably, like a nervous twitch.

"It's her," he says after examining the nun. "The old leech!"

The reverend twists and turns, and her eyes bug out in terror. The one-eyed man identified her, and it seems that she recognizes him too. She tries to yell something, but her gag stifles her cries.

"Spare your saliva, Mother," he tells her. "You never bothered to grant me an audience when I was at the Incurables, and it's too late now. It's not like I didn't beg you a hundred times to reexamine my file so I could leave the asylum." His mouth is seized with a nervous spasm. "Yes, I was struck by lightning. Yes, it took out one of my eyes and gave me the tremors. But that doesn't make me crazy. In my opinion, you stuffed me into that hole for twenty-one years just so you could drain me of blood every week and improve the quotas of the hospice, true or not?"

Every week? That's four times more often than the monthly tithe imposed on commoners. I remember that during my first visit to the Incurables, Mother Incarnadine congratulated herself on running an excellent establishment, one that supplied an exceptional amount of blood to the Faculty. It's not surprising, not the way she was draining the lunatics, taking advantage of their real or imagined insanity to keep them imprisoned.

"It's your turn to see what it feels like to scream and not be heard," One-Eyed shouts at her.

Gasping for breath and filled with terror, the nun wobbles. Her legs give way under her, and she faints. Two young people catch her just before she crashes to the ground.

"What do we do with them, Martial?" asks a girl who can't be much older than me, her cheeks pockmarked by smallpox.

"Take them to the mouth of the Devouring, Belle," One-Eyed orders. "The lady will judge them all together once tonight's activities are over. Remove the gags from the two mortals so they don't die of suffocation before the ruling. And careful with the vampyre; wait until you've secured him in a pillory before you ungag him. You don't want him biting off one of your fingers."

I was right to despair. Sterling's bullet never reached the Lady of Miracles, and our lame attempt to stop her turned into a debacle.

The pillory I've been enclosed in consists of a pole fitted with two wooden planks cut with holes: one for the head, two for the hands. Once my neck and wrists are inserted, the planks closed against each other and locked, it's impossible to get out of the restraint. I can feel the onyx ring on my left hand, knowing full well that I won't be able to give it the final turn to unscrew it. Anyway, of what use can the *essence de jour* be in these depths that are so brightly lit, almost as intensely as by daylight itself?

In spite of the pain and frustration, I turn my neck to look at our surroundings, what One-Eyed called the *mouth of the Devouring*. It's a rocky crevice with walls oozing dampness. Heavy droplets fall here and there, splashing onto the ground in a throbbing rhythm. The air smells of moss, wet stones, and metal. Is there an iron deposit somewhere?

For the rest, large black curtains block my view. Suspended from a rod that's driven into the rock face of the ceiling, they totally hide the underground valley. You can still hear the paddle wheels turning, but the river and the hundreds of orbs that illuminated it have disappeared from my field of vision. Only one remains, hanging from the rod, dispensing its strange white light.

"The glass of that miraculous lantern seems impermeable, with no openings," I reason, thinking out loud. "How can a flame burn without any air? Is it a phosphorous powder? No, it could never shine so brightly . . ."

"For a courtier from Versailles, you seem to know your alchemy."

Quickly, I turn my head, which will probably give me a stiff neck.

Sterling is imprisoned in a pillory similar to mine, the second in a line that has a good fifteen of them. Behind him, Mother Incarnadine lies unconscious in her own pillory, her religious veil hanging limply through the opening.

I thought the silver chain had damaged the vampyre's mouth so that he couldn't speak anymore. At least, not until he regenerated himself. But he's able to talk, in spite of the dark burns the chain links have dug into his lips and cheeks.

"Phosphorous has nothing to do with alchemy," I rush to tell him. "It's just a mineral that glows a little at night. My father, the Baron of Gastefriche, had a small piece in his curio cabinet."

It was really in my apothecary father's laboratory that I discovered the phosphorous, but that's something I'll keep to myself.

"I see," Sterling says. "You're an enlightened aristocrat. So to speak."

He raises his eyes toward the miraculous lantern that floods us with its white, implacable light. His ability to maintain his cold, detached sense of humor after the torture he was subjected to impresses me.

"Whatever sorcery makes those lanterns shine, something tells me it's what's keeping the ghouls at bay," he says. "Otherwise, this underground valley would be infested with them."

"I think those miraculous lanterns are doing a lot more than simply protecting the Court of Miracles," I add. "The Lady of Miracles' people also use them aboveground, I'm sure of it. My teammates and I found fragments of glass a lot like the ones these orbs are made of in several of the devastated places. And I'm dead certain that when we were in the reverend's office earlier, it was the same magic that blinded us."

My stomach somersaults at the mention of our botched mission. But Sterling doesn't depart from his insufferable cool composure.

"You're decidedly a beacon of thought, Diane de Gastefriche," he says.

"Well, what if you lit our way with your brilliant thoughts instead of mocking mine? Do you have any idea where we are, since you know Paris? Is the river we saw an underground tributary of the Seine?"

"I don't think so. There's only one underground river in Paris, the Bièvre. A long time ago it crossed the capital south to west and flowed into the Seine. But over the centuries, it got buried. Successive embankments completely covered it. Streets and dwellings rose up above the riverbed."

With each word Sterling utters, his brutalized mouth grimaces in pain.

His wounds are deep. In spite of the disgust bloodsuckers inspire in me, I can't help but sympathize. After all, even with all his repeated threats, he's always helped me until now.

"You should stay quiet," I counsel him. "Wait until you're better. It hurts to see you talk."

A smirk stretches across his bruised lips.

"The pain doesn't bother me. Otherwise I wouldn't wear a silver earring."

Silver?

I assumed the safety pin in his lobe was made of iron. But now I see the ornament is too shiny to be a base metal. I also notice the skin irritation around the area where the earlobe is pierced.

"Why inflict such pain on yourself?" I ask in disbelief.

His black eyes meet mine.

"I told you, I like to chew on a toothpick and wear a safety pin in my ear so that I remember I was a mortal living through hard times not that long ago. But that's not all. The toothpick is made of applewood, like a miniature stake, and the safety pin of silver, like the swords belonging to those who hunt abominations. Both so that I remember who I've become—a monster of the Shadows."

The confession troubles me. After having described his existence as impious, now Sterling calls himself a monster. It's a far cry from the narcissism of an Alexandre who, like all the lords of the night I know, takes pleasure in wallowing in the vampyric condition.

"Let me tell you what's really funny," the lord adds. "My name, Sterling, means *starling* in Old English. The irony is that the same word used to refer to the most common silver alloy before the advent of the Shadows: *sterling silver*, from which coins and silverware were forged. And that's the name I, a vampyre, bear."

He laughs drily, making his pillory shake. I take particular note that he was baptized after a bird, like the ones he magically speaks to, as if even before his transmutation he already somehow belonged to the feathered crowd in the skies.

"There's little chance of us escaping," I say. "The judge's ruling is only going to come down one way."

"True. That charming expression, *mouth of the Devouring*, doesn't inspire optimism. I'm fairly sure said mouth is right behind us. Don't you feel a draft down your back? And smell blood in the air?"

Now that he mentions it, I'm aware that an icy wind lifts the folds of my flannel dress. Firmly shackled by the pillory, I can't turn to see where this blast of air is coming from. Still, I'm guessing there's a tunnel behind us, plunging into the depths beyond the halo of light from the magic orb.

As for the metallic smell . . . if Sterling says it's blood, he must be right. After all, he knows what he's talking about.

"I bet that alchemical light is our only defense against the things lurking behind us," Sterling says, sighing wearily. "Ghouls fear bright light more than anything. When it goes out, nothing will protect us from them."

"It doesn't seem to worry you."

"*When remedies are past, the griefs are ended.*"

"Shakespeare again?"

"*Othello.*"

The mysterious Sterling Raindust truly baffles me.

"You told me you were once a stagehand at a London theater and, obviously, you memorized the actors' lines, just like a parrot," I tell him. "You're always quoting verses as if you were playing a role and nothing really mattered to you . . . not even your very life."

"And what of your own existence, which I'm sure you believe is crucially important? You're like every mortal, full of arrogance. You probably think you're the most precious thing in the world, and you can't imagine that Earth could continue to go round without you."

"Not true!" I shout, louder than I intended, all indignant. "You don't know what I think."

"Every courtier, without exception, is obsessed with one thing: assuring their promotion at the court."

"You're the one who's arrogant if you think you know better what's going on in people's minds. Who says I'm not serving a higher cause? Just as you serve the Crown of England."

A hiccup catches in his throat. At first, I think he's choking on his own saliva, a consequence of the death-silver he had to endure for more than an hour.

But no, he's not choking. *He's laughing.* That tragic raspy laughter, in this grotto where so many others before us must have been nailed to the pillory, chills me.

"Is it the words *higher cause* that amuse you? If you're only serving your country out of personal interest, then you're no better than the courtiers you were mocking, who don't begin to understand the meaning of the word *sacrifice.*"

"You're the one who doesn't understand, Diane," he says. "*Serve*: that's the only word out of your mouth. As if our lives on earth have to serve any purpose. Not for a second have you entertained the idea that we can exist with no purpose at all. No enrichment, no elevation, no allegiance to a crown, no nothing."

I'm growing dizzy.

I think I'd be swaying if the pillory wasn't holding me firmly in place.

"No . . . no one exists without a purpose," I stammer. "Our existence is always reaching toward something. Even if it's just . . . the future."

"There is no future. None at all."

Those words drop like a lead weight from the lord's tortured mouth. *No future.*

Three syllables, a succinct phrase, a master key that finally opens the door to Sterling's soul.

"More Shakespeare?"

"No. This time it's from me. It's too late. The Shadows have won. They'll swallow the world and all of us with it."

His head turned toward me in the pillory, he stares at me more intensely than ever, and for the first time I detect a kind of fragility in him.

"The thirst of vampyres is increasing everywhere in the world," he says softly. "Soon there won't be enough mortals to feed them, so they'll kill one another. It's already begun, with the stryges on the eastern front. The nocturnal abominations proliferate there. They'll end up killing each other, too, until there's nothing left but a complete void."

I take a deep breath. The humid air of the grotto fills my nostrils with a rocky scent, old as time itself.

"If you think the end of the world is inevitable and that everything will sink into the abyss, then why did you give me a weapon the other night? Why are we here tonight, in the lair of an enemy we swore we'd kill?"

"For the simple beauty of the gesture, Diane."

"Excuse me?"

"If the King of Shadows seizes the ghouls from the lady, his rule will be absolute. His merciless empire will spread over the entire earth, all the while gnawing at itself from the inside like an insatiable Moloch. The Immutable will be the last being to disappear, after he's siphoned the blood of every nation, every people, including that of his closest advisers.

"But if the ghouls elude him, war will break out, yes, though with a more balanced playing field. Time won't end under the murderous order of an all-powerful empire but in invigorating anarchy. Even if the final outcome is certain—universal annihilation—at least everyone will be able to wage their own battle, however briefly. Have their voice heard.

The Magna Vampyria will disintegrate into myriad nations and cliques fighting against both the Immutable and each other. Vampyres and mortals, aristocrats and commoners, death-lickers and rebels: what a polyphonic concert it will be. What a finale! England is already the laboratory of this gestating chaos. Hopefully it'll spread to the Continent and the entire world. That's what I wish for.

"I'm telling you again, Diane, our lives have no meaning, and there is no future. But all things considered, I'd rather that the world end in polyphonic fury than choked under stony silence."

Sterling expressed himself with such conviction—such rage—that the wounds in his mouth have opened up again. Streams of blood flow out, a dark vampyre blood obscured by the shadowessence.

I've known moments of despair before, but now I realize they were nothing compared to the profound nihilism that haunts the lord. More shattering still, this dark discourse, which seems dictated by the Shadows themselves, paradoxically makes Sterling more . . . *human* to me.

And what if he's right?

What if all the battles were lost in advance, both the Immutable's to rule forever and the Fronde's to restore the Light?

What if there is truly no hope, not for mortals, vampyres, or anyone?

What if there's no future?

Numb from the pillory, I mull over the dark thoughts that Sterling put in my head.

I don't know how many hours go by. Nothing allows me to measure the passing of time that flows as unrelentingly as the underground river in its invisible bed. The hum of the paddle wheels that reaches me, muffled by the thick curtain of dark fabric, evokes the grinding wheel of the eons that crushes everything in its way: individuals, families, and civilizations.

No future.

Abruptly, one of the curtains opens. The lady's henchmen bring in another prisoner.

That patched tunic with the black hood . . .

That bare head with suture points around the neck . . .

And, most of all, that scent of decaying leaves, both subtle and slightly pungent . . .

My heart jumps in my chest as I recognize Orfeo's massive shoulders, bound by silver chains.

"We found this creature wandering in one of the tunnels near the Gobelins neighborhood," says One-Eyed by way of introduction. "He'll face his judgment with the rest of you, in a pillory."

Under normal circumstances, Orfeo's endowed with colossal strength. But tonight, he's visibly weakened by his restraints. As a creature of the Shadows, he's sensitive to silver, just like vampyres.

The lady's henchmen place him in a pillory right next to me. Then they throw a bucket of ice water over Mother Incarnadine's head to wake her up.

"Huh? What?" she shouts, coming to. "Sister Garance, did the morning bells ring?"

"More like *your* hour will be ringing soon!" One-Eyed yells at her. "The Lady of Miracles is going to make her ruling any minute now."

The reverend suddenly realizes she's enclosed in shackles. Gripped with panic, she trembles, her lips moving in an incoherent mix of prayers and curses. But One-Eyed and his gang are already on the other side of the curtain.

Without paying any more attention to the reverend's ramblings, I twist to get a better look at Orfeo. His muscular neck is so large that the pillory barely contains him. He turns his bare head, protruding as it does from the wooden yoke, toward me. In the harsh light of the miraculous lantern, his pale-green complexion looks even more translucent, like the surface of a puddle.

"What are you doing here?" I ask.

His bloodless lips, resembling those of a drowning victim, mouth three syllables.

Na . . . o . . . ko.

My heart melts as I recognize my friend's name, which Orfeo's tongueless mouth can't articulate. So he came to Paris to save her. He must have developed a strong bond with her during the few weeks they lived in the basement of the Grande Écurie—a friendship so strong he couldn't bring himself to abandon her.

"You know this abomination?" Sterling asks.

"I forbid you from calling him that. Orfeo is like my brother."

Orfeo's jade-green eyes seem to tremble, just as they did when I gave him my mother's pocket watch.

"How did you manage to enter Paris, Orfeo?" I ask softly. "Did . . . did you remember the secret passageway that goes under the outer ramparts?"

His long black lashes blink over his strange eyes, confirming my intuition. His desire to find Naoko must have stirred up fragments of memories from the depths of his foggy mind. And now it seems his pained expression isn't because of the fate that awaits him. It's because he failed to save our mutual friend.

"Don't worry, Orfeo," I say. "Naoko was captured by the bandits, but I made a deal with them. Tell me, do you remember the Lachryma?"

He shakes his head, the pillory that constrains his spine shaking along with him.

"It doesn't matter. All you need to know is that the Lachryma promised to let her go."

As he hears this, the pale-green features of the living dead relax, and he gives a hint of a smile. It's just a crease of tiny lips, as fragile as a water lily on the puddle of his greenish face. And yet it's enough to light up my soul, dissipating the melancholic fog that Sterling's words spread in my head. If I was ready to renounce hope for myself, I'm not about to renounce it for those I love. I did what I could to save Naoko from a terrible fate, and now I'll do everything I can to save Orfeo.

I've barely made this resolution in my mind when I hear the bellowing of a horn, a sound that masks the monotonous churning of the paddle wheels.

"The Lady of Miracles!" announces a booming voice that reverberates under the invisible vault.

The black curtains that surround the pillories shake from top to bottom.

Then they open fully, all at once.

21

JUDGMENT

Total dazzlement.

Just as at the hospice earlier, the sudden difference in light is so brutal that I'm forced to shut my eyes. It takes me several long seconds to reopen them, time enough for my pupils to adjust. Even then, my eyes stay drowned in tears.

In front of me, a star seems to have risen: the occult moon from the depths. It's a luminous circle of radiant white so large and so bright it eclipses the constellations of miraculous lanterns filling the underground valley.

An imposing figure stands out against the blinding light.

The contrast is too strong for me to make out any of its features. But I perceive contours enveloped in a long dress, loose hair in a strange double-horned raised coif.

It's her.

The one I've been chasing all these weeks.

In that suspended moment, a memory from Butte-aux-Rats rushes back to me. The little Chinese shadow-puppet theater that Bastien set up on winter evenings to entertain me. It was just a modest sheet of a screen where he projected shapes that he made with his nimble fingers.

How many hours I spent dreaming and trembling in front of his mermaids and ogres, his wizards and dragons.

Today, once again, I'm a spectator at a shadow-puppet performance, and part of me becomes a captivated little child again.

A clear and regal voice echoes under the vaulted grotto.

"We, Hecate, Lady of Miracles, will proceed with your judgment before our assembled court."

Even if I can't see the courtiers the lady refers to, I hear their breathing. A sizable crowd is in attendance.

"Two of you were captured in Mother Incarnadine's office," the lady states. "Are you mercenaries she paid to protect her in the wild hope of escaping our vengeance? Speak."

"I didn't pay anyone!" the reverend yells before Sterling or I can answer. "Those intruders came to the hospice without me asking them. The girl . . . is called Diane de Gastefriche. She's a squire to the king who vowed to crush you. She brought a foreign vampyre with her and his pistol with death-silver bullets to destroy you. They're the ones you should be taking revenge on, not me."

The nun shoots me a look of pure hatred from under her veil. The radiant light of the occult moon illuminates the smallest of her wrinkles, each of her features contracted by bitterness. In her cowardice, she hopes to save her head by offering mine.

"I never sought to harm you," she goes on to the lady, pretending. "Oh, how I blamed myself for not having saved you from yourself. And why did you feel the need to go to the mass grave at the Barrière du Trône two and a half years ago, exposing yourself to that vampyre who abducted you? When you came to me after your illegal transmutation, I lost all reason. Yes, I planted a quill pen in your heart, but I was panicked. Later, when I lifted the lid of the coffin after the wake, it was to free you. In turn, you got scared, and you fled. But I only wished for your well-being, I swear it."

The old woman's hypocrisy flabbergasts me. Hours earlier, she confessed to me that she'd tried to decapitate the young vampyre with a saw. How can she think the victim forgot?

"Spare me, for old times' sake," the reverend implores. "Let me go back aboveground, and I'll tell no one. I promise you, Sister Amarante."

"Sister Amarante is no longer here. Only Hecate remains."

The lady's crystal-clear voice hardens like a diamond.

"You killed Sister Amarante," she accuses. "Not with a quill pen or a saw but with a look. The one you gave her when she sought refuge in your arms. A look of horror, of disgust, one you give to a monster."

"You . . . you're not a monster," the reverend stammers, twisting in her pillory.

"Yes. We became one. A cruel monster without pity, who now condemns you to death. You'll be handed over to the ghouls. As soon as the curtains fall again and the bulb is extinguished, they'll come out of the mouth of the Devouring to butcher you alive."

This confirms Sterling's intuition. The miraculous lanterns are holding back the ghouls with their light. What did the lady just call them? *Bulbs?* The only bulbs I know belonged to my father's laboratory: they were glass vials in which he kept different serums and concoctions.

Ignoring the reverend's cries for pity, the figure wreathed in light turns toward me.

"As for you, Diane de Gastefriche, you'll be subjected to the same death. Let that send a message of our resoluteness to your master, the King of Shadows. May he understand that we won't stop before we have Paris."

"And *he* won't stop until he has your army of ghouls in his grasp," Sterling intervenes.

I give him a furtive glance. With his head locked in his pillory, he braves the torrent of light that spills down on him, never blinking.

"I'm Lord Sterling Raindust, attaché to the ambassador of England. The reverend is correct: the gun with the death-silver bullets belongs to me. I admit that one of those bullets was meant for you, so the Immutable could never learn your secrets."

"At least you have the courage to admit it, unlike others who lie in hopes of saving their hides," the lady says. "But our sentence is irrevocable. The squire must die. And so must you, Lord Raindust."

"Such is your sovereign right," Sterling replies, slipping with ease into his role of diplomat in spite of the irons that bind him. "But allow me to insist: Louis the Immutable will never grant you any crown. I read as much in his personal missives. He'd rather reduce his own capital to ashes than share its control. And you, madame, do you prefer to be holed up in this city under siege until it smolders, or to carve a real realm under an open sky, under different latitudes?"

Has Sterling lost his senses? No, in the flood of white light, his black eyes, with their penciled underline, sparkle with acuity.

"And what latitudes might those be?" the lady inquires.

"The British Isles, or farther still, the English colonies of the Americas. Vice-Queen Anne, my mistress, also reigns on an empire, a vast territory that's about to escape from the King of Shadows' control. As I said, Anne ordered your assassination to ensure that your loathsome army doesn't end up in the hands of her rival. But I'm sure she'd be far more delighted if that army entered into an alliance with her. This realm that the Immutable refuses you, she will gladly offer up. You could establish it wherever it pleases you from among her numerous dominions."

Those words awaken a frenzied murmur among the invisible audience. For a few seconds, the figure that pops out against the backdrop of a gigantic moon remains immobile, like an angel suspended precariously from a sky of light.

"Never."

The swift answer comes down like an axe.

"We will never abandon Paris, do you hear me? *Never!*"

Her voice clear at the start of her remarks, then harsh when she addressed Mother Incarnadine, the lady now sounds enraged.

"Fleeing the capital would be a defeat, a renunciation. Never will we fold in front of the Immutable. It is he who will fold before us, forced to recognize us as his equal before the eyes of the entire world."

This voice that resonates and smolders, I know it all too well. It's the voice of obsession. Not that long ago I, too, was devoured by a fixed goal, focused on the Immutable. Such is the malevolent power of the absolute monarch—he attracts and fastens to himself the fiercest willpowers. Even as we loathe him, we remain under his thumb.

"I understand your fervent wish for revenge, madame," I shout, unable to hold back anymore. "But careful that it doesn't blind you, for vengeance can be a blaze more dazzling than all your bulbs combined."

The lady's silhouette stays mute a second, a silent effigy in the middle of a deluge of light. Even if I can't see her through my partially closed eyelids, I sense that she's staring at me.

"At your age and given your current position at the court, what could you possibly know about vengeance?" she finally says, full of scorn.

"I know plenty, believe me, Hecate . . . or should I say, Iphigénie."

As I speak those words, I know I'm taking a huge gamble. If the lady reacted with cold fury to the name Amarante, how will she respond to the one she was given at birth? But I don't have a choice. I have to appeal to the sensitive young woman she once was, who may still remain behind the cruel vampyre. Not so much to save my life but to save Orfeo's, and to propose a deal to the lady. The idea of an alliance suggested by Sterling has inspired me with another. A crazy possibility: *What if the Lady of Miracles and her army joined the Fronde?*

"I know your story," I hurry to add. "I learned about the injustices you were dealt. Your merciless upbringing, your banishment from Versailles, the brutal transmutation that was imposed on you, right up to the betrayal that you endured at the hands of the institution you took refuge in."

"Enough, or we'll have your tongue ripped out!" the lady thunders.

"All right, I'll stop talking. Everything I have to say is on my finger."

At the risk of gashing my skin, I extend my wrist through the hole of the pillory and stretch out my left index finger, the one where I slipped Marcantonio's signet ring.

The lady's impressive silhouette comes slowly toward me. With each step, the glacial aura that precedes her grows stronger. Little by little, the contours of her figure define themselves in the glittering halo of the occult moon.

Her sumptuous dress, a deep midnight blue with folds that glisten against the light, has the gleaming appearance of the most precious moiré fabric.

Her long chestnut hair undulates in ample waves on her shoulders, animated by that supernatural vitality belonging only to immortals.

The horns of her coif are in reality the two extremities of a large diadem finely wrought in the shape of a crescent moon, the crown of the goddess Hecate herself.

But most striking is her face, which I discover once she's no more than a few feet from me. The resemblance to Hélénaïs leaves me breathless. The same Madonna oval, same perfectly curved nose, same golden-brown eyes that seem poured from pure gold. Hélénaïs's sister, older by seven years, could be her twin. The real difference is her expression: while the squire flaunts a swaggering bravado at all times, Iphigénie seems to carry the weight of the world on her forehead. There's something heavy as lead in her celestial features.

"I beg for your lenience!" Mother Incarnadine cries out, seeing her victim, now a judge, for the first time. "I . . . I recognize former patients from the asylum among your people. You obviously took pity on them by welcoming them here, so why not on me as well? I'm more deserving than Martial, the epileptic . . . or Pierrot, the possessed, who's just behind you."

Narrowing my eyes, I make out a second silhouette, someone so still and silent that I hadn't noticed him until now. It's a child about twelve years old, frail in his dark woolen frock coat, the sleeves a little too long. His midlength brown hair falls on his gaunt face as if he wanted to hide behind it.

Without paying attention to the reverend's pleas, the lady continues to advance toward me, her strange valet at her heels.

She directs her magnetic gaze on my hindered hand.

I see her glance at the Gastefriche signet on my ring finger . . .

. . . then at the onyx on my middle finger . . .

. . . until her eyes rest on Marcantonio's signet ring on my index.

Her eyes go wide. Her pupils retract. In a vampyric reflex, her canines burst forth from the gums where they were hidden.

"Him!" she says in an animallike growl.

"He is no more," I shout, breaking my promise not to speak again.

I know that in a moment of fury, the lady could sink her fangs into my pilloried neck. I'm entirely at her mercy. With each second and each word, I'm risking my life and the future of the Fronde.

"I gave him ultimate death," I rush to explain, not taking a breath. "I used Lord Raindust's pistol when we were at the ball at the Louvre earlier, where the Immutable thought he'd set a trap for you. I tore that signet ring from Tarella's fleshless finger after my very own eyes saw him turn into a shriveled corpse."

The lady's face freezes a few inches from mine, her long canines resting on her parted velvety lips. She's petrified like a statue, as only vampyres can be, without the beating of veins to pulsate her alabaster skin, without a breath of air to make her nostrils quiver.

"By fulfilling the vendetta demanded by a group of bandits called the Lachryma—in exchange for my best friend's release—I avenged you as well," I say, breathlessly.

Under her crescent-moon crown, the vampyre's features come to life again.

"You don't understand, Diane de Gastefriche."

She's so close to me now that her chestnut curls brush my cheeks like silk serpents come to life. But her dead mouth doesn't project any breath in the hollow of my ear.

"Our vengeance does not stop with that swine. He's an insignificant detail. What we want is—"

"To make the King of Shadows bite the dust. I know. And I can help you."

The lady takes a step back to get a better look at me.

The child accompanying her also eyes me between his wild locks.

And I feel Sterling's puzzled eyes on me, too, and those of an outraged Mother Incarnadine. For the lord as well as the reverend, I'm supposed to be a courtier at the beck and call of the sovereign. I was even his favorite squire, until recently. No doubt they attribute my flip-flop to resentment at having been stripped of my responsibilities and the desire to save myself. They don't need to know the truth.

"Unshackle me, and I'll tell you how I can help you," I say.

The lady gestures slightly with her hand. Immediately, two men emerge from the light and, with one turn of a key, unlock the planks of my pillory.

My back cracks as I stand upright after having been in a hunched position for so many long hours. I pretend to massage my neck and numb wrists as I hurry to think of my next move.

Already, the lady's men drag me behind their mistress's footsteps, toward the occult moon. I just have time to glance at Orfeo and mouth a silent promise: *"Count on me."*

Suddenly, the light decreases.

It takes me a few seconds to adjust to the change in luminosity. I realize I've passed onto the other side of the occult moon, or, more precisely, onto the other side of the gigantic lamp that dazzled me. For that's what it is, a round lamp more than a yard wide, mounted on wheels. It's turned toward the pillories and, behind them, toward the mouth of the Devouring—the entrance to a dim tunnel.

"Another marvelous bulb," I say, torn between horror and wonder.

"No, not a bulb," the lady replies beside me. "A projector."

I look up at her.

Her face is no longer lit by the relentless light she called a *projector*, but by a gentler one, by the hundreds of bulbs strung across the rock face of the valley. Is this why her expression seems less severe?

"By . . . by what miracle?" I stammer.

"That of electricity. We can reveal it to you, for you'll never leave the underground valley of the Bièvre. At least not before we have complete confidence in you, as with all the subjects of our court."

The Bièvre. So Sterling was right. On the other hand, try as I may to search my memory, the word *electricity* doesn't ring a bell.

As for the lady's subjects . . . I blink, taking stock of the hundreds of people assembled at the foot of the projector. I recognize one-eyed Martial, and Belle, the girl with the pockmarked cheeks. The other "courtiers" are of the same sort: lame, dragfooted, scar faced, rebels with wild expressions. It would seem that the old medieval Court of Miracles has been reconstituted here—the one with beggars and swindlers. These people look like the miserable lot I saw rushing to the soup tents at the Incurables. But instead of wearing rags, they're dressed in furs and rich velvet coats. Instead of being hunched and crushed by woes, they proudly puff out their chests. All of them sport the strange orange metal tube at their belts, same as our abductors.

Behind them, the underground valley stretches out in all its expanse, vaster than I had imagined when I arrived a few hours ago. Now that we're on high ground, some fifteen yards from the riverbed, I can better see the lay of the land. I'm able to distinguish cave dwellings carved into rocky slopes that go down to the water. A small city has sprung up here, in secret, under the Paris cobblestones.

"To start gaining our trust, you're going to explain why and how you plan on making the king *bite the dust*," the lady orders.

"Here?" I ask, glancing at the men holding me by the arms, at the entire court that surrounds me.

"Do you think our subjects are unworthy of hearing you speak? Disabuse yourself! Aboveground, they were considered the dregs of the Magna Vampyria, but down below they're the salt of our kingdom. As for you, the courtier from Versailles, your noble titles hold no value here, even if the Immutable's blood runs through your veins."

I take a deep breath, like a diver before a deep plunge. The moment has come for me to find the right words, to try and recruit the most powerful ally the Fronde has ever dreamed of.

22

ALLY

"You're right, madame," I say. "I wouldn't want to take advantage of the Immutable's blood running in my veins to claim any privilege. But the king is likely to use the blood link that unites me to him to locate the Court of Miracles. At any time, if he suspects I've been abducted, he can use his sixth sense and send troops into the valley of the Bièvre. A large army was assembled in Paris this very night."

In showing my hand, I expect that my revelations will alarm my host, but she just gives a clear laugh, cold as an icy shower.

"No army will ever vanquish mine," she says. "Legions of ghouls live hidden on the edges of this underground valley, not only behind the mouth of the Devouring but also in the hundreds of other corridors that lead here. Thanks to the power of the electric light, my people come and go as they please, clearing a path among the abominations with the beams of their flashlights. The Immutable's soldiers will be shredded to pieces should they decide to penetrate here armed with simple torches that a gust of wind will instantly blow out."

To illustrate her point, she takes the metal tube attached to the belt of one of the men escorting me. I notice that one end is covered with a thin coat of rounded glass, exactly like the debris my teammates and I found during our search. With her long white finger, the lady pushes a button and . . .

. . . a luminous ray floods out through the glass.

"Flashlights allow us to navigate at will in the depths, without fear of the abominations that swarm here," the lady says. "The batteries last all night long. This flashlight is actually on its last legs."

The beam, in fact, starts to make a crackling sound, its intensity rapidly decreasing.

The lady shuts it off by pushing the button again.

"Come morning, we recharge the flashlights here, in the valley. The bulbs that burn permanently make it a safe haven where monsters won't ever dare venture. As for our projectors, not only do they dazzle perpetrators in the pillories; we mostly use them to herd ghouls in waves, pushing them toward the surface, in coordination with the sound of the horn. Such a powerful light, for the sensitive eyes of those creatures, sends them into a total, devastating panic. That's the power of electric light. That's *our* power!"

So this is the "*terrifying and pale celestial body*" that those on their deathbeds at the Incurables were referring to with their final breaths, as recorded by Sister Vermillonne. I vaguely sense that if the lady hits me with these revelations, it's because I'm her enemy's representative. Through me, he's the one she's humiliating. She refers to a magic I'm totally ignorant of. On the other hand, the way she speaks about it is something I know only too well. It's like hearing the King of Shadows himself, so sure of his power and invincibility.

My resolution wavers. Can such a despot ever put herself at the service of the Fronde? Am I truly ready to reveal my rebel identity to this assembled court?

"So, tell us," the lady orders, cutting my thoughts short, "is it to save herself that one of the Immutable's squires is prepared to betray her master?"

"I'm no longer a squire, madame," I say cautiously. "The king stripped me of my duties because I was unable to find you. From now on, I prefer to serve *you* rather than him."

"Very well. But what's your plan to make him buckle and snatch Paris from his grip?"

"Lord Raindust is right. You'll never be able to wrench Paris from him as long as you stay in these walls."

"What?" the lady says, a cold fury freezing her features. "Is this what you had to tell us when you asked to be unshackled?"

"But you'll be able to take far more away from him," I rush to add. "You could topple his crown, even his throne. To achieve that, you need to retreat for a while in order to counterattack later on. You need to form an alliance. You'll use the power of your *electricity* all the better by deploying it on a vast territory, rather than in this grotto."

"Are you also going to tell us to forge a pact with Vice-Queen Anne?"

I try to look the lady square in the eyes, measuring all that I say. One word out of place and everything will collapse.

"Many are dissatisfied with the Magna Vampyria," I respond. "Vice-Queen Anne among them, yes, but she's not the only one. For personal reasons, I seek vengeance against the Immutable for the dishonor he brought upon me. Countless other nobles throughout the kingdom suffer the tyrant's temper every day. And it's not just the nobility. The fourth estate, more than any other, can't take it anymore. Seeing whom you've welcomed at your court, it would seem that the fate of the people matters to you, does it not?"

An innocent question to probe the heart of the one who was once a compassionate young woman, if Sister Vermillonne is to be believed. Given the lady's expression, I try to draw snippets of this former sensitivity, hoping to see the gold melt from her eyes. But it stays cold and opaque.

"You're mistaken if you think our court is open to the fourth estate," she replies. "Those who live here are lower than commoners. They form the *quint* estate, the fifth and lowest of all." In a sweeping hand gesture, she embraces the assembly that's listening intently to us. "Outcasts of society, spit upon by the bougies of posh neighborhoods as well as by the people of working-class areas. Those who have a roof over their heads only have contempt for pariahs. I saw that firsthand when

I worked at the Incurables. That's where the untouchables wound up, those even the most humble didn't want: crazies rejected by their families, prostitutes stripped of their good looks by smallpox and booted out of their brothels, beggars disfigured by disease and misery."

The lady's words, hard as bronze, reverberate in the cavernous vault. Her previously impassive face is racked by a violent emotion. Unfortunately, it isn't the compassion I'd hoped to awaken in her; it's bitterness.

"I myself thought I'd known total degradation when I was banished from Versailles, disowned by my father, imprisoned at the hospice," she says, abruptly switching to the first person singular to evoke her past before becoming the Lady of Miracles. "But I hadn't yet drunk the cup down to the dregs. Only after I was illegally transmuted did I fully comprehend despair." She looks over at the pillories where the three other prisoners are restrained, too blinded by the projector to see us. "The reverend, whom I trusted completely, sought to eliminate me like you squash a roach. So I tried to find refuge with the families of commoners who had relatives at the Incurables, the very ones I had cared for with love and respect. But the doors were shut one by one; some tried to pour boiling water on my head through the windows; those who had dogs let them loose on me. So I really hit rock bottom. I contemplated suicide as the only way out, the only deliverance. I just had to lie down on one of the quays that runs the length of the Seine, out of sight, and wait for the morning sun to turn me to ashes. Yes, that's what I would have done had it not been for Pierrot."

Pierrot?

I turn my attention to the silent boy accompanying the lady.

Is he mute like Orfeo? Or just exceedingly shy?

His elusive eyes remain half-hidden between his long strands of brown hair.

The lady places a hand on his shoulder with unexpected, almost maternal gentleness.

"The reverend calls him *the possessed*, probably what his parents who abandoned him also believed, before he landed at the Incurables. A lunatic with a head full of demons. But when I was on staff, I listened to him closely. I lent him an ear that had never been extended to him. I made sense of his strange dreams and elaborate visions—the secret of the electric light."

What the lady is saying captivates me. The words she uses—*dreams, visions*—resonate with my own experiences these last few weeks.

I look at Pierrot anew. So he's the one responsible for the formidable magic by which the Lady of Miracles organizes the ghoul attacks. This upends everything. By ordering me to capture his rival, the king aimed at the wrong target; by asking me to kill her, Montfaucon also erred. The unrecorded vampyre's alchemical power isn't innate. She got it from a boy barely out of childhood.

"When Count Tarella raped me, I had gone to the communal grave at the Barrière du Trône," she continues, lost in her thoughts. "I wanted to try out a tool I had taken weeks to fashion in secret in my cell at the Incurables, something based on Pierrot's exact instructions—the first flashlight. Oh, it was still just an experiment. I used a jar instead of a bulb and lead graphite by way of a filament. As for the battery, I fashioned one out of coins and pieces of stacked cardboard, all macerating in vinegar. I was dying to test this invention under real conditions— against the ghouls. I had witnessed too many painful agonies at the Incurables, too many deaths following a poisoned scratch. I thought I finally had a weapon to fight against those abominations. But before I could speak about it to the reverend and the Faculty, I had to try it out so I wouldn't be accused of listening to the rantings of a lunatic."

Graphite, battery, filament . . . all this alchemical jabber makes my head spin. Still, one thing stands out: Pierrot's visions are definitely the source of the flashlights, bulbs, and projectors, of all the magic of the electric light.

"No ghoul came to the Barrière du Trône that night," the lady goes on. "And that's probably for the best. My flashlight prototype was only emitting a single filament of light, probably too weak to push back the least nocturnal abomination. Instead of a cannibalistic monster, a vampyre attacked me: Tarella. The rest, you know . . ."

She heaves a deep sigh.

"While I was dragging myself through the streets of Paris, covered in blood and rejected by all, thinking about Pierrot saved me from suicide. The prospect of what he and I could accomplish together helped me survive. For many months, I lived as an unrecorded vampyre, barely evading the inquisitors of the Faculty, living off the drunken students who staggered around the streets after the start of the curfew. Come daylight, I took shelter in a public dump on the southern edge of Paris, near the Gobelins. It was a hole full of refuse, going deep into the ground. If you listened closely on windless nights, you could hear the distant murmur of a river: the underground Bièvre, covered up by streets and dwellings over the centuries.

"In the heart of the dump, I gathered the ingredients necessary for my revenge. Coins taken from my victims, copper torn from the gutters of buildings, glass bottles stolen from badly shored-up taverns. Then I went to the Incurables to free Pierrot and the prisoners in the asylum. They didn't reject me as if I had the plague; they recognized the person who had cared for them without recoiling at my newly cold skin. They followed me up to the dump at the Gobelins, and under my guidance, and with the materials I provided, they fashioned countless flashlights nonstop. As they worked, I combed through all the old books I'd stolen from the hospice to learn as much as possible about ghouls, in preparation for our expedition into the depths."

Once again, the lady's face becomes emotional as she relives the memory of that first entry into the bowels of Paris.

"Relying on old geographic maps also stolen from the Incurables, I pinpointed the course of the Bièvre. Instinct told me that it was the perfect place to set up my court. I just had to locate the most favorable spot.

"Through a manhole cover at the Gobelins, we transported rafts right up to the black stream. Then, armed with our flashlights, we descended into the tumultuous water. Half the crew died during the crossing, cut down by the ghouls because our flashlights weren't as powerful as they are today. But enough brave souls survived and made it here, into this vast grotto where we established the colony."

The lady's golden gaze wanders over the audience. Today there are hundreds of them, but only a handful were here in the beginning. I assume Martial, who's looking at his mistress out of his good eye, one that gleams with loyalty, was a member of these pioneers.

"This area used to be an open-air swamp," the lady resumes. "Before flowing into the Seine, the Bièvre used to irrigate the king's Garden of Plants. But ever since the embankment work began in Paris, the surface of the garden is only watered by human hands. Parisians have forgotten all about this buried valley, but we rediscovered it.

"Over the months, the colony grew. Thanks to Pierrot's visions, we learned how to tame the river. Ever since it's run underground, it never freezes. In fact, it flows impetuously in all seasons. We erected turbines to produce more electricity that gets transported up to the bulbs via copper wires sheathed in waxy fabric."

She points to the paddle wheels that I had thought were intended to grind grain. I notice long wires suspended from wooden poles coming out of the riverbed, rising up to the string of lights attached to the rock face.

"Little by little, the valley was illuminated, snatching more territory from the Shadows and nocturnal abominations. Then we led our first expeditions aboveground. It wasn't about unleashing the army of ghouls yet. We were content to raid granaries and merchants' warehouses at night to steal food and warm clothing. We also recruited orphans who were too old to find a foster family, and the deprived of all stripes. Last of all, we abducted the artisans we needed for our expansion: iron-workers, blacksmiths, carpenters, and glassblowers. Those who agreed to cooperate became my full subjects. As for the others . . . they ended up under my fangs, for I had to feed myself."

The lady's face, which opened up at the stirrings of her memory, abruptly closes.

I shiver in my flannel dress. In the aquatic ambiance of the grotto, my host suddenly reminds me of a mermaid, attracting mortals to the bottom of the abyss to feast on them. The breeze rising from the riverbank makes her chestnut curls flutter. They look like amber algae dancing around her opalescent forehead.

"After a year and a half spent expanding my court and equipping it with miraculous weapons, I sensed the time had come to claim domination aboveground," she goes on. "That was my plan of vengeance against the Immutable—tearing the capital away from his empire. I took the name Hecate, goddess of the occult moon of the depths, mistress of ghouls and nightmares. With the help of the projectors, I unleashed the first ghoul attacks. Those raids allowed us to tend to the growing needs of the colony in terms of nourishment, clothing, and prisoners— the ones who managed to barricade themselves to survive the ghouls would not resist our explosives. We constantly need more manpower to generate ever more electricity. The Bièvre alone is no longer enough."

She gestures toward the top of the grotto on the other side of the river, on the slope opposite the pillories.

Above the cave dwellings, I can make out silhouettes going round and round, chained to wheels like slaves to their galley. Those engines aren't activated by the running water but by human chattel. Which means L'Esquille's hypothesis was wrong. The Court of Miracles doesn't harbor a vast number of the unrecorded, as he reckoned. The thousands of Parisians who vanished these past months didn't end up under the fangs of thirsty vampyres. They didn't pay with their blood but with their sweat, to produce the mysterious electricity that feeds the lady's crazy ambitions. I shiver as I think about the son of poor Mère Mahaut of Mont Parnasse and how he's surely tied to one of those wheels, same as his wife, maybe even his child.

"The most deserving are freed after a time and join my court," the lady says, noticing my concern. "Of course, on condition that they prove their loyalty."

"The dead left by the ghouls after each attack don't get a second chance," I venture to remind her, my throat tight.

"In all wars there are victims. That's how it goes."

"But what of the innocent?"

"*No one is innocent!* I told you. All those supposedly well intentioned have, in fact, no consideration for those lower than themselves. Worse: the poor feel rich knowing there are others worse off; the weak feel strong exercising their contempt on the lowest of the low."

This hopeless vision of human nature floors me. I'd like to tell the lady that she's wrong. I'd like to tell her about my father and how he tended to his patients, never hesitating to wipe the slate clean for those who couldn't pay. I'd like to tell her how Bastien offered his writing skills to illiterate peasants at Butte-aux-Rats. Finally, I'd like to tell her that the humblest cottage dwellers always had room around their hearth for the traveler who'd lost his way, braving the laws of the sequester and curfew.

But I don't reveal anything about my rural background. No more than I talk about the nobles who hold the fate of the people deeply rooted inside them, like Montfaucon and Naoko. I'm not ready to divulge my true identity yet, especially not to an immortal who considers all humanity a lost cause. I have to bring up her past, not mine, to soften her.

"Sister Vermillonne," I say, "she's all about self-sacrifice for her fellow human beings."

For the first time since the start of our exchange, the lady looks away. Maybe because I hit a tender spot, and she doesn't want her eyes to betray her?

"I know she was close to you at the Incurables," I persist. "She knew the young nun you were, the one who worked tirelessly to care for the patients. And she continues to devote her life to the dying despite her old age. She's proof that humanity isn't so bleak."

"Sister Vermillonne is naive," the lady says between clenched teeth. "I was too. But my transmutation opened my eyes. By being reborn in the Shadows, I saw the world in all its darkness. It's governed by selfishness. Vampyres and mortals, nobles and commoners: everyone is guilty. And all must atone. The only possible redemption will come by force, by establishing a kingdom of pariahs here on earth!"

The lady spreads her arms out, deploying the long sleeves of her midnight-blue dress as if she wanted to engulf the world. More than ever, the horns of her diadem resemble those of a demon: the demon of vengeance.

"Through me the terrible goddess Hecate lives on. When I'm crowned, Parisians will have to grovel in front of those they looked down on yesterday. They'll have to grovel before *me*. Recalcitrants will be executed. For destiny chose me to be queen of this iron kingdom and sent Pierrot to be my prophet."

The frail boy hasn't said a word during the entire time his protector spoke, and he remains silent. His elusive eyes prevent me from discerning anything. Does he also believe that he was destined to establish a dictatorship in the city of Paris, the mirror of the tyranny exercised by the King of Shadows? For that's what this is about. The lady isn't dreaming of liberty, fraternity, and progress for all, ideas I associate in my heart with the Fronde of the people. There's nothing egalitarian about her vision. She wants to create a new aristocracy of the wretched. What's really motivating her is an unquenchable thirst for revenge. She disguised it in the trappings of a political vision, but deep down, she's consumed by hate. As I once was myself . . .

I look away from her face, unable to bear the crazed intransigence reflected there. That's how I notice her pale wrist. A clear metal bracelet glistens around it. Made of white gold. Or platinum. Engraved with one letter.

H for Hecate . . .

. . . or for . . .

"Hélénaïs," I whisper.

Then louder.

"*H* for Hélénaïs!"

23
SISTERS

Hélénaïs's name echoes for a second in the silence.

"Let her go," the lady suddenly orders her men.

They hesitate.

One look from their mistress and they do as they're told. The hands that gripped my arms loosen, but the lady herself grabs hold of me.

She drags me away from the projector, far enough so the audience can't hear us. Pierrot also stays a few yards behind, observing us.

"You mentioned my sister's name," the lady says. "Why? Just because you rubbed shoulders with her when you were a squire, you think you can soften me up?"

I realize the lady was itching to talk about her sister all along. She's very up on what's happening aboveground, as she's proved with numerous allusions. As soon as she learned I was a squire, she assumed I knew Hélénaïs. But she held back from questioning me on the subject . . . until now.

I answer with a question of my own.

"The bracelet you're wearing is engraved with her initial, isn't it?"

I think I can feel the lady's hand trembling slightly on my arm.

"It's just a silly trinket from bygone days. I don't know why I keep it. I told you: Amarante and Iphigénie are dead. I don't mean anything to Hélénaïs, and she means nothing to me."

The lady's emotional voice belies her coldhearted words . . . exactly the same as Hélénaïs sounded hours earlier, when she claimed any memory of Iphigénie was *dead and buried.*

Suddenly, the facts hit me at gale force. I was mistaken about the significance of the platinum bracelet on the squire's wrist, a bracelet so similar to the one worn by her older sister. The symbol *I* that I had interpreted as the prideful number one isn't a roman numeral.

It's a letter.

The first letter of Iphigénie's name.

"You're wrong, madame," I say. "Hélénaïs hasn't forgotten you. She wears a bracelet identical to yours, engraved with *your* initial."

No doubt about it this time. The hand that's holding me is definitely trembling. And it finally releases my arm to touch the bracelet with fervor, as if it were an amulet. What if Hélénaïs were the last link in the chain connecting the Lady of Miracles to her humanity?

The thought makes my heart race. Away from the crowd of courtiers, far from her sulfurous *electricity*, Hecate seems to have gone back to being Iphigénie. I barely hear the paddle wheels that continue to turn.

"We had these bracelets engraved together one morning in May 293, six years ago," she remembers. "It was my last day in Beauce before I left for Versailles. My father had secured me a position as a lady's companion to the Marquise de Vauvalon. He wanted me to rise at the court and become the first Plumigny to be granted transmutation by the Faculty. I never dared tell him that the vampyric condition disgusted me."

My heart constricts as I observe the lady's trembling face. Contrary to what Sterling said, every noble doesn't aspire to being transmuted. Iphigénie de Plumigny is a poignant example. The brutal fate that Marcantonio imposed on her is all the more tragic.

"I was terrified to leave the Plumigny estate," she says, lost in thought. "But I didn't reveal any of this to Hélénaïs. I didn't want to scare her. She was only twelve, and I knew that one day the hour would arrive when she would be sent to the court too. I swore I'd be there for her when the time came. We exchanged bracelets, promising to reunite."

The lady strokes the *H* engraved in the platinum.

"I know she misses you," I say. "I sensed it. I also sensed the bitter poison your father instills in her on a daily basis with his letters and admonitions."

The lady's face continues to change before my eyes, more strikingly than ever. Her gently arched brows start to quiver; her delicate mouth partially opens; her golden eyes finally melt.

"That poison seems to agree with her, since she's succeeding where I failed," she says. "The fortune my father spent on Hélénaïs's alchemical surgeries won't have been in vain. Her beauty radiates at the court, while mine ended up shrouded under a veil."

I don't believe my ears. Hélénaïs's beauty was fashioned by alchemists? It would explain why the younger sister looks so much like the older one. Their monstrous father molded them after one another like wax figures. Like dolls! He tried to turn them into his puppets, inside and out, mentally as well as physically.

"You . . . you can save Hélénaïs from your father," I stammer. "You can save her from herself."

"She's the king's squire," the lady snaps back, her voice choked. "She's my mortal enemy now. My rival."

It's my turn to grab her arm, which is cold as marble.

"Don't speak like that. Rivalry is the way your father thinks, not the way gentle Iphigénie does. You have the power to break the vicious cycle."

Blood rushes to my head.

The sparkling bulbs on the rock face of the grotto diffract in front of my eyes.

My head spins. It's time for me to leap, to jump into the void without a safety net—to reveal who I am to Iphigénie so I can touch her soul.

"Refuse a confrontation with the King of Shadows. It can only end in a bloodbath for Parisians and your people," I say, my voice shaking. "Leave the capital with your courtiers, your Pierrot, and your bulbs. Establish your court somewhere else, in England or another region, wherever many rivers allow you to produce your precious electricity without the need for slaves. Create a kingdom where everyone has the chance to live free and happy. Not just the few. The force from the electrical magic gives you that power." I try to smile despite my trembling voice, and I look headlong into the lady's eyes. "As for Hélénaïs, she'll join this new court, I'm sure of it. She'll choose you over the King of Shadows, over your father. She'll choose freedom."

"You don't talk like a courtier at Versailles, or like one of the Immutable's squires, even a fallen one. You sound more like—"

"A Fronde rebel. That's because I am. And you can be one too. The most powerful of all, capable of changing the world."

"Changing the world . . . ," she repeats dreamily. "So that's your mysterious plan."

"I could help you," I assure her, burning with hope. "Introduce you to the right people. Accompany you along the way. It would be an honor."

The lady stays mute, as if lost in thought. Her long chestnut hair undulates around her like a golden ocean at sunset as she mulls over all that I've said. I would give anything to be able to read the thoughts that unravel behind her marble forehead, as cold and indecipherable as a statue's.

"You've convinced me," she says softly after several minutes that seem to last an eternity. "You're worthy of my trust. I accept you among us."

I let out a deep sigh of relief—no, of joy.

"Thank you! You won't regret it. Orfeo also has his place by your side."

"Orfeo?"

I gesture toward my strange-looking friend, still restrained in the pillory before the mouth of the Devouring.

"He belongs to the rebel camp, same as me. And he's been rejected by everyone, same as you. But his heart stayed good and pure, to which I can attest. You can free him without fear."

"Well, you can free him yourself, Diane, since you're now part of my court."

Without losing a second more, I hurry over to the mouth of the Devouring, the lady hot on my heels. I'm barely aware of Pierrot, who's following in our footsteps.

Under the horrified glare of Mother Incarnadine's and Sterling's startled eyes, I rush onto Orfeo's pillory.

"We've come to liberate you," I tell him.

Beside me, the lady asks Martial to give her the keys to the pillories.

My heart rejoices when I see her take the correct key with long delicate fingers bathed in the irradiant light of the projector.

She's joining the Fronde.

And with her comes a power that Montfaucon himself could never have dreamed of.

I'm eager to see the grand equerry's face when I give him the news. What irony: the one I was supposed to destroy is about to become his most precious ally.

She hands me the key to my friend's pillory. As I take it, I whisper in my new ally's ear.

"Lord Raindust doesn't know I belong to the Fronde. I'd like to keep it that way. Besides, he doesn't need to be clued into this bit of information to arrange our passage to England."

"No need to arrange it at all," the lady answers softly.

"You'd rather find refuge elsewhere? So be it, we could release the lord once we leave the valley of the Bièvre."

"Releasing him is also out of the question."

I raise my eyes toward the vampyre's face as it stands out against the light of the projector. Her features are once again hardened, with the same rigid inflexibility as the Immutable's gold mask itself.

"Do you want to make Raindust one of your subjects?" I ask.

"There's room for only one immortal at our court—ourself."

After letting me into her confidence and using a familiar form of address, the lady now sizes me up haughtily and returns to the formal *we*.

She's close by but feels suddenly frighteningly far, as if the light of the projector at her back was propelling her into another dimension.

"We will never quit the valley of the Bièvre," she declares. "We will never abandon Paris. It's the Immutable who will deliver it to us. And you, Diane de Gastefriche, will help with that."

Her statement is like a cold shower.

Getting swept along by my own enthusiasm—my own vanity!—I thought I'd converted someone responsible for thousands of deaths into a universal savior. In just a few words, I thought I'd erased Hecate and resurrected Iphigénie. How did I ever imagine I'd so easily purge this all-consuming desire for vengeance when I myself had such a hard time vanquishing it?

"The tyrant must be quaking by now," the lady proclaims, a vengeful grin on her face. "Our arm reaches far beyond this valley, and he knows it. Gathering the saltpeter that grows in these damp depths, we fashioned the powder for the fireworks that engulfed his gallows. And to think we didn't even have to pay that survivor of the La Roncière conspiracy to stick our letter on the mortuary door."

"A . . . a survivor of the conspiracy?" I stammer, crushed by this vindictive avalanche. "Lo . . . Lord Serpent?"

"He doesn't know who we are, we don't know who he is, but it doesn't matter. Louis is surrounded by enemies, that's all that counts." She turns to face her court, so they can all hear her distinctly. "Tomorrow, for the Night of Shadows, Paris will erupt in chaos!"

"Tomorrow!" the courtiers shout, a war cry that spurts from the light of the projector.

The lady takes my hand, the one in which I'm still holding the key to Orfeo's pillory, and lifts it high.

"And tonight, we welcome someone new among us: Diane de Gastefriche, former squire to the King of Shadows, now squire to the Queen of Miracles."

The outcry redoubles in ferocity.

My head rings like a warning bell.

The burst of light from the projector prevents me from seeing the hundreds of shouting mouths. The only one I can make out is Pierrot's; he's standing near me and the lady, his lips still tightly sealed.

"I thought you wanted to change the world," I yell.

"Yes, you convinced us of that," the lady says. "But we'll do it our way, and without anyone's help. First Paris, then France, followed by all of Europe. Millions of prisoners will be made to work the wheel to produce unlimited electricity and flood our kingdom with light."

My legs turn to jelly while the garlands of bulbs dance in rhythm to the war cry of the court.

A kingdom of light? The light the lady speaks of has nothing to do with the one I imagined would chase away the Shadows and illuminate the future. No, hers is a tyrannical beacon made to blind and subjugate.

"But . . . Hélénaïs . . . ," I stammer.

"Our sister will choose sides when the time comes."

As she says this, the lady slides her hand into the bodice of her dress and takes out a dagger with a horn handle that she places in my free palm.

"The blade is made of death-silver," she says. "Use it to decapitate the Englishman. That's the first order we're giving our new courtier. It's the first test of loyalty we demand of our new squire. Don't disappoint us, Diane, for with just one blow of the sword, our people could quickly take down Orfeo."

I notice Martial is standing next to my friend's pillory, a few yards from me. He's holding a heavy sword inches above the neck held in place by planks of wood. Other armed courtiers are on either side of their mistress, glaring at me menacingly.

"Madame . . . ," I plead with her.

"The vampyre's head," she demands as she pushes me toward Sterling's pillory.

I lower my eyes onto the back of the lord's neck, where it's flooded with light, defenseless. There's no need of a stake to immobilize him. The pillory serves the same purpose. Bent over him, I see his crest of black hair, the arch of his brows, and the contours of his cheeks. He doesn't raise his face to implore me; he doesn't engage in any of Mother Incarnadine's gesticulations. None. He remains stoic, immobile.

"His head, now. Hecate demands it!" the lady roars.

The dagger shakes in my hand.

Why am I hesitating when Orfeo's life and my own depend on this? What does Sterling mean to me? Nothing! I decided to cut the throat of Tristan, a boy I'd fallen in love with, when duty demanded it. So why is it so difficult to do the same thing to the bloodsucker?

Because Sterling is more human than Tristan ever was, that's why, the voice of my conscience says.

"Say . . . say something," I stammer.

Instead of pleas, he's content to spout another aphorism.

"The stroke of death is as a lover's pinch, which hurts and is desired."

"Still your damned bard," I say, my throat tight. "And of course you managed to whip out a verse where *pinch* means *bite*."

"Not bad for a vampyre's final words, wouldn't you say?"

My blade rests on his neck.

The edge of the death-silver is so sharp it leaves a nick without my having to apply any pressure.

A thin trickle of blood starts to flow on Sterling's olive skin.

Tears also flow from my eyes.

"Go on, Diane," the lady says impatiently behind me.

I'm wildly tempted to spin around and plant the dagger in her throat. But she's surrounded by her people. I'd only injure her, not destroy her. In doing so, I'd condemn Orfeo to certain death, without even saving Sterling.

Unless . . .

My onyx ring . . .

Would it have any effect in this harshly lit space?

As a storm of doubts erupts within me, a shout bursts out from behind.

"Look, the turbines! They've . . . they've stopped turning."

24

DELUGE

Stunned, I realize I don't hear the continuous motion of the paddle wheels that had accompanied me since I entered the forbidden valley.

I venture to glance over my shoulder.

The light from the projector seems suddenly weaker, less dazzling. Yes, it's diminishing with a quiver, so much so that the silhouettes of the courtiers gathered behind it come into focus.

"What's going on?" the lady snarls, momentarily losing interest in me.

The projector isn't the only thing growing weaker. All along the valley, the string of bulbs is dwindling in intensity. Down below, the paddle wheels aren't moving. They're not sending the mysterious electricity into the suspended wax-covered wires that until now supplied the light at the Court of Miracles. The flow of the Bièvre has slowed down—or, more accurately, the river has stopped flowing out. If water is still coming upstream, it's not flowing downward anymore. In fact, the water is stagnating in the valley, slowly covering the banks inch by inch.

"A dam!" comes a shout. "Someone's dammed the Bièvre!"

"Impossible," the lady roars back. "The entire length of the river is embedded."

"Except at its mouth, madame, where it runs into the Seine," Martial clarifies, his sword still raised above Orfeo's neck.

The courtiers, who seconds ago were clamoring with warlike zeal, exchange worried looks in the semidarkness.

The lady, who was haranguing them, can't find the words to reassure them.

"It's the king!" I shout at her. "I warned you that he would try to pinpoint my location thanks to the blood link that unites me to him. He knows I'm here, underground, in the hidden valley of the Bièvre. He didn't dare descend into the depths with his troops because he doesn't need to. He's counting on the water to make you confront him in his place."

The lady's lips begin to tremble. "But how could he have built a dam so quickly?"

"You've kept us in the pillories for hours, the others and me. Meanwhile the Immutable assembled an army of thousands of soldiers in Paris, an army that's become a crew of excavators." With the tip of the death-silver dagger, I gesture toward the rapidly overflowing river. The first cave dwellings already have water up to their windows. "This valley is going to be completely flooded."

I've barely announced my prediction when the projector that illuminated the pillories goes dark.

The light from the bulbs starts to crackle more and more violently, bathing the valley in a trembling flicker. The buzzing of these hundreds of dying stars blends with the raging flood.

Above, near the vault of the grotto, the enslaved chained to their wheels have also stopped, frozen by the approaching cataclysm.

Now grasping the situation at hand, the lady turns toward her subjects.

"Don't just stand there! Electricians, turn on the main lighting circuit to the manual turbines. Guards, out with your whips and get the slaves back to work. Fast! What are you waiting for?"

"The manual turbines won't be able to compensate for the ones in the river," Martial says. "Maybe . . . maybe we should run?"

"You dare doubt your queen? No one is running off!"

The lady's silhouette is visible against the light of the few bulbs weakly flickering and twinkling at the top of her crescent moon.

Martial shakes his head forcefully, casting off his doubts—and his instinct for survival—to recover his devotion, body and soul, to his mistress.

"Yes, madame."

"And put the squire back in the pillory. She hasn't proved her loyalty yet, far from it."

"No, you can't!" I shout, my hand tightly gripped around the dagger.

Lightning fast, she grabs my wrist before I can even decide where to strike at her. Obviously, the shadowessence endowed her with the same vampyric power as her sister, Hélénaïs: superhuman speed. She forces me to let go of the dagger, which falls on the rocky ground, and shoves it away with a kick of her pumps.

"We'll deal with you later," she declares as Martial grabs me by the waist.

The lady turns away from me, the long panels of her moiré dress flapping in the air.

My heart racing, I see her descend the valley escorted by her people, and soon she's just a shadow in the waning light.

"Lower your head," Martial orders.

He's the only courtier still beside me, the others having rushed down the slope toward the turbines. He pushes me forcefully toward the pillory I occupied earlier.

"Your gut was right. The valley is going to be flooded," I say. "There's still time to escape, and you can . . . *aaah!*"

The first punch to my stomach takes the wind out of me.

The second makes me fold in two.

My neck lands brutally in the notch of the pillory.

The plank closes on my neck with a thud.

As I hear the clinking of keys in Martial's hands, a hooting reverberates near me, to my right. I turn my head, my eyes filled with tears. It's Sterling, and he's yelling.

Before I understand what's happening, I see a flutter of wings above me, then hear Martial cry out.

"My eye!"

The ring of keys falls to the ground in a metallic din.

Now's my chance.

Abruptly, I get to my feet, pushing up the heavy circle of wood from the pillory that the lady's henchman didn't have time to lock. He's busy battling against a grayish bird whose talons grip his hair, whose beak is trying to puncture his only good eye. It's a small tawny owl.

I rush to pick up the set of keys, then the death-silver dagger lying inches away.

When I stand back up, breathless, Martial has managed to pull the owl from his face, a long stream of blood flowing from his eye.

"Damn sparrow! I already lost one eye, and now I'm blind!" he yelps as he tosses the bird to the ground.

Blind? I don't believe it. Only his brow is torn. When he realizes it, he'll just wipe the blood with the back of his hand and see again . . . which can't happen.

I pounce on him and hit him with all my strength. Situated directly in line with the pillory, he tumbles right into the gaping opening. Instantly, I shove the top plank down and secure it in place, frantically searching for the key that corresponds to the lock on the ring.

"You'll pay with your life," he shouts, thrashing awkwardly.

He tries to blindly grab me with his hands, which I couldn't restrain. But I dodge his grasp and finally find the right key. Once I've closed the lock, I step back, panting, and look down toward the valley. It's teeming with activity.

Did someone witness my maneuver?

No, I don't think so. The panic resonating in the grotto is such that Martial's screams were drowned out, and the intensity of the bulbs has diminished to the point that everything has gone to an indistinct semidarkness. To ensure we're concealed, I hurry over to the tall black curtains and pull them shut around the pillories.

Only then do I run over to Orfeo to free him.

"Rip off the bottom of my dress," I yell at him once he's rid of his yoke.

He looks at me with his jade eyes, the crackling of the one dying bulb above the curtains reflected in them.

"Hurry! We need to gag the cyclops!"

Orfeo kneels and tears the flannel fabric with his strong hands near my calves, as easily as if it were paper.

"Well done, dear child!" Mother Incarnadine gushes in the pillory beside me. "The Faculty will reward you accordingly for having saved a respectable nun like me."

Ignoring her pleas, I go straight to Sterling's pillory.

"If I free you, will you jump at my throat?" I ask him between two wheezing breaths.

"That wouldn't be very elegant after you spared my life."

He raises his eyes and looks at me with that phlegmatic air of his, which I instantly want to slap away.

"More of your nonsense on the beauty of the gesture? But it's no longer enough. I need more. I need an oath."

"Just a few hours ago you said you didn't lend weight to a vampyre's words, even less to a spy's."

"I changed my mind, Sterling Raindust. So make up your mind because I'm not waiting forever."

The lone bulb goes out completely for a brief second, plunging us in total darkness, then lights up again, weaker than ever.

"I swear I won't bleed you," the lord promises, his black-underlined eyes looking directly at me.

Should I believe him?

My gut tells me yes. And I'm doubly safe with the death-silver dagger in my pocket and Orfeo beside me. I hurry to unlock his pillory.

He stands up and stretches his stiff body out from head to toe.

"At *last*. That yoke was even narrower than the hold on the ship I took to cross the Channel."

"Don't get too excited. What comes next won't be all fun and games. You do remember the reason we came here, don't you?"

He nods seriously. "To destroy the lady."

I step closer to a curtain panel and part it slightly, just enough to glance out.

The luminosity in the valley has gone so low that I have trouble recognizing the area at first. The chaos that's gripped the Court of Miracles makes everything even more confusing.

"I can't be seeing clearly. It looks like the flood already came halfway up the valley, which is impossible."

"Yet it's true," Sterling says. He sidled up next to me, and his eyes are perfectly capable of seeing in the semidarkness. "I don't think the Immutable was simply content closing off the mouth of the river. By some evil spell, he seems to have also succeeded in increasing the flow to speed up the flood."

He's barely finished talking when the string of bulbs emits a surge of renewed energy.

In an instant, the valley appears in all its chaos. The foaming water has in fact risen over nearly seven feet in several minutes, engulfing dozens of cave dwellings and largely covering the paddle wheels, which are now useless. The courtiers are struggling in the middle of this deluge. Their legs in freezing water, some of them are trying to save what they can from their homes. Farther up, those the lady called the *electricians* are changing the connections of the suspended wiring in a frenzy. The slopes upstream of the river, over which we arrived earlier, are completely submerged. As for the heights still clear of water, those across from the pillories, where the manual turbines are installed . . . a worse tide awaits, even more menacing.

The fresh burst of luminosity makes the whitish, churning . . . living tide momentarily ebb—ghouls that spurt forth from the depths to attack the enslaved and shackled. The latter let out shrill cries as they see the fleeing monsters who were ready to feast on them in the twilight. Terror, more than the whip of the frightened slave wardens, drives them to redouble their efforts. *Faster! Faster still! Make the turbines turn to produce the light and repel those horrors.*

A voice rises above this deafening concert of screams, grinding wheels, and roar of water: the lady's.

She's on the opposite riverbank, at the edge of whirling torrents of water, standing erect in her moiré dress that blows with the wind coming from the depths.

"Listen! The main lighting is now linked to the manual turbines," she declares, addressing her troops. "The rising flood is slowing down. Our court is saved."

It's true; the water seems to be coming up more slowly. The flood reached the intermediate tunnels, midway up the slopes of the valley, which function as drains, at least for now.

My fingers tighten around the partly open curtain panel.

"The lady is out of reach," I note. "We don't have a pistol or any means of striking her now. We've failed."

"We haven't failed, not if she's really saving her court and continues to hold her own against the Immutable," Sterling replies behind me.

It was his objective and mine that Hecate's secret never fall into Louis's hands. This to safeguard the Crown of England as well as the Fronde of the people. But now that I know the Queen of Miracles' intentions are as violent and absolute as those of the King of Shadows, this outcome leaves me with a bitter taste. If she were to supplant Louis, her reign would be as ghastly as his.

"Don't worry about the Immutable's fury," Sterling says in a hushed tone, his cold lips whispering into my ear. "I'll obtain your passage to England, if we get out of here, of course."

"If we get out of here." Those words pull me brutally back to our precarious predicament. And to Orfeo, whom I've pledged to myself to save.

I look at Sterling. He's holding the owl battered by Martial against his chest, delicately wrapped in his shirt.

"This small owl told me she came here through the mouth of the Devouring," he says. "And that's how we're going to get back to the surface, or at least try to. I took the cyclops's flashlight."

I'm about to close the curtain when someone places a hand on mine.

I look down. It's Pierrot. I hadn't seen him approach. In the confusion, he slipped away from his mistress and climbed back up the valley slope to us. For the first time, he looks at me squarely, his deep-blue eyes diving into mine with greater force than he used to avoid them until now.

And for the first time, his thin lips let out a soft voice.

"Take me with you, please. I'd like to see . . . to see daylight again."

"The child," Sterling says. "He's the one who holds the secret of the electric light."

Quick as lightning, Sterling grabs his arm.

Scared, Pierrot cries out.

Over in the hollow of the valley, the lady abruptly raises her eyes toward us, as if a blood link bound her to her protégé as intimately as the one that binds me to the king.

"The prisoners!" she thunders, pointing her finger at us. "They've captured the prophet. Seize them."

Hundreds of faces turn in our direction, illuminated by the restored light.

The lady dives into the water.

I grab hold of the curtain, petrified by the scene of courtiers hurtling down the slopes of the valley, none hesitating to follow their mistress into the glacial black water to swim toward us. The movement of the crowd causes the walls of the grotto to shake, along with the shimmering bulbs and half-submerged poles.

One of the poles vacillates . . . and comes crashing down on several others, toppling them like a game of dominoes.

Bulbs and copper wires fall in a big splash.

A sinister sizzle rings out.

The water starts to bubble furiously.

The submerged bodies are caught in a demented dance that's even more outrageous than the never-ending jig. Intuitively, I understand that it's the alchemical power of the electricity, forcefully released into the water, that's making them dance this ball of death.

The lady, half-immersed, is gesticulating as well. Her long hair stands on end like lightning bolts; her diadem vibrates as if it were struck by lightning; the panels of her moiré dress catch fire as easily as straw. And blazing fire, whether it comes from the sun or from this mesmerizing electricity, is the ultimate way to destroy a vampyre.

The bulbs radiate stronger than ever, flooding the lady's face with light, her eyes wide open like those of a Pythia awakening after a long trance. I think I see sparks running the length of her eyelashes, bolts of lightning ringing her forehead. A black mist oozes from her alabaster skin—the shadowessence that's evaporating as ultimate death nears.

Her mouth opens on a word I'm too far away to hear but that I'm perfectly able to read on her electrified lips.

"Hélénaïs!"

Suddenly, nothing.

All the bulbs go dark, all at once, never to shed light again.

25

DEVOURING

A concert of screams echoes against the walls of the grotto.

The shouts of men and women consumed by the terror of the Shadows puncture my eardrums. The inhuman growls accompanying the cries are even more terrifying. Here in the valley, nothing is holding back the ghouls from complete carnage.

A weak slither of light suddenly pierces the black night. It's our only flashlight, which Sterling just turned on. His face appears in the trembling beam. He's still holding Pierrot's arm with his free hand. Behind them, I can make out Orfeo's massive silhouette.

"Hurry, there's not a minute to lose!" the lord orders. "Let's hope this light holds out long enough for us to find a path up to the surface."

He's already heading toward the mouth of the Devouring. I can't see it, but I can feel its glacial breath.

"What about me?" Mother Incarnadine shouts hoarsely from somewhere in the dark.

I grab Sterling by his shirtsleeve. "We can't abandon them like this, not her and not Martial."

The vampyre sweeps my face with the beam of light.

"Pity for your enemies? That sounds like a far cry from the portrait of the king's merciless squire."

"You benefited from that pity just an instant ago. I gave you a second chance. They deserve the same." I swallow. "Sometimes I've had to kill to save myself, which I'm not proud of. Looking back on it, it's like plunging a knife in my heart. But it's not about self-defense today. I have a choice. I won't abandon these defenseless people to certain death, enemy or not. So help me free them."

I remove the key to Martial's pillory and toss it at Sterling. Counting on his eyes to see in the half darkness better than mine, I take the flashlight from him and hurry over to the reverend's shackles.

"None too soon," Mother Incarnadine yelps as she stands up once she's liberated. "I nearly had a heart attack." She gets a grip on herself and with effort tamps down her anger. "Thank you, dear girl—"

Before she can say any more, Martial runs off in front of us.

Still gagged, he hurtles through the curtains and onto the obscure slope that tumbles down to the river and death. Loyal to his queen to the very end . . .

"Come on!" Sterling shouts.

All five of us run toward the corridor. I lead the way, Sterling and Pierrot at my heels, Orfeo and Mother Incarnadine bringing up the rear.

The mouth of the Devouring extends into a narrowing passageway where we're forced to proceed single file. The beam of the flashlight only extends a few feet in front of me, barely enough to see the rocks before tripping over them.

A strong wind gusts in this narrow conduit, blowing my hair back and making the panels of my torn dress flap against my calves. I think about what L'Esquille said at the start of our investigation: he told us that the underground drafts of air systematically blew out the torches of those who ventured there. The flashlight is holding up, but for how much longer?

I hurry as fast as I can up the hill, my chest tight with anxiety. The agonized screams from the valley have disappeared behind the whistling wind. Impossible for me to chase away the last dream I had from my mind, the one where I was pursued by an army of ghouls into a narrow tunnel that looks more and more like the one we're moving through right now.

"Praise be the Shadows!" Mother Incarnadine's voice resonates behind me. "The mouth of the Devouring is empty. All the ghouls are busy devouring the beggars back in the valley."

That thought fills me with sadness. The subjects at the Court of Miracles may have chosen a bad road, but what alternative did society give them? As for the unhappy souls chained to the turbines, none of them deserved the end they got. Even the lady, in all her folly, was serving a sort of perverted ideal, a distorted reflection of justice, whereas Mother Incarnadine is serving solely herself. She reminds me of Madame Thérèse, the cynical governess at the Grande Écurie.

"I'm finally rid of that demon whose memory poisoned my nights," the reverend rejoices. "I'll be able to sleep soundly again back at the Incurables. What am I saying! Having helped to neutralize the Lady of Miracles, the Faculty will most surely reward me with an offer to run a more prestigious establishment. Maybe Les Invalides? I'd be delighted to set up my office under the cupola with its unobstructed view of the esplanade."

"Be quiet," I tell her, both annoyed by her chatter and worried that she'll attract attention to us.

But she babbles on. "Oh, rest assured, my child, I won't breathe a word to anyone regarding that business about an alliance with England. I won't say anything about your schemes with that foreign vampyre and that . . . huh . . . that *creature* you call Orfeo. Same for Pierrot, not a word. You can do what you want with the boy. You can deliver him to the king and take sole credit for capturing the prophet of electrical alchemy. As for me, I'll be as mute as the grave that Sister Amarante should never have left . . . *aaah!*"

The reverend gives a piercing cry.

Quickly, I turn around, pointing the torch beam toward the back of the line. In the half darkness, the nun is fighting off something hanging from her vestment . . . two long, pale arms spiked with claws.

"Help!" she shouts. "Help me!"

Orfeo rushes to her aid, but she pushes him away in panic.

"Don't touch me, you abomination! Get away!"

Three other pairs of clawed hands join the first, bursting from the dark to draw their prey toward them. The thin woman is no match. She vanishes in the dark, snatched by the ghouls. Her shrill cries chill my blood. The sound of her cracking bones makes me want to puke.

"Hurry, while the ghouls are busy with their victim!" Sterling yells. "Diane, open the way for us!"

I surge forward, running faster than ever.

The flashlight shakes in my clenched fist, sweeping the ever-narrowing corridor with its ever-weakening beam.

The hollow acoustics echo the gasps of the pack that's busy tearing up the old woman, giving me the dreadful feeling of participating in a macabre feast.

How long will the reverend's lean carcass hold them back?

The corridor suddenly forks.

Opening onto a cul-de-sac.

"An impasse," I say, out of breath.

"No," Sterling says. "The owl came this way, she told me so. Don't you feel a draft of air? Look more closely."

I sweep the fallen rockslide with the flashlight's waning beam and end up locating a tunnel right here at ground level. In fact, the cold air seems to be coming from there. The opening is too small for us to enter standing up; we can only get through by crawling. My stomach knots up at the thought, which again reminds me of my frightening nightmare.

"Go first," I say.

"What about you?" Sterling asks.

"I'll scare off the ghouls with the flashlight before I go in last."

"The flashlight is dying!"

I grab the lord's cold wrist and push up against him to look him in the eyes in the dim light.

"I have another asset, Sterling. No time to explain. You just need to promise me something."

"Again?"

"Once you're aboveground, you'll let Orfeo take Pierrot with him."

I anxiously lower the flashlight on the boy that Sterling is still holding by the arm. Our frantic pace blew his brown hair back, clearing his high, pale forehead and eyes that are too large for his refined face.

"Orfeo will take you to a safe place, Pierrot, I promise you."

"You mean straight into the Immutable's hands, along with his secret about electricity," Sterling says. "That's what I call landing on your feet, baronette, with your promotion at the court all but assured."

"You're wrong. The Immutable will never learn of Pierrot's existence, or his secret. Orfeo will place him under the best protection possible, out of the Immutable's reach and that of Vice-Queen Anne. You don't need to know more."

I shine the light onto Orfeo's green eyes. No need for words for him to guess who I'm talking about—his master, the grand equerry.

Already, the sound of claws grating the rock face resonates in the corridor. The ghouls are done with the reverend . . . and they're still hungry.

"Promise!" I yell at Sterling. "It's what you wanted—to prevent the kingdom of France from gaining an asset in the upcoming war. Anyway, you don't have a choice: Orfeo is strong enough to tear you apart, even though you're a vampyre."

"All right, then. I promise to let the child go."

I push him toward the tunnel, my heart beating in rhythm with the ghouls' approaching clomping.

"You, too, go, and don't let them out of your sight," I say to Orfeo. "I promise I'll meet up with you."

Never has a promise tasted so bitter in my mouth.

If my dream showed me the truth, my chances of survival are slim.

But I can't tell Orfeo that. In spite of his massive body, I know he's capable of slipping through the narrowest passageways, like in the chimney flues at the Grande Écurie. But nothing must slow him down as he heads on the final leg toward the surface . . . toward life.

Orfeo has barely gone into the tunnel when I plant my legs firmly, facing the dim corridor.

The flashlight vacillates in my trembling hands, emitting such a weak beam that I can't see more than a foot in front of me. But I hear the monsters approaching. Yes, how I hear them and smell their putrid stench.

Suddenly, the flashlight goes out.

Overwhelmed with terror, I let it fall.

I bring my trembling fingers to my left hand, searching for the onyx stone.

I find it, close my eyes, and give it one last turn to unscrew it.

A blinding light shoots from my hand.

Against the light, I see the network of my veins pulsating through my closed eyelids.

I hear bestial screams bursting from dozens of mouths.

Then a din of legs scuttling off.

Finally, complete silence.

I open my eyes again onto the night that was momentarily chased away but is already back; then I throw myself headlong into the tunnel.

Right now, whether my eyes are open or closed makes no difference. The darkness around me is total.

I wriggle along as best I can along the uphill slope, knocking my elbows into the rock face, groping for asperities to grip and propel me forward.

If Sterling was right and the draft moving over my sweaty forehead is really coming from the surface, I may have a chance of getting out.

Maybe the exit isn't far off.

"Sterling?" I call.

No answer.

But a growl comes from behind. The ghouls are hot on my trail again.

I remember my nightmare, more suffocating than ever.

No, it can't be. I'm not going to end like this.

My palms slip on the slimy moss.

These last few days, each of my premonitory dreams was a warning.

My nails break on the hard stones.

I always found a way out, and tonight again, I'm going . . .

"Aaaaaah!"

A horribly calloused hand closes around my ankle, stopping me dead in my tracks.

I scream, kick, rear up, but nothing helps. Other repulsive arms grab my legs. In my dream, I'd tried to unscrew my onyx stone but couldn't find it. Now I know why: I already used it. And stuck as I am, it's impossible for me to turn around and use the death-silver dagger I took from the lady.

This time I'm done for, and all my contortions are only prolonging my agony.

My body goes limp.

"Maman . . . ," I say as the wet jaws go up my calves.

Spongy, cold tongues smack onto my knees.

"Bastien . . ."

May my torture be as brief as my brother's, killed with the single stroke of a sword. Why haven't the ghouls already pierced me with their claws and fangs? I distinctly heard Mother Incarnadine's bones crack and crunch minutes ago.

Are these despicable monsters . . . toying with me?

In response to questions that swirl in my head, a hollow voice comes from behind me, a voice so deep it seems to rise from the very bowels of the earth.

"Who are you?"

That voice . . .

That question . . .

It's as if I've been thrust back to the Temple, when I thought a ghoul was talking to me. Only now I realize I didn't imagine it.

Today, like before, one of the creatures is speaking to me . . . and I can understand it.

But can ghouls, creatures supposedly devoid of thought, comprehend the meaning of my words?

"I'm Diane de Gastefriche, squire to the King of Shadows," I choke out. "Let me go or you'll incur the royal wrath!"

My threat doesn't seem to make the ghouls quake. Their limbs don't loosen around my legs.

"*Gastefriche . . . ?*" the voice from beyond the grave repeats. "*No, you aren't a Gastefriche.*"

My heart pounds a little faster in my ribcage, crushed as it is against the rock face.

How can this thing know I usurped someone's identity?

It's impossible.

"*What does a Gastefriche taste like, anyway?*" asks a second voice, huskier than the first.

"*Sounds like the name of a human,*" says a third voice, whistling like the underground wind.

"*But this prey doesn't taste human, you know that as well as I do,*" says the first voice.

This surreal conversation makes my head spin. Am I delirious? Did the ghouls inject me with their devastating venom, and has it already gone to my brain?

I could swear I didn't feel their claws dig into my skin. And this bit about taste reminds me of what Sterling said when he claimed my blood had a flavor as complex as my unexpected gray hair . . .

It's coming back to me now. The ghoul at the Temple spoke to me *after* it had smacked its tongue against my cheek, wanting to know who I was.

There seems to be something about me that leaves the creatures of the Shadows puzzled, be they ghouls or vampyres . . . What's this about? The Sip of the King? No. The ghouls didn't taste my blood. It's the flavor of my skin that discouraged them . . . Why? I don't have a clue. All I know is that the wolves in my forests back in the Auvergne would attack sheep but avoid the shepherds. Wild beasts are innately wary of what they aren't used to. Unless hunger or fear push them to attack, wolves only become truly dangerous once they develop a taste for human flesh.

"You said it, I don't taste like good prey," I pant. "I'm sure I'm not even edible. So let me be on my way."

A confab of growls greets my suggestion.

"*Maybe we could just bite off a small piece and see if it's fit to eat?*" suggests the huskiest voice.

"*Too risky. She could be venomous,*" says the whistling voice. "*Maybe we're being poisoned just by touching her . . . yuck!*"

The arms suddenly release me.

Seizing this unexpected chance, I start to crawl again, using every ounce of strength, skinning my limbs. Not waiting to catch my breath, I drag myself blindly toward the direction of the wind that whips my face.

Blindly?

Am I not seeing the jagged contours of the tunnel after all this time in total darkness?

Yes. A translucent glimmer wreathes the narrow tunnel, its intensity increasing as I move forward.

The exit is here, straight ahead, so near.

The surface, fresh air, and . . .

. . . daybreak.

26

CITY OF LIGHT

My eyes damp with tears, I crawl the remaining yards separating me from daylight.

The tunnel widens toward the opening, allowing me to stand again.

Between my tears of joy, the diffracted light breaks down into a multicolored rainbow.

"Morning . . . ," I say, rolling the magical word on my tongue. "It's amazing."

"More like burning, you mean," says a weary voice close by.

I realize that three figures are standing inside the tunnel entrance, huddled against the rock face, on the edge of the halo cast by the dawn.

I make out Orfeo's muscular frame, Sterling's lean silhouette, and Pierrot's frail body. Behind them, the oval of daylight is streaked with a curtain of vines.

"Glad this light enchants you, baronette," the lord adds, his earring gleaming in the half light. "Because it's singeing my skin and burning my eyes. I need to burrow somewhere for the day."

"If you want, you can backtrack. The path is free of ghouls . . . at least for now."

I'm not about to tell what I've just experienced—not to him, not to anyone. In fact, now that I'm in daylight, my conversation with the ghouls seems suddenly as unreal as a bad dream.

"No way I'll . . . backtrack . . . into the depths," Sterling says.

His voice trails off more and more, as if each word is increasingly difficult to say. Like all vampyres, he's supposed to spend his days restoring his energy in a coffin or vault. That's the way of bloodsuckers.

"I'd rather brave daylight . . . a second or so . . . and bury myself in the garden."

As he says this, I discern the landscape beyond the tunnel entrance through the vines partially covering it. A sprawling greenhouse stands there, invaded by sleeping vegetation: trees barren of leaves but heavy with ivy, crates of withered flowers, orange trees covered in tarps, bags of dried bulbs. If the imposing glass roof protects this patch of land from snow, the slack season has sent the plants into a deep slumber, as if by magic.

"We're in the king's Garden of Plants," I whisper.

"A fallow garden," Sterling points out. "The gardeners took in all the plants susceptible to frost . . . they won't be coming back to this greenhouse . . . before springtime." He lets out a big yawn. "And I . . . won't be coming out of my tub of potting soil before this evening."

He points shakily toward a large wooden crate that the burgeoning rays of light haven't reached yet.

"Would you help me one last time . . . Fearless Diane?"

"You can count on me, No-Future Sterling."

He opens his shirt, releasing the small tawny owl, which flies off and perches on the branch of a willow tree. Then, using the last ounce of his energy, he dashes out of the tunnel and runs to the crate, where he plops down his exhausted body.

I hurry after him to close the lid. A strong odor assails my nostrils when I bend over the crate. It's filled with dark soil.

"Compost . . . ," Sterling says, sighing, his pale face popping out against the black fertilizer. "Just my luck . . ."

"Hush, my lord."

I rake the compost to cover his limp hands, his pale chest, and his immobile forehead.

Do not spread the compost on the weeds . . . to make them . . . ranker . . ."

His mouth, lips bruised by the silver, freeze before he can finish this last quote. I toss a final handful of manure over his face, burying it completely.

Then I place the lid on the crate just before rays of sunlight reach it. Only then do I return to the tunnel.

I realize it's actually a small artificial grotto that embellishes the greenhouse, so obstructed by vines and roots it's impossible to see the entrance. The gardeners probably don't know that it leads directly into the bowels of Paris.

I push aside the vegetal curtain and see Pierrot and Orfeo.

"You also fear the daylight," I say to the latter.

He nods, clearly frustrated by this flaw. Already his head is bobbing. Still, he finds the strength to stuff his hand into the pocket of his leather tunic and takes out the slate board and piece of chalk that he's never without. Battling fatigue, he traces out some words in his precise handwriting, the refined penmanship in stark contrast to his large hands.

> Don't worry about Orfeo.
> He's going to sleep here until dusk.
> He'll return to Versailles at nightfall.

"Are you sure you'll be able to find the secret passageway under the outer ramparts again?" I ask.

He nods a second time.

"All right," I say. "But we need to find you a daytime refuge as well."

"Over there, it looks like a tool shed."

Surprised, I look at Pierrot, who's just spoken. It's only the second time since I've met him that he's said a word. He's clutching Orfeo's hand. Two innocents bullied by life, one mute, the other silent.

"You're right, Pierrot," I say softly. "That shed is the perfect size. Come."

Orfeo pulls the leather hood over his head to protect himself from the pale winter morning, and both of them follow me to the small cabin at the corner of the greenhouse.

Inside, it's dark, and there's enough room between the shovels and rakes for Orfeo to lie down if he curls up. Even the scent blends with his, a soft fragrance of decaying leaves gathered last autumn that still clings to the tools.

He's barely lain down when his eyes close and he sinks into a slumber. I grab two long gardening coats attached to the wall, one for Pierrot, one for me. I spread a third coat over Orfeo's shoulders. Even if his body is energized by the Shadows and therefore not susceptible to the cold, I gently tuck him in like a child. Then I quietly close the shed door, certain that no one will come bother him before he wakes up.

"Now we need to leave Paris," I say to Pierrot as I hand him one of the coats. "The sooner you're gone from these walls, the better."

The boy's eyes widen between his brown locks. "Gone from these walls?"

When he asked that we take him with us, it was just to see daylight again. Now the rays of the sun illuminate his high forehead, pale and translucent after two years spent underground. I can only imagine the strange sensation of freedom that he must feel. The idea of leaving the city where he's lived all his short life must be even more dizzying.

I place my hands on his frail shoulders to catch his eyes as they try to look away.

He's rather small for the twelve-year-old I size him up to be. I'm a head taller than him.

"Do you have somewhere to go in Paris?"

He shakes his head. "I just know the Incurables. I spent lots of years there, and before . . ." His ethereal blue eyes widen a little more. ". . . I only remember the street where I was found."

"You don't remember your family? Your parents, who named you?"

"Mother Incarnadine baptized me. She called me Pierrot, like in the song, after the one who ends up getting eaten by ghouls. She wanted to remind me that without her charity, that's how I would have wound up."

The reverend's cruelty sickens me. I can hear the verses from the popular song: *"Poor homeless Pierrot, / His blood they will steal. / Leaving just marrow, / A grim ghoulish meal!"*

"But when Sister Amarante came to the hospice, she told me that my name was also given to dreamers and seers," he goes on. "She'd smile nicely and call me *Pierrot la Lune.* She said I wasn't crazy, that my visions were a precious gift."

As he mentions the person he continues to call *Sister Amarante* and not *Hecate*, and still less *Lady of Miracles*, Pierrot's eyes cloud over. He knew the best side of the young woman. For several months, before bitterness transformed her into his jailer, she replaced the mother he doesn't remember.

"Well, if you don't have any attachments, you must leave Paris," I say, stroking his cheek. "You must avoid getting picked up by the soldiers of the Royal Watch and getting shut away in a new orphanage. Most of all, you must stay out of the Faculty's reach. Understand?"

He nods. "And afterward?"

"Afterward, you'll decide your future. If you choose to continue and use your visions for a worthy cause, you can do that. I promise you one thing: Whatever you decide, you're free. No one will ever lock you up against your will."

The promise, which I vow to keep to the best of my ability, seems enough to reassure the strange child.

He bundles up in the gardener's coat, pulling the deep hood over his head.

Then he takes my hand and squeezes it tight, just like he was holding Orfeo's hand earlier.

Pierrot and I squeeze through the gates of the Garden of Plants: easy enough to do since it's closed for the winter.

Farther to the east, we notice a sprawling work site that sprung up during the night. Mules are loaded down with stones pulled from adjoining streets, and cranes have been erected in haste to block the mouth of the Bièvre. The silhouettes of hundreds of soldiers are still busy working on the dam. Turning our backs to them, we follow the course of the river due west and head toward the snowy banks of the Seine.

My goal is to reach the Porte de Versailles, the one that opens onto the road leading to the royal city . . . and the Grande Écurie . . . as fast as possible.

Presently, the sun sits high in the sky, making the snow on the cobblestones of the banks glisten.

We've already gone by the Île Sang-Louis and the Île de la Cité, leaving behind the outlines of Notre-Damn and the Pont au Change. On the opposite riverbank, I see the long silhouette of the Louvre where, just the night before, the king hosted his ball. I've barely slept in over twenty-four hours. My limbs are exhausted and my eyelids heavy. As for Pierrot, he stumbles now and then on the badly cleared clumps of snow. He isn't used to walking any great distance since being cloistered for so long underground. But he bravely hangs on to my hand. There's no way we can afford to slow down.

"Time for us to leave the riverbank and cut through the city to the south," I tell him after we've gone past the Tuileries Gardens. "Make sure your hood is secure."

I head toward a wide street bustling with activity.

The merchants' and onlookers' shouts resonate, blending with the scraping of shovels clearing the snow.

A surprisingly light mood runs through the city. Rumor has it that the Lady of Miracles was defeated. No one knows how or what tomorrow will bring; all that matters is surviving the present day. The Night of Shadows threatened to be a hideous slaughter. Maybe now it'll just be another celebration of the vampyres' tyranny, as it's been for three hundred years.

All the hubbub lifts me up, carries me forward, and lulls me.

I notice the gold dome of the Hôtel des Invalides.

I feel Pierrot's warm hand in my palm.

I sense a certain softness floating in the air, something out of season.

But yes, it's suddenly a lot warmer.

And the sun is more luminous.

The facades of the buildings seem different, lighter in color and more solid, as if they've been cleaned.

The passersby have shed their gray rags for colorful, strangely cut clothing. I recognize the denim that Poppy loves so much, but the other fabrics aren't familiar. The haircuts don't look like anything out of Le Mercure Galant, *and the faces don't show any of the resignation found on the commoners of the Magna Vampyria.*

A bell rings at my back, forcing me to jump to the side with Pierrot to avoid a fast-moving wagon on the street. Made entirely of metal, it isn't pulled by any horses and moves on its own as if drawn by some mysterious magic.

I look around at this Paris that's both familiar and different, splashed with sunbeams—not a City of Shadows but a City of Light.

That's when I spot it, standing erect above the neighboring rooftops, a formidable tower of iron that points toward the radiant sky, higher than the Hunting Wall and all the other buildings I've ever seen. Its four enormous pillars made of delicate lacelike beams soar upward, coming together in a triumphant arrow.

Stunned, I let go of Pierrot's hand so I can grab the nearest wall.

My fingers have barely detached from the child's when the tower disappears.

The sky takes on its normal leaden cast; the cold bites again; the facades look their usual gray; and faces appear tired. The carts in the street are now pulled by beasts of burden.

"Did you . . . did you see that?" I ask Pierrot.

He looks at me between his long strands of hair, seemingly as surprised as I am.

"You mean . . . you saw that too?"

I nod.

His pale-blue eyes shine, tearing up. Equally overwhelmed, not knowing what to do, I press him against me.

"Calm down, Pierrot," I whisper in his ear. "Let's not call attention to ourselves."

But he's overcome with emotion. "It's the first time . . . the first time that someone else sees what I see," he says through strangled sobs. "Oh, if you only knew what that feels like."

I hold him tighter in my arms, the same way I hugged Bastien when he had nightmares. Pierrot has the same hypersensitive nature. He needs to talk. I sense that he won't be able to take another step until he pours his heart out. I back up enough to hold him by the shoulders, a reassuring gesture, and look at him encouragingly.

"Those visions come to me out of the blue," he whispers, as if it's a shameful secret. "They fascinate and terrify me all at once. And they keep swirling in my head for days after. As I think about them . . . I try to analyze them. To dissect the machines I see. To understand how they function. It's like an obsession." His eyes flutter under his hood. "Maybe it's just *my* mechanism I'm trying to figure out."

I realize what his life entails, with one foot in this world and the other . . . somewhere else. I'm struck only with brief fragments of dreams, here and there. But he lives between two realities permanently, in the same way that the Eye of the Innocents was haunted by visions in his reclusory. Even free, Pierrot remains a prisoner of himself.

"It'll be all right, Pierrot," I say, forcing myself to smile.

Gently, I take his hand, vaguely expecting to veer to the other side again.

But no.

Nothing happens.

The strange moment has passed, or maybe I'm too awake to tip into a trance.

I hurry until we reach the gloomy mass of the outer ramparts, and I stop only once we come to the huge toll gate.

"Do you have a pass?" one of the guards asks, leaning on his halberd.

"Signed by the king himself," I reply, taking out the precious document from the pocket of my torn dress.

The guard immediately stands at attention, stammering excuses for his listlessness.

He's too impressed to think about checking the identity of the hooded figure accompanying the bearer of a royal pass.

And so I cross the city wall of Paris, not as a prisoner like last time but free.

The main road leading to Versailles is deserted.

The king, his courtiers, and his army returned to the palace at the end of the night. Only deep ruts hollowed out in the ground and snow are left in their wake.

Still, Pierrot and I stick to the shoulder, shaded by frozen willows. I'd rather keep a low profile during the last miles that separate us from our destination. No one must catch me with the child before I've found him shelter.

"Courage, Pierrot," I say. "We've covered most of the way. Soon you'll be warm, with a nice bowl of broth."

He nods under his hood, shivering, his lips blue from the cold.

All of a sudden, I hear the crunching of twigs behind us. Someone else is walking, avoiding the road . . . or following in our tracks.

I turn abruptly, ready to draw the death-silver dagger that's still in the pocket of my dress.

The person at our backs also freezes, some thirty yards away.

The long light-beige coat blends in with the snow-covered landscape, just as it did one week ago, when the Lachryma dragged me to the Bois de Boulogne and a mysterious rider tried to save me.

"Naoko?" I call out, my throat tight.

The person removes her hood, revealing my friend's black bun and porcelain face.

"It's you, Jea—?" she starts to say.

The rest of her sentence stays stuck in her throat.

I remove my hood in turn, then Pierrot's.

Whatever path the child chooses to take, I don't need to keep secrets from him.

"Yes, it's . . . it's me, Naoko," I stammer. "You can speak freely. Pierrot's a friend."

I'm choked with joyful tears, unable to say more.

Naoko stays mute, too, her eyes shining.

She starts walking toward me and me toward her, our steps crunching the snow.

"The godmother kept her word," she manages to say. "The Lachryma freed me once they heard that Count Tarella had been destroyed."

A smile spreads across her delicate lips.

Right then, a sunbeam pierces the blanket of gray clouds, illuminating this wooded area. The icicles hanging from the tree branches instantly morph into crystal garlands, the coat of snow under our feet into a sequined carpet.

"Stubborn mule," Naoko says loudly, bursting into triumphant laughter.

We cover the last yards between us in a run.

The cold air burns our lungs; joy warms our bellies.

Here, between the frosted willow trunks, we throw ourselves into each other's arms.

27
NIGHT OF SHADOWS

"I'm going to book passage for Pierrot on the next ship bound for the Americas," the grand equerry says.

He looks at me with eyes that glisten in the light of the candelabra. Raymond de Montfaucon isn't the type to express his feelings, but, today, in his underground room at the Grande Écurie, he has trouble hiding his emotions.

First, it's due to seeing us—Naoko and me—alive again after he thought he'd lost us both. For I believe he grew as attached to his guest as much as he did to me. Second, the incredible story I told him about the demons and wonders at the Court of Miracles brought up a slew of reactions on his large, weathered face.

Right now, Pierrot is resting in Naoko's cell, my friend by his bedside.

I myself slept soundly on a straw mat at the foot of Naoko's iron bed, completely crushed by fatigue after walking for half a day. I didn't wake up until hours later, then went to the vaulted room where my mentor set up his quarters.

"I don't know where the young boy's visions are coming from, but they could change *everything*," he says. "Here in France, he's in constant danger. Let's hope that by flooding the underground valley of the Bièvre, the Immutable destroyed all trace of that magic, which would have a devastating impact if it fell into his hands. But we shouldn't rejoice too quickly. It could be that in the days and weeks to come, remnants of the Court of Miracles will spew to the surface from the manholes of Paris. Debris from what you call *bulbs* and *projectors* might be found. Who knows if other nuns or boarders at the Incurables are aware of Pierrot's strange visions? I heard there were many survivors from the last ghoul attack, thanks to an old nun who evacuated people through a door reserved for funeral services . . . some nun named Vermillette."

"Vermillonne!" I shout, relieved to learn that the Sister of Final Care is alive. "I know her. She's a discreet woman, totally devoted to her work."

"Maybe. But if the inquisitors of the Faculty investigate and discover Pierrot's existence, they'll do everything they can to capture him."

Pensive, Montfaucon smooths his thick goatee. Behind his anxious forehead, I imagine meticulous gears at work. Over these past weeks, I had to concentrate on the mission he entrusted me with, focusing all my attention on one objective. But Montfaucon pulls the strings of a secret and complex operation spanning many continents, where the slightest hiccup can have drastic consequences. He's under immense pressure, and I know I still have a lot to learn from him.

"Over in the Americas, the Fronde will know how to hide and protect Pierrot," he says. "The New World has lots of wide, uninhabited open space where surveillance by the Magna Vampyria is a lot looser than in old Europe. Guided by the prophet of magical electricity, the American rebels will be able to recreate the paddle wheels of the Bièvre, only on rivers ten times bigger to produce ten times more of this mystical energy."

Even if I'd like to keep Pierrot near me, Montfaucon is right. The child will be both safer and more useful on the other side of the ocean.

"I agree with you," I say. "But we should let Pierrot decide whether he wants to make the long voyage. I promised him that he'd be free from now on."

"You've been known not to keep your promises to friends in the past."

"True. But that's in the past. The new Jeanne keeps her word."

The grand equerry acquiesces. "All right, the child will decide. Seems you only needed a few hours to grow attached to him, am I right?"

"Yes, monsieur. He's an orphan, like I am. He touches my heart and reminds me of my brother Bastien at that same age. His visions also mean something to me . . . I got a glimpse of them as we made our way through Paris together. I thought I was seeing a different city . . ." I hesitate to let the words out of my mouth. ". . . another world."

The grand equerry raises his bushy brows. "Another world, Jeanne?"

"Yes. And it's not the first time. I never told you because I thought I'd dreamed it up, but when I was in the king's mortuary chamber on the night of the La Roncière conspiracy, I had a vision. I saw my home in Butte-aux-Rats bathed in a bright light. My family was alive, similar yet different."

Tears well up in my eyes as I think about this image that seemed so real.

"You miss your family, and their souls visit you on occasion. Nothing unusual," Montfaucon suggests, his voice unexpectedly soft for a man like him. "Come on, Jeanne. It was probably nothing but a dream, as you just said."

He puts his large hand on my shoulder, clumsily, to comfort me.

"No, monsieur. I'm now sure it wasn't a dream. My brother Valère was wearing an undershirt stamped with a date I remember very clearly. 2014."

"2014, you say?" Montfaucon says, his hand trembling on the hollow of my shoulder blade.

He furrows his brows, doing a mental calculation.

"At the time, I didn't pay attention," I reply. "But now, I'm doing the same math you are. 2014 is the sum of 299 and 1715."

"1715: the year Louis XIV was transmuted into the Immutable . . . ," Montfaucon says in a whisper.

"Plus 299 years of his reign. If the Immutable hadn't pushed the calendar back to zero to deduct the era of the Shadows, today we'd be in the year . . . 2014."

We're silent a moment, lost in each other's gaze, trying to understand what this means. The fire crackles softly in the hearth. Time itself seems somehow suspended.

"Could . . . could you have glimpsed a parallel world to the Magna Vampyria?" Montfaucon finally stammers.

"Or the promise of a possible future beyond the Shadows?" I venture to say.

"Or simply a vision of what could have been and never will be," the grand equerry concludes darkly.

I'd like to talk to him about my premonitory dreams and my experience with the ghouls, but I don't dare. I'm afraid he'll withdraw his trust if he finds out I understand the language of the nocturnal abominations. I know he hates them and spends his free time hunting them. What would he think if he knew the ghouls had described me as *nonhuman*? I'm too afraid of how he'd react. Most of all, I'm afraid of myself.

As I'm filled with doubt, the door to the armored room opens with a creak.

A fragrance of decaying leaves wafts in, warming my heart.

"Orfeo!"

For it's really him in the doorway.

Time flew by as I rested in Naoko's cell, then as I filled in the grand equerry about my crazy adventure, and so night must have fallen a while ago. Orfeo sneaked out through the outer ramparts, and now he's back, as he promised.

Presently, he's looking sheepishly down at his leather shoes, avoiding his master's gaze.

"I just learned about your nocturnal escapades," Montfaucon growls. "You deserve to be shackled to learn obedience . . ."

Poor Orfeo sulks even more.

". . . but Jeanne told me you'd found the secret passageway used by the Lachrymas to get in and out of Paris without being seen. That crucial bit of information could be a big help to the Fronde in the months and years to come. Therefore I forgive you . . . this time."

Orfeo finally risks raising his head.

At that moment, Naoko bursts into the hallway behind him.

"Orfeo!" she shouts as she rushes to hug him.

My friend's clear laughter fills me with happiness. The wide smile that spreads across Orfeo's pale-green face melts my heart.

Montfaucon also starts smiling, his austere face momentarily taking on the features of an emotional grandfather.

A fuzzy feeling warms my heart in this blind cave, the last place in the world I would ever have thought I'd find a home again. And yet it's the wholehearted truth. I feel good, the best I've felt since my loved ones were taken from me. What a team we make! The old repentant executioner, the young markswoman with a hybrid body, a stitched-up abomination, and me, the girl with the gray hair and vampyre blood who's plagued by nightmares . . . and the clairvoyant child sleeping nearby. We're like characters out of some strange fairy tale, haunting some insomniac writer under a full moon. But for me this fairy tale is the gentlest of all.

In the depths of the basement, a clock chimes eight times, interrupting this blissful moment.

"The celebrations for the Night of Shadows are about to begin," Montfaucon reminds me as he turns serious again. "Jeanne, it's time to make your comeback at the court."

Two months ago I entered the Hall of Mirrors as a nobody, trying to compete for the Sip of the King. Today, December 21, as I enter the central aisle at the Royal Chapel of Versailles, everyone turns to look at me, and my name booms from everyone's lips.

"It's Diane de Gastefriche."

"She's back."

"She's not a squire anymore, but she's accompanied by the grand equerry."

Montfaucon is in fact walking beside me, dressed in his most luxurious black velvet waistcoat. He's even waxed his goatee for the occasion and curled the locks of his old wig with an iron.

As for me, I took off my torn flannel dress in favor of one of Naoko's beautiful dresses, made of black silk with embroidery. With her dainty hands, she confectioned my hair into an exquisite braided bun.

Thus attired, I cut through the rows of mortal and immortal courtiers who are already lining either side of the aisle. They're all dressed in black, as befits the Night of Shadows, the longest night of the year—as well as the most sacred.

Tall dark tapers are planted in iron candelabras.

A heady scent of incense floats in the air, myrrh and still rarer herbs—ancient secrets of the pharaohs that were used to preserve the bodies of the dead, a fragrance pleasant to the noses of the lords of the night.

Immense Doric columns encircle this magnificent architecture erected to the glory of the greatest vampyre of all time, the absolute monarch by the grace of the Shadows.

He's here, in the first row, in front of the choir, where an imposing and dazzlingly bright organ rises up. Tonight, the King of Shadows is clad in an immense fur cloak made from the black pelts of a wolf pack. Dotting the royal cloak are dozens of dead, yellowish gleaming eyes that recall the gold of the solar mask.

That mask is turned toward me as I walk down the aisle, the air growing colder with my every step.

Impossible to read the eyes hiding behind the two obscure slits.

On the other hand, those of the most prominent and highest-ranking courtiers surrounding the sovereign are all focused on me. Those of the Marquis de Mélac, minister of the armies, vacillate between surprise and bitterness. Those of the Princess des Ursins, minister of foreign affairs, express a certain admiration.

The five other squires are here too.

Hélénaïs is the first to catch my eyes, her gorgeous chestnut hair coiffed à la Fontanges, an elaborate aerial style of curls and lace. She looks just like her sister, Iphigénie, with a face that I now know was shaped by alchemical surgery. But unlike her elder, something in her golden eyes hasn't quite frozen. Even as she tries to clench her jaw, she can't help but smile as she sees me. Yes, despite our differences, she seems relieved that I'm not dead. We've shared room and board and danger during these last few weeks. Maybe one day we'll grow closer and I'll be able to pull her away from her father's toxic influence, in homage to Iphigénie.

Next to the heiress, Suraj stands tall in a shimmering maroon jacket embroidered with gold. He doesn't hesitate to smile broadly. I can't imagine the tribulations he must have lived through during our stay in Paris, forced to lie to me to fulfill the Immutable's orders when his heart told him to tell me the truth. He looks incredibly happy and probably also relieved that the moral torment is over with.

To his right, Rafael didn't need to change his everyday attire for the evening. As always, he's dressed in black, the style at the Spanish court. He looks at me with his green, vibrant eyes that seem to be encouraging me. The way he stands next to his secret lover, so close but not touching, moves me.

Poppy displays no such reserve. Flouting etiquette, she mimes words with her deep-blue-glossed lips, daring to use English behind the Immutable's very back: *"Welcome home!"*

At the end of the row of squires, Zacharie's mysterious face is as impenetrable as the king's himself.

Now two yards from the sovereign, I curtsy deeply and remain kneeling on the icy tiles. The mortal cold emanating from His Majesty chills me to the bones.

With one word, the master of the Magna Vampyria can raise me up or deal me a death blow. I know him well enough now to recognize how much he relishes creating suspense around the fate of his subjects—until he deigns to speak through his metallic lips, always doing so in front of the largest possible audience.

"Diane de Gastefriche," his Olympian voice roars above my head. "We instructed you to bring us the Lady of Miracles and her army of ghouls. You failed in your mission."

"She more than failed, sire," an angry voice quickly says to my right. "She committed a heinous crime."

Still kneeling, I glance discreetly at the first rows of the chapel, reserved for the elite of the kingdom. That's where the cry came from. A tall woman draped in a black crepe dress has stood up, quivering in anger. Her attire isn't just dictated by the current style du jour—it is mourning attire. I raise my head ever so slightly to look at the veil covering her face. It's Edmée de Vauvalon, her canines erect with fury.

"She killed Count Tarella," the marquise accuses me, pointing her fingernail at me as if she wanted to lacerate me. "No one knows how exactly, since the murder weapon wasn't found. Oh, sire, render justice and crucify her!"

I thought the marquise was sufficiently versed in the ways of the court to avoid such an outburst in front of the king. Maybe the disappearance of her despicable lover truly shook her. Maybe he was the mirror image of her own moral decrepitude. Whatever the case, she chose the wrong time to vent. If there's one thing the Immutable detests, it's having the spotlight stolen from him.

"Where do you think you are, Marquise?" he lectures her icily. "At the commedia dell'arte? Get a grip on yourself! According to the Viscount de Mortange's eyewitness account, your Tarella attempted to bleed this demoiselle without our prior authorization. It was legitimate self-defense, regardless of how she disposed of the scoundrel."

The assembly doesn't make a peep, but an excited thrill ripples through the crowd.

"Mort . . . Mortange . . . ?" Edmée stammers, her face wilting under her veil.

She looks toward the opposite row. I turn my head, too, taking care to remain kneeling before the sovereign. Alexandre is there, his magnificent red hair pulled back into a ponytail, the better to display his defiant face to his enemy . . . a face that softens with tenderness when he lowers his eyes to me.

"I . . . I thought Gastefriche was worthless to you now, Your Majesty," Edmée stammers in a last-ditch attempt to win over the sovereign.

"Spare us your thoughts, for our mind hovers far above your comprehension," the king lashes out, shutting the marquise's mouth for good.

I feel the royal attention returning to my lowered head, as glacial as the rays of a frozen sun.

"Where were we before this annoying interruption? Ah yes, your failure. Well, what do you have to say in your defense, Gastefriche?"

The monarch's question reverberates under the gigantic vault of the chapel.

The mortal courtiers hold their breath. You can't even hear the rustling of a dress.

"Nothing, Your Majesty," I say, bending forward a little more. "You had every reason to relieve me of my duties as squire. I returned to Versailles and proceeded to the Grande Écurie so I could come tonight and deliver my body and soul into your all-powerful hands."

It's the declaration of a courtier submitting wholly to the royal will.

Or, as Sterling would say, it's an actress relinquishing wholly to the director.

"Our hands have, in fact, guided you exactly as we intended," the monarch says gleefully, falling into the prideful trap I set for him. "You were the instrument that led us to the Court of Miracles. Are you not asking yourself how?"

"I . . . I don't know, sire," I say, feigning ignorance to flatter him even more.

"A sip of our blood runs in your body and is uncontestably the better part of your humble being. It was likely too ambitious to ask that you bring us the lady, for aside from that sacred sip, you are a simple mortal. One can't ask too much of a little gray mouse. But at least, in spite of yourself, you fulfilled your task. Our blood in your veins allowed us to locate the Court of Miracles. Not only did we erect a dam at the mouth of the Bièvre going downstream, but we also diverted the sewers upstream so that they emptied out into the underground riverbed. That rebellious principality is now drowned under a torrent of filth, its mistress swallowed up and her army disbanded. Our triumph is complete. Rise, Gastefriche!"

Slowly, I get to my feet, displaying an expression of passionate gratitude.

"We reinstate you in your duties, here and now," the king declares.

A murmur of emotion ripples among the assembly. I sense the resentment of those who were expecting an execution and the overblown wonder of those who praise the royal magnanimity.

"Oh, sire, that's too great an honor!" I shout. "I don't deserve it."

"We alone decide who among our subjects is deserving. And we hereby order you to take your place by our side for the ceremony."

Reining in my jubilant victory, I finally straighten, reassuming my restored dignity as squire. My heels click against the tiles, marking the silence with solemn steps. I take a seat next to the sovereign.

Exili approaches the choir to begin the celebration, followed by the archiaters in their ritual funereal robes, collars bursting with jet-black ruffs.

The colossal organ intones a requiem that shakes the somber silks, nighttime-hued dresses, and lustrous heads of hair.

The highest ranking in the regime turn their pale palms up toward the baroque vault to give thanks to the Shadows.

No one suspects that in the heart of this dark ocean, a spark is catching, one that has vowed to restore the Light to the world.

EPILOGUE

For the first time in weeks, I wake up in my spacious room at Versailles.

Last night, I went to bed as soon as the ceremony ended. Exhausted, I immediately fell into a dreamless slumber. No recollections of the past, no premonitions of the future. Nothing but a deep, restorative sleep.

The palace now bathes in the silence that precedes the dawn. The clock at my bedside, under the oil lamp that serves as a night-light, indicates that it's seven fifteen in the morning. I still have a few minutes before I have to get ready for the king's Grand Retiring.

I linger on the soft mattress, so different from the coarse straw mat at the Yellow Cat. In spite of the trials I've gone through, I wouldn't change anything that's happened to me. I take a deep breath, gathering my hopes and fears, my memories and questions.

In this very room, one month ago, Paulin sacrificed his life. Yesterday in Paris, Iphigénie de Plumigny and her courtiers also gave up theirs. The carpenter wanted to render justice at its humble human level and avenge his sister Toinette. The subjects at the Court of Miracles dreamed of a universal Last Judgment—destroying this world in order to erect another on top of the ruins. Although I don't share the extremes of this battle, I sympathize completely with the suffering that inspired it. I don't want to remember Iphigénie as a despot but as a martyr. I tell myself I'll honor her memory and that of her people. I'll do all I can to build the better world that these men and women aspired to. Not on ruins—but on fertile soil.

I throw off my bedcovers and get up.

My chest swelling with newfound optimism, I walk to the window and open the interior shutters.

Through the cold pane, the gardens of Versailles are still shrouded in semidarkness.

Still, I sense the pink of the coming dawn over at the other end of the obscured Grand Canal.

Just like this promise of a new day at the end of the night, maybe the visions that struck me twice announce this future world. I would have liked to talk to Pierrot about it. But he agreed to leave for the Americas. He'll be sailing toward new shores today. I hope to see him again someday.

I also hope I'll cross paths again with Lord Sterling Raindust, who gave me a glimpse of the complex political games played among vampyric nations . . . and who touched me more deeply than any immortal before him. He pretended there was no hope—"*no future*." I wonder what he'd think of my visions. Would he mock them with his inimitable cold humor? I still can't decide whether I should consider him an adversary or an ally.

On the other hand, I know that the Court of Shadows overflows with fierce enemies. Starting with Edmée de Vauvalon, who'll do everything she can to avenge Marcantonio's death. Other assassins will prove more treacherous, trying to kill me in the shadows, like Lord Serpent, a survivor of the La Roncière plot who brought Tristan back from the dead.

But what if the most dangerous enemy of all resides within me? That somber spot hidden in my soul that I'm barely aware of. By what magic am I able to understand the language of the ghouls? And what is that taste on my skin that dissuades them from devouring me like any other human being?

I look away from the Grand Canal and focus on my reflection on the windowpane. Between my silver strands of hair, my face looks like an enigma. I think I hear the hollow voice of the ghouls: "*Who are you?*"

The Eye of the Innocents' tarot-card reading pops into my head.

The Death card—the obstacle—is the one I met when I thought I'd die under the claws of the abominations. But the Moon card—the future—remains a mystery. I was so obsessed with the lady during the reading that I absolutely wanted to see her in the arcana. I didn't pay attention to the seer when he explained that the Moon actually reflected something amorphous deep within me, a secret that was gestating and that I needed to question myself about. The old man has vanished now, as mysteriously as he appeared in my life. I'm alone as I face my future, as I face myself.

I heave a deep sigh.

The mist covers the pane and veils my reflection.

Enough introspection.

As uncertain as I am about the future, at least the present seems clearer. I found my adoptive family with Montfaucon, Naoko, Orfeo, and Pierrot. Behind the palace walls, the longest night of the year is about to end. Soon, the sun will rise. And the days will start to lengthen—a few minutes more each morning, like many lilliputian victories won over the Shadows.

I leave the window to go and dress in my squire's attire.

My battle has only just begun.

ACKNOWLEDGMENTS

I'd like to thank all those who accompanied me on this journey into the heart of Paris through the Shadows.

My family, of course, who made sure I didn't wander off into the catacombs of the imagination.

My intrepid editors, Elsa, Glenn, Constance, and Fabien, who were by my side for the duration of this investigation.

The fabulous artists, Nekro, Loles, Misty Beee, and Tarwane, who continue to dream up with me the dangerous and captivating world of the Magna Vampyria.

The entire team at Éditions Robert Laffont, my French publisher, but also the wonderful crew at my American publisher, Amazon Crossing. A well-fitting name indeed: they really made this story cross the Atlantic ocean to reach the Americas! Kudos to my virtuosa translator Françoise, my fantastic editors Adrienne and Clarence, and the supremely talented artist Colin who created a stunning cover for the novel that you hold in your hands.

I wrote this story during bouts of insomnia, immersed alongside Jeanne in the bowels of the City of Shadows. Deep into my nighttime writing, I would sometimes look out the window in search of the secret moon that my heroine was also looking for. It seemed the Eye of the Innocents whispered a few words in my ear: *"In the darkest of nights is when stars shine the brightest!"*

AS YOU TURN THIS PAGE, DEAR READER,
YOU CLOSE IT ON THE COURT OF MIRACLES.
BUT A NEW COURT ALREADY BECKONS,
MYSTERIOUS AND SAVAGE,
SHIMMERING AND DEADLY ...
LET'S RENDEZVOUS THERE!

ABOUT THE AUTHOR

Photo © 2019 by Samantha Rayward

Two-time winner of the Grand Prix de l'Imaginaire, Victor Dixen stands at the forefront of French fantasy. His acclaimed series include Animale, Phobos, Cogito, Extincta, and Vampyria. A nomadic writer, he has lived in Paris, Dublin, Singapore, New York, and now Washington, DC, drawing inspiration from the promises of the future as much as the ghosts of the past.

In the second volume of the Vampyria Saga, Dixen transports readers into a shiver-inducing and fantastical adventure—a breathtaking search into the depths of Paris, where the City of Light becomes the City of Shadows.

Find out more about Dixen's universe at www.victordixen.com.

ABOUT THE TRANSLATOR

Photo © 2023 by Elisabeth Bui

Françoise Bui spent twenty years as an executive editor at Penguin Random House, where her list of edited books included numerous novels in translation. Of these, four received the Mildred L. Batchelder Award for outstanding children's book books initially published in a foreign language; two others were Honor titles. Originally from France, Bui lives in New York City.